MONEY FOR MAYHEM

By Scott Malensek

"Money for Mayhem" by Scott Malensek. ISBN 978-1-947532-53-3 (hardcover).

Published 2018 by Virtualbookworm.com Publishing Inc., P.O. Box 9949, College Station, TX 77842, US.

8/20/1990

Alan Conferra was just another guy in a suit, at the local coffee shop, in the mornings. Standing six-foot-two and 190 pounds, his most distinguishable features were his tailored black suit, bright white shirt, and a constant 5 o'clock shadow. He liked his charcoal-colored haircut high and tight like a Marine's, and he wore his suit with the same sort of meticulous attention to detail. Beyond that, and a remarkably warm smile, Alan looked like anyone else in Washington, DC. He seemed largely unremarkable to most people.

In truth he had always been a noteworthy accountant. He graduated top of his class from the University of Michigan as a CPA with a BA in accounting and a BS in economics. He followed those degrees with both a master of science in public and corporate accounting as well as a PhD in outsourcing and business management. Months before graduating Alan had job offers from all over the country, and he settled on an entry-level position in the office of Congressman Jerry Henderson (D-SC). After his first year there he enrolled in Georgetown University, where he earned a certificate in forensic accounting.

Despite a lifetime of exceptional grades, Alan had never fully fit in. He wasn't an outcast or someone who had authority issues, but he was certainly no after-school football hero. He never played any sports or joined in any clubs. Still, he was blessed with a special smile and a rare sense of understanding that others infectiously sensed. For as long as anyone knew him, he could look anyone in the eye, and the person looking at him had a feeling of empathy, understanding, and lightheartedness. Alan could connect—even without words—to anyone for a few moments, but he was always so engrossed in school that he'd never developed any significant relationships.

For years he had been a student and intern with little more perspective than a desk or a cubicle. Now, his position in Congressman Henderson's office opened the world to him. After his classes in forensic accounting were complete at Georgetown, Alan's job changed. He had been little more than an overqualified accounting associate for those first few months, but a foreign policy crisis on the other side of the planet yanked him from cubicle duty.

During the Iran-Iraq War, Iraq's military adventure was funded by both the Soviet Union and nations in the West that feared a greater Iran/Saudi war should Iraq fall. Even that, however, was not enough. Near the end of the war the failing Soviet Union supported the war less and less—preferring to spend more money on a nuclear arms race with the United States. This compelled the Iraqi government to seek funding elsewhere, and no one was more eager to keep Iraq in the fight than neighboring Kuwait, which was surely Iran's next conquest if Iraq fell.

After the war ended, the Iraqi government and the Kuwaiti government came to odds. Iraq still saw the Emirate of Kuwait as a lost province of Iraq, and the Kuwaitis viewed Iraq with both concern as a possible aggressor as well as the disdain of a bad debtor. Iraq refused to pay back the money it had borrowed from Kuwait. To make matters worse, Iraqi drillers were drilling diagonally from Iraq, into Kuwaiti oil fields, and then selling the stolen Kuwaiti oil to Trucial Energy as a way of making payments to Kuwait. The matter escalated. The Emirate of Kuwait threatened to take the dispute up through the international community and compel the rest of the world to stop illegal Iraqi oil activity.

The Iraqi government quietly asked other nations' ambassadors how their nations would react to an international dispute between Kuwait and Iraq. None of the ambassadors envisioned an invasion, and so all agreed that they would abstain from getting involved. Saddam saw this as a "green light," and did, in fact, invade Kuwait in August 1990. His intent was to "reclaim Iraq's nineteenth province;" i.e., Kuwait.

The world, however, had not expected an invasion. The risk of having Iraq control all the Iraqi oil and Kuwaiti oil, and threaten the oil reserves of Saudi Arabia and/or the other Gulf emirates, was just too much of a threat. The United States put together an international coalition to protect Saudi Arabia and the Gulf States. Then, the United Nations empowered the Coalition to drive Iraqi forces out of Kuwait.

America was going to war again. Carl Von Clausewitz wrote, "There is nothing more common than to find considerations of supply affecting the strategic lines of a campaign and a war." Modern masters of war put things more plainly. "Amateurs talk about tactics, but professionals study logistics," stated General Robert H. Barrow, USMC. For the most part this meant beans and bullets to military leaders, but to leaders of empires and states...logistics meant money and morale. Wars are waged with money, and won with the will of those who wage them.

As congressional staff began to get stretched thin assisting constituents with the concerns of an upcoming war, Alan was pulled from the data entry side of accounting, and was assigned as lead on a new project. Representative Henderson wanted a favor from a K Street consultant. The lobbyist, Gillian Knight, had a contract with a lesser known yet certainly global oil company, Trucial Energy. If Henderson could help him out, then he could help the congressman on a vote for a project in Colombia, South Carolina. That project would help the friend of the congressman in the city of Colombia, and thus political friendships were made and maintained.

The professionally renowned Trucial Energy had built several offshore drilling platforms just off the coast of Kuwait and Iraq. These platforms had been built with permission from OPEC and Kuwait, but not Iraq. Since Iraqi forces were occupying and effectively tearing Kuwait apart, there was concern that the oil rigs would be seized at a huge loss. Though the sites were fully insured and supposedly still protected by those insurers, by the UN, by the Gulf State Security Agreement of 1988, and by OPEC, no one knew if Saddam would honor those commitments.

Starting on Monday, August 20, 1990, Alan's new job was to "...monitor and maintain the condition of Trucial Energy resources in the Persian Gulf region, and ensure that Trucial Energy assets were accounted for properly." There was a lot more to it on the official memo. It seemed a simple task, but the scale of it was daunting. Trucial Energy had hundreds of billions of dollars in the region, and on that scale even simple tasks get big fast. Still, Alan assumed that he would basically be collating reports from the region as they came in, and then he'd write a report. It was the naiveté that came with both inexperience and his lifelong pursuit of a quiet bureaucratic lifestyle.

***

1/29/1991: 0430hrs

Sergeant Brian Assana stood on the roof of a closed gas station just a few miles south of Khafji, Saudi Arabia. They were literally in the absolute middle of nowhere. Below them the rest of their platoon was in rest mode, but no one slept. Everyone kicked back and waited to be ordered to do something. A few were walking around and marveling at the historic and expensive light show to the north.

Sergeant Assana stood five-foot-eleven and weighed 185 pounds, and his face was a reflection of both his father's Eastern European parents as well as his mother's Spanish family. Compared to most of the marines in his unit, he was slightly more disciplined in the way he wore his uniform, but he still displayed a few field customizations and personalization as every enlisted US Marine has done in any war. Brian's character was that of a man who did his job. What was most unique was why: Some people serve their country for fame, glory, family heritage, excitement, or money. Brian was one of those who served to serve. He saw a way to serve others, to do a duty to his country, and he was committed to that—not loudly, but quietly. That kind of dedication was always rare.

After successfully invading Kuwait, and as nations from around the world gathered to force Saddam to order a withdrawal, he instead ordered an attack. Operation Desert Shield's main objective had been to keep Saddam's forces from seizing Saudi Arabia's Persian Gulf oil fields. Instead, the UN Coalition had forced him to choose between withdrawing and effectively surrendering his power in Iraq or attacking. Centuries earlier the Sun Tzu had written his guide to waging the art of war, and preeminent in that text was the claim that the best time to attack was just before an enemy attack was initiated. To that end, Saddam had sent three reinforced brigades of tanks, armored personnel carriers, and sixty thousand troops across the border in Saudi Arabia.

At first no one could stop Saddam's forces. There were only a few small outposts of US Marines positioned along the Saudi/Kuwaiti border. Most of the Americans were quickly overrun or driven away from their positions by massive Iraqi fire, but two outposts were able to survive thanks to air support from a few Cobra helicopter gunships. Another outpost was forced into the town of Khafji itself. Even though the marines trapped in Khafji were completely surrounded and outnumbered tens of thousands to one, they still called in close air and artillery support, which decimated the Iraqi forces.

The men at the gas station to the south had been sent there to prevent the Iraqi forces from moving further into Saudi Arabia. They were part of two entire USMC divisions, Saudi divisions, and several brigades from neighboring Persian Gulf States. Hundreds of ships and thousands of aircraft were all being called to battle as the word passed through the lines that the Iraqis had moved south.

From the roof of the gas station the Marines watched. Millions of small arms tracer bullets glowed as they rose into the sky from the Iraqi troops. Larger AAA (Anti-Aircraft Artillery) spewed long streams of glowing explosives into the dark sky. Missiles launched from unseen aircraft raced toward the ground with flashes and thunderous explosions, marking the end of their race toward targets. Thousands of laser-guided bombs directed by the handful of Marines trapped in Khafji silently dropped out of the sky from unseen aircraft, and flashes burst all along the horizon and in the darkened sands of the surrounding desert. Red, yellow, green, orange...the colors of the fireworks were amazing. And they were deadly. Years later an Iraqi who had survived a decade of trench warfare during the Iran-Iraq War would claim that he lost more troops and tanks that night than he did in his entire career combined.

The Marines watched. Some cheered like it was a game. Others oohed and aahed like it was the Fourth of July. Some who were exhausted by the heat rested and ignored the billions in munitions being spent. The three men on the roof felt all of those things as well, but after a few hours of war watching they began to mentally record the scene. They knew they were witnessing history. The fourth most powerful nation on Earth at the time was being killed.

***

2/22/1991

Alan Conferra was swamped. Sitting in his gray-carpeted cubicle in Congressman Henderson's office, he had been inundated with boxes of reports and information regarding Trucial Energy assets in Kuwait, Saudi Arabia, the Persian Gulf, and even Iraq. The stacks of boxes and three-ring binders around his cubicle were starting to resemble a small castle. Unlike most people who would have skimmed the avalanche of documentation, Alan had stayed late and read each word on each page. It had taken him months—of sixty-, seventy-, and eighty-hour work weeks—but he was now the leading expert in Washington, DC, on Trucial Energy. Even most Trucial Energy executives didn't have the overall data that had filled the space between his ears.

Outside it was unseasonably warm, almost sixty degrees. Most people were taking long coffee breaks or extended lunches so that they could enjoy it. Alan didn't even consider it. He had work to do. Congressman Henderson wanted a summary report on Trucial Energy's Persian Gulf interest by Monday. For Alan, it was going to be another long weekend.

***

2/28/1991

After Alan had been mentally glued to his computer's monitor reviewing the offices' budget for the month, Wayne Kowalski, Congressman Henderson's chief of staff, came up behind him.

At six-foot-six and 270 pounds, Kowalski was a physically imposing figure. He'd been a defensive end for South Carolina until he broke his ankle in his senior year (no one found out about it until after the game; he'd played with it broken). He graduated with a degree in political science, and was close friends with his boss, Jerry Henderson. As big as he was physically, his character was bigger, and far more imposing. Generals had met with Congressman Henderson, and more than once their mouths opened as they stepped aside to let Kowalski pass.

Wayne was one of those people who truly believed that it was better to be a kingmaker than a king, and to that end he loved his job. In the congressman's office it was sometimes more unnerving to exchange a few words or even a glance with Wayne than it was to talk with the congressman himself.

"Alan!"

Kowalski was always a loud man, but he raised his voice even higher to get Alan's attention away from the numbers on his computer screen. Exactly as he'd hoped, Alan shot straight up and around in an instant while doing his best to look professional and hide the deer-in-the-headlights expression he felt.

"Alan, the congressman and I have just come back from a West Wing briefing."

He paused for a moment to let Alan's shock wear off a little, then he continued.

"The president's going to give Saddam twenty-four hours to get out of Kuwait later today. No one thinks that asshole will accept the offer, but he's making it anyway."

Everyone had expected the air attacks on Iraq would be followed up with a ground war, but everyone still had the Vietnam experience in their minds, and the thought of ground combat was daunting.

"So we're really gonna do it? We're really going in, huh?" Alan asked.

"Yeah. Looks like it's gonna happen. And you're gonna go see it."

Alan's face was unshaken, but his mind was dumbstruck. First, his boss' boss' boss was giving him a sudden one-on-one, then the news that the country was going to war again, and now it sounded like they wanted him to be there too? He couldn't believe it.

"Um, did you say I'm going to see it? My name is Alan Conferra, sir. Are you looking for the right Alan?"

Kowalski laughed. "Yes, Alan. I know who you are. I get your reports. The congressman knows you too. Trucial Energy's been raising some hell with the West Wing. They're going apeshit over their losses, and no one knows them better than you do. So, you're gonna go over there, meet with their reps, and coordinate with them."

"Sir, I'm just a numbers guy. I don't even have a passport. What am I supposed to coordinate with them? Are you serious? Is this a joke?"

Kowalski was not a man who ever accepted "no" or even a tinge of reluctance when he wanted something done. In this case, the congressman himself had told the president that his office had the best man in DC for the job. This was not a negotiable discussion, and even if it were Kowalski rarely negotiated.

"Look, I know who the fuck I'm talking to. I know what the fuck you're being sent to do. You won't need a passport since no one'll be stamping 'em anyway. Now get your fucking shit together, and get the fuck over to Andrews to get a ride out. I'll have a memo for you that'll get you wherever you need to go. You sank all that time reading these fucking reports, and you're the fucking guy! This isn't a discussion. Now move!"

"Yes, sir! Uh, I'll just get some of my, um..." Alan was as confused and hurried as a new recruit getting off the bus for basic training.

"Fucking MOVE!" shouted Kowalski. His temper was like a flash in a pan, and if someone showed fear and acquiescence it only gave him satisfaction. The more nervous they seemed, the more he had to fight to keep from grinning. At this point everyone in the office could hear him. Those who worked closely with the chief of staff were either smiling with laughter or shaking their heads in disgust at the man who took genuine joy at scaring people.

"Sir, uh, what will I be coordinating with them about?" Alan asked.

"How the fuck do I know? Just go over there, hold their hands, document what damages they have, and report back here as often as possible. Some Trucial Energy execs'll meet you when you get off the plane. Just tell 'em what you know, reassure them, hold their fucking hands, and get 'em off everyone's backs for a few days. Then come home. We're asking you to go stay in a luxury hotel for a few days on our dime. Hang out with some billionaires, kiss their ass until this is over, then come home. Show 'em some numbers or something. Just get keep 'em happy for a few days. You're a numbers guy, and they love numbers guys."

Kowalski yelled again, "Karen! I know you can hear me!" He started stomping off toward the office manager's desk. "Write up a memo giving Alan clearance to anywhere he needs to go in service of the congressman, and then have the congressman sign it. Alan'll be there in a few minutes so hurry it up."

With no wife, kids, or immediate family, it was relatively easy for Alan to gather his things for a trip. Still, he wasn't sure what clothes to pack. He'd spent so many late nights at the office that he'd brought a bag with a shaving kit, toothbrush, toothpaste, and deodorant. He even had a spare suit in the trunk of his car, but he wasn't anywhere close to being packed for war, and the shock of it all was still paramount in his thoughts. Kowalski could see it too.

"Alan? You with me here?"

"Yes, Mr. Kowalski. Just, uh, figuring out what I'm gonna bring."

"Alan, this isn't just a job that you have here, okay? You work for the United States government. More to the point you work for a congressman who is asking you to serve, and the president of the United States is specifically asking you to take care of something. If you wanted a nine-to-five accounting job there's banks and corporations for that. You knew that, and instead you came to work here. This is more than a job. Here, we serve. Here we do our duty. You got that? Are we clear? I know this is a huge deal, and it's clearly not what you expected when you came in this morning."

The words rang true with Alan. He wasn't a Navy SEAL commando or some Medal of Honor soldier in waiting. He was, however, committed to his country. Alan had chosen to work at the congressman's office over other jobs because it appealed to him more than just making money. He wanted to do some good; to make a difference...not just make money. Something about being a lifelong accountant had shown him that money was a thing that came in many forms. He'd learned a million ways to invest his regular earnings and make a retirement nest egg, and any job he would take would pay him enough to live well. He wanted something else, and the congressman's office gave him that.

Alan rose with his briefcase in one hand and his bathroom bag under his arm.

"Yes, sir, I get it. I'm happy to serve. You're right, it's why I'm here, but you're wrong about one thing, though. It's not what I thought I'd be doing when I came in yesterday morning. I never went home last night."

Kowalski gave him a gentle nod with a tinge of a half grin. It was then that he realized that Alan had pulled another all-nighter in the office. Clearly he was one of those guys, he thought. It's a good choice. He moved his coffee mug to his left hand and tapped Alan on the shoulder and then shook his hand.

"You'll be okay, son. Any problems you call me. I'll make some shit happen faster than you can say greased goose shit. You got it?"

"Yes, sir. Thank you."

"All right then," Kowalski said with a flash of a supportive smile, but it was just a flash. He stormed off again.

"Karen?! Where the fuck is Alan's memo?! I need it five minutes ago!" Then Kowalski stopped, turned to Alan, and took advantage of the opportunity to be cruel. "Oh, and Alan...don't get killed." With a subtle and not-contained laugh he finally disappeared around the row of cubicles.

Alan wasn't laughing

It took only minutes to change Alan's life, and in less than thirty minutes he was at Andrews Air Force Base arranging for a ride on a C-141 transport to Ramstein, Germany. From there he'd catch another ride on a C-5 Galaxy to Saudi Arabia. In less than twenty-four hours after Wayne Kowalski's spot rant, Alan would be meeting with Trucial Energy executives at a hotel in Dhahran, Saudi Arabia. All the while he kept asking himself, "How in the world did I get myself into this?"

***

3/1/1991

Alan's odyssey was so surreal that he couldn't grasp it as reality. All he was doing was going through the motions of what he could do and what people asked him to do. Immediately after getting on the plane for Germany he had fallen asleep to the hum of the C-141's engines. In the cargo bay, next to the foggy accountant, were a pair of 155mm howitzers and pallets of artillery rounds. When he landed in Germany it was as if he had time traveled. Before he could grasp where he was, what he was doing, or even what time it was he was already on another plane bound for Saudi Arabia.

In Saudi Arabia he got off the plane wondering where he should go or who he should talk to. What he really wanted was a place to take a shower and change clothes. That wasn't going to happen. He wasn't able to walk ten paces before a pair of jeeps and a Mercedes pulled up next to him. The jeeps were escorts with .50-caliber machine guns and gunners standing in the back, and inside the Mercedes were his contacts.

It was clear they weren't there for the howitzers so Alan tightened his tie as the doors to the Mercedes opened and two men in suits stepped out. One of the men appeared Middle Eastern, and the other Western.

"Mr. Conferra?!" shouted the Middle Eastern man.

Alan nodded and reached out his hand in a practiced handshake. While they shook hands the Middle Eastern man tried to speak over the sound of hundreds of jet engines in the area.

"Mr. Conferra! I'm Ibrahim al Douri! I represent the House of Saud and Trucial Energy. This is her majesty's Lord Terrence Tryphine from Tryphine Banking House. He represents the concerns that have brought you here! Shall we step in the car where we can speak if you have a moment?"

Lord Terrence Tryphine was the very model of a modern major banker. His tailored, three-piece pinstripe suit, royal accent, and nonchalance gave him a stereotypical British aristocratic look. His character, however, was not as divisive; he was as comfortable and respectful in a conversation with the world's most powerful people as he was sitting on a park bench talking to a secretary on her lunch break. At five-foot-eleven and 180 pounds, his size wasn't particularly imposing, and he appeared neither weak nor Napoleonic. Lord Tryphine came across to any and all who met him as a man of quality as well as humility.

Ibrahim al Douri, on the other hand, was an elitist. While both men came from wealthy upbringing, Ibrahim was not comfortable with anyone who lacked in wealth or power. He was a snob, pure and simple. Ibrahim wore a traditional Saudi bisht, a long, white cotton robe with a square, cotton ghutra on his head, held there by a gold braided cord—an igal. The gold was gold thread. The cotton was the finest from Egypt. Underneath he wore several rings, bracelets, and a decorative gold watch on his hands and wrist. Though he was an inch taller than Lord Tryphine, his attitude did give a Napoleonic appearance.

Everyone smiled and half laughed as they crammed into the car and it headed away from the airport to an unknown destination. Ibrahim sat in the back with Alan while Terrence rode next to the driver. The car was cramped but luxurious, certainly fit for modern royalty. Alan suspected that Ibrahim was one of the five to ten thousand Saudi royals who ran the country. People without relations to the king or high prince just didn't get to positions of power, money, and interest in this country. Then again, Alan thought, he could just as well be a member of one of the emir of Kuwait's family, or any of the emirs in the Persian Gulf. The western shore was packed with rich royals.

"Gentlemen," Alan started, "I have to admit I feel a little out of my league here. Am I the only one without a royal title?"

They all laughed—even the driver. He'd broken the ice.

"Seriously, gentlemen, how can I help you?"

"Straight to the point then, hmm?" Terrence began. "All right then. Trucial Energy has been a client with Tryphine since the 1920s. Prior to that, the gentlemen who formed Trucial Energy were our clients as well. As you may or may not know Tryphine Banking House is England's oldest and, we believe, finest private investment firm. We've expressed our concerns over Trucial Energy's assets to our friends here in the House of Saud as well as through members of our government, and I imagine that's why your government has sent you."

It made sense to Alan, but he had lots of questions. "Why not have someone from the UK out here? What assets are you talking about more specifically? I'm familiar with the platforms and drilling equipment and so forth, but I don't imagine you'd raise a fuss like this if we were just talking about a few drilling rigs and tanker trucks."

In perfectly clear English, Ibrahim replied, "You're completely correct, Mr. Conferra. We could have had anyone in the UK or a Saudi or anyone from any of the Gulf States. I'm not sure how things are viewed in America, but the world sees this as an American war. Without America Saddam never would have invaded Kuwait. That's why your president sent an army here, why your president is sending men to turn off the oil fires that Saddam and his terrorists started. It's why your president shut down the oil spill Saddam started, and it's why you are here. This is America's war, and America is responsible."

Terrence interjected, "You see, Mr. Conferra, Alan, many Kuwaitis hold America responsible for being invaded. The Saudis hold America responsible for protecting them, and while Trucial Energy assets are Trucial Energy's, we hold the loans on those assets. Those assets are insured by the UK, and the UK will be pressing your country to cover losses on our assets. Is that clear?"

Alan was in business mode, and the unreal surroundings no longer called for comprehension. When it came to work, and money, he was focused.

"Thank you, sir, your Lordship. I still—"

Terrence interrupted. "You can call me Terry, if I may call you Alan?"

"Thank you, Terry. That answers a lot. Still, let's face it, gentlemen...we're not talking about losing a few tanker trucks in combat."

"No, Alan, you're right," Terrence replied. "We're talking about everything—beyond the platforms, pipelines, trucks, and other equipment."

The three looked at each other. It was time to address the elephant in the car. Terrence opened a briefcase at his feet, pulled out a small three-ring binder, and handed it back to Alan. While Alan was opening it, Terrence continued.

"Alan, we're talking about the assets that matter. They're all listed in this report: paper assets, digital assets, and hard assets."

As he was flipping through the report Alan finally learned why he was here. He saw that "paper assets" meant currency; cash. "Digital assets" meant electronic data stored on tapes and discs; data that was in effect electronic money. "Hard assets" meant gold, silver, diamonds, oil, and equipment. All total the report listed over $5 billion (US) in lootable monies that Saddam's forces were believed to have stolen from Trucial Energy sites in Kuwait. Money stolen from Trucial Energy would be repaid by Tryphine Banking House, and that money would be repaid by the UK, and the UK would make the US pay, and that's why the US government had sent someone to confirm, contest, or protect $5 billion in missing money.

Alan took a deep breath, but tried to hide it from his royal contacts. The report detailed the type, amount, and last known location for all the assets, and it instantly became clear that Alan wasn't just going to a war zone, but to the war itself. He would have to visit each site to make a full report, and if anything was missing there was no doubt that Kowalski would send him to the ends of the Earth looking for it.

The car rolled on silently for a while as Alan was given a chance to first skim the report and now read it in detail. When he was done, he closed the binder, tugged at his chin, and looked out the window in thought.

"We're going to have to check out all of these locations, aren't we?" Alan asked.

Ibrahim answered, "Alan, I am your host in this endeavor. Whatever you need I can provide. By the way, when was the last time you ate or slept?"

"I slept on the plane, but haven't eaten in two days, so if we could stop off and grab a bite I'd—"

"There is no need," Ibrahim responded. We're pulling up to your hotel in a moment. The concierge will get you anything you need, and there is a fine restaurant next to the lobby."

The Mercedes pulled up under an awning next to a large hotel. Attendants opened the doors for everyone, but no one got out.

Ibrahim shook Alan's hand. "Take some time to rest and recover from your journey, but please, things are changing here every hour so don't take too long. We'll be in touch soon."

Alan took the hint, gave his pleasantries to both men, and then stepped out of the car. Walking into the lobby of the nicest hotel he had ever seen, Alan was both physically and mentally lost. Despite having been in the same suit for more than forty hours, and extremely hungry, all he could think about was the $5 billion that he was supposed to find in a war zone. Here he was, somewhere in Saudi Arabia, and he had to get to places in Kuwait that he couldn't even pronounce, let alone find.

Serendipity struck.

Alan looked around and spotted the concierge. One of the many men in various military uniforms walked over and got between Alan and the concierge.

"Alan Conferra?" he asked.

"Yes."

"I'm Jim. I'm with the CIA. Come with me if you want to stay alive," he said as he walked back out the door.

Alan couldn't believe it. This had to be some sort of dream or fantasy. Maybe he'd fallen asleep at his desk and was dreaming. There's no way he could—

Jim laughed. "Yeah, I know. You're freaking out. Relax. I was just kidding with ya. I really am with the CIA, though. Come on. You can't stay here. Saudis have the whole place bugged. We've got a safe house nearby. By the way, Wayne Kowalski called me. That's why I'm here. What the hell is this greased goose shit thing he keeps talking about?"

Alan sighed, rolled his eyes, and laughed. He was calming down. Jim seemed legitimate even if it was surely a fake name.

Though he lacked a Western American accent, Jim had the appearance of a cowboy: poorly shaven, aviator sunglasses. He even wore a yellow neckerchief. He was big too: six-foot-two, two hundred pounds. Jim was the stereotype of what many in the world saw as an average American—for better or worse.

Alan was confused by the entire adventure so he figured, Why not go with the man? The thought that Jim could be someone untrustworthy and might just leave him in a hole in the desert never occurred to Alan. They walked out to the employee parking lot rather than have the parking attendants bring a car forward for them. There Jim pointed to an unlocked white Toyota pickup truck, and both men got in.

"Wouldn't they bug this too?" Asked Alan.

"They could, but I've got a spook toy," replied Jim as he pulled out a cassette tape player. Jim pressed play without a cassette in the player. "It's a jammer. Range is only about five feet, but it does the trick."

They pulled out of the hotel lot and headed east on a desert highway.

"So, where we going?" Alan asked.

"We're gonna go up to a little town called Al Jubail about sixty clicks to the north. Call it miles. Then we're gonna stop, get some food, I'm gonna make a few calls, and then we're gonna get to work. You slept on the plane, right?"

Alan looked at him suspiciously and said, "Yeah."

Jim smiled, looked at Alan, the road, then back at Alan again. It's the Middle East, bud. Everyone's listening. I bugged Ibrahim's driver this morning. So, $5 billion in gold, eh? Damn, talk about the worst kept secret in the entire war zone. Everybody knows Saddam invaded Kuwait 'cause of money. He owed 'em billions; money he borrowed during the Iran-Iraq War. Back then Saddam was too busy to do a lot of drilling so the Kuwaitis were letting other companies slant drill under Saddam's border and into his oil reserves. He got pissed, refused to pay; they bitched, and so he invaded. Then yesterday he got caught running away with everything that was possibly valuable in Kuwait. You're gonna be lucky to find any of that gold left in the banks. Iraqi Republican Guard probably blasted the vaults with their tank cannons. It's why they're stopping the war. Couple of flyboys spotted a traffic jam on Highway 80 coming outta Kuwait. Bombed the crap out of 'em, and that's where all the loot is. Truckloads of TVs, stereos, you name it. They took everything including the kitchen sinks. I guess the Air Force hit 'em with everything. No one coulda lived through it."

"It's not all gold, Jim," Alan said. "Money takes a lot of different forms. Hey, I've been on a plane for days, Jim. What are you talking about, stopping the war?"

The map labeled the road "Highway 80," but stretching from Kuwait into Iraq, the road was coming to be known by the rest of the world as the Highway of Death. America's president was ending the war with Iraq after only one hundred hours of ground war. Saddam had been driven from Kuwait, and the UN mission was accomplished. One of the main reasons were these miles of devastation on Highway 80 and Highway 8.

Saddam's forces from Kuwait had not only tried to escape Kuwait, but they also tried to take as much loot with them as possible. It was an army of thieves that had been caught on the open road by US airpower. First to hit the mass theft were a few US Navy A-6 Intruders—Vietnam-era bombers in their last campaign. They'd spotted the packed road and dropped dozens of rockeye cluster bombs on the leading elements. Each rockeye broke open above the ground and released hundreds of softball-sized bomblets; thousands of bomblets in total. Traffic backed up as more aircraft were scrambled and sent to the area. Within minutes scores of American and Coalition bombers were dropping bombs and launching missiles at the trapped Iraqi forces. They had nowhere to go. Tens of thousands were killed or wounded, and the rest were forced to run for their lives in the desert. The slaughter had lasted all day and into the night with flames, smoke, and wreckage under the umbrella of smoke from burning oil wells. It was a scene straight out of Dante's *Inferno.*

"How far away is that from where we're going?" Alan asked.

"Couple hours by truck, couple minutes by helo."

Alan sighed, but he was still in business mode, so his focus was on his job. "All right then, can we get a helo and head up?"

Jim looked at Alan, the road, Alan again, then the road again. After a few moments' pause he determined that Alan might be a desk jockey but he was a professional. It was time to work. He turned north on to a new highway.

"Okay. We'll head to the airport in Al Jubail, then grab a ride up. Air space around here is packed with military out of Bahrain and our carriers. It'll take me some time to make some phone calls. We're gonna need security. There're people from all over the world up here with guns and tanks. While I'm doing that you better get some food. Grab something to go too. Might wanna get something a little less out-of-place to wear. Not gonna see many suits north of Al Jubail. You can loosen your tie too, ya know."

The small city of Dhrahan slipped away in the background, and open desert lay in front of them. The farther north they went the more military vehicles they saw. He could see the smoke from the hundreds of oil well fires that the Iraqis had started. After about half an hour it looked as if they were driving through one long military convoy. Alan was in the war now.

It was midafternoon when they finally got to the tiny airport at Al Jubail. Getting a helicopter didn't seem like it was going to be too hard to arrange. The place was filled with a half dozen different types of military helicopters from as many different nations. It was a beehive of activity with heavy security everywhere. If Jim couldn't arrange a ride, he could always call Ibrahim or Kowalski. In the middle of the night in Washington Kowalski would definitely be in a mood to grease some goose shit and make something happen.

Jim told Alan to "rustle up some grub" while he made the calls. Thankfully the airport had several fast food kiosks, and Alan bought a few pizzas from one of the American-based franchises. The local gift store in the war zone had souvenirs, books and magazines written in Arabic, and some T-shirts, but nothing Alan figured would help him blend in in the war zone. He found a dry cleaners and a tailor, but no one was selling any army chic. Jim found Alan and was thrilled to see the pizzas, but laughed at him about how he was still wearing the same suit he was wearing days earlier in DC.

"Okay, we've got a ride on a US Army bird up to the highway. There we're gonna have our own platoon of Marines to watch over us. It looks like everyone's more concerned about the frontlines now than the damage behind. Not everyone believes Saddam's really gonna give up, so everyone's locked and loaded. You ever handle a weapon?" Jim asked.

"Heh? Uh, no."

Jim thought for a moment and then gave Alan the only briefing he'd have on security or how to do his job. "Okay. Plan B then. We won't go in subtle. Keep your suit on. Don't talk to anyone. *Do not* introduce yourself. Let everyone introduce themselves to you. Don't say your last name, and don't be specific about where you're from in DC or what you do. You're just gonna be Alan-the-important-suit-from-Washington. Got it? Since we can't make you blend in, we're gonna make you stand out so much that no one would dare fuck with you."

"Got it."

"Okay then, our bird's at the end of the line over there. Remember, let me do the talking."

"What do I do with my briefcase and bags?" Alan asked.

"Leave the shaving kit bag here. You're not gonna have time. Just pitch it in a trashcan. What all is in the suit bag?"

"Just a fresh suit I kept on hand at the office."

Jim looked around. "Pitch that too. We'll get you a new suit when we can. Make sure there's no ID or anything else in there. Where we're going, you're gonna be the cleanest thing around even if you've been wearing that for three days now. One more thing, you're gonna see some things you wouldn't see in an office. Shit that's so bad they can't even put pictures in the newspaper or show on TV, and it's gonna fucking smell. Try to focus on the job. This is war. Guys in the field just call it "The Suck." It's okay if you puke; just try not to look like a pussy about it. We want people to see you as someone so important that they wouldn't dare question us or fuck with us."

The two men passed through the crowd with Jim in the lead. His pace changed, as did the way he looked around. He now had the appearance of a personal bodyguard rather than just one person walking with another. They caught a few glances from others, but few stared. Most tried awkwardly to look away and walk away. Alan threw away all of his belongings except his briefcase, and they headed out of the concourse and began walking down the deafening flight line.

A few hundred yards from where they exited, Jim walked up to a UH-60 Blackhawk helicopter. He stopped, then slowly twirled around to do an obvious security check. It was all a show as he was only armed with a hidden nine-millimeter Beretta pistol that even Alan hadn't seen yet. At the helo the crew was already on board and two US Army soldiers were waiting on the left side to meet them. Just like in Dhahran the ambient noise made conversation almost impossible. When Alan and Jim reached the two soldiers, Jim greeted them. He and the Army lieutenant gave each other a thumbs-up, and then everyone climbed inside. Once the doors were slid shut they were given headsets, and everyone could talk.

The lieutenant spoke first as the helicopter lifted a few feet off the ground and began to hover its way down the flight line. "I'm Lieutenant Baker. This is Sergeant Aristide. We've been told to watch out for you guys. Headed up to Highway 80, huh? What are we gonna do up there?"

Alan stayed quiet as he'd been instructed. It was his first time in a helicopter so he ignored the conversation and deliberately focused on the experience—the view outside the window. Jim spoke instead.

"I'm Jim with SAG—Special Activities Group. This is Alan from DC. He's here to assess the damage and report back directly. We've got you two, this bird, and a platoon of Marines once we get up there. That's about all you wanna know, Lieutenant."

Not far down the taxiway the helicopter was cleared for flight. They rose a few hundred feet and headed north. Normally they'd fly a lot higher, but the smoke from the oil well fires was turning day into night with every mile they continued. Flying low was the only way to maintain any visibility. The smoke contained high concentrations of flammable gasses as well, and some aircraft had been lost to engine flameouts. This was dangerous flying, but Alan had no idea. He saw it as a dangerous part of the entire planet.

Wherever he looked out the window he saw flames shooting from the hundreds of oil wells, black-stained sand from oil that had sprayed out, and military vehicles everywhere; tens of thousands of them. The other day he was in a snowy Washington, DC, with cherry blossom trees budding early. He'd gotten on a few planes and gone to Hell.

Then it got worse.

Forty-five minutes into the flight the helicopter was forced to switch to nap-of-the-earth flying. They cruised just high enough to avoid power lines. The smoke was as black as night, but ahead in the distance they could see the lights of Kuwait City to the north. As they drew closer sporadic tracer rounds raced into the sky—fired not by Iraqis, but jubilant and careless Kuwaitis. The town was partying the way Paris did when liberated from the Nazis.

Starting from the left side of the city and heading north Alan got his first glimpse of the Highway of Death. It was a line of black smudges, smoke, and flames. Even with the oil wells burning all around, the line of burning vehicles clearly marked the road. Miles away, Alan was already fighting back a gag from the smell: oils, chemicals, melting metals, and organic stink of every type. Jim moved forward and told the pilots to go all the way up to the top of the road, where the Navy bombers started the traffic jam. On the way Alan had a crystal-clear view of the wrecks and flames just a few feet below the low-flying helicopter.

Eventually they landed in a clear spot ahead of the main traffic jam. Jim took an MP-5 submachine gun from one of the pilots and hopped out the left side. Lieutenant Baker and

Sergeant Aristide stepped out the right side. The helicopter crew shut down and waited for orders.

Jim took control of the situation. "Lieutenant, you guys stay with the helo. Check your targets carefully. I'm expecting to meet up with some other guys who are not going to be in a familiar uniform. If the Marines show up have them set up a perimeter. Alan and I will be right back."

Alan was about to leave his briefcase in the helicopter when Jim stopped him.

"Sir," Jim said loudly enough for everyone to hear, "you'll want to hold on to that. That chopper could get called away." Then he continued under his breath and closer to Alan. "Okay, don't touch anything. If you see something, ask me. There's bound to be lots of unexploded ordnance around here."

Alan adjusted his tie and began walking through the wasteland as if it was something he'd seen every day. The burning bodies of drivers and passengers in the vehicles would be seared in his mind for the rest of his life. Pieces of metal, flesh, and everything imaginable were everywhere. Most vehicles were barely recognizable, having been shredded by American firepower. On his left he might see a truck with a burned Iraqi still at the wheel, and on his right a tank missing its turret. The ground had shredded metal, tires, pieces of meat that were surely human, radios, TVs, and even a decorative lamp. How Alan was supposed to find anything in all this was beyond him.

Jim was right by his side. "Alan, follow me. I have something I want to show you."

"You've been here already?" he asked.

"Yeah. In some ways I guess I'm the reason you're here." Jim looked around to make sure no one could hear. "I was here the night it happened. I was working with some guys who should be still around here. We'll bump into 'em. Just don't lose your cool. Unless I tell you to do something, everything's okay."

"Got it. Where are we going? How am I here because of you?!" Alan asked.

"Well, we got wind of the Navy causing a backup, and so we came over here and started guiding in more airstrikes. One of the guys I was with had a laser designator, and we had an Air Force combat air controller with us. It was just another night at work. So we're out here kickin' ass and blowin' the shit out of everything we can see. We had planes stacked up and waiting to come in and bomb stuff, but there were still targets up on the frontlines and in Baghdad and everywhere else. The guys we were using ran out of missiles and bombs, and we had some Saudi gunships do some work, but after a while we were down to this pair of A-7 Corsairs—planes left over from Vietnam. The guys were loaded with dumb bombs, but the plane's a great airframe for doing precise hits. Anyway, first guy comes in, blows up a few trucks and some cars n' stuff. The next A-7 rolls in, drops a string of bombs, and took out a pair of BMPs—armored cars. Now, this last guy's last two bombs straddled a dump truck but didn't so much as blow out its tires!"

Alan and Jim kept walking and talking, and thanks to the conversation Alan was distracted enough not to see a pile of civilians who had made it out of their van but were mangled by shrapnel in a ditch.

Jim went on. "After we were told to stop bombing the crap out of everything on the road, we waited to make sure there was no one left alive that might smoke us. Then we came out of our hide on that hill over there to the west. The guys and I were checking things out when we found the truck that wouldn't blow up."

"Yeah? What was up?" Alan asked.

"Truck's loaded with what Ibrahim called 'assets.'" It wasn't the kinda thing we wanted to announce on any radio no matter how secure. Guaranteed someone would be listening. I know for a fact the Russians have heard every word of every transmission from last July to now. I told the guys to stay here and guard it, then I went back, made a few calls back home, and you're here."

Alan didn't understand. "You said someone would hear you?"

"Yeah, if you say certain words the satellites monitoring electronic communications—radio, phone, fax, even digital messages—the sats'll record that communication. I just told the guys in Langley that I found Trucial Energy's files a mess and that they were clearly missing stuff. I was as vague as possible. Even with that, you saw firsthand that the Saudis and Brits knew and jumped on it. It wasn't Terrence Tryphine's connections that got the president involved. It was my guys. They told the White House, who asked around for an accounting expert, and you're here."

Alan was again in disbelief at the cloak-and-dagger life.

"Okay, so what kind of assets are we talking about specifically in this dump truck?" he asked.

Jim pointed down the road. "It's probably less than a mile now."

"Jim," Alan stopped and asked, "what are we looking it specifically?"

"Gold, man. The truck's loaded with gold, boxes of documents. There's a box with hard drives, discs, tapes...one of the guys found a briefcase of diamonds—some cut and in rings and necklaces, and others not. Look around, man. Most people see burnt meat and metal on this road. You do this job long enough, and you look beyond that. You can look in every single car, truck, APC, or tank and you'll find loot. Doesn't matter if it's a big-screen TV or pieces of expensive medical equipment, these guys were stealing a country, man."

They continued walking, Jim at the ready with his submachine gun, and Alan in his suit, tie, and briefcase. When the orange dump truck came into view, Jim stopped and shouted, "Hey! It's me! Don't shoot us! We're coming in!"

An unseen voice responded from somewhere down the road. "All right, James Bond, come on in!"

Alan had to ask, "James Bond? Really? CIA guy with a name like Jim? Jim Bond maybe?"

Jim laughed, "Yeah, I didn't think of that until I started using it. Just don't ask me anything else about it, okay? Policy, secrets, and it's embarrassing so...shut up."

They smiled and kept walking through the junkyard. Alan wasn't noticing the pieces of people anymore, but the smell made him grimace no matter how hard he tried. As he went to wipe some dust off his face, he noticed that his suit was sticky. Smoke from the oil fires was slowly raining down a fine mist of tar. Soon enough he'd be without any clothes at all.

Finally they came to the truck—the reason he wasn't asleep in a bed with fluffy white snowflakes and pink cherry tree petals on the windows outside. It was a big rig with the dump bed as its own separate trailer. The body of the truck itself looked like Swiss cheese given the hundreds of holes from shrapnel. All the windows were shattered and/or partially missing. The driver was long gone, thankfully. As they got closer several armed men came out from the surrounding wrecks.

One of them called out, "Jim! Took you long enough! Where the hell've you been? We've been on half rat[ion]s since you left. If you didn't bring us something to eat I'm gonna waste you right here and now." Jim reached over and gave him a big hug. Then he began the introductions.

"Guys, this is Alan. He's from DC. He's a desk jockey, but he's a good guy. They pulled him out of cubicle yesterday, and he just got here a few hours ago. He's here to help us sort this thing out."

"What the fuck's to sort out?!" another one of the soldiers called out.

Jim laughed. "Alan, the guy who wants your pizza is Sam, and the guy who wants to play Finders-Keepers with the truck is Ian. They were with me that night, and they've been out here since making sure no one messes with a truckload of trouble. Where's our wing wiper with the designator?"

Sam responded, "We sent him and the interpreter up to meet you at the helo when we saw you fly by. You didn't see 'em?"

Jim replied comfortably, "Nah, but in that mess it's not unbelievable. We'll meet up with them when we go back up there."

Alan looked each man in the eye, gave his best disarming smile, and then he began shaking hands. "Hi, guys. Alan from DC. Man, I'm sure glad to see you. James Bond here wanted me to have dinner with him at the hotel, but I was eager to get out and see this beachfront property. Love what you've done with the place. I always thought the sky wasn't dark enough. What do you call this color—Oil Slick Gray or Saddam Sunset Orange?"

Jim punched Alan in the arm, called him an asshole, and everyone laughed for a few moments. Alan even loosened his tie.

"Okay, guys." Alan looked around and began to try and sort things out. "We've gotta get this out of the middle of the desert. You're right that this is a truckload of trouble. Jim says the Brits and Sauds probably already know, and that's way too many people. We gotta move. Ideas?"

Sam suggested getting a Chinook helicopter from the Army or a Sea Stallion from the Navy. Ian wanted to get a small Army or Marine convoy to escort it. Jim wanted to bury it or move it into another truck and sneak it out of the war zone. Alan took a moment to look in the bed of the dump truck. It was filled with dust/oil-covered gold bars. That's what made it too heavy to blow up from the bomb blasts. The passenger section was packed with boxes just as Jim had described. There was even the briefcase of diamonds and jewelry.

There's no way this is Trucial Energy's—at least not all of it, he thought to himself. Jim was right: Iraqi troops were stealing a country. Exhausted as he was, Alan's adrenaline was flowing. Anyone who had seen that much gold would get excited.

"Has anyone tried starting the truck?" Alan asked.

The three men all rolled their eyes. None of them had even tried. Sam quickly jumped up and inside. The key was still in it, and it started right up.

"Alan, you've got some serious luck."

"Jim, if I had any luck I'd be in DC, asleep and well fed right now."

Again they huffed in semi-laughter as by Alan's standard they were all unlucky.

"Nothing except a battle lost can be as melancholy as a battle won," Alan said.

All three looked at him.

"Britain's Duke of Wellington—the guy who beat Napoleon at Waterloo?" Alan was in disbelief that none of them had heard it before.

They stared right back in disbelief that an accountant with a suit and tie and briefcase was standing in the middle of the Highway of Death quoting Wellington. Everyone shook their heads and nodded off the unreality they were living. Then Alan turned to Jim and asked to use the satellite phone that was strapped to his waist.

"Who in the world are you going to call?" Jim asked.

"Kowalski in DC. We're gonna need a ride."

The two Navy SEALs and the CIA Special Activities Group agent were all confused, but Alan was getting into the groove of doing his job and completing his task.

"Karen? It's Alan.... Yes, I'm fine, but I need to speak with Mr. Kowalski right away please.... Thank you."

Alan turned to the elite warriors around and smiled again. "It's okay, guys. We're gonna do this. I've got a plan." Then Wayne Kowalski came on the line.

"Alan?! Can you hear me?!"

"Yes, sir. I can hear you, but I can't say much, and I've no idea how long we'll have the connection, and it is *not* a secure line. I need your help, sir."

"Are you okay? What's going on?!"

"Mr. Kowalski," continued Alan, "I'm fine, but I cannot say much! Listen! I need a C-141 like the one I flew in on! I need it ready to go at Al Jubail airfield! It's gotta be empty. Repeat, it must be empty, and I need it there in the next hour or two with no questions asked!"

Kowalski heard, but the "no questions asked" part bothered him. "Are you sure you're okay, Alan?"

"Yes, sir. Fine, sir. I just really need a shower. Can you do this—can you get me the plane, sir? Remember, no questions asked, and it has to be empty."

Kowalski didn't know what was going on, but it was clear to him that Alan was being deliberately vague, and that it was important. Alan was given a huge task. If it was important to get that task, to monitor Trucial Energy's assets, then he'd get that plane there. "You got it, kid! I'll have your plane there faster than you can say greased goose shit!"

Alan hung up.

Jim jogged back up the road to the helicopter to arrange for an airborne escort for the truck. Once there he saw that there was a Marine Corp LAV armored personnel carrier and a squad of Marines. He needed a battalion, hoped for a company, knew he could only expect a platoon, and instead got a squad. Lieutenant Baker had already met the Marines. A few were milling about while others wandered and looked into the wreckage.

"What the hell are you people doing?!" Jim shouted. "This is a high-value secure area. Get that perimeter locked down and stop dickin' around the dead bodies."

Just then a shot rang out. Everyone turned to identify the threat. It was Lieutenant Baker. He'd just decided to fire his pistol into the skull of an Iraqi corpse.

"Lieutenant!" Jim shouted even louder this time. "What ROTC nursery fucking school did they find you crawling out of?! I've a mind to put a cap in your ass myself right here and now! Get in the bird!" He turned to Aristide. "Soldier-boy! You get in the bird with him!"

Jim turned to the Marines. "Who's in charge over here?"

"You are, sir!" shouted the Marine in the commander's hatch on the LAV.

Jim smiled. "Damn fucking straight! Finally, a professional! What's your name, Marine?!"

The Marine climbed out and off of the LAV, and in a more subdued voice replied, "Sergeant Brian Assana, sir. They told us to come up here and meet somebody named Jim. It looks like you're him 'cause no way that Army butter bar looey has enough muscle to make a call and get us up here."

Jim smiled large and openly now. He asked Sergeant Assana about the rest of the men in the squad. They were down several men due to combat wounds and a form of dysentery they called Saddam's revenge. The three of them were all that could be spared, but since they were only able to scrounge the three men, the Marine Corps decided to assign an LAV as well to make up the difference. True to the greatest and most universal military tradition, the orders were messed up, and the LAV crew returned to their unit after bringing the LAV to Assana's unit.

It didn't matter. The empty space inside the LAV would be a nice ride for his laser designator team as well as himself and Alan.

Jim told the Blackhawk pilot to head down to the big dump truck where he'd see several men standing around trying to get it out of the traffic/wreckage jam. Then he told the others to get inside the LAV and drive down there as well. The helicopter had to circle three times before it saw the dump truck, and both the Blackhawk and the LAV arrived at the same time.

Sam and Ian had managed to ram some of the vehicles off the road, but the truck was too big to handle for non-professional big rig drivers. Without having to say a word Sergeant Assana and his Marines stopped and began to hook up a tow cable between the LAV and the semi-tractor trailer dump truck. Alan, the Air Force combat air controller, and the interpreter all moved small pieces of debris out of the way in an effort to keep from losing any tires.

It didn't take long to secure the truck and get it out of the road of wrecks and on to the desert. Once there the Marines reset the tow cable. With eight-wheel-drive on the LAV and eight more wheels on the truck, they were able to move slowly across the tar-covered sands. Behind them lay the white lines of clean sand turned over from the wheels—and images of death than none of them would forget.

Alan fell asleep in the back of the LAV despite its loud diesel engine. With the smoke blotting out the sun, the time zone differences, and the jet lag he had no idea what time of day it was, let alone what day or date. It seemed like a week had passed, but it was only a few more hours until they were away from Highway 80, passed Kuwait City on their left, and headed for Al Jubail. Somewhere along the way the Blackhawk with Lieutenant Baker and Phillipe Aristide on board was called away to carry some media people up to the Highway 80. "If it bleeds it ledes," and there was plenty of blood there.

It was late at night (though the smoke from the oil well fires made it hard to recognize) when the LAV escorted the truck through the gate at Al Jubail. Kuwaiti security guards, of course, wanted to see paperwork and search the truck for explosives. Jim tried to stop them, but he was getting nowhere. The Marines had guessed the truck was packed with money, but they hadn't seen it.

Alan stepped outside of the LAV, tightened his tie, and walked over to the security checkpoint with his briefcase. Jim was trying to physically keep the checkpoint guards away from the truck, but their English was limited. Sergeant Assana had everyone dismount the LAV and take up guard positions to help Jim.

As Alan approached the gate he looked to identify who was in charge. There was a Saudi soldier standing in the background telling another to give orders, and Alan deduced he had to be the man in charge. Even better, he'd figured out who was second in command. He smiled and approached the two men, reached out, and shook their hands. Then, using hand signals, he motioned for permission to open his briefcase. They nodded in agreement. It was clear that neither spoke English, and that made sense as most of the interpreters were up front in combat. Alan pulled out the memo that Kowalski had had drawn up, then he called out to the interpreter who had been with the laser designator team to come over and join them.

"Hi. Hey, could you please tell these men that I have a letter from the president of the United States?"

The interpreter relayed the message.

"Tell them that the president has demanded that as soon as Kuwait is liberated we bring him a truckload of free Kuwaiti soil. The president of the United States will take this personally if we are not let through immediately." Alan presented the letter from the congressman's office. It wasn't from the president, had nothing to do with Kuwait, or soil, and didn't have a presidential seal on it, but the Saudi soldiers would never know.

The interpreter relayed the message. The Saudi officer nodded, and his second in command waived them through.

Jim hopped on to the back of the truck as everyone else jumped back into the LAV and both vehicles headed for the tarmac. Once they had found a spot away from all the other aircraft and vehicles, they parked. Jim thanked the Marines and told them to head back to their unit when they saw fit. Then he asked his Air Force combat air controller to report to the duty officer. The interpreter went with him. Sam, Ian, and Jim stood with the shredded dump truck.

"Okay, so what do we do now?" Alan asked.

Jim looked at the others, then at Alan. "Hey, man, it's your show now. We'll get you on the truck, and then we're off your clock and back in the game here."

Sam and Ian looked around for threats, and spotted a C-141 coming in for a landing.

Sam smiled and reached to shake Alan's hand. "Looks like your ride's here, bud."

Ian asked Alan the big question. "What're you going to do with it?"

"Well," said Alan, "I've been thinking a lot on that. It's not ours. It can't all be Trucial Energy's. It can't be all Kuwait's. I'm gonna bring it back to DC. We'll put it in an escrow account there, make some local bank happy as hell, and then we'll sort it all out. Trucial Energy's gonna get paid back whatever losses they claim. Same is true of Kuwait. Right now, this is nobody's and everybody's."

They all paused. Then they looked at each other, smiled, and as one voice Jim, Sam, and Ian all said, "Naaaaaah, too heavy to carry. Besides it'd just get us in trouble." They'd all thought about taking at least a bar, but none of them did. Like Alan, they all certainly liked having money, but there was something else that they liked more. Some would call it self-respect, or honor, or integrity. Few would understand it.

Twenty-four hours later, Alan met Wayne Kowalski and Congressman Henderson at Andrews Air Force base. His suit was crumpled, wrinkled, ruined with a layer of tar, stank of chemicals and death. He hadn't showered in days, but when he walked off the plane he had his briefcase in hand and his tie tight. Alan looked like he'd been through Hell, because he had been. The cubicle-cruising accountant who no one had ever heard of had done the impossible, and he'd done it with little more than a memo and some phone calls.

The truck's engine had succumbed to battle damage. It refused to start. Kowalski arranged for an aircraft tow cart to drag it off the plane. They stored it in a secure hangar where Air Force guards protected it until Alan could arrange for an armored car company to offload the "assets." The same guards who watched over stealth bombers, Air Force One, and other high-value assets could be counted on to keep the truck and its content secret for the time being.

Congressman Henderson was in awe.

Kowalski was in shock.

Alan was dead-dog tired. He asked for a raise, a new pair of suits, and a week off. He got two weeks off, but that was it. It didn't matter. His mind was numb having been on a reality trip that could make LSD look like cough drops.

A few days later Alan would begin dispersing the truckload of assets amongst various banks. It was a fast and easy way to make sure other people had to do the specific counting, ensuring that he could tell the congressman exactly what was recovered. To avoid even the appearance of impropriety he made sure that the accounts were only manageable by himself, Kowalski, the congressman, and "an officer of the Department of Treasury authorized by the president of the United States." The president would have to decide who would bear that title. In doing this Alan had made the president involved in the dispersal of fund decision, but it would be up to Kowalski and the congressman to decide if they informed the president. Until then, the money was safely spread out, turned into electronic funds, completely counted, and hidden from all the entities—American and foreign—who wanted to claim it as their own.

***

3/10/1991

Sergeant Brian Assana rode inside a Marine Corps LAV-25 armored personnel. They'd been detailed away from their company almost two weeks previous for a special escort assignment. Since then their unit had moved up through Kuwait and was dug in along the Kuwait/Iraq border. They, however, had become the company errand boys. Rather than sending the remnants of their platoon out on patrols or any of the other platoons, Assana and his friends had been sent on multiple supply duties, escort duties, and innumerable patrols into Iraq. Saddam had been defeated, and all that was left now was to make sure the hundred-hour war didn't start back up again with another surprise like the one they had at Khafji before the war. For them, it wasn't one hundred hours of combat, but one hundred hours of running errands and getting almost no sleep at all.

The platoon had taken losses too, but none to direct combat. Of the thirty-two men they brought across the border into Kuwait, six were taken off the line by a local form of dysentery. Two others were sent back because they'd gotten into a brawl that ended with both young men having broken bones. Four were taken from the platoon to act as a security detail for a reporter who was following the company commander. Another man had been sent away by the company commander for unknown reasons (everyone suspected he just wasn't ready to see the carnage in Kuwait and was sent home). That left the platoon with basically one squad to do the work of three. When put in hour shifts it meant that at any time only four or five Marines were watching a stretch of the frontline meant for thirty-two or more.

Their company commander had been given the LAV to make up the difference, but in classic military organization the crew never came. Brian had been sent to find them, and when they couldn't find the crew, he took it upon himself to take the LAV and return with it. Stealing an armored vehicle that had been assigned to the platoon anyway wasn't really stealing, but since he was already qualified in its use, Brian not only appropriated the vehicle but the new duties that came with it.

On this particular Sunday they'd been sent back to Kuwait to try and get the four men who'd been assigned as a security detail off of that duty and back up to the line. With thousands and thousands of military vehicles going all over Kuwait and Southern Iraq as well as countless of destroyed Iraqi vehicles, traffic was a mess. Few road signs, and fewer road signs in English, made it even worse. Brian, stood in the LAV turret's commander's hatch. They had gone off of Highway 801, headed west to avoid the traffic, and gotten substantially lost. After less than two hours of driving they had managed to find a farm in the middle of the Kuwaiti desert, and from that they determined that they were west northwest of Kuwait City.

The Mohammed Al d'uut farm was a disorganized maze of palm groves and thousands of shredded plastic greenhouses. Arab troops from Saudi Arabia, the Gulf States, and free Kuwaiti forces seemed to wander in every direction. Melting plastic from the greenhouses mixed with the smell of the oil wells and the hundreds of thousands of tons of high explosive that had been used over the past few days.

The Marines had their goggles on and cloth wrapped around their faces. It was of little use. Sand particles—smaller than talcum powder—caked the makeshift masks. Millions and millions of flies were already swarming everywhere, having hatched from the dead bodies of a scattered and slain Iraqi army. There was a stench of melted greenhouse plastic and burned human meat everywhere.

They drove for more than an hour, asked for directions three times from different Coalition troops that they passed, and finally made it out of the farm's maze of access roads. "Murphy's Law" had struck, and the shortcut on their journey south had left them north of where they had started hours earlier. They were now in Southern Iraq.

Not long after re-entering the traffic jam from Hell (in what actually looked like Hell), there was a giant flash of light to the north. The Marines looked and while shockwaves spread out and at least eight giant fireballs rose into the sky. US Army demolitions troops had found one of Saddam's ammunition depots and destroyed it. The explosion at the Khamisiyah depot was the equivalent of a tactical nuclear weapon.

After two more hours of crawling through traffic and wreckage they were finally in Kuwait City. What had once been a jewel on the Persian Gulf was peppered with bullet holes, rampant robbery, and destruction for destruction's sake. Once-pristine beaches were covered with thick layers of barbed wire and land mines. Fires burned from buildings even days after the war had officially ended. Still, the people were out and already cleaning things up to the best of their abilities. Countless waves and smiles greeted the three Marines as they drove through the streets to the division headquarters.

At division headquarters Brian began asking officers where he should look for his lost security detail. No one wanted to help him. Everyone was busy with their own lists of things to do. The entire Coalition army had moved faster than any other army in history, but the price was that all the units were now mixed up, and untangling the mess while trying to send people home as fast as possible was a bureaucratic nightmare. Already some troops—the ones who were first deployed half a year earlier in Operation Desert Shield—had landed at home to parades and cheering families. Meanwhile, in Kuwait City, it was Situation Normal, All Fucked Up (SNAFU).

By late afternoon, Brian had found a media center and located the four missing Marines. They were having dinner and sitting around a pizza place that had been flown in and set up already. Aside from the uniforms and war zone, they might as well have been a few eighteen- and nineteen-year-old kids sitting at a shopping mall, camouflaged and armed with rifles. Despite the business of the people all around them, everyone was in great spirits. They had come and faced the fourth largest army in the world, decimated it in one hundred hours, and now were headed home. There was a certain level of frustration since their unit hadn't been involved in any of the combat for which they'd trained months, even years, but the victory and the impending trip home made everything good.

***

4/5/1992

Sarajevo was no longer an idyllic European tourist destination. The 1984 Winter Olympics had brought a boom in international prestige unlike any previous host city. Just a few years later, however, Yugoslavia no longer existed. The Soviet Union, which had supported it, no longer existed. Order no longer existed. Now it was the capital of Bosnia-Herzegovina. On this Sunday the triangle-shaped valley floor upon which the city rested echoed with church bells, Muslim calls to prayer, and the thunder of Serbian artillery fire.

Eighteen thousand Serbs from the former Yugoslavia had encircled the city. The United Nations, fresh off of its victory over Iraq, recognized a new Bosnia-Herzegovina state. Serbs and military leaders from the former Yugoslavia drew a border and declared their own Bosnian state, Republika Srpska. As with all wars there was a long list of causes, and a long list of reasons people fought, but more than anything the Serbs who had controlled Yugoslavia since the end of World War II wanted to maintain a continuity of the Yugoslav government even if it meant under a new name.

Many in Yugoslavia wanted to live under governments that more directly represented the people in different areas. Slovenians wanted a portion of Yugoslavia to separate and become Slovenia. The same held true with Croats who wanted to live in a country called Croatia, and they didn't want to be part of a Yugoslavian government dominated by ethnic Serbians. Bosnians and Herzegovinians wanted their own independent nation that would understand and represent their regional Muslim heritage. Historic heritages, different nationalities, different religious views, even ethnic prejudices all led to a pile of tinder, and as that pile grew taller and taller by injustices (real and/or perceived) the pile threatened to catch fire by friction from its own weight. By 1992, a simple spark at a wedding—over a Serbian flag—set a twig in the pile on fire, and it grew to set another burning, then another until there was war.

Over the next three weeks the booming sound of artillery would grow and grow as would the constant popping of automatic weapons fire and the crack of sniper rifles. By May 2, Sarajevo would be completely cut off from the rest of the planet. More than half a million people were trapped by thirteen thousand to eighteen thousand Serbs in the hills. When the Bosnian military units in the city fortified themselves, the Serbs redirected their fire at the civilians. Mortars, artillery, and snipers would kill fourteen thousand people in the city. Marketplaces, women, and children were prime targets of the Serbian artillery units and snipers.

The siege of Sarajevo would go on for 1,425 days until it ended in 1996. It would hold the record for the longest post-World War II siege of the twentieth century. For four years it went on and on. Governments around Europe and the rest of the world would come and go, but for those years the people in the valley struggled to find clean water, food, and medicine, and they struggled to stay alive despite the thousands of snipers and an average of 377 artillery shells a day (peaking at three thousand plus on one day). As with any siege, conditions inside the city deteriorated rapidly.

Houses were razed. Trenches and bunkers were dug. Mass transportation ceased along with all city services. Tall office buildings burned uncontrollably as Serbian tanks fired shot after shot into them. There weren't even firemen in Sarajevo.

Groups of people acted like police forces, but there was no effective police force. No electricity or running water. People starved. Money became useless as bartering ruled the streets.

Outside Sarajevo the world watched, and diplomats debated, but nothing substantial or effective was done. Charities were formed, and aid was sent from time to time, but only at the whim of the Serbian antiaircraft artillery units in the hills surrounding the city airport. Peacekeeping military units were sent to surrounding areas, but they were not allowed to use their weapons. Baby blue United Nations helmets and peaceful-looking, white armored cars of the UN were laughed at—even targeted—by the Serbs as there was no fear whatsoever of international retaliation.

Besides the UN and occasionally NATO, militant Muslims from all over the world saw the siege as an opportunity to wage a holy jihad against infidels in the city. Hundreds of these jihadis came from Turkey. Thousands more came from Syria, Iraq, Lebanon, Libya, Tunisia, and East Africa, and absent a Soviet Union to fight in Afghanistan, thousands of "Arab Afghans" came from various brigades. Bosnia became a training ground for those who followed a violent form of Islam.

Sarajevo, Bosnia, Croatia, the Balkans...in the early part of the twentieth century the area had been on the cusp of chaos, and the assassination of a single person, Archduke Ferdinand, had set off the first world war. At the end of the twentieth century it was in chaos again. Support from former Turkish provinces, and from Russia, was in the hills above Sarajevo. On the other side, all around Europe there was fear and shame at the war in the former Yugoslavia; fear of taking action that would again spark a world war, and shame of having been paralyzed by that same fear.

Erwin Zimmermann wasn't European royalty, but by the end of the twentieth century Europe just didn't have as many people with titles as when it began. Kings, queens, emperors, and czars were largely extinct, but princes, princesses, barons, and so forth still ruled over the most exclusive social circles. After the first and second world wars those same circles were now open to the new power brokers of Europe—occasionally even the outside world—but a noble family was still a noble family.

Erwin hadn't grown up in aristocratic cliques. After years of successful banking and having accrued remarkable wealth for himself as well as (more importantly) others, he was, however, part of the "in" crowd. Whenever and wherever there were dinner parties, weddings, funerals, or any excuse to meet others of their class, it was not at all unusual to find him and his wife walking around, shaking hands, and giving polite kisses to Europe's oldest families. Erwin Zimmermann was not a particularly flamboyant or famous person. His ego fit in almost as well as his wealth. There was money and power and information to be gathered, and all it required was Olympic-level social graces. Besides, just as everyone likes a good party, Erwin liked being at the best parties.

On this particular Sunday afternoon he had been invited to a tea party for one of his clients just outside of London. Specifically, the wife of Lord Terrence Tryphine from Tryphine Banking House, Joan, had asked Erwin's wife, Roese, for tea. The two were longtime friends. Their friendship had led to a professional friendship with Lord Tryphine and a solid relationship between Erwin and the oldest private bank in the United Kingdom. The Tryphines and Zimmermanns would never be family, but they were certainly close couples.

Out in the country west/southwest of the London metropolis, the Tryphines had a home in the little town of Guildford. It was a cute home by American standards, small, even modest to their wealthiest friends, but large enough to make modern peasantry who lived in townhouses and apartments extremely jealous. The home had been built in the late eighteenth century on a one-way street/alley called Castle Hill. The brick walls along the alley hid most of the homes, but a gate in the wall opened up to the estate's parking lot and garages. Here, in the backyard of their Guildford home the trees and brush had been cleared to provide a beautiful view of Guildford castle on the neighboring hill, and its lovely gardens in the swale between the two.

Though Guildford Castle was technically a national historic site, it wasn't a normally busy place. On Sundays it was closed to the public, and in the wake of restoration funds amply provided by Tryphine House Bank, Lord Tryphine effectively had has own private castle and gardens with which to have a monthly tea such as this one. This month, however, there was no crowd of sycophants and snobbery. Instead, it was just the two families.

After the normal handshakes, hugs, and faux kisses, the ladies moved to the gardens while Erwin and Terry watched from a veranda at the rear of the house.

"Erwin, my friend, I'm going to advise you of something, and I wonder if you could return the favor?" Lord Tryphine asked.

"Of course, Terry."

"Erwin, this is of the highest level of privilege, you understand. Tryphine House is of course deeply involved with many members of Parliament and such. Just as I value the conversations you and I have, I also value the ones I have with those particular ladies and gentlemen. It's come to my attention from a number of these privileged conversations that there will, in fact, be a move to remove the pound sterling from the ERM later this year—perhaps in a few months."

The ERM, European Exchange Rate Mechanism, was an agreement between most of the nation-states of Europe designed to maintain stability in the exchange rates between states. This was intended to make trade in Europe easier and faster, and add stability between the European and world markets. Removing the British pound sterling from the agreement would allow the British government to raise interest rates on bonds with the intent of luring investors to buy British debt and bring more stability to the United Kingdom's budget.

Erwin was shocked at the information, and it was impossible to hide. This change in monetary policy was a very risky endeavor. At best it could spell the end of the ERM and encourage other nations to leave as well, thus creating a dramatic change in the value of various European currencies. At worst it could fail and the UK might default on its current bondholders, risking an economic collapse. Surely there was some middle ground, Erwin thought, but in any event the change would be significant, and those privy to this in advance could speculate on currencies before the withdrawal from the ERM and make millions, even billions.

"How certain are you of this?" Erwin asked.

Terry sipped his tea and looked outside, down the hill, into the gardens, and up at the castle.

"I'm certain of it."

Both men paused for a moment and considered the ramifications of this coming change in monetary policy. How they could profit from it was obvious to each, but when people reach a certain level of wealth where money is a plaything, they more often than not look past their own futures, and consider the wider future. Would Britain survive or thrive? Would people still have money to buy milk and bread, or would their money be useless? It had happened in the past, countless times, and to every country. They both knew that it was profitable information, but that it was so valuable they dare not share it with anyone else lest they risk a run on the banks and markets.

"You can see where this is both an opportunity and a challenge, and as such it puts Tryphine House in a position where hard currencies and valuables will be more important than the soon-to-be chaos of paper and electronic monies. To that end I'm looking for something that was lost last year."

"What would that be?" Erwin asked.

"Last year some of our clients lost track of a sizeable amount of hard currency assets when Kuwait was liberated. The emir of Kuwait, sultan of Oman, many of their princes, and of course Trucial Energy were all victims of Saddam's great robbery. All of them have had their insured losses reimbursed by various entities. The United Nations, the International Monetary Fund, the House of Saud, even your government and mine have contributed to the reimbursement. Still, the question remains: What happened to all that hard currency? Some say Saddam managed to steal it and get it into Iraq, but we've had some American clients who have individually suggested that the American government recovered truckloads of gold and more. A few of these rumors corroborate."

As Terry paused to sip his tea, Erwin interrupted.

"I've heard similar allegations from a few of my own clients. The most detailed story that I've heard was that the CIA found it and took it back to America. Other stories say US Army commandos seized it. Some of my Trucial Energy clients are very frustrated—even after they've been reimbursed. I had one claim that an American congressman stole it."

"An American congressman?"

"Yes, I'm trying to think of which one."

Terry put down his tea. He remembered meeting someone from a congressman's office when he was in Saudi Arabia just after the fighting in Kuwait ended. What was that congressman's name? No, it wasn't a congressman, it was a congressman's staff member...an accountant. It couldn't have been that person, though. He was no commando or soldier or CIA agent. It had to be someone else, Terry thought.

Erwin continued.

"Henderson. That's who it was. I was at a wedding reception in Dubai last winter, and Ibrahim al Douri told me that the American Department of Treasury planned to repatriate his losses, but that the funds were temporarily under the control of Congressman Henderson's office. He was very upset because apparently he met with someone from the congressman's office as the war was ending, and the person from that office had been sent to monitor and report on his losses, not steal them—as he put it."

Both men looked at each other and thought the same thing. The Americans had untraceable hard currency—

specifically gold—and both Lord Tryphine and Erwin Zimmermann would need hard currency to survive and even thrive in the forthcoming economic crisis that was about to shake the United Kingdom, Europe, and the world.

"You know, Terry, this change in monetary policy couldn't come at a worse time. Yugoslavia is looking worse and worse by the day. Everyone remembers where the First World War began. Now, with Sarajevo surrounded, the Russians arming the Serbs, and all of NATO quietly arming everyone else, it could explode."

"I know, Erwin. You're absolutely correct, of course. Tryphine House clients are terrified that the 'trouble' will spread. Here you and I stand watching our wives in the garden, and a mere 1,600 kilometers away there is Hell on Earth waiting to spread like a cancer. Truly, I can't see it ending until larger entities force the peace. The United Kingdom can't afford it—certainly not now. France has been averse to all sorts of military action since the Great War. Germany can't be seen conducting foreign military operations. That leaves the Americans and the Russians to dominate what happens in Europe—yet again."

As a German himself Erwin understood the antiwar stance of the German people very well. He'd grown up surrounded by a hatred of war. During the Cold War Germany was a planned nuclear battlefield. No, Germany would not fight. Not a particularly religious man, he prayed he'd never see his nation at war again.

"I don't think the Americans have the desire to get involved—not now at least." Erwin suggested.

"I don't either," Terry replied. "That's awful for the people in Yugoslavia, but best for Europe and the world, I'm afraid. Still, something has to be done about the suffering there. Do you have any clients in that area?"

"I've only a few. I believe two are Croatian and one is Slovenian. Of course, we both have friends in Montenegro and Albania, I'm sure. Why do you ask?"

"Sarajevo is surrounded, but United Nations flights and convoys are occasionally allowed into the city to bring humanitarian supplies."

Erwin looked at him with a tilted head and concentrated eyes. "Yes, but I don't understand. What are you thinking?"

"We're going to need hard currencies as soon as possible. I doubt the Americans will just hand us over that which they robbed from the Iraqi robbers. Without letting your clients or mine know about the removal from the ERM, if we could suggest that they withdraw their hard currencies from the region, Tryphine House could serve as a safe haven from a war zone. Perhaps they could put some pressure on NATO or the Americans to fly out their reserves from Sarajevo?"

Erwin was confused. "I'm not sure I understand. How much hard currency could there be in Sarajevo? If there was that much, the city could have paid the Serbs to leave them alone and ended the siege. I understand that the clients would surely be eager to move hard currency out of a war zone, but this has been going on for months now. What would make them suddenly want to make a move?"

Terry smiled, put his tea down, sat down, and clasped his hands. "Erwin, you're an advisor, and they seek your advice. They respect it—value it. For centuries now Tryphine House has been a place for treasures to be kept safe. People often covet their treasure. If you and I advise the right people that their treasures are not safe, and need to be moved to a safe place...that's the easiest advice to ever give our clients. We can't let what happened in Kuwait happen again here in Europe."

Erwin smiled and gave a slight chuckle. "Advise our clients to advise the Americans and NATO nations to help them get their gold and other hard currencies our of a chaotic war zone that has in the past and may in the future be the epicenter of world war.... I suppose you're right. I suspect that once provisions are made for a few clients and other investors, and once that's known, it's likely to create an avalanche of pressure for a currency air lift. Deliberately causing a run on banks is not something I've ever considered, but in this case it sounds like the soundest action anyone can take."

It was of no consequence or thought for either man that the fate of hundreds of thousands of people in the Balkans or hundreds of millions in Europe had just been altered. Days later both men began advising specific clients that they should put pressure on the Americans and NATO members to help them fly hard currency out of Sarajevo so that they may put gold and other reserves into Tryphine House for safe keeping.

Erwin walked to the window and looked out. In the distance he saw their two wives. They reminded him of beautiful little girls in a garden. The sun was getting low on the horizon, and the low, puffy clouds were casting perfect shadows that flowed across the scene as in a painting. How he loved Roese. Money, accounting, war...none if it meant as much as a heartbeat to him. Though the moment and view were in his mind, they belonged to her. For the moment, she was in perfect happiness, and he lost himself in that moment as well. Absorbed as he was in the imagery, he'd managed to forget just for a little bit that Roese was dying of ovarian cancer. Instead, he could hear their distant laughter through the window's glass.

***

5/4/1992

Though he'd been "on the job" at the East Cleveland Police Department for several months, Officer Brian Assana was still considered a rookie. That would change in time. As with rookies in the military, in other first responder jobs, or in many other fields, "the new guy" tended to get the least savory of tasks. This night was to be one of those moments.

In the wake of a racially charged verdict regarding a case in which police officers in Los Angeles were caught on camera beating a suspected drunk driver, things in the area were similarly charged. There had been race riots in Los Angeles and in other places around the country, and East Cleveland had a distinctly simmering atmosphere—particularly toward white police officers like Brian. People in town were already coming to recognize him on patrols, and some had come to respect him—even liked him—but America's age-old racial division held ancient wounds that would still take decades to heal.

One of Brian's "new guy" tasks was to work late nights. This provided him with complex situations while at the same time a slower pace in which he could gain his experience. His wife didn't like it, but he did. As most rookie officers, he liked being a policeman. Older veterans always tended to be more salty and laissez-faire, and he looked at them as dark shadows of what kind of cop he didn't want to become. He'd been partnered with a veteran officer who was not jaded, who was supposed to mentor him, and who did so as if Brian were his son.

Around 11:30 p.m. the two men responded to an "officer needs assistance" call at George Peake Elementary. They were only eight blocks away and were there in a minute. Two other cars responded, and all six reinforcements headed for the school. Out front two other officers were hiding behind two large oak trees with their backs to the school. They were tucked in tight. Brian and the others ran up to them to see how they could help, and one of the veteran officers behind the tree looked Brian square in the eyes. "You better not stand there, kid," he said, but it was already too late.

From inside the school a fire hose blasted out. One of the doors was half glass, and the man inside had broken it, gone into the school, and was using a fire hose to keep everyone away. Brian was hit with the full force of the fire hose and was blasted off his feet. He slid down a small brick wall and on to the sidewalk, where he lay flat, out of the fire hose's angle of attack.

Dazed, soaked, already cold, and fully embarrassed, Brian shook his head. He found his hat, put it back on, and looked up at the officers behind the trees.

"I told you," the one hiding officer said.

Brian shook his head, called him an asshole, and maneuvered to him—also using the tree to block any blast from the fire hose. His partner had made it all the way to the school and was standing next to the door with two of the responding officers who had also made it. Two others were hiding behind trees.

"C'mon, dickhead," Brian told the officer behind the trees. Then he led the way to the school so that they might meet up with his partner and the others. The other three police officers who were hiding behind trees ran as well. Again the firehose blasted from where the window on the door had been, but this time it only knocked down two of the responding officers. Brian and the first two officers on the scene made it to the school.

They stacked up like a SWAT team with their batons at the ready. There was a "Ready, Set, Go" from Brian's mentor, and then they all tried to swamp their way through the school door. Two men went down from the firehose immediately. Brian managed to get the door open before he was sent summersaulting down a grassy knoll. Then the rest of the police charged into the stairwell where the man with the firehose had been standing.

The hose was unsecure and flying all over—blasting everyone and keeping everything slippery. All of the policemen jumped on the man and were trying to subdue him, but he was large, very drunk, and very naked; i.e., very slippery. As the police wrestled, punched, and tried to stand to get a better stance against the man, the hose kept blasting, and the man began screaming, "Rodney King! Rodney King!" It was no one's finest moment.

Brian was the last inside. He walked past the mountain of Cleveland police officer and down the hall, where he turned off the firehose. Immediately thereafter the man was cuffed and carried out by five officers. All the while the man kept screaming, "I'm gonna burn all you mothafuckas with my flamethrower!" In reality, the alleged flamethrower was, of course, an elementary school firehose that had just completely soaked half the entire East Cleveland Police shift to the bone.

Racism and prejudice was nothing new to Brian. He'd seen it in the Marines. He's seen it among the different Sunni, Shia, and Christians in the Middle East. It was easy enough to see for him. Judging how such divisions were expressed was going to take time for Brian to really grasp, however. What was clear, after the firehose battle, was that even a naked drunk with a firehose could be a serious force to be reckoned with when prejudices were in the mix. Funny as the story was to tell his wife, he imagined what it would have been like if the man had a gun, and he didn't share that thought with her.

***

2/26/1993

At 12:11 p.m. a yellow rental van gently rolled into the underground B-2 level of the parking garage below the North Tower of New York City's World Trade Center. Two men exited the vehicle. One lit a twenty-foot fuse, and they ran away. A few minutes later, a 1,300-pound homemade bomb made of urea nitrate-hydrogen exploded inside the van. The overpressure from the blast exceeded 150,000 pounds of pressure per square inch on everything in its path. Extra-reinforced concrete floor disintegrated on four floors. Vertical steel support beams were stripped clean of all fire-resistant coatings. Hundreds of parked cars were torn to shreds in less than half a second. The blast cut power and phone service to two entire zip codes. Refrigeration units were ruptured as well as a waterline to the Hudson River, causing the basement and part of the subway system to fill with water. Part of the blast shattered the walls around some of the elevator shafts and stairwells, and toxic smoke rushed up through to the 93rd floor of both buildings. Over a thousand people were seriously injured in the terrorist attack. Six died.

Many of the parked cars caught fire and weakened the vertical beams that held up the tower—beams that had already lost the horizontal support that the floor provided and were at the moment carrying five to ten times the normal stress they were designed to bear. Left unchecked, the fire would soften the steel and the weight of the tower would bend them, allowing it to fall on to the South Tower. A quarter million people were at risk in an instant. Thick smoke hindered the fire department's efforts, and no one knew how long the tower would stand—if at all. Few even knew what had happened.

No one knew it was a terrorist attack.

In Washington, DC, Alan Conferra's phone rang just before 1 p.m.

"Senator Henderson's office—Alan Conferra speaking."

"Mr. Conferra," a rushed male voice answered. "My name is Dan Hurt. I'm with the Department of Treasury's Federal Reserve liaison office. We're notifying all the congressional offices with members who are on the Banking, Housing, and Urban Affairs Committees. I don't know if you've heard or not but there's been a blast at the World Trade Center. No one seems to know what caused it, but there's a problem starting, and action will need to be taken very soon. Arrangements are already being made to have a joint committee conference call with all the members, but Senator Henderson's chief of staff suggested I brief you on what's happening."

"Sounds bad. What's going on?"

"It is. We don't know much, but power and communications are out at the World Trade Center and spotty around the area. We're already seeing what could be a run on the banks and investment firms. It's clear the banks in the immediate area are seeing plenty of reallocations, but without communications, funds can only be removed in the transfers and not accepted."

"Is there any way to reroute? Is anyone talking about halting trading yet?"

"No, sir, on both," Dan replied.

"Isn't there any contingency planning or suggestions from your office? What's the Fed want to do?"

"Sir, if there was a plan, no one knows it, and the Fed's still assembling. We've got major banks refusing to take transfers, but withdrawals aren't being stopped. New York's just a mess."

"Who's taking lead?" Alan asked.

"Right now, no one. It only happened about half an hour ago, but someone's going to have to do something in the next hour or less, we think."

"Okay, I'll brief the senator and sit in with him on the call. When is it?"

"We're hoping to have it in about ten minutes," Dan replied.

Alan thought for a moment. If withdrawals weren't made between institutions, America's financial system could collapse, and even if they were then it could be choked to death. The control mechanisms were all in multiple departments in Washington and New York. DC had no plans in motion, and New York had no controls. A simple boiler explosion in just the right place could bring down the country in economic collapse if something wasn't done right away.

"Dan, is there an offsite that the Fed can use in the interim? Why can't transfers and so forth be moved through one of the other Fed locations?"

"We've got several offsite support options available in New York, but we haven't been able to connect with them yet. Over the past few years now we've been trying to get everything digital, but so far Cleveland's the only one that's close enough to a secure Internet hub to have been hooked up. I'll find out if we can just switch to them for a while, but no one has any idea how to do the non-digital transfers."

Alan thought for a moment. "All the banks and everyone know how to do digital transfers and reallocations, right?"

"Most should, but a lot of people haven't because...well, it's New York, it's what they know, and—wait..." Dan picked up on Alan's idea. "Yeah, maybe if we just reroute to Cleveland, tell the major banks to go digital, and then ask everyone else to work through all the other locations then it'll disperse their calls enough for the different Federal Reserve branches to handle...at least for a few hours. I'll run it up the flag pole and see what happens. Either way, we'll call you in nine for the conference call."

Alan smiled and shook his head. It was a simple solution, but multiple departments and agencies often made simple solutions hard to find. This was particularly the case with Washington, DC, as well as with any major corporation...like the big banks. Adding even further to the problem was the generational difference between an older generation of bureaucrats and bankers who grew up using heavy rotary dial telephones, and the younger generation of new, usually lower-level staff who understood the digital world. It was a recipe for confusion that too often Washington did so well.

So simple, he thought.

He got up from his cubicle, walked down the aisle, and found Kowalski. They walked together to the congressman's office while Alan tried to explain what was going on. Kowalski and Senator Henderson were familiar with how banks and the market moved money around all day, but the specific cash flow problems resulting from the World Trade Center explosion needed some explaining. The short-short version was that the world was going digital, and there was no stopping it. Digitalization made things more vulnerable to things like the explosion in New York, but it also made it a lot easier to shift the way things got done without much of a problem.

When the conference call came, there were the usual list of government pleasantries and thank yous. However, instead of being a call for ideas, it was a briefing on what the Fed and Treasury Department were doing to handle what could have been an economic meltdown. They announced that digital transactions were being routed through Cleveland, and all other transactions were being directed to other Fed locations. They announced Alan's idea and took credit for it.

Frustrated, Alan hid his expression by flipping through some notes he had taken. Kowalski, who was sitting next to him, patted him on the shoulder. The senator looked at him too.

Wayne smiled, leaned close to him, and whispered, "Alan, I think we're gonna have to get you an office."

They laughed quietly. Senator Henderson didn't laugh. Instead, when the crisis call/briefing was complete he asked about the elephant in the room, the question no one else had been concerned enough to ask. "What caused the explosion at the World Trade Center?"

The Treasury Department had an assistant to the Secret Service sit in on the call. "Sir, preliminary thinking was that it was a boiler, but from what we're hearing it's far too big to have been something like that. No one is going to call it a terrorist incident without any solid, physical evidence, but the FBI was apparently expecting some sort of incident in New York, and they're confident that this is it. They even had an investigation going with some excellent sourcing, we're told, and there's speculation that it might even have been state-sponsored. I must stress, however, that this is all preliminary and speculative. People are still being evacuated from the buildings. The smoke is extremely bad—as I'm sure everyone has seen on TV. No one has really even been able to see the entire damaged area all at once. The city has engineers already there checking out the structural integrity of each tower. They are, of course, very concerned about one collapsing—or worse, falling over. I'd direct everyone to the FBI and the intelligence services for better information on the blast itself."

Senator Henderson thanked them, and after a few more questions from some of the other members of Congress—as well as their banking and accounting staff—the call ended. Then he turned to talk to Alan with his rich southern accent and "down-home charm."

"Alan, those people at the Fed panicked today, and you pulled 'em out of the frying pan in a big way. Wayne, get Alan an office, a nice one, and double his pay. He needs a new title too. We should've done that when he came back from Iraq. I want

Alan to dedicate all of his time to following the money. Alan, you'll give me a report every day on what you're seeing. I want to know how the money is flowing here in the US, and I want to know what kind of financial threats we're seeing from other nations. This very well might be an attack aimed at our economy. If it is, I want to know as much as we can. You'll be coming with me to the Banking and Urban Affairs Committee meetings, and we're going to get you a security clearance so you can sit in the Intelligence Oversight Committee meetings too. Any problems with this kid?"

With a firm and confident smile Alan shook his head. "No, sir. No problems at all. Happy to serve."

"Good," Senator Henderson continued. "Listen, you literally brought home the bacon when we sent you to Iraq. No one saw that coming. We thought it was going to be a simple meet-and-greet and hold-hands kinda thing. Sending you off like that...it was a mistake. We should have never put you in that position, and at least not alone. Wayne's still on my shit list for doing that. Where are we on that? Is Treasury still deciding what to do with the escrow account you opened when you got back?"

"Yes, sir. Everybody wants a piece of it. CIA, DoD, even the DSS wants to take it over."

"I bet they do. The Brits, Kuwaitis, Saudis...everybody wants it I'm sure. Money that's not on anyone's books is the most lucrative kind, in my experience. It's been years now, and no one seems to be getting a better claim on it. In fact every few month it seems like someone else tosses their hat in the ring looking for taste of the honey pot. What do you think we should do with it? I've read your reports on what everyone else wants to do with it, but not your ideas."

"Sir, as you know it's not just one simple account. There are actually several, all under the umbrella of one entity: this office. Some of it's in CDs, other in money markets, bonds, and that kind of thing. I'm an accountant. Money that's not earning interest is money that's losing value. Besides, someone has to pay taxes on it. Altogether the various accounts are averaging 8.25% a year, bringing in just under $500 million a year to pay the taxes. I didn't think it reasonable for this office to be responsible for over $6 billion and have to bear the tax burden as well."

"Wayne...." The senator laughed hard, interrupted, and smiled. "...get Alan a new car too. Okay, kid, so what do you think we should do with it?"

"Sir, I think we should keep it."

"That's what everyone wants to do—keep it for themselves."

"No, sir, that's not exactly what I'm saying," Alan continued. "I think we should keep it and then let everyone have it. Assuming you're reelected, the interest alone will double the money before the year 2000, and then we can just let the Treasury dole it out. From then on we could use the money garnered from the interest to pay for programs and projects that Congress can't. Every program belongs to a department of this or that, and everyone's going to be laying claim to the funds. We'll just make sure that after Treasury gets the original funds, everyone else gets the portion they lay claim to as well. Everybody gets what they want."

Senator Henderson laughed. "Alan, I think that sounds perfectly reasonable, extremely fair and responsible. It doesn't sound anything like DC accounting to me, though. You sure you work here on Capitol Hill?"

***

7/4/1993

Erwin and Roese Zimmermann had been married for some time, but to them every day felt as if they had just started dating. Time had passed, and they aged in course, but their love was still as pure and exciting as any first love. Each kiss stirred hearts.

Both knew their time together was fleeting, eroding fast. Roese's cancer was spreading. Coupled with the constant tests and treatments, she had less and less energy. It wasn't uncommon for her spirits to fall, but Erwin always raised her back up. Sometimes all it took was a smile, or a kiss, but other times...well, Erwin was a romantic—a very rich romantic.

One of the things that gave them both strength and joy was the children's hospital in Munich. Roese had visited there once to check on a servant's daughter. She compelled Erwin to visit the hospital with her, and millions of dollars in donations followed immediately afterwards. Twice a week they'd come talk to the administrators and doctors to see how the operation was performing and to visit the children, to be inspired by the children. In later weeks the inspiration became more important. Now, as the end was becoming clearer, and hope less imaginable, they visited to be distracted.

On this day, however, Roese was not inspired. She wasn't distracted. She found no hope, and they ended the children's hospital visit early. Her heart was fading—not physically, but spiritually. Erwin could see it, but he denied it, confident he could make her smile and live again rather than just be alive.

They went home, and Roese asked to sit in the garden for a while, the one overlooking the pasture where their Arabian horses grazed and played. Behind her was their huge *Schloss*—castle/mansion. All around were rose bushes that Erwin had brought from around the world. There was a bush grown from a cutting at the White House in America. There was a yellow one grown from a two hundred-year-old shrub in Texas given to her by one of Erwin's clients. There were roses grown from cuttings of ancient bushes at the Vatican and Buckingham Palace, and a pink grandiflora from her grandmother's home outside Frankfurt. Each bush was part of history. Each had its own smell and unique color.

As Roese sat watching their ponies chase each other, a perfect breeze passed through the garden and the air was a circus of natural perfumes. Erwin, who had gone back inside, came out with a present. It was heavy, and heavier for Roese in her weakened state.

A client of his was in Washington, DC, and Erwin had asked him a favor. Roese opened the wrapped box and found a crystal bottle with a gallon of water. The bottle had a note explaining the water. Outside the National Cathedral in Washington, between the church and the bishop's house, was what appeared to be a large fountain. There was a picture in the box as well showing the structure surrounded by a rose garden almost as large as theirs. It was, in fact, the baptismal font of Emperor Charlemagne. Erwin's friend had collected rainwater from the font, had it blessed by the bishop, and sent it to Roese. He asked that she water all her roses with some of it to bring further blessings and life to her garden and thus her.

Roese and Erwin both wept. Such was the character of Erwin and Roese Zimmermann as well as the company of friends which they kept.

***

8/1/1993

Alan Conferra stepped into Senator Henderson's office for a scheduled meeting to prepare for a weekly conference of the Senate Select Committee on Intelligence. It was clear from the moment he entered the room that their pre-meeting meeting would have to wait as another meeting was still taking place. While the senator was from South Carolina, he and the nation were transfixed on the center of the United States. The Army Corps of Engineers was calling it a "hundred-year flood." Everyone just referred to it as "The Mississippi."

Senator Henderson, Wayne Kowalski, and two women were watching one of the congressman's televisions when Jerry Henderson spotted Alan walking past his open door.

"Hey, Alan!" he called out. "Come in here. This is Congresswoman Kinzel of Iowa and Melony Rose, her senior intelligence advisor."

Alan shook hands, smiled, and gave the usual polite introductions. Then Senator Henderson continued. "These lovely ladies were just briefing Wayne and me on how the flood is affecting their district. Apparently they've heard rumors of unallocated funds that we might be able to free up for some relief efforts in their district."

Congresswoman Kinzel looked at Melony and gave a nod for her to speak. "Last week we approached the Treasury Department to see what aid might be available to help fight the flood in my district as well as elsewhere upstream and downstream. They told us about the usual FEMA and other relief efforts, but things are being stretched thin in the area. There is a sincere risk of a natural disaster turning into a national security risk. We've asked local authorities not to give details to the press, but many people are getting cut off by the flood. There's a steady increase in the incidents of looting, but it seems largely contained to food and other basic supplies. There have been some non-supply related incidents, and some violence. We've seen at least a dozen reports of people deliberately bulldozing or even blowing up levies to make the flood move to one side of the river instead of the other. The efforts do work, and the Corps of Engineers is even considering doing some of this on their own, but when Americans start destroying one town to save their own...you can see where this is getting to a tipping point."

On the television behind Melony, Alan watched news footage of a break in a levy. There was an excavator on the levy that looked like it had been trying to stop the breach, failed, and was backing away as fast as possible lest the driver get sucked into the break. In seconds it had gone from a small trickle across what appeared to be a causeway to a dam break. Hundreds of millions of gallons were flowing out and already flooding the crops of the same farmer who was driving the excavator. A moment later as a camera on a helicopter circled, the water surrounded the man's home. By the time Melony had paused, the house was lifted from its foundation and was floating through the crops.

"My God," Alan said quietly. "What do you need specifically?"

The congresswoman answered, "We need cash, lots of it, and we're not going to be getting receipts from the people who we give it to. My constituents are going to get loans and all kinds of help from state, local, and federal agencies, but right now people need to get out of the area and find places to stay. I've got entire cities being abandoned with no time to even hit an ATM. Davenport, for example, was almost entirely evacuated. Downtown is filled with several feet of water, and the other day when a fire broke out at a store, there weren't even enough firemen in town to stop it. Three men drove their truck as far as they could, then waded out with fire houses and kept the town from burning down in the middle of a flood. It's pretty bad. I want to be able to get cash in hand to Iowans so they can buy gas to get some food, and get a place to stay until the water recedes. The Corp's telling us that could be months."

"How do you plan to distribute cash?" Alan asked.

"There's a company in my district that makes the physical credit cards and gift cards and identification cards, and things of that nature. Our thought was to have them make a run of Visas to distribute at post offices, and set up a call center where post offices can call and confirm the recipients. All someone would need to do is give a Social Security number and a valid ID. My office would set up the call center."

"Then you really don't need cash. You just need a ready funding source that doesn't need receipts. But if people are giving their Social Security numbers and IDs, then you could use that list as a receipt. You'd just have to have the office validating the card recipients record the person, place, and time that the card was given out, right?"

"I believe that's workable, but we still need that 'ready funding source' you're talking about, and Treasury isn't gonna bend on that," answered the congresswoman.

Wayne Kowalski loved and hated politics, but he also preferred a more direct/less tactful conversation method.

"Let's cut to the chase. How much are you looking for, Congresswoman?" he asked.

Like anyone else, Congresswoman Kinzel didn't like to ask for money. Melony saved her the shame and answered for her.

"The flood will affect everyone in the state, but only about half will need the immediate aid we're talking about. That's a million people."

Senator Henderson looked past the congresswoman and her aide, made eye contact with Alan, and his face made his wishes clear. He wanted to use some of the money that Alan had obtained in Kuwait to help the people of Iowa. Knowing the senator's personality, Alan knew his wish to do so was likely to help the people first, and to gain a large political favor second.

Alan looked at Senator Henderson, then at Kowalski, who had the same look and even added a nod. If the message wasn't clear enough from the senator, Wayne Kowalski's stern face and body language made it abundantly understandable.

"I understand, Congresswoman. Treasury's job is to protect funds. We've known for some time that too often there's been a sluggish response. Most of the time it's people ruling their cubicle kingdoms, but toss in the regular DC political leanings, and it can be difficult. I can't count the number of times we've been stalled and stopped dealing with them over there. Every failed effort has a lesson, and we've learned ours to be sure. I've been lucky enough to find some people over there who do prefer to get things done regardless of partisanship. I'm sure the senator could make a few calls to the right people on your behalf. You may even have funds as early as tomorrow. If you'd like, I can establish an escrow account for you to use."

"Tomorrow?"

"Yes, Congresswoman. It's midafternoon now. I'm sure it'll take at least a day. I'm sorry."

Congresswoman Kinzel stood up and everyone else did the same—except Alan, who never had a chance to sit.

"Jerry," she said to the senator. "If your man here can get funds tomorrow, we can have the prepaid Visas start printing by the end of the day, and distribution by the end of the week. I won't be able to thank you enough. If you can't, well, you know how it goes."

Senator Henderson laughed as he shook her hand and patted her on the shoulder.

"If Alan says he can get it done, it'll happen. That much I know!"

The ladies said their goodbyes and stepped out of Senator Henderson's office. Wayne closed the door behind them.

"How're we gonna handle this, Alan?" Wayne asked.

"Well, she's right that any financial aid has to go through the Treasury Department, and technically those funds that we're all thinking about...technically those are available to Treasury. Treasury knows about all the accounts. I sent them a memo myself. I even made a point to let them know that the accounts required a Treasury Department officer to access them. I just didn't mention that the terms of the accounts require that said officer be recognized by the three of us. Besides, they haven't picked anyone to even try. The paper shuffle over there is incredible. In the meantime, yeah, we can shift the funds. I am the only trustee."

"How much can we move without breaking into the principal you brought back?" asked Wayne.

Alan did the quick math in his head. "If she wants to help a million people, we can give each person $600. It's not enough to live on for several months, but I'm sure it'll help a lot. With all the other aid that her state's going to be getting through the normal channels, $600 million in fast cash should be pretty appreciable. I would think that it would at least cover a couple of weeks until other funds come available. I know most insurance issues will take a few weeks, but from that point on they should be covered by the insurance as well as state, local, and typical federal relief."

"I think she's going to be happy as hell if you can do it," the senator replied.

"Yes, sir. We can do it. I think it might take her a while to actually create an account for her plan—get staff, offices, and so forth. Come to think of it, I think I'll just log in to one of the banks and set up an account for her. I can have it all ready for her in an hour or so really."

Senator Henderson and Wayne Kowalski looked stunned, and nodded slowly in appreciation. Alan saw that he was confounding them.

"Should we prepare for the Intelligence Committee hearing, Senator?" he asked.

Jerry Henderson cleared his throat, sat down, and finally invited Alan to have a seat. "Good idea Alan. Great work. The Intelligence Committee...okay, so what do you see as important to bring up?"

Kowalski laughed, and stood up to walk out.

"Okay, you two. I'm getting some coffee. I know what the senator wants. How about you?"

"Cream, no sugar, please. And thank you, sir. I appreciate it." He smiled and continued, "Senator, as you know the UN has demanded that Serb forces pull back from Sarajevo. They've even threatened to use air strikes against the Serbs, and it's only been a few days, but it does appear to be working. I have learned, however, that the UN airlift of supplies into Sarajevo has also been used to remove valuables and hard currency from the city. Generally speaking only people with the right connections have been able to get on the flights out. Regular civilians just can't buy their way out."

"How'd you find this out?"

"One of the planes flown out of Sarajevo by our Air Force was piloted by a colonel who had been a crewman on the same plane that we used to extract from Kuwait. He saw a crate of gold bars in his plane, tried to have it removed to fit some civilians on board in its place, and he got in trouble. Long story short, he remembered the flight from Kuwait, asked around, heard the rumors that this office was involved, and called us. Kathy put the call through to me, and we had lunch last Friday. He's in some hot water for rattling the cage of some powerful people apparently. Seems the UN guys on the ground and in the chain of command for the airlift have their thumbs on the scales, and people just don't weigh as much as gold. Word's even reached the White House, and this guy's career is gonna be at best stumped until the next administration, or until something better comes along and he retires. His flying days in the Air Force are over, though."

"Dammit, dammit, dammit. DAMMIT!" Henderson shouted.

Alan's eyes stopped, and he stared down at his notes. Only Wayne Kowalski's reentering the room relieved the tension in the air.

"What the fuck is going on?" Kowalski called out. "I leave to get coffee, and he's all pissed off. What the fuck did you do, Alan?!"

Senator Henderson answered, "It's not him, Wayne. That Yugoslavia thing's a clusterfuck. Alan found out that the airlift bringing in food isn't bringing out wounded and civilians. Someone's using it to get all the valuables out of the city, and to get the rich folks out. Pisses me off. Alan, who's behind the airlift out? Is it UN skimming, locals, or is this a large, organized thing? Is someone profiting off this—other than the usual arms and supplies?"

"Sir," Alan answered. "From what I've been told it looks like it's a case of anarchy with players taking advantage. This has likely been going on since the city was first encircled last year. I have very little information, and I really can't draw any conclusions on that limited data."

Wayne handed out the coffees and interrupted. "Ya know, you can't bring this up at the committee hearing, right?"

"Why not?" asked Senator Henderson.

"Jerry, if we start a conversation about people being bad guys because they move money out of a war zone, it's just not going to go well. Those who don't know about Kuwait will want to keep a close watch and investigate on things like this, and those who suspect about Kuwait—which is a growing number of people I might add—would look at us as being extremely hypocritical...or worse."

"What do you suggest I do then, Wayne? We just let these people get bombed, starved, and now pillaged? What's your idea?"

Alan weighed in. "Sir, there's a genocide going on over there. I've no idea how much of value could have been in Sarajevo to begin with. Getting involved in any way over there risks setting off another chain of events like the ones that started the First World War."

"Okay Alan, so what in the Sam Hell do you think I should do? We've got this hearing in less than an hour."

"Sir, I think we should let it slide today. Congresswoman Kinzel has obviously been butting heads with the people at the Treasury. I'll be busy with her emergency aid package the rest of today or tomorrow depending on how long the committee hearing runs. After that, I'd like to go over to Treasury and see what I can find out."

"Alan, you can't do that either," answered Kowalski. "It's the same problem; same reason the congressman can't bring it up at the hearing. Better to go to the Pentagon. The congressman's pretty popular over there. See if you can find out who's commanding the flights in and out of Sarajevo, then talk directly with him, but make sure he knows you don't want names. You want information on the cargo. He can have one of his subordinates work with you to get more information from the crews making the flights. Let 'em know that they don't have to do anything special, and that they need to continue to follow the operation's chain of command. Those guys are solid on chain of command things. What you want to do is to talk with the crewmen off the record, and you have to do it in a way that everyone involved from the airmen to the generals can deny they were ever involved. Got it?"

Alan nodded, and the pre-meeting meeting about the Intelligence Committee meeting moved on to other, far less expensive issues.

***

10/22/1993

Shortly after Operation Desert Storm ended, Phillipe Aristide reenlisted in the US Army. He then managed to get into

Ranger School, and became one of the Army's elite. Like many Rangers he wanted to go where there was a fight—a chance to use all the training he'd had and share his limited exposure to combat in Kuwait and Iraq. Operation Restore Hope gave him that opportunity.

While the world's attention was on Operation Desert Storm in January 1991, Somalia collapsed. Its dictatorial ruler was overthrown by a collection of clans and factions from all over the country. What followed was the perfect portrayal of anarchy. The continuity of any central government or even local governments evaporated. Law and order disappeared. Police were replaced by groups ranging in scale from clans to small rebel armies. There was rarely electricity in the country to begin with, but with violence rampant in every corner of the tiny nation, generators and fires were providing what little night light there could be seen. Seaborne commerce disappeared and was replaced by small, local fishermen and historic numbers of modern pirates—armed with AK-47 rifles and rocket-propelled grenades (RPGs) instead. Fresh water was scarce, and armed groups fought to maintain control over food supplies, leaving hundreds of thousands of their enemies to starve.

After Desert Storm the news media turned their attention to the hundreds of thousands of Iraqi Kurds and Shiite Iraqis driven from their homes as Saddam fought off rebellions in the North and South. Then world attention shifted to the Balkan powder keg, but the world's fear of getting involved brought embarrassment and shame to everyone, so reporters looked elsewhere. Northern Iraq, Southern Iraq, and the Balkans were hard, shameful, and very dangerous stories, though, and it was easier to report on Somalia where starvation was being used as a genocidal weapon.

In Somalia the world had an opportunity to do something good without risking another war like Desert Storm. From this shift in coverage came attention by the United Nations, and demands to send in food aid, but when the largely rhetorical United Nations finally did take action and arranged to have food sent to Somalia, the food was seized by warlords, and it was used to further their support while civilians continued to starve.

Operation Restore Hope was initially thought of as a simple show of force. Leaders imagined that surely massive military might that had just decimated the fourth largest army in the world would deter clans and warlords in a backwater place like Somalia. The plan was to send in UN peacekeepers to stand watch over food aid distribution, and larger American forces would bring back order to the airport and seaport.

Internationally, however, people and leaders saw what had happened in postwar Iraq, the cost of the war—a million Iraqi soldiers, Kurds, and Shiites dead, millions more homeless—and they saw the millions of people suffering by war in the Balkans, and no one wanted to see more war. No one wanted to see intimidating images of giant American tanks aiming cannons at crowds of civilians where a militia could blend in and hide. Operation Restore Hope's objective of using huge military force as a deterrent was destroyed before it began because no one—not even the Americans—wanted to deploy a huge military force. Of the twenty-five thousand troops promised by the Americans in late 1992, by June '93 only 1,200 remained.

Things had fallen apart quickly. UN observers and international units were under extremely limited rules of engagement so as to not offend or upset locals. American Marines were limited to their small areas of interest, and served more as targets for brazen clans than as a deterrent. Efforts to seize combatants' weapons failed and only managed to unite clans and factions against the UN forces.

On October 3 a US Army Ranger force attempted to capture the leaders of the largest clans who were struggling for control of Somalia. These clan leaders were caught, but the mission went awry as a pair of American helicopters was brought down by Somalis in Mogadishu. What followed was an eighteen-hour-long gunfight that left almost a hundred Rangers killed or seriously wounded and one pilot captured. Three days later the president ordered the withdrawal of all American forces in defeat.

Americans had come to Somalia with the best of intentions—to stop genocide by starvation—and they were driven out in national shame. In postwar Iraq, the Americans had encouraged the Kurds and the Shiites to rise up and remove Saddam, but when the rebellions started, the Americans provided no help, and because of the national and international fear of a fight, millions suffered. In the Balkans the world watched as hundreds of villages were burned, as long ditches were filled with the corpses of mass executions, and fear of getting involved in another war led Americans to watch the suffering in shame.

Whether it was Northern Iraq, Southern Iraq, Croatia, Bosnia, or Somalia, the United Nations offered little more than rhetoric, and in many cases UN observers or peacekeepers were attacked, kidnapped, or in any way possible rendered useless. Americans and the world had grown so use to the shame that people and leaders had come to deny it, watch it, and believe that what happens elsewhere was sad, but somehow they should not be involved. Certainly, when a nation suffered a flood, engineers and aid came from around the world. When a country had a disease outbreak, doctors came from all over the world to help. Where there was famine, food was sent. But when there was war and anarchy, no troops dared be sent.

Phillipe had been part of that strategic defeat in Somalia. He'd joined a convoy sent out to rescue the surrounded Rangers. He saw women and children with rifles shooting at elite Americans soldiers. He saw the poorest people on the planet waging war against some of the most powerful, most well-trained soldiers in the world. Sophisticated Blackhawk helicopters with motorized mini-guns that could fire thousands of bullets a minute were shot at by starving, half-clothed, illiterate people armed with rocket launchers left over from the Cold War. Once his convoy managed to get to the trapped Rangers, he saw young men just like him with bodies and sometimes minds shattered. Chaos reigned. Everyone Somali was out to kill Americans.

The Rangers themselves were not defeated. When they returned to the airport perimeter, even as dead bodies and wounded friends were being removed from the vehicles, many Rangers were re-arming, reloading, and preparing to go back into the city. Many wanted to get back out and kill everyone who had shot at them. Orders from higher in the chain of command kept them secure in the airport, however. The Rangers were ready to continue the fight, and given an hour or two would have again become an effective, organized, well-armed fighting force, but Washington, DC, had had enough. The policy makers were no longer a fighting leadership.

Phillipe's frustration and anger were mirrored all throughout the American military and with many of the American people. When French news footage showed bodies of American helicopter crewmen being stripped naked, desecrated, and torn apart by a Somali mob, the Rangers were infuriated and shamed. Their creed stated that they would never leave a comrade behind, but they'd failed and left the bodies of the helicopter crew as well a living crewman behind, captured. To Rangers, this part of their creed was literally part of their being.

Phillipe was officially wounded in the action of October 4. An RPG hit the right side of the Humvee he was in. When it detonated his friend and fellow Ranger took the brunt of the blast and was severely wounded. Phillipe was firing out the left window. Three pieces of shrapnel had hit him in his back, close to his right shoulder—one steel, one copper, and a piece of bone from his friend. All were small, and the pain was manageable. Penetration was at worst a half inch, and he was still completely mobile. The chaos and confusion of combat mixed with the shock of the blast and the apparent loss of his fellow Ranger, even the pain...all was ignored as there was a great deal of soldier's work to be done.

On the night of the 4th he was among the last to get medical treatment. All three pieces were removed and some stitches were given, as was dressing and some antibiotics. He was still bitter about the mission, and even angrier that—because of his wounds—he wasn't allowed to give blood and help his fellow Rangers. There was some satisfaction in hearing that his friend was likely to survive the direct hit from the RPG. Like many of the Rangers he took a small amount of pride in the knowledge that they did manage to capture a pair of Somali warlords in the raid.

Because he was "wounded" Phil was one of the first 105 Rangers evacuated by plane from Somalia. The three small holes in his shoulder had already healed, but still rated top of the list. He took his seat on the plane, and while many were happy to be going home, the plane ride wasn't anywhere near as joyful and celebratory as the one he had taken home from Kuwait after victory in Desert Storm. There were no victory parades in Washington this time—not because he and the Rangers had failed, but because his leaders had.

***

1/1/1994

On New Year's Day Roese Zimmermann died in a hospital bed with her husband at her side. She had fallen victim to a rare form of ovarian cancer. She did not die in her beloved rose garden, or in a hospice, or even in a hospital, but in a children's hospital with young and hopeful patients down the hall, patients who had brought her fleeting smiles near the end.

Erwin was lost. The five phases of coping circled his soul like a whirlpool. He was angry that she'd been taken from him, and he was angry for the suffering she'd endured. He went to pass his hand through her long, silky blond hair, but it had been lost to the cancer treatments, and he could only go through the motion, remembering what it once felt like. He tried to convince himself that if he just continued on, taking care of the children's clinic, doing his work, maintaining the *Schloss*, then she'd still live on in him, but the bargain wasn't reasonable enough to grasp yet. He tried to deny that she was really gone, but the body in front of him was that of a lifeless corpse. It was not his precious Roese.

Erwin was a practical man, a man of numbers, accounts, and order. So he went through the motions of the funeral, and of going back to work, and he went on with life the way he was supposed to. He rarely cried, and when he did he was careful to ensure no one saw. Roese was his love, and now his rich and perfect life was without the one thing that mattered: love.

***

4/7/1994

Jim Smith had only recently left the CIA. His short and successful career as a case officer was remarkable, and he was extremely proud of the work he'd done. Following the liberation of Kuwait, he'd been disappointed time and time again by American leaders in DC. He saw leaders choosing Procrastination as a policy. Jim had personally helped encourage Shiite Iraqis to rise up against Saddam after Operation Desert Storm. He'd promised them that American firepower would back them up, but exactly as America had abandoned Cubans at the Bay of Pigs, so too had American leaders abandoned the Iraqis; so too had he personally abandoned them. The Balkan wars and the unwillingness to stop genocide there further confounded his loyalties between obedience and morality. When pure evil was faced in Somalia—where a few warlords were starving hundreds of thousands of people—his bosses told him America was powerless to help. That's when he gave up on the system that he'd devoted his life toward.

In January 1994 Jim Smith left the CIA and joined a private security company called RoeseDefender Security and Consulting Group (DSCG). Some called it a private military contractor (PMC) because most of the security personnel had advanced military service of some kind, and some of the security contracts they fulfilled were closer to military security tasks. Others called it a company of modern mercenaries. The company was run by a flamboyant and popular former FBI agent, and it had a good reputation. It also paid very well—five times what he was making at the CIA.

On Wednesday, April 4, a rare double presidential assassination took place in Rwanda. President Habinyarimana of Rwanda and the president of Burundy were both killed when their plane was shot down by Rwandan rebels near the Kigali airport in Rwanda. In the following hours there was an immediate and total collapse of the entire country. Rwandan Hutu rebels took control of all communications outlets, travel centers, and services. Hospitals were surrounded and put under lockdown by rebel forces. Power was cut, water was cut off, and the Hutu had seized control of everything.

Then they moved to the people. Machetes were passed out by the tens of thousands, and Hutus all over Rwanda began killing their long-standing rival ethnicity, the Tutsi. By the end of the first day thousands had been killed.

Yet again, the United Nations was impotent. A UN peacekeeping mission that had been organized in Rwanda earlier had thousands of people flee to their camps, but even inside the UN peacekeepers camps the slaughter continued. Blue-helmeted soldiers were told specifically not to intervene as their mission was only to monitor, not to protect. It was the same familiar formula:

Protests led to violence.
Violence led to vandalism.
Vandalism led to coordinated attacks.
Coordinated attacks became a war.
War would lead them to societal collapse.

In Rwanda the formula for collapse went further, however:
Anarchy erupted.
Civilians were slaughtered en masse.
The UN talked about intervening.
The world refused to intervene.
Anarchy ruled.
Genocide succeeded.

Jim Smith had seen it too many times before. This time, instead of the CIA calling him to make sure he didn't get involved, he got a phone call from his boss at DEFENDER SECURITY.

"Jim, Dan Dempsey here. I'm the Africa regional director here at Defender Security."

"Hi, Dan, what can I do for you?"

"Jim, there's some trouble in Rwanda, and we've been given a contract for some work over there. I could use someone with your background on the team. I know you're still going through the corporate paper shuffle, and you haven't had any sort of assignment yet. You interested?"

Smith didn't even hesitate. He wasn't eager, but he was kind of bored with everyday life back in the states. "Sure, where do you want me and when?"

"Kigali airport in Rwanda's capital is shut down. The others are either in rebel hands already or unsecure at best. You're in the DC area right now, correct?"

"I am in fact." Clearly Dempsey had done some homework, Smith thought.

"Okay, you'll be in Africa before morning. Got it?"

"I'm packed and ready now, Dan."

Dempsey laughed. "I figured as much. That's why the car should be in front of your house right now."

Jim looked out the dining room window and saw a stretch limo. DEFENDER SECURITY knew how to treat their people. He smiled. "Heh, yeah, I see it Dan. It's here. Nice job. I'm on my way. Thanks for the opportunity."

"No problem. I'll see you when you get here."

Jim locked up his house, walked outside, and began a journey that took him from his couch to Entebbe, Uganda, via a very luxurious, company-owned Gulfstream IV private jet. It took eighteen hours with three stops. He was the only one on the plane besides the pilot, copilot, and a flight attendant, but they'd been replaced at each stop. Nine people came and went while Jim sat and read his mission brief as well as information on the region, Uganda, and particularly Rwanda, where his mission would focus.

Defender Security had been hired by a wealthy Rwandan. They were being paid to get the man and his family, all of whom were Tutsi, out of the country, which was even more chaotic than Somalia had been at its worst. In Somalia the genocidal threat came in the form of empty rice bowls, but in Rwanda it was bloody machetes.

Finally, his plane landed at the Entebbe airport in Uganda and pulled up next to a hangar. It shut down, the door opened, and six men dressed in American woodland camouflage came on board. They all shook his hand and introduced themselves, first names only. All were aliases, including two who liked the name Mike. As they took their seats, the flight crew disembarked, and Dan Dempsey came on board.

"Hello, Jim. I'm Dan. Nice to finally meet you in person."

They shook hands, and Dan knelt down facing the aisle with his back to the cabin.

"I see you've met our little team here—including the 'Mikes.'" Everyone laughed. It was as if old friends were going out to a pub for some beer.

"Okay, so here's the latest info: The other day the president of Rwanda and the president of Burundi were assassinated at Kigali airport. They were brokering a peace accord with the rebels in the hills surrounding the capital city of Kigali as well as rebels in the north and the jungles all around. It's Africa. There're rebels of one sort or another everywhere. In response some extremists took power and refused to cede power to the prime minister. The country has a long history of racial divide between Hutu and Tutsi forever. There's a UN peacekeeping force there of about 2,500 with French paratroops, US Marines, and others on the way, but they're all under strict orders not to use force. The UN troops are only allowed to watch. The French and the Marines are taking Kigali airport as we speak, and they're only there to get the white people out."

The faces on the men sank. Even the flight crew, which hadn't been deliberately eavesdropping, stopped what they were doing and froze to listen in.

Dan continued, "That's right, everyone who's white. They're bugging out. Orders came down yesterday from all over the world. Story is that a few Belgian UN peacekeepers were sent to help some priests or someone get to the airport. Hutu extremists stopped 'em. They disarmed the Belgians, tied 'em up, and chopped 'em up with machetes, then they killed the priests and a hundred to two hundred Tutsi civilians who had been hiding in the church. The Hutus figure that if they kill a few, the UN will leave like they did in Somalia, and they're right. Everybody's getting their people out."

There was silence, disappointment, and shame on the plane, and Dan let it sink in before he continued.

"I guess it's like that all over the entire country. Right after the presidents' plane was blown up, the Hutus took over the radio and TV stations and locked down all the border crossings. This is gonna be an ugly scene, and a hard nut to crack. That's why we got the call. We go where governments can't, and in this case won't."

Dan unrolled a stack of papers that he'd rolled up and been holding.

"Business. Defender Security's been hired by Pasteur Kagame for an exfiltration. We're to get Kagame, his wife, his sister, and their three kids out of Rwanda ASAO. They're Tutsi, and the Hutus are reportedly slaughtering Tutsis in the street; pulling people out and butchering them one at a time in their front yards is what I was told. No wonder he wants out, huh? Everybody does, but he's a banker in the west/northwest part of town, and he can afford us."

Dan paused for a moment and made eye contact with each man for a moment to personally communicate the importance and danger of the job.

"What I want to do is get in and out quick. There's no telling how long that airport will be in operation. The Americans are already talking about getting the embassy staff and others out by road to meet up with some Marines in Burundi. I guess there's some antiaircraft fire, and no shortage of people shooting at whatever they've got into the air. The French are planning a more direct exit by air. The pilots we just took on are pretty good; both have some combat hours under their belts. We're in good hands with them. They're gonna get us into that airport regardless of authorization. Then they're gonna park someplace where we're not gonna be the center of attention, and we're not gonna be all by our lonesome. Jim's here to take lead outside the airport. You guys'll secure a vehicle by any means you choose. If there's a convoy headed into the Kiyovu area, hook up with it, and get our guy and his family. If not, don't wait. Just go and get him. There is no Quick Reaction Force to come help you if you get into trouble. No backup plans."

Dan passed the papers out to Jim and the others. Everyone was told to memorize the map, the picture of the Pasteur Kagame, and the briefing notes.

The plane was refueled, and the flight crew started the engines. Minutes later they flew across the dense jungle of Africa's Great Lakes region. As the sun was setting the flight crew donned night-vision goggles and turned off the lights inside and outside of the plane. They circled Kigali from several thousand feet. Below them the city had fires everywhere. Occasionally a stream of small arms tracer bullets streamed randomly into the sky. At the airport below they could see hundreds of vehicles in and around the airport, a few larger aircraft, but no small planes. The pilots brought the plane around, descended rapidly, and landed just above stall speed at 108 knots.

They were immediately surrounded by French paratroops. Dan got out and spoke to their lieutenant in French. Then the paratroops left. He came back and pointed to a white BTR-60 armored car. Jim and the others were told they could use it, but that they had to be back in two hours. It was expected to be a fifteen- to twenty-minute ride so no one was concerned.

They left the airport in BTR and began the roughly three-mile trek. It looked like anything one might see in a middle-class area of Florida or Southern California. The only difference was the roads were dirt, and savage killers meandered in the streets everywhere. Small groups were going door to door through the thousands of homes.

Even over the sound of the armored car's diesel engine, driving down the streets they heard gunfire and screams, and they saw bodies every hundred feet or so. Other people walked around like nothing was happening. Some carried machetes, hatchets, clubs, and AK-47s. The only living people they saw were Hutu. All of the Rwandan Tutsi were hiding/waiting to be killed.

They turned left out of the airport on to KN5, a paved four-lane road like anyone would see in the US. It took them past gas stations, hotels, a Chinese restaurant, a multistory office building, and government buildings. Next they headed right on RN3 and right at the KN2 roundabout, the one with a decorated garden in the middle. They drove down Embassy Row, and beyond that the office of the president immediately followed on the left. RN3 continued around the national police headquarters, past hospitals and libraries. Finally they made their way into a residential neighborhood, one that resembled something in Southern California with grocery stores and small restaurants.

There was a distinct difference between the middle- and upper-class neighborhoods and the typical third-world shanty towns, and often the two were side by side with only privacy walls dividing them. A simple left turn on to KN1 took them out of the shanty areas and immediately into the financial district, with tall banks casting shadows on the poorest people in the world. Finally they turned left on to the KN3, passed an Indian food restaurant and the Congolese embassy, and turned left into another middle- and upper-middle-class neighborhood where they turned on to Pasteur's street.

His was the biggest house in the neighborhood. They managed to fit the armored car into the walled, gated parking lot in front. It was a large rectangular house with a flat roof and L-shaped additions on the left and right side. There was a square garden with a fountain in the backyard and wooded area beyond.

Jim went out to meet Pasteur. His wife answered the door as if nothing else was going on in the world. Inside it was modern, minimalist, and sparsely decorated with African art and artifacts. A few houses away, as if on cue, there were screams as a neighboring family was being butchered alive by a gang. Jim introduced himself, was invited in, and was introduced to Pasteur.

Their bags were packed, and the children began walking outside where one of the Mikes helped them get into the BTR through the back hatches. The rest of the team had split up and one man was at each corner of the house pulling security. Mrs. Pasteur followed along with her sister-in-law, her husband, their two kids, and all of their suitcases. It was immediately clear there was no room for everyone; certainly no room for everyone and their baggage. The BTR was a big machine, but it was cramped inside normally.

The mission was for seven men to evacuate three adults and three kids, not nine people with a remarkable amount of baggage. They might be able to cram everyone into the BTR if they left the baggage or strapped it on top, but Jim and the other six Defender Security team members knew they weren't all going to fit in the plane. He explained the space problem to Pasteur, who in turn informed his family. There were tears of loss, and fears of what was happening.

Pasteur's sister had married a Hutu, but Hutus who had intermarried were being murdered as well as Tutsis. Children of Tutsis were even being singled out for particularly savage mutilation. Outside Pasteur's walled home, boogeymen walked freely and literally ruled the land.

Pasteur asked Jim if there was any other way besides leaving part of his family.

"We can get everyone to the airport if we dump most of the luggage. Maybe some of them can get on another flight if we hurry. That's all I can think of right now, but we have got to get out of here immediately. There's not a second to waste."

Pasteur's family understood English, and despite some tears from two of the children, everyone understood the gravity of the situation. Only carry-on luggage was allowed in the armored car. Minutes later everyone was aboard. The rest of the Defender Security team left their security positions. They entered the BTR through its rear hatches, closed them securely, and as the vehicle began to move four members of the team opened the top dorsal hatch to deter or respond to any threats.

As the armored car began to crawl out of the parking area, through the gate, and onto the street, four men with freshly used machetes shared a moment of eye contact with the Defender Security team members. The vehicle pulled out, and behind them the four murderers walked into Pasteur's front yard, looking to kill Pasteur and his family. They were close enough to the vehicle that one of them rubbed upon its side and turned sideways to get through the gate as the BTR was pulling out.

Out on the suburb-like street it was incomprehensible to see the natural peace and tranquility of a nice residential area decorated with the macabre. Jim saw bodies and body parts sprawled out in one front yard with killers still standing amongst the blood, laughing and smiling. The next few houses were normal, then there was another house where a family had been systematically taken out front and slaughtered. A few more normal homes were passed and then there was another where a handful of men literally hacked people apart as if chopping wood; differing only in the chilling screams—screams that didn't seem to bother anyone who was visible.

Looking back inside the white interior of the BTR, Jim saw the Pasteur family. They heard the screams but forced themselves not to look outside. Everyone was on edge. They were being saved in the nick of time, but some wondered if they would find safety at the airport or be abandoned like everyone else in the country and so many other countries before. Emotions were running so hard that no one could feel a single one at a time, and instead a deep sense of concentration seemed to come over them all.

The rest of their three-mile move to the airport happened quickly. On the one hand it was a normal drive through a normal city under blue skies and with people going about their daily business. On the other hand, as Hutu families went about their normal business, people with Tutsi heritage on their ID cards were hidden from view, hiding from the genocide that was occurring. Jim occasionally glanced out the firing port of the thirty-yearold BTR-60, and he'd see someone eating at a café while men with blood-spattered clubs and dripping machetes calmly walked by. Then he'd turn, look back inside, and see the wealthy family who had the money and connections to escape.

They entered the airport through the same North Gate from which they'd left. Where there had been a sober and sickening normalcy outside the gate, inside was international confusion and chaos as everyone with white skin from all over the world rushed to get into a plane and out of the country. There were three hundred US Marines and half a dozen USAF transport planes to take out hundreds of American citizens. Hundreds more UN peacekeepers—many from Belgium—were being evacuated, and to make sure that evacuation went safely they'd sent another eight hundred troops to help hold the airport. France's four hundred paratroops were also protecting the perimeter. African nations had also flown in troops and transport aircraft to get their small contingents of peacekeepers out as well as to evacuate their embassies as fast as possible.

Thousands of well-connected Hutus had also made it into the airport perimeter, and while many were evacuated, there was hysteria as hundreds were not being allowed on planes.

As per the plan, they pulled up next to the Defender Security private jet and exited the BTR-60. Jim walked over to Dan to brief him.

"Got a bit of a challenge here, Dan: a few extra relatives want a ride. I'm not sure if we can all fit."

Dan watched as his team helped Pasteur and his family out of the armored car.

"Well, the brochure said the plane can fit nineteen people. We've got two pilots, you, me, a half dozen shooters. I supposed we can fit 'em. Not sure where everyone's gonna fit, though. You're right."

Both men looked at their plane. Dan's head slumped back on his shoulders, his eyes closed, and then he turned to Jim. Jim realized it at the same moment, and both said it simultaneously.

"Seats."

Jim nodded, and they walked quickly into the plane. Dan pulled out a knife, cut the carpet, and revealed how the seats were connected to the plane. Each row had a track running from left to right, and the seats were held in place by spring-loaded clips that locked them in place from fore to aft. While Dan went to work cutting out the rest of the carpet, Jim started prying the springs back and unlocking the seats. The flight crew then carried them out and tossed them in a pile.

It took them almost half an hour to get all the seats out and strip down the cabin. When they exited the plane to start cramming everyone in, both men were stunned. Well over a hundred Hutus had surrounded the left side of the plane, held back only by the Defender Security "shooters," as Dan had called them. Children were crying and screaming while their parents and grandparents begged for their lives profusely. There was also a pair of UN diplomats trying to calm the crowd, but they were clearly failing in their efforts to bring rationality, logic, and understanding to people who were likely to be tortured and killed at any moment.

One of the men-in-white came right over to Jim, believing he was in charge. Dan stopped him and told him in no uncertain terms that the plane was over-capacity and could fit no one else. Jim could barely hear them arguing, and could only determine that they were speaking French—nothing of what they were saying exactly, however. Finally, as the diplomat raised his voice and pointed vehemently at the plane, Dan smacked the man's face while at the same time pulling out a Colt .45 pistol from his holster. The crowd's volume fell.

Then Dan aimed the pistol at the crowd and yelled, "Listen up! This aircraft is already full! Small plane, small number of people... Get it?! If you want to get out of here, go find a big plane! Big, like those over there!" He pointed to the row of American C-130 transport planes.

The crowd started to walk in that direction, and those who stayed were silent. That's when his shooters started aiming their weapons at the crowd as further encouragement. Jim shuffled Pasteur and his family into the plane, and the crew started the engines. Finally, Jim, the six "shooters," and lastly Dan got into the plane, pulling up the step door even as the pilots already had it moving away from the BTR-60.

There was no call to a control tower. They taxied to the runway, spun up the engines, dropped the flaps, and took off. No one heard the small arms fire aimed at them as they raced over the bleeding city. Hours later, when they safely landed at Entebbe, Uganda, they realized how close they'd come to being shot down or stranded in Rwanda. Several bullets had hit the rudder and grazed the port engine's nacelle.

What they had witnessed in Rwanda was the worst result of a breakdown in government: anarchy. When the president was killed, the supporting legislature was terrorized, then individually hunted and killed. There was no effective plan for a continuity of the government. What had once been a largely successful African government evaporated before the president's plane finished smoldering; chaos reigned.

***

9/22/1994

It had been over a year since Alan had started looking into the question of favoritism and war profiteering in the Balkan Wars. In that time he'd made several trips to Italy where he personally interviewed USAF transport plane crew members and squadron staff. Everyone he talked to had a story about the horrors they'd seen in the former Yugoslavia—particularly in Sarajevo. People told him "off the record" stories about rampant corruption among the civilians on the ground and how it went hand-in-hand with corruption among UN officials. He'd come to the conclusion—as had everyone he spoke with about it—that there was no real peace process, but rather a latent, undercurrent of corruption and violence ruling the day.

On this day, Alan had been speaking with a crew of a British C-130 aircraft who were about to fly another relief mission into the former Yugoslavia. They were to deliver pallets of food, bottled water, and basic first aid kits to a small airport called Resnick in southeast Croatia. From there the plane's supplies were supposed to be unloaded onto UN trucks and driven over the mountains into Sarajevo. The plane was packed, and it was hard to walk through the space between the pallets. The British airman who was in charge of maintaining the cargo was checking to make sure everything was secure, and while he did so he was telling Alan a story about flying paintings and sculptures out of Resnick months earlier. The airman had to pause for a moment when he told Alan about closing the rear cargo ramp with artwork behind him and a crowd of refugees watching him from the gate.

Alan heard the engines warm up. He went to shake hands with the crewman, who looked surprised. "What's this? You're leaving? Oh, come on. It's a short hop across the Adriatic, and Resnik's right on the coast. Nothing to be afraid of, mate. You haven't talked to the boss up in the cockpit yet. Right, you're takin' a ride with us, and that's all there is to it," he said with a comfortable smile. Being so close to the military, Alan felt confident that he was safe, so he agreed to fly over to Resnik with the crew. Why not? he thought to himself.

Alan sat down in a cargo seat next to the British airman as the plane taxied. While it was taking off, the crewman told him about how one time they had to fly a planeload of pallets from South Africa marked "eggs" over to Resnik. When the crewman looked inside one of the crates to see if the eggs were actually packed well enough for a trip, he found they were actually wooden crates of grenades packed in cardboard boxes. War was a strange thing with secrets, alliances, and lies everywhere.

Earlier the British airman had told Alan that the flight to Resnik was only about an hour. After an hour and a half of listening to the airman's stories of strange and unusual cargo, he asked if perhaps he should go speak with "The Boss"—the pilot. That was, after all, the reason he'd stayed on the plane. Naturally the airman was a bit embarrassed at having rambled on so long, but as he took Alan to the ladder up to the cockpit he pretended that he was upset to have been interrupted in favor of conversing with an officer.

The large cockpit of the C-130 had glass everywhere. Visibility was incredible. Alan introduced himself to the pilot, copilot, and navigator, all of whom laughed that he'd been stuck listening to their only enlisted man for so long. There was room to stand comfortably in the cockpit, and as he stood behind the pilot he could almost look straight down through the surrounding glass. While he'd been around military aircraft for years, this was his first time flying in the American-built C-130, and the view was breathtaking.

It was breathtaking...until he realized that there was no water. It'd been an hour and a half into a flight to a coastal airport that was supposed to take an hour, and there was no water to be seen anywhere.

"Say, um, guys...where are we?"

Everyone laughed and the navigator answered. "We're over the Blidinje Nature Park. That's Blidnije Lake on the left. You might have to look straight down to see it."

"Oh. Okay. So, where's Resnik?"

"Not going to Resnik, Alan. Orders changed while you were down in the bay listening to crazy cargo legends and tales. Gonna drop this stuff off at Sarajevo International Airport. Apparently the Serbs agreed to let in flights today, but only for a four-hour window. That's not enough time to set up an airlift in Italy, get supplies there, unload, and leave. The Serbs know that, but agreeing makes it look like they're being humanitarian. There were only four planes in the air at the time they agreed, and by the time the word got from the UN to the Ministry of Defence and then to Italy, well, we're all they can get in today."

Alan had the same feeling he had when he was being flown to Iraq on a simple paperwork mission that turned into a worse memory. The crew noticed his face, and his silence.

"It's okay," the copilot said. "We've done this plenty before. It can be a bit sporty, and you have to take it seriously—it is a real war after all, but we should be okay. If they were gonna shoot us down we'd have been hit a while ago."

"What?"

"Right, we've been over Serb territory for a bit now. Even at Resnik we'd be in range of their fighters and surface-to-air missiles. We're low enough now that even their AAA [antiaircraft artillery] could give us a bad day. Should be all right, though. Besides, you said you were here to see what was really going on, right?"

Everyone laughed. Even Alan shook his head in disbelief. He even managed a smile that seemed to ask without words, "I can't believe I stayed on the plane—geesh."

"Okay, so how's this work, guys?" he asked.

The laughing faded quickly and the crew got serious. "It'll go like this. We'll be flying on for another ten minutes or so. We should make contact with the airport any time now. They'll give us a route to fly. We'll fly parallel or so to the current Serb lines—wherever those are today. Then the tower will tell us to make our approach. They usually do that when the runway's directly to our left so the turn's almost always a hard left with a rapid descent. You'll definitely want to be strapped in and holding on to something. When they clear us for landing we're dropping down about three miles as fast as we can. Anything not tied down tends to float up and fly around the plane. If it goes like normal we should make it down before you toss your lunch all over. We've got bags under all the seats. Don't be embarrassed. It happens to everyone—even us from time to time. They have us go through all this because the Serbs are afraid we're gonna pull a trick and drop bombs on their front lines. That's what they claim anyway. It works for us too, though, since there's always some idiot who either doesn't know or doesn't care and decides to pop off a few rounds at this big fat bird."

"Anyone ever get shot down?"

"Had a few get shot up pretty bad, but it hasn't happened in a couple of weeks. Most of the time it's rifles and stuff, but we've had 'em drop mortars on the airport after we land. Everyone gets sniped at so don't stand still outside the plane when we're down, okay?"

Alan looked outside at the multi-colored fall forest below. It amazed him how fast he could go from peaceful Italy to flying over hostile territory with missiles and guns aiming at him—at that very moment.

"Hey, Yank," the copilot asked. "You're really here to see what's happening, huh?"

"Yep. Back in Washington there's the official briefings from the State Department, and Pentagon, and intelligence agencies like the CIA, but members of Congress don't always get the real picture. Politics are everywhere, and everyone's got their agenda, their party agenda, and a lot of other wants. It's hard to know what's really going on. Sometimes people like my boss send out staff to see what the truth is, and if they're getting the truth."

"So what do they tell you back home?" the navigator asked.

"Well, they tell the people that the war's very confusing, and terrible, and important, but that right now all we can do is send in food and UN peacekeepers. Everyone sees the news about the peacekeepers being useless—even targets. After Desert Storm there hasn't been a lot of support for getting involved in other people's wars anymore. The disaster in Somalia cemented that feeling. I'm not sure the average American even knows why we were involved in World War I let alone how bad it was or how it set the stage for World War II. Most people would rather go about their lives than be concerned about stuff that happens over here."

The navigator tried again. "Right, but what do they tell you or your boss?"

"We get the same crap, but everyone knows better. We know how important it is; how bad this could get if it's not stopped. I'm here mainly to look into this bit about the rich getting out and the poor being left to die. From what I can tell it's true. It's probably that way in every war. There's always grifting and profiteering—and money, power, those things get you privileges. I have to say, though, this does seem worse than anything I've read about or seen anywhere else. How about you guys?"

This time the pilot chimed in. "Look, Alan, we're here to do our jobs. Officer in Italy tells us to take stuff to wherever, and we do. An officer in Resnick or Sarajevo tells us to fly stuff out, we load up and fly. That's our job."

"You don't care about who gets left behind or what you're carrying?"

"Of course we do! Alan, we've seen things you can't believe. We do our job. Sometimes it's shit work, and sometimes it's a planeload of little tikes and their mas. Don't think we don't care. You better go back down and strap in. The tower's on the radio. We'll be down in fifteen minutes. Hold on, and you'll see. You'll see what this is all about."

It was clear Alan had touched a nerve. It might have been the subject, or the way he asked, or a cultural difference. In any event Alan had been politely and seriously told to leave the cockpit so he did. He took the strapping-in advice seriously too, and the airman helped him tied down tight until the straps on the cargo seat were almost painful. Then he waited. He waited and waited almost ten long minutes until the plane suddenly dove and turned left. It felt as though they were crashing. The engines howled. He heard the landing gear and flaps deploy as the plane leveled out, and the instant it did, he heard the gear rumble on the runway.

He could smell the rubber from the tires as the plane rolled down the runway to where it would be unloaded. While it was taxiing from the runway the airman opened the cargo ramp until it was level with the ground. Then Alan could smell the brakes as well as the exhaust. He could smell burning wood as well...and plastic, and trash, and sewer...and when he looked outside it was clear why. All around him was a smoking city under siege. This was war.

The British C-130 rolled past the terminal and to an area where normally planes would be refueled. There hadn't been fuel at the airport for months. Few, if any, vehicles were still running in the city, and those were on homemade alcohol or gasoline that had been smuggled into the city. Before the plane's engines were shut down, and before the plane even stopped rolling, a white SUV with "UN" letters painted on the doors pulled up between the tail and the left wing. Soon a propane-powered forklift and a French military cargo truck (also painted white with giant, black "UN" letters on the side) moved into position behind the C-130.

The British crew knew the routine. While the pilot and copilot did the shutdown flight list, and the airman guided trucks to the rear for unloading of the pallets, the navigator stepped out of the plane's port side hatch and met with the men from the UN vehicle: the United Nations airlift manager (UNPROFORHO; United Nations Provisional Force Humanitarian Operations), the British UN liaison officer, a Bosnian official, a driver, and a Pakistani soldier/UN peacekeeper with an FN-FAL rifle to protect them. Alan didn't want to stay on the plane and get in the way so he stepped off and met with the group as well. While they talked, everyone walked around the UN SUV to make it harder for a Serb sniper to take aim. It was nothing new to them, but to Alan the thought of being in someone's crosshairs unnerved him greatly.

When the moment came Alan introduced himself by name only. He didn't want to offend anyone by passively accusing them of war profiteering or smuggling or worse. The British navigator understood the nature of the situation as well and didn't explain who Alan was or why he was there. Instead, he evaded the issue, and that gave the officials the idea that perhaps this American was from the White House or more likely the CIA. They accorded him the respect due such offices.

"Mr. Conferra," the UN official asked, "what can we do for you?"

"Once you've got everything arranged with these Brits, perhaps you and I could talk someplace? Someplace more secure?"

The UN official nodded and waved over the airport noise. No sooner had they agreed than the first French truck of aid was full, pulled away, and another one was backing up to the C-130. Things moved quickly. As the first truck disappeared out of sight, the navigator returned to the plane. The UN and Bosnian officials motioned for Alan to join them in the SUV with the Pakistani soldier/peacekeeper/driver, and the British liaison officer stayed with the plane and crew. The driver didn't even wait for all three of the other doors to close before he stepped on the gas and headed back to the airport terminal.

"Okay, Mr. Conferra, what brings you to the war?"

Cool as a smiling spy Alan half-pretended/half-convinced himself that everything was normal, and he belonged in Sarajevo, not Italy. "I'm here to see about getting some special people out."

With a thick Swiss accent the UN official laughed. "We should have left you at the plane then. You'll want to talk with your British friend. We here are the ones getting supplies in. He gets people out."

"Are you sure? I'm talking about some very special people here. I thought you were the one to speak with?"

"No, Mr. Conferra. There's no need to be indirect here. You want to get rich people out. That British officer—says his name is MacLean—he's the one to talk to. It is clear you are not CIA or you would have known this. Who *do* you work for?"

Alan smiled and imagined he was a spy. "I'm with the United States government. That's all I can tell you." He laughed. They all laughed. Sarajevo and the Balkans in general were a web of secrecy, alliances, and deals, and the war's newfound purpose was more like a camouflage net to cover and connect them all. There were no more sides, only the deals and the prices to be paid: with blood inside the war zone, and with currency outside.

In the terminal Alan was briefed by the UN and Bosnian officials. They told him about the terminal, the situation on the ground in Sarajevo, and about the airlifts. In the background the occasional *wump*/ pause/*pop* sounds from Serbian mortars could be heard in the distance. To Alan it sounded like it was far away, but the Serbians were shelling the airport outside, and the thick walls and sandbag barricades inside the terminal muffled the sounds. After a few minutes the British liaison officer arrived and joined them.

"Mr. Conferra, I'm Major MacLean. They say you've been looking for me. How can I help you?"

"Major, I'm with the United States government. There are some people and packages that are important to us, and the time has come to move them from the war zone. These gentlemen say that you're the one to talk to."

"That I am. Where is your cargo?"

Alan motioned for the two men to step aside and isolate their conversation from the crowd.

"There's no need to be coy here, Mr. Conferra. There's no more Yugoslavia, so there's no more need for tact and delicate conversations."

"No more secrecy, huh?"

"Oh no, there's more secrecy than ever, but in a world of secrets there's simply no reason to pretend there are. Look around you. There are hundreds of people in earshot, and every single one of them has a secret, or a thousand. Trying to be coy here is like trying to hide blood in a butcher shop. Now what is it you need from me?"

Alan wasn't expecting such frank behavior in an illicit operation. It caught him off guard, and MacLean knew it.

"Right then. Well, Mr. Conferra, I know you're not with the CIA because that's your CIA man over there, three gates down on the couch. I can tell you're not military because, well, let's face it...you don't seem like you've ever held a weapon in your life. My guess is you're not with any agency. That makes you either private sector, and that's not likely because they're usually more trained in what we call tradecraft, or you're someone's errand boy. Are you someone's errand boy, Mr. Conferra? Let's have it: Who are you, who do you work for, and what do you want from me?"

Alan smiled humbly and half-laughed in a successful attempt to hide his embarrassment. "I'm just an accountant, Major MacLean. I do work for the United States government, and (with honest humility and self-deprecation) yes, I could definitely be described as someone's errand boy, I suppose."

"Right, and you're here to do what errand exactly?" MacLean recognized Alan's situation, but he remained the serious career military man in a war zone.

"My bosses want me to see if the airlift is really doing a humanitarian job, or if it's being misused to get out more powerful, wealthy people. I was just supposed to interview people. One thing led to another, and I find myself here as a sort of accident borne of poor judgment. Care to give your thoughts on the matter?"

"The matter?"

"Do you think the airlift is being humanitarian, or is it being misused by the elite?"

"Dear lord...you can't be serious?"

"I am. That's my job. If I'm here I might as well find out what's going on, and I've been told you're the man to talk to. What do you think?"

MacLean shook his head in utter disbelief.

"Mr. Conferra—"

"Alan, please."

"All right then, Alan, here it is. Life is a lot different in the rest of the world than it is in Washington, DC. It's a lot different in the rest of the world than in America. Outside your country's little bubble there's an uncivilized planet. Oh, there're pockets and areas where there's peace, but by and by the large part of the planet is far more ruthless. Yes. Yes, the airlift is being used to fly in humanitarian aid. Yes, we try to get civilians out. Yes, if the powerful and the rich want to get out first, they get out first, because without their support and their money there is no airlift. I may have a flight out that just has a mayor or minister on board with his family and their belongings, and that flight inevitably leaves dozens or even hundreds of women and children waiting in bunkers while artillery and snipers pin them down, but by getting that minister out, we get the political capital and or money to continue the flights, and get even get more flights and convoys out. That same minister might be the prime minister when things calm down here, and he can come back. We're ensuring that there's some continuity to even the slightest government structure. Last week I had a C-130 fly out with no one on board. Just art from the Sarajevo art museum and private collectors. The plane left while fifty elderly people waited in that building down at the south end of the terminal."

MacLean pointed out the window, but Alan didn't see the building.

"It's gone, Mr. Conferra...Alan. The Serbs shelled it with artillery from the other side of the hills. It went on for hours. There was nothing that could be done. Even if someone could get to the building, there was no way to get the people out through the barrage. Fifty people died for a planeload of artwork. That's war. That's what's going on here."

Alan's smile was gone. His face was apologetic, and his jaw lowered with shame just a bit. MacLean saw it, and hard man that he was he still understood that there was intelligent ignorance as well as lawlessness on the planet. He was familiar with the lack of civilization, and even had an "at home" feeling in war zones, but he'd seen bureaucratic types like Alan before. Most of the time they bore an arrogance to shield them from their naiveté, but it was clear Alan was different; it was clear this was a different bureaucrat. MacLean had already surmised that Alan was some sort of accountant, and perhaps in the same way that most accountants could see a spreadsheet as black and red, profit and loss, it seemed Conferra could accept the black smoke and red blood of the real world's math as well. That and he felt a bit of pity for the errand boy who took a wrong turn into the real world.

"Look, er, Alan, you're out of your element here. Why don't you just go back to America and tell your 'bosses' that the airlift is still humanitarian. It is. There are times when people get left behind, but tragedies like that building over there...they happen every day here. If they want to save more people, the airlift's not the way. The only way to do that is to end the war. That means forcing the Serbs back to Serbia, and making the Bosnians accept Bosnian-Serbs in a new government. You and I both know that's not going to happen, however. The only way to get both of those things to happen is to get America and NATO to put actual troops in this war—not this United Nations observer/peacekeeper farce, but actual troops. And I mean enough troops to actually force the Bosnians and Serbs and everyone else to stop or be destroyed. Anything short of that, well...it just won't work...and the fighting will go on and on until everyone is bled bone white."

"I see your point. How bad is it here in the city? When do you think it'll fall?"

"The situation in the city is grave. There's no food, no water, no electricity, no fire or police, and the government is in exile. All these people have is their ability to scavenge, to make do, and the militias. The militias are just ordinary people who have one way or another obtained a rifle and been told by someone that beyond a certain point there's only Serbs. I've never seen such resiliency on a large scale. These people are amazing. Without government services and authority, the civilians have become the authorities. Truly, I've no idea why the Serbs haven't just rolled in with their tanks and crushed them. The only possibility is that they're using the suffering here to make a point in the region and to the world; to show that they have power—maybe not in arms or ammunition or skill, but certainly in the most important thing on a battlefield."

"What's that, Mr. MacLean?"

"Brutality, of course. War is about being as brutal as possible to make the other side do what is wanted. The Serbs have it in spades. And they've got artillery too I suppose. My apologies for being direct, Alan, but that's the way it is."

Alan's expression parroted MacLean's.

"No need to apologize. I appreciate your candor. All things considered it appears you're clearly correct in your assessment, and the occasional need to balance the flights makes perfect sense. Thank you. I mean that sincerely." Alan smiled and continued, "I better get going before I miss my plane out."

"Too late," MacLean laughed. "They left before I came back here and we started talking. You can stay here till the next one comes in, but I'm not sure the Serbs are going to let anymore come in—at least not today. There's a UN convoy that came in this morning. It was supposed to turn right around, but the Serbs have been delaying it all morning. I can get you in on that if you'd like?"

Alan's polite goodbye smile had evaporated—replaced by a sigh and the face of a deer caught in headlights.

"Thanks. I'd appreciate that."

MacLean patted him on the shoulder. "On me then. We're gonna get you outta here."

The two men walked through the airport terminal and back to the white United Nations SUV outside. The same Pakistani soldier/UN peacekeeper drove them out of the airport, through the Pejton suburb, and to the still-parked line of UN vehicles that were lined up on the M17 highway—stopped at the bridge across the Miljacka River.

"There you are, Mr. Conferra. No telling when they're leaving, but it's the best chance you have of getting out of here for the next few days at least. Good luck."

"Don't you have to talk to someone, get permission, or something?"

"No. You're an American. Everyone wants the Americans to come into the war and stop it. They'll do anything to help you. Remember when you asked if rich or powerful people were given preferential treatment? Well, you're one of those people now. Americans are bloody rich compared to anyone here, and just because you're an American makes you powerful. All you have to do now is climb into one of those vehicles. If anyone bothers you, just tell them who you are, and that should do the trick. If it doesn't, tell them I put you on board. This convoy has a British escort. We'll take care of you."

In disbelief, Alan stepped outside, waved at the SUV as it sped off, and walked toward one of the British armored vehicles. As he did so he straightened his tie and attempted to look calm while walking swiftly. There was no shaking the sense that some sniper on the other side of the river was looking through telescopic sights with crosshairs tracking every step.

The convoy consisted of eighteen white trucks, "UN" painted on their sides, and about a hundred civilians inside. In the front there was another white UN SUV and a pair of what appeared to be tanks with small cannons. In fact, they were British Warrior Infantry Fighting Vehicles (IFV). Three more were at the tail end of the convoy.

The British Warrior IFVs had a crew of three with the capacity to carry seven soldiers. The commander and gunner sat in the turret—most often with the hatches open for better visibility. Between them a 30mm RARDEN autocannon was ready to use, even though United Nations rules of engagement strictly prohibited it. To most people it was just a tank—twenty feet long, nine feet high, and almost ten feet wide. The Rolls-Royce-Perkins V8 Condor diesel engine allowed it to run at forty-five miles an hour while a few inches of aluminum armor could protect both crew and passengers from small arms fire and shrapnel. The armor would never last in a fight with a tank or stand up to any antitank weapons. Still, to Alan, they looked like tanks, acted like tanks, and in his mind acted like tanks with room for passengers—passengers like himself.

Sitting in the commander's hatch and the gunner's hatch on the top of the turret, a British soldier/peacekeeper spotted Alan. They made eye contact, and the soldier motioned for Alan toward the back of his Warrior. Alan walked over, through the stink of diesel exhaust fumes and the deafening engine noises. As he did he waved at the soldier, who again motioned to Alan—this time to enter the back of the Warrior and put on a set of intercom headphones once inside. As he did so a hydraulic ram opened a door in the back of the Warrior, and Alan could see three more British soldiers inside. They handed him a headset.

"Can you hear me?" he asked.

"Yes, yes. I can here you, but who are you, and what the bloody Hell were you doing out there—trying to get us all killed?"

"I'm not sure what you mean, sir, but my name is Alan Conferra. I'm with the US government. A British officer back at the airport told me I could get a ride out of town with you."

The Warrior's commander shook his head, but since Alan was inside the vehicle, and the commander was standing half in/half out of the vehicle's turret, the two couldn't see each other.

"A Yank. Well that figures. Explains the suit too, no doubt. Who did you speak with back at the airport?"

"His name was Stan MacLean."

The commander shook his head again and made eye contact with the gunner next to him, who was also shaking his head.

"That figures as well, Mr. Conferra. Welcome aboard, I suppose. Major MacLean's our man out here. The rumor on the [radio] net is that we've finally been given permission by the

Serbs to move out. We'll be leaving any time now. Luck is apparently on your side."

Another voice joined the intercom conversation. It was one of the soldiers sitting next to Alan.

"What's a bloody Yank doing here? You some sort of spy?"

Alan smiled, tilted his head to the right, and looked to the soldier on his left who was asking.

"No. I'm not a spy. I'm an accountant—"

The intercom broke in with 5 different voices. It was impossible to make out who was saying what. One was clear, "Bloody Hell! The bean counters are here! We're in for it now! I thought this place was shoddy before, but now accountants!?"

Alan laughed, "No, seriously. I'm an accountant for a senator back in the states. He wanted to see if the situation was as bad as the reports we get."

The Warrior's commander interrupted, "Well what do you think Yank? Is it as bad as it looks back in America?"

Alan's smile disappeared replaced by a sincere, frank, matter-of-fact look. He shared it by making eye contact with each of the three soldiers sitting in the cramped compartment with him.

"It looks terrible back home. It's definitely worse, but I don't know if people back home can really understand. A lot of the time, when things get too ugly or hard to believe, people just change the channel or turn the page in the newspaper. I'm guessing you men know what I'm saying. People back home just can't believe it."

Heads nodded, and the conversation ended.

Outside vehicle engines droned on and on while inside there was silence. One of the three soldiers tried to sleep. Another stared off into a corner lost in thought. The last endlessly fiddled with his weapon-stroking and rubbing each part as if it had been dropped in sand despite having been cleaned incessantly earlier that morning. In the turret the commander scanned the far river bank and nearby buildings. The gunner did the same, but with a set of binoculars. The driver sat with his hatch open for better visibility as well, and he sat, and he sat.

An hour passed, and finally the commander said something.

"Right gents, just got the word, we're moving out."

Everyone could hear the engines of the trucks and Warriors outside rev louder and begin to move. Several minutes later, the Warrior that Alan was riding in jerked forward and began to move. There were no windows, or open hatches, or even firing ports to see the outside world. The convoy drove forward on the highway. They crossed the bridge into Serbian territory without incident. No other vehicles were in sight. There were few people left in the area—only soldiers and civilians hiding in basements. The M17 highway rolled through a quarter mile of destroyed industrial area followed by a few small residential areas. After a few minutes they rolled left and began proceeding through the most dangerous part of the trip—an area with pastures on the right and thick woods on the left.

The driver cut in on the intercom, "Taking fire from the woods. Repeat, taking fire. I'm buttoning up [closing the hatch and driving with periscopes instead of his head exposed]."

The commander responded with immediate coolness. "Taking fire, roger, buttoning up."

No one knew it except the driver, but a sniper at the far end of the pastures on the right was taking shots at each of the vehicles. It was a sort of revenge, hate, fun, but mostly the sniper was shooting out of boredom. One of the shots hit the Warrior and missed the driver's face by a few inches. Other shots wounded four people in the unarmored trucks. Inside the Warrior there was no chance of hearing the sniper's shots or even the snap/tick sound of the one that almost hit the driver. The engine was just too loud and the compartment too thick.

A minute or so later the commander came on the intercom and reported that the convoy was taking heavy small arms fire near the front of the column. Alan and the soldiers exchanged looks. There was no fear on the soldiers' part, but certainly apprehension. They'd done plenty of convoy escort missions through the area, and they knew that this was how serious situations started; first with a bullet, then a few, then, like a waterfall's first drop, the deluge could follow.

While the British soldiers were expecting it to rain high-velocity steel and lead, there instead came a loud blast from the front of the column. Even inside the Warrior's compartment Alan and the soldiers could hear it. The Warrior stopped abruptly, and the commander's voice came on the intercom.

"Right, lads, someone caught a mine up front. Driver, open the hatch. I want you three in back to run up to the front of the column, see how bad things are, see if you can help, and return back. I can see the smoke from up here, and the CO's [Commanding Officer] not answering on the net. Check it out."

In the front of the Warrior the driver unlocked the hydraulics and pulled a lever to activate the ram to open the hatch in the back of the vehicle. With the beams of sunlight passing through a blue veil of diesel exhaust, all three soldiers bolted out the door, and the smell of spent high explosive was unmistakable. Even though the lead Warrior had been hit almost a quarter mile ahead, Alan could smell it burning.

The sound of the engines was louder with the hatch open. So too was the sound of battle. A rifle is not a quiet thing. Alan could hear the deep staccato of AK-47s in the distance, and precision rifles farther away: above them on top of the steep mountain ahead, to their right and across the pastures, and on their left from the woods. The tenor and tone of the rifles was interrupted by the rare reply from a British soldier's L85 IW (SA80) assault rifle.

Minutes passed, and finally the three soldiers ran back to the Warrior.

Alan could hear their report from inside the infantry fighting vehicle.

"Boss, the lead Warrior's hit a big antitank mine on the left side."

"Anyone hit?" asked the commander.

"No, boss, but—"

"Anyone tell you when we can get moving and out of this shooting range?"

"No, boss, but you'll never guess who was in the front! The bleedin' general! That's right! He wanted to see if the Serbs were being up 'n' up and see what these convoys are all about. And of course a general's gotta ride up front so naturally he was in the Warrior that got hit!"

Another of the soldiers interrupted. "You should see it, boss! That mine blew off the front bogey and at least three road wheels. Track's blown all over the place, and the whole damned Warrior is sitting on its right side like some kid kicked over a toy!"

"Shit, it'd have to be the damned general, wouldn't it?" answered the commander.

"Oh, boss, he is pissed off too! Word is he's calling in an airstrike himself! You imagine that poor sap on the other end? Guy's just flyin' around doing nothin' at all like they always do while we get our asses kicked, and all of a sudden a general's on the net tellin' him to come down and do his fuckin' job!"

All three soldiers and the Warrior's three crewman laughed hard.

"Right, well, do they need anything?" the commander finally asked.

"They're taking the tow cables off all the trucks and putting them together so the next poor sod in the Warrior behind the general's can pull over their wreck. Not sure if they can fix it or how long it'll take, though."

Starting April of the previous year the United Nations and NATO had worked together to create Operation Deny Flight. The initiative was set in motion after Serbian aircraft were allegedly bombing civilian centers in the disputed Bosnia-Herzegovina war zone. At first air superiority fighters were the only aircraft involved, but after several incidents where Serbian-Allied forces had held UN peacekeepers hostage, ground attack aircraft were added to Operation Deny Flight. The United States contributed F-16 fighter planes, which could function as both air superiority and ground attack aircraft. The British contributed several SEPECAT Jaguar fighter-bombers.

The SEPECAT (Société Européenne de Production de l'avion Ecole de Combat et d'Appui Tactique) Jaguar was a joint venture between Britain and France. Initially the program was to build a training aircraft. Politicians in both nations, as well as in other NATO nations, saw an opportunity to develop a small affordable bomber to help cope with shrinking defense budgets in the 1960s. Modifications to the trainer were made. Others saw an opportunity to make the plane into a nuclear-capable bomber, and more modifications were made. When Cold War plans showed that NATO airfields were vulnerable to Soviet attack, the Jaguar design was modified to have exceptionally strong landing gear, which would enable it to take off or even land from grass fields. Air Force leaders in several NATO countries saw a need for a fighter role, and the Jaguar had air-to-air missile mounts put on top if its wings. As integrated air defense systems increased in capability and as Soviet-made surface-to-air (SAM) missiles proved they could even shoot down American U-2 spy planes flying at the edge of the stratosphere, modifications were made to make the Jaguar into a fast, extremely low-level ground attack plane. It was here where the "Jag" really fell into its element.

Ground attack aircraft were not an uncommon thing. They'd been around since World War 1. During World War II the American Thunderbolt and various US Navy bombers excelled at the specific mission type. Those same aircraft were still used in Korea, and even in the Vietnam War. Post-Vietnam modern fighter planes that were designed for air-to-air combat were often modified for ground attack. The Jag, however, was amalgamate of infinite committees and wants and desires. In its core it remained an extremely agile training plane. Operation Desert Storm proved that the American A-10 Thunderbolt II was the ultimate close-air support plane. In that same war, the Jag proved that when there were ground attack targets in heavily defended areas, the Jag could get there and get the job done.

While Alan was sitting in what tank crews call a "steel coffin" out over the Adriatic Sea, south of Aviano Air Base, a pair of British SEPECAT Jaguars had been cruising at thirty-five thousand feet, waiting for a call. The pilots knew that when the call did come, good people were in dire need. The call came.

As one, both pilots banked to the left and headed toward Alan. The sky was clear at thirty-five thousand feet, but below them a layer of clouds hid the Adriatic, Slovenia, Croatia, and then Bosnia-Herzegovina. Slowly they descended. Fifty miles west of the Bosnian/Croatian coast one of the planes had a CAUTION light and alarm go off. The flight control system had indications of an oil pump about to fail on the port engine. He had to abort the mission and return to Aviano. Contrary to protocol, the other pilot decided to continue on the mission alone. He knew that if he got the call for help, help was desperately needed.

The remaining pilot descended into the thick cloud bank and emerged under it at three thousand feet. For most planes three thousand feet was low level. The Jag was more comfortable under a hundred feet. Pilots called it "shaving the rocks." At five hundred miles an hour trees and houses appeared as blurs while they raced past the canopy. Still, this is where the Jag lived—not dodging SAMs and antiaircraft-artillery (AAA), but by dodging trees and powerlines. Why? In the rocky mountainous terrain of the Balkans, air defense networks were often put near the tops of hills and mountains where weapon-mounted radars could acquire and track targets. The Jag would literally fly "under the guns," and they did it fast—extremely fast...too fast for even soldiers on the ground to shoot at them effectively.

The pilot rolled left and dove for the ground near the town of Gradac. From there the valley snaked its way all the way to Sarajevo. He passed the village by dodging a medieval tower on his right. Continuing into the valley he dropped down lower—almost fifty feet above the small river. The valley opened for a moment into farmland. Here he began to follow a road, the R424, though he didn't know what road it was. He only knew it headed toward the waypoint on his guidance computer. In no time the mountains closed in again. The pilot continued forward, banking left and right to evade mountain cliffs. Near Sretnice he climbed and rolled upside down to hop over a mountain and dive back down while staying as close to the changing ground as possible. The town of Mostar and its historic arch bridge passed below faster than one could say "passed below." A quick turn to the left and then right, and he approached his target—climbing slightly to ensure that he wasn't blown out of the sky by his own bombs. The computer showed him where the target's coordinates were.

He only caught a fleeting glimpse of the trapped convoy. The image of a Warrior IFV sitting upright on its side was too unusual to miss, and that made his focus all the better. He lined up the bombing symbol with the target symbol on his heads-up display (HUD), and let half a dozen 450-kilogram bombs fall exactly where the general wanted them. Even though they were only dropped from a few hundred feet, the shockwave from the blasts shook the tiny Jag. He continued forward, turned low over a piece of farmland where the valley opened up, and then headed back down the way he came. Once back over the convoy the Jag's engines puffed from a momentary lack of oxygen as he flew through the smoke from his own bombs. With that he wagged his wings and continued flying down the mountain roads—all the way to the Adriatic, and then back home to Italy in just a few minutes.

Alan was sitting tensely inside the Warrior when he heard the six loud explosions—or rather one large rolling thunder. Even inside the armored vehicle he could hear the Jaguar's twin jet engines scream overhead and the cheers of all the people in the convoy that followed. The shooting stopped immediately, so Alan asked to step outside, and the driver opened the Warrior's rear hatch. He removed his intercom headset and then stepped outside just in time to see the Jaguar come straight at him as it passed through the smoke and waved its wings. Then it faded from view like the smoke from the bombs.

From on top the turret, the commander yelled down to Alan, "There's your airlift, Mr. Conferra!"

Alan smiled and waved back.

The battle was over. There was no more resistance or interruptions on the rest of Alan's journey out of the Balkans. He'd been to war a second time, even under fire, and survived. Alan thought such an experience would have turned him into a hardened man, weathered, and left staring off in the distance, but it hadn't. He was still the same man, still an accountant, still a bureaucrat. Still Alan.

He didn't know it, though, but deep inside he had changed. He'd seen the women and children at Sarajevo airport. He'd felt the despair of an entire city under siege. Thanks to Stan MacLean's frank conversation he'd also learned about the limits of what the world can do. He'd also seen that a community can come together even in the absence of a government or power or water.

***

12/24/1995

The holiday season and Christmas in particular has tremendous emotional effect on billions of people. In the northeastern United States memories of Norman Rockwell paintings mix with Santa Clause imagery and the modern commercial advertising to move people out of their normal lives and take them on a journey to another world. It's a world where children's innocent fantasies and dreams come to life by recreating those Norman Rockwell snow scenes with snowmen and fireplaces and by buying gifts that open hearts. For a few weeks every year people rush everywhere and with everything, and amid the tensions of combat-shopping in strip malls or demolition derby détente in parking lots, people tend to open their hearts more to the ones they love.

It's a time when memories are created: family dinners, the morning ritual of opening gifts, and seeing pure, unadulterated joy that children have when they are given the most well-marketed toys instead of socks and underwear. Husbands and wives often take the time to reflect and share their gratitude for each other and all the good things in their lives. It's a time of the year when people reflect.

And that reflection can be hard. Suicides rise sharply during the holidays. As much as the time brings families together, those who are left alone can feel deathly abandoned. Normal financial troubles are exasperated by the perceived need to spend so much more on gifts for other people. And for everyone, the New Year holiday brings reflection.

This Christmas was a great one for the Assana family. Brian and his wife had been together for four years now; they had married immediately upon his return from Operation Desert Storm. They had three children since—twin two-year-old daughters and a one-year-old son—and they were comfortable. There was the occasional month where unseen expenses made it hard to pay the electric bill, but for the most part his job as a patrolman on the Cleveland Police Department paid well. Brian's wife, Kim, worried about his safety on the job, but she also had a great deal of confidence in him.

They were a happy, loving family. The kids were thrilled with the toys Santa brought them. The house was decorative with the best (albeit cheapest) décor. Kim, an elementary school teacher, was off for the holidays, and Brian had incredibly managed to get three days in a row off to spend with the family. Everything was perfectly 1995 Americana.

There was even the inevitable holiday error, something that would go wrong and do little harm beyond giving the kids a memory to mark the event by in the future. Kim had decided to take part in the holiday feast tradition by baking a ham and having "a big family dinner" with her inlaws visiting. The house was a small one, built in 1900 on a street with forty-nine other homes almost identical. There was no real distinction from one to the next, and likely the same could be said about many neighborhoods in any northeastern United States city. The kitchen was cramped, and it was definitely Kim's lair. Everyone else was exiled to the living room in the front of the house to sit around the Christmas tree and watch the girls play or hold the baby.

That's when Murphy's Law struck. Kim heard the baby crying. It was indiscernible to most people, but a mother knew her child. She recognized the cry as one for food. Kim had been basting the ham when she heard it, and she pushed the ham back into the oven to go feed the baby. What she'd forgotten was that she had left the plastic baster in the oven with the ham. After a few minutes the smell of pineapple- and cherry-glazed ham roasting began to smell of melting plastic. It didn't take long for the plastic smell to overcome the ham's scent. Brian was the first to the kitchen with Kim in tow. He opened the oven door and smoke rolled out.

All at once it hit him. The smoke billowed. The smoke alarms went off, and Brian projectile vomited all over the ham. He'd tried to cover his mouth, but that just made it worse. Kim was shocked, and Alan bolted through the kitchen and out the backdoor of the house. Next to the cement stairs leading down to the driveway he fell to his knees. At the same time that he continued to vomit, he wept uncontrollably. His heart raced. His head pounded. He felt small, icy snowflakes on his face and neck. He also felt the cool air, but the cold that he felt the most was inside. He felt as if he was suddenly lost in some dire way.

Kim was only a few seconds behind him. She took one step outside, and the sight of Brian shocked her. He motioned with his left hand for her to go back while he tried to say "go back inside" in a manner that would both compel her and not cause her to feel even more concern. The screen door shut immediately.

A few minutes later Brian regained control of himself. The shaking continued, and he wiped the tears from his face as best he could while kicking snow over the vomit. While being a relatively humble man, Brian was still terribly embarrassed. Going back inside to face his wife, children, and his parents gave him a sense of shame. They loved him immensely, but still, he'd clearly ruined dinner and created a spectacle.

As he sat on the cold concrete steps, the screen door opened. It was his father.

"How you doin'?"

"I'm okay."

"Not the first time, huh?"

"No."

"You talk to anyone about it?"

"No."

"You remember that time at the Fourth of July, back when you were a kid? The big Bicentennial thing?"

"Yeah, I remember. We had a block party back at the old house on Merriman Road."

Brian's father stepped outside, carefully closed the door behind him, and sat down next to Brian on the small steps. He pulled out a pack of gum and handed Brian a piece to help clear his breath.

"Do you remember the fireworks that year?"

"Can't say I do."

"Well, I do. It was the combination of flashes, explosions, and the smell that got to me. When I got back from 'Nam, me and a lotta guys had a real tough time. It wasn't just the political bullshit, but it was like no one understood. Hell, we didn't understand. I lost more friends at home than in my entire first tour over there. Some guys just couldn't handle getting back into The World."

Brian interrupted, "Dad, that's not me. It was completely different for us. We—"

His father interrupted him. "Yes. It is you, and it is me, and it is a lotta guys. It's not because we're crazy or weak or anything else. It took a lot of time to understand for me. You've gotta talk to someone, and get some help. You're not insane, but your head's been trained to act certain ways, to react other ways, and some of the stuff we've been through just makes us feel like we're right back there."

"Dad, this doesn't happen very often. I dunno what makes it happen. It just happens out of the blue. It's got nothing to do with the war."

"Really? Every time I smell burning metal my muscles lock. It reminds me of this one time I saw this "track" [an M113 armored personnel carrier] that'd been hit by a Viet Cong RPG. Thing melted like a candle! That melting aluminum gets me every time. Fireworks remind me of that last day at Khe Sanh. You couldn't believe the noise, the artillery, the rifle fire. When I first came back, every time I'd see an Asian kid I felt afraid, like the kid was gonna get me with a frag. Took me years, and it still happens sometimes. God knows how many times your mom's had to wake me up at night.

Brian was silent. He'd had similar things happen. The nightmares were the most poignant similarity.

"Son, let's go back inside. Your mom knows what's going on, and I'm certain Kim does too. The girls have their dolls, and could probably care less."

Brian sighed, nodded, and again tried to clean himself up with a handful of snow.

"What about dinner?"

His dad smiled. "Brian, Kim's great, but she's the shittiest cook I've ever known. That woman could burn water if you gave her a chance. Better idea, I'll tell the girls that you and I are gonna go look around for a dinner replacement. All the grocery stores are closed, but the VFW down on Cedar Ave's got a potluck Christmas dinner today. Good guys down there. I'm sure they'll help us out. Besides, it'll give the girls a chance to air the place out, and I dunno about you, but I could use a break from being in your house with four women!"

Later, the Assana family had a memorable Christmas dinner of BBQ chicken wings with green bean casserole and pasta salad. They managed to make the entire thing a laughable moment, but only because they all understood. No one but Brian knew the specific sights and smells he'd had in the Kuwaiti desert, but they knew he was having a bad memory. They all knew it. That meant he wasn't alone; he had support.

The memories of the hydrocarbon smell from all the oil well fires were similar to that of the melting/burning plastic. He was also reminded of being lost in the desert, at the Mohammed Al d'aoud farm, and smelling the mix of melted greenhouse plastic with the stench of burned human flesh. Brian didn't know it, but that unique combination of smell—burned meat and burned plastic—memories of those scents were part of the memory he had of being lost in the war, the fear. In the same way that a dog learns to salivate whenever its food bowl is filled, so too had Brian Assana learned to feel scared, lost, and near panicked whenever he would smell that unique combination in just the wrong way. His father had his post-traumatic stress syndrome triggers too. Together, with the support of their wives, the veterans would learn to deal with the mental scars of their wars.

***

12/25/1995

Sergeant Phillipe Aristide, veteran of Iraq and Somalia, spent this Christmas in the jungle along the south side of Firestone, Liberia. There was torrential rain instead of snow, and the temperature was over one hundred degrees. The rain masked any movement. That made Phillipe and the six other Rangers who were with him feeling comfortable in moving undetected, but that benefit was a double-edged sword. They knew that anyone or anything could sneak up on them as well. Visibility in the thick, triple-canopy jungle was rarely more than fifteen to twenty feet, and while it was the middle of the afternoon the rain-heavy clouds and layer upon layer of greenery made it seem like dusk. They sat there, in the rain, in the dark, and in the steamy heat, without saying a word.

He and his team had been sent into Liberia on a reconnaissance mission. He was second in command. With him was a staff sergeant who had responsibility for the mission. Phillipe's mission was to make sure the team could do the mission. With them was a corporal responsible for communications and a pair of two-man scout/sniper teams with an observer and shooter in each. None of them had worked together except the team leader and the corporal doing communications. The sniper teams had only worked together as individual teams. Still, they had all gone through Ranger training, as well as specialty training for this Long Range Surveillance Detachment [LSRD] mission, and they were professionals.

Liberia was founded just after the War of 1812 by an American group that sought to create a refuge for freed American slaves. Its capital, Monrovia, was even named after American President James Monroe. Over the years more and more former American slaves came, and eventually they declared their independence in the model of the United States. The Liberian Constitution was actually written in Washington, DC. English was the official language. They even created a flag with red and white stripes and a blue field with a single star...looking almost identical to the American flag. To the people of Liberia, America was their big brother.

Things were never all that well with Liberia, however. Many of the former American slaves who returned to Africa actually enslaved populations of the indigenous people, and formed plantations based on the model in the southern United States from which they themselves had been freed. This practice continued until the first African-born president of Liberia came to power in 1980. In 1989-90 he was overthrown by rebels. One of them, Prince Johnson, actually captured him, tortured him on video, killed him, and ate his heart while drinking Budweiser...all for the world to witness on live TV. Johnson was then overthrown by fellow rebel Charles Taylor, who was in the process of being overthrown by at least a dozen different Liberian warlords.

Like many African nations Liberia was rich with natural resources desired by the industrialized world. Before the nineteenth century it was known as the Grain Belt of Africa, then it was seen as the hub for the ivory trade, of which its neighbor would later adopt the name Ivory Coast. After World War I and the avalanche of automobile technology, American tire magnates saw Liberia's rich rubber tree resource and sought to secure it. Leading the way was the Firestone and Rubber Company, which loaned the developing country of Liberia huge sums of money in exchange for ninety-nine year leases on hundreds of thousands of acres filled with rubber trees.

Firestone developed a massive plantation. Processing buildings were built. Schools, hospitals, roads, even an airport were also built. Tens of thousands of people were employed, and—flush with corporate investment—the area around the plantation grew until it actually became its own town: Firestone, Liberia. Firestone flourished, and Liberia grew.

Beginning in the 1980s a series of coups followed one after another, and by 1989 the country had dissolved into full-blown civil war. Neighboring countries like Sierra Leone and Guinea as well as other African nations fueled the civil war for their own interests. When the Soviet Union collapsed, its weapons went to market and many found a home in Liberia. The original army units were long shattered and dissolved by 1995. Anarchy ruled. There were several competing rebel groups, but the streets of Monrovia, Liberia's capital city, were filled with detritus, garbage, and dead bodies. Any resemblance to a continuity of government control was gone.

The West promised help. The United Nations promised help. Larger African nations promised help. The charitable people of the world promised help. None came. Some charities tried, but with no sense of security at all they only became targets...exactly as had happened in Somalia, and Rwanda, and so many other places.

Finally, the American embassy in Monrovia came under attack itself, and the Firestone plantation was threatened. The Americans promised action, but Big Brother was slow to act. Americans still feared another Black Hawk Down incident like the one that was so humiliating just two years earlier in Somalia. Those bodies of American soldiers being dragged through the streets had as much influence on American foreign policy as the Soviet Union's tens of thousands of nuclear warheads.

Help was coming, however. A US Navy amphibious assault group was positioned off the coast of Liberia. A US Marine Special Forces unit had been sent in to secure the embassy while helicopters flew people out to sea and safety. US Navy SEAL teams were already surveying the coastal areas, swamps, and rivers (albeit usually at night and very covertly). And other US Army Long Range Surveillance Detachments (LRSD) like Phillipe's were scouring the countryside to gather as much intelligence as possible before any potential American involvement began.

Phillipe and the young men with him were to circle the entire Firestone plantation, gather as much intelligence as possible, and patrol the road from the plantation to the nearby airport. Military planners in cubicles at the Pentagon in Washington considered using that airport as a way to bring in larger US Army infantry units and supplies if needed. The American people had an interest (though a momentary one) in the suffering of the Liberian people, but the American government—and the lobbyists who steered it—were interested in Liberia's resources. An American resource like the Firestone plantation was top on their list, but even with that much value and attention, only Phillipe and six other US Rangers had been sent to check it out.

The plantation itself was large—almost eleven miles by six miles. Inside the perimeter were twelve different "Division Areas," a river, a road network, nine different processing areas, and on the southeast corner a shantytown. Gathering intelligence on any one of these elements would have taken weeks and perhaps a second team. They had six days, and they'd already used a full day to parachute in and stash their supplies.

The team leader divided his force. He assigned each sniper team three "Division Areas" to check out. Phillipe and his team were to check out the processing facilities and shanty town to the southeast. The plan was for everyone to meet back at where they had stashed their supplies on the fifth day. Then they'd head for the extraction area in the southwest corner of the plantation. Sending half the LRSD off on their own without even radio communication was a very risky and dangerous proposition. Everyone knew it, but everyone believed they could manage it.

The plan was communicated at a whisper. First one sniper team, then the next stuck their heads under a plastic poncho that the team leader used to cover the map as he illuminated it with a blue flashlight. After getting their orders, the first team left into the jungle and was gone before the second team even saw the blue light. When they understood their orders and disappeared into the jungle, Phillipe was told to take the lead position and head southeast into the jungle—navigating only by a compass; able to see only a few feet in front of his face at any moment.

Phillipe led the team for the rest of the afternoon. When the sunset and night was fully upon them, visibility dropped to less than ten feet and they had to stop. Trudging through the brush without being detected by man or animal was hard work. The men were tired. They paused, formed a circle for security, and began to stand down. The team leader made a radio check, and he let commanders in snow-covered Washington know that he and his men were fine in the dark steamy jungle of Liberia. Then they ate some energy bars and rested two at a time.

A little after 2 a.m. the rain stopped as if someone had turned a knob to turn off the shower. Instantly the jungle's insect population came to life. The sound of a hundred different species of cricket and other noise-making bugs was deafening. Their ears were highly tuned to listen for any approaching threat, but the bugs didn't care. To them, their city of green and wood was alive. The only way to fight it was for the men to stand up. Resting on the ground with everything that crawled was just not smart.

Sunrise came, and the larger wildlife that fed on the insects came to life. As such, the insects' mating and territorial calls were replaced with that of birds, monkeys, gorillas, and even a forest elephant somewhere on the plantation. The Liberian jungle would have made most people feel they'd time traveled to a prehistoric era.

The team headed out. This time the assistant radio operator took the point position and led them southeast. Twice the jungle suddenly opened up to large fields where rubber trees had once been planted and harvested once they'd reached low production levels. On each occasion the Rangers stayed inside the tree line and made their way on the edge of the fields. The third time it happened, the field was ten-foot-tall elephant grass, and they decided to cross the field through it.

Eventually even the elephant grass ended. When it did the team had come to a road that crossed their path to the southeast, but on the other side they could see a small encampment, a village or perhaps a latex processing area. In any event, they could see people there. Since learning about the people in the area was paramount to their mission, Phillipe and the team concealed themselves along the edge of the road and began to watch the encampment.

The camp was barely two hundred yards away. There were five buildings: three cinder block structures that had once been painted white, and two shelters made from aluminum sheeting and corrugated tin. There was also an old station wagon that was dented and shot to pieces, but still seemed to function, and at least twenty armed men wearing a variety of faded, once brightly colored t-shirts, shorts, jeans, and in some cases underwear. They didn't look like plantation workers, and a motley collection of Soviet-made small arms added to that suggestion. They looked more like a local militia, a gang, perhaps marauders, and surely saw themselves as some sort of rebel faction.

Phillipe took some digital pictures. The team radio operator was able to send those pictures back to Washington. They also went to several other intelligence agencies and military command units around the world. In this way analysts could study the potential enemies in the region and make educated guesses on their armaments, their training level, their discipline, their supplies, even their nutrition—or malnutrition as it were. Nutrition would be the real shocker to Phillipe's commanders.

Using a small parabolic microphone, the assistant radio operator was able to eavesdrop on some of their conversations. Everyone else had to listen from a few hundred yards away using just the ears that nature gave them. At first it was just a few of the armed men talking and yelling at each other. Then more of the T-shirt troopers joined in to the indiscernible debate. After a while an older man, almost twenty, stepped out of one of the cinder block buildings, and when he yelled at them all they fell silent either with fear or respect. Wind, jungle noise, and local slang made much of the conversation unclear in any way.

"You babies think you are men, but you are [unintelligible]!" he yelled. "I will show you a lesson! I will show you! Who is the baddest [unintelligible] in you?!"

One of the child T-shirt trooper soldiers, fourteen, stepped forward with an AK-47 at his side.

"I am the baddest, general. I killed the most soldiers, and no bullet ever kill me."

The man grabbed the kid by the back of his neck and threw him inside the cinder block building. There was shouting, then a gunshot. The kid remerged with his fist raised high, glistening in dark red blood, and his shirt heavy and wet with the same.

"I told you I the baddest! I drinked the blood, I lifted it up to the temple, and I ate the heart and the liver!" the kid shouted.

By this time everyone had come out to see the commotion. Others had emerged from beyond the buildings, and Phillipe—as well as everyone on his team—recognized that they were in a bad location. There were at least a hundred people armed with rifles and machine guns, all chanting and screaming wildly around the "baddest [child] soldier."

Then the leader of the ragtag T-shirt troopers came back out of the cinder block building. This time he threw a man out before him. The man was almost twenty years old—old by Liberian standards. He was dressed in American woodland camouflage, and his hands were tied behind his back. The commander had another man, similar to the first, whom he dragged with a rope around his neck.

Phillipe took more pictures. The zoom lens showed him instantly that it wasn't anyone from either of the sniper teams. They appeared to be local government troops loyal to President Charles Taylor (Taylor himself had been a rebel leader until a few years earlier when he took power in one of the coups). While it was impossible to tell one militia or gang or rebel group from another, Taylor's government troops wore American camouflage on at least part of their body—something everyone else avoided.

"Now you show me how baddest you all are! Take the heart of this general, and you will all be generals!" the commander shouted over his "men."

As one, the mob pounced on the man wearing camouflage who was on the ground. First they beat him, then they kicked him and then stabbed him. Phillipe used his zoom lens get even closer pictures, and so he saw it first. One of the mob stuck his face into the dead man's chest to cover his face in the man's blood. Another did the same, and then another, and the third man emerged not just with blood but with entrails in his mouth.

Phillipe took more pictures.

The crowd backed up as a few of the child soldiers began to cut out the heart and liver from the young man's body. They cheered and danced and began firing their guns into the air.

Christianity had been brought to the area almost two hundred years earlier, but local traditions and customs still carried weight, and a form of voodoo ruled the day. It was common for Liberian fighters to eat their enemies in the belief that they would then take on their enemy's strengths while bringing fear to remaining enemies as well as respect/fear among their own peers. Phillipe and his team knew war was different for people in different parts of the globe. So too did their commanders sitting at desks back home, but when Phillipe's digital pictures arrived on their computer screens they were reminded of it very clearly.

Phillipe spent his Christmas in a ditch, watching, recognizing, and learning what happens when mobs rule and civilized values have faded away in lieu of more martial ones.

***

2/28/1996

Senator Jerry Henderson and Alan Conferra were at the New York City offices of The Beauregard Investment Group LLC with its leader, George Whittaker. A few weeks earlier in the midst of a global economic crisis, it was Whittaker and his staff who noticed that the crisis was in fact an attack by a small group of men who were controlling the Japanese government behind the scenes. Jerry's pre-political career had been in currency and commodities trading as well as other forms of investment. Along with Alan's growing reputation for forensic accounting the two had helped stave off a global economic meltdown. Now the three men, along with some of Whittaker's staff, sat in a conference area and watched the latest presidential address to the nation.

While no one would call it "war" between the United States and Japan, there was certainly a conflict—one that even involved both sides shooting at each other in the Pacific Ocean. Cooler heads and incredible heroism had staved off a nuclear war between the two nations. The public was largely left in the dark about Japan's secret nuclear arsenal, as well as the covert missions that destroyed it.

President Durling had given a calming national address when the economic crisis hit. He gave another when—at the suggestion of George Whittaker—they orchestrated an international recovery. He'd also given a national address when it was leaked that two American aircraft carriers had been damaged and two submarines were missing as a result of the Japanese navy. In the midst of the military and economic crisis, he'd also accepted the resignation of Vice President Kealty, who was involved in a media-sensation sexual affair(s). Now the president was about to go on TV and address a special joint session of Congress.

The president talked about the "conflict" with Japan. He talked about the resolve of the American people, and he talked about how—as he'd promised—America had weathered the economic crisis (attack). In a surprise move, the president requested that the Senate immediately approve National Security Advisor Jack Ryan to replace former Vice President Kealty. Senate leaders came forward while the nation watched, and when they called for a yea/nay vote, there was no opposition. The president called for Ryan to come to the speaker's seat and be sworn in on the spot. It would have been easy since the entire Supreme Court was only a few feet away.

Suddenly there was movement in the visitor gallery. Secret Service people ran to grab the first lady. There was confusion. One of the Secret Service agents fell. Other agents ran toward the president, grabbed him, and turned to take him out in a rush. Everyone rose in confusion and fear as it was obvious there was a life and death threat. Cameras swiveled, then there was a white blur, and the feed was lost.

In the conference room there was shock. Since they were veterans of thousands of stressful transactions, there was no panic but certainly shock and fear. The room was, after all, filled with men and women who moved more money in a day than twenty countries' combined GDP. They were people who'd felt panic. This was shock, fear, and concern, and everyone suspected the worst. While they looked at each other and wondered, Senator Jerry Henderson sat down. Alan did the same right next to him. The only question in their minds wasn't "what" had happened but "who" was going to be left.

Henderson feared the worst—a nuclear attack. Maybe one of Japan's secret ICBMs had survived the American Special Forces raid that he'd learned about in the Senate Intelligence Committee briefing. Maybe it was another nation taking advantage of the confusion in the US government. Maybe it was a terrorist somehow. He didn't know, but he knew that confusion and a flash like that surely meant Capitol Hill had suffered a bad blow.

A few minutes later the networks cut to cameras outside of Capitol Hill. A 747 jumbo jet had crashed into the House of Representatives—flown by a despondent Japanese father who had lost two sons in the recent Conflict Other Than War (COTW...as the Pentagon called it). Flames shot into the sky through the hole, and only the tail of the plane with its red stork Japanese markings could be seen. Fire trucks were already responding. Jerry Henderson would be one of only nine senators remaining in the United States; ninety-one had been killed. So had most of the members of the House of Representatives. The Supreme Court justices were all dead, buried, and burning in the rubble. So too were all of the joint chiefs of staff, all but two Cabinet members, dignitaries from twenty-plus nations, guests, family members, and the president. Former Vice President Kealty was nowhere to be found.

Newly approved Vice President Jack Ryan had been in the tunnel between the House office building and the House of Representatives when the plane crashed. Flames had rushed down toward him and his family, but were miraculously sucked back into the House before reaching them. He would be sworn in as president within the hour, and address the nation immediately afterwards.

Alan tried to call Kowalski, but all the lines were busy. Cell towers were overloaded and direct lines broken. It didn't matter. Kowalski's body would be found a week later in the rubble that once was the House visitors gallery.

America was in shock. It was Pearl Harbor redux complete with a Japanese pilot, Japanese plane, and sneak attack. There was anger and hate, but more than anything there was fear. No one ever doubted that there were plenty of bureaucrats to step in and fill vacancies, but members of Congress represented the people, and the attack was viewed as an attack on people personally. Sadness and resolve would win out as it always has and always does with Americans, but until then the planet held two types of people: angry Americans and everyone else, who worried what the Americans would do.

***

3/1/96

Jerry Henderson had returned to Washington immediately, and things moved quickly. The government was rebuilt with remarkable speed. The Department of Defense had switched to deputy commanders before the fire trucks even arrived at the Capitol. Deputy cabinet leaders had already met at the White House along with a few new temporary appointees. State governors were already looking at appointees to replace departed senators. Election officials were already looking at holding special elections for the members of the House. The new president was already examining possible replacements for the Supreme Court. As had been done so many times before, the nation mourned, and then began rebuilding.

While the February 1996 attack was devastating, it was not the first time the United States government had faced destruction. Even before the Constitution, the Continental Congress had been routed from the nation's capital of Philadelphia as British forces seized the city. Later, in the War of 1812 British forces again scattered Congress and tossed the government into disarray, and this time they burned most of Washington, DC, including the White House. Barely fifty years later at the outbreak of the American Civil War, half of the government left and formed their own nation, and more than half of the government workers left. Another fifty-plus years later, with the dawning of the Atomic Age as well as the Cold War, the entire federal government came to life with the knowledge that at any moment of any day, the entire country could be annihilated within twenty minutes of Soviet ICBM launches. In fact, on no less than forty-six occasions either the United States or the Soviet Union had come within minutes of starting such a war—often by accident, and always through poor communication. The Japanese pilot had devastated the United States' government, and while it left the nation and world stunned, historians knew better.

What could have and should have been a complete destruction of the American government was in effect little more than a fast and brutal changing of faces. The institutions remained intact. The federal government's leaders were quickly replaced. State leaders remained in place. There was a continuity of government, and most of all, while the United States government was surely impacted, the nation—the people of the United States—drew resolve. The attack brought unity rather than division. History repeated.

For his part, Senator Henderson found himself suddenly cast into a leading role in the Senate. The freshman senator now had his choice of committees to chair...and reform. In the three weeks before the attack on the Capitol and the three weeks after, Jerry Henderson was at the center of a hurricane. Normal Senate rules limited participation to two committees, but those rules also allowed for "special circumstances," and this was clearly one of those situations. He was already a member of the Senate Intelligence Committee, but because of the casualties he was now the ranking member. He'd also been on the Senate Finance Committee and now the Foreign Affairs Committee.

Luckily, he was not the most senior senator to survive, and was not put in a Senate leadership role.

Through his positions on the Senate Finance Committee he knew before the public that the collapse of the dollar's value and the near global economic meltdown had been a deliberate attack on the part of a few Japanese leaders. He also worked hand in hand with American and global bank leaders to orchestrate an economic counter-attack that revived the dollar's value, saved the global economy, and dealt a devastating blow to the Japanese yen...all without the public at large knowing.

Through his position on the Senate Foreign Affairs Committee he knew that the minor military skirmish between Japan and the United States was in fact one of the largest military operations since World War II. That "skirmish," as most knew it to be, nearly ended in nuclear Armageddon between the two nations. He'd also learned about numerous confrontations between American and Pakistani military units, and confrontations between the United States and Iran/Iraq.

Through his position on the Senate Intelligence Committee Henderson had learned the scariest secrets. He knew of covert American missions that destroyed Japan's secret nuclear-armed ICBM complex. He knew all about American assassinations abroad. He knew that as scary as a recent Ebola outbreak was, it was in fact a great deal more terrifying, as it had been a deliberate biological warfare attack on the United States by joint Iranian/Iraqi elements. He knew that China and Japan had worked together and almost invaded Siberia. He knew about nuclear proliferation efforts in a dozen countries that could bring annihilation if brought to fruition.

Yet in the wake of all those secrets—all those nightmares that he kept so Americans could sleep—there was one concern that rose to the top each time: What if the attack on the Capitol had succeeded? Most of the federal government's leadership had been wiped out, but by a strange twist of fate they had just the right man to step in as president when the moment came. President Ryan had been in the CIA and high finance most of his career. He was integral in both the pre-attack economic crisis as well as the conflict with Japan. He knew the world's threats like few others. Had it been anyone else, would America have survived?

Henderson learned a lot and he learned it fast. He learned that the world as most people understood it was infinitely more fragile and dangerous that most dared imagine. He'd learned that America is vulnerable. He'd learned that the American people are resilient and the American government could rebuild, but it took time and more than a bit of really good luck! Senator Jerry Henderson had gone from being a freshman senator to one of the few people on the planet who really knew humanity's secret horrors.

Alan too had been drafted on to those committees at the behest of Senator Henderson. With Wayne Kowalski gone, Alan found himself senior advisor to the senator. The world's secrets were Henderson's secrets, and they became Alan's too. Alan, however, drew different lessons. Most striking to Alan was the speed and efficiency with which the continuity of the federal government's operations had undergone. Like Jerry Henderson, he recognized all too clearly that if anyone else had been forced to take the reins as president—anyone with less understanding of the world's darker clockwork...well, they were incredibly lucky that the new president was a former deputy director of the CIA.

***

6/25/1996

Senator Henderson and his new senior advisor, Alan Conferra, stood in the senator's office surrounded by several dozen staff. Many were new faces showing a bit more confusion and concern than those who had survived the latest historical attack on America's capital. Everyone circled around a wall with six large TVs hanging on it. All at once, the political announcers on each network stopped talking and the scene was that of the Oval Office with President Jack Ryan sitting at his desk and addressing the nation.

He explained to the American people and the world that a terrible and highly contagious virus was loose in the United States. Senator Henderson and Alan already knew that and more from the latest Senate Intelligence Committee briefing earlier in the morning. They also knew that it was Ebola, and that it was probably deliberately sent to the United States by elements in Iran or Iraq.

After explaining the threat to the "general welfare" of the United States, the president explained the actions he was taking by executive order. First, every single school and every college, every institution of learning, was to be closed. Second, all businesses—except those providing food, healthcare, or media—were to be closed as well. First responders were also, clearly, not sent home, but rather called to report to duty. All "places of assembly" like restaurants, bars, theaters, clubs, and so forth were to be closed immediately. All interstate travel was suspended except for healthcare services, food transport, and first responders. Flights were ordered grounded. Lastly, the president activated the National Guard under federal service to enforce martial law.

These actions were taken in an effort to stem the spread of the virus. Henderson, Alan, and a few others knew that the actions were taken to prevent the death of hundreds of millions, even billions, of people. What the president didn't say was how deadly the virus was. He had to treat it as if it was worse than the black plague while not allowing the public a conduit or reason to panic.

Jerry Henderson turned around and looked at his staff. Everyone had been shocked by so many things over the past few months that there was a sense of ordinary about the room. It almost seemed as if the sense of fear, chaos, confusion, and disorder...that same sense that had followed after the attack on the Capitol...was gone. The room Jerry saw was a room of professionals. He saw faces that knew they had jobs to do, and that their jobs were important to the people of South Carolina, the United States, and the world.

"Okay, everyone," Jerry began, "I know a lot of you are new here. To those of you who've been here a while, I'm sorry if you've heard me say this before. You all work here, you all came to Washington for a reason. If you came here just to get into the rat race or to get your ticket punched on the way to something more lucrative...well, we wouldn't have hired you. Those people work—"

Jerry paused. He almost said such people worked for other members of Congress, but there weren't many of those around anymore. Then he went on, correcting the sad error he almost made.

"...those people just don't work for me. Period. That means you already know we've got a lot of work to do. Stay off the cell phones for a while. Call home. Call your family. Call your extended family. Call all your friends. Call everyone you were friends with growing up, in high school, college, whatever. Use the landlines. There is a lot to do, but the president and the Cabinet have most things moving. Our job is to be the connection between Washington and home. Call people and reassure them. Even if we have to do it one by one, make it happen. I'm gonna have Alan and some of you get working on a list of people back home we need to contact. I want every county executive, every mayor, every school board director called. Pass the word that people are controlling this thing, and we want everyone to call each other and comfort each other. Alan, I want a mailing to go out as well. Kathy, draft up a letter. Send it to every business and home we have on file. Don't just tell people things are under control. Convince them. The Surgeon General, the CDC, and others will all be putting out statements. I want copies of those included in the mailing that goes out. This is a time to get people to hold each other up, and I'll be goddamned if that's not what we do."

"Sir," Alan interrupted. "We've got another briefing in half an hour. I'm sure by the end of the day the White House will have a printed statement and more detailed information that we can send out. I figure the briefing and so forth...about one to two hours. Can I suggest we have everyone make their calls to family and friends now? We'll make a clean mailing when we get back. We can start setting up some phone interviews for radio and TV then as well."

"Good idea. Okay, this office building has some uniqueness to it. One of the things is that we've got some of the best phone network access in the world. Put it to use. Call people, and have them call people. Our job is to prevent a panic, and since we don't have answers to all the questions, just do like the president said: Tell everyone to use common sense, and we'll get it sorted out. Get to work."

The staff applauded, completely taking Senator Henderson by surprise. Politician or not, he was a man, and a man is usually humbled by genuine appreciation. He was, and with a stiff yet thankful smile he motioned for everyone to get to work. Many already headed back to their desks. Everyone was focused on their jobs as he headed into the hallway and toward the elevators for his next briefing.

Once in the hallway Alan took his place at the senator's side.

"Sir?"

"Yeah, what is it, Alan?"

"Sir, new government, new president, a fight with Japan, looks like a fight with Iraq or Iran or both now. This virus...we've been hit hard lately. The people of this country might be looking to Washington not just for reassurance and default reactions to events. I think the people might be looking for something more than that."

"What the hell are you talking about?"

"Well, we'll either all get through this or we won't, and assuming we do...I think maybe we should start looking at better ways of handling a national crisis. There are too many plans, too many agencies, too many leaders, and not enough connection with the people. Best I can figure you're the only one suggesting people call each other to 'hold each other up.' And what if things do get out of control? What if the government and agencies do get taken out, destroyed, disconnected from the nation? There has to be some sort of last-ditch, restart, or reconnect mechanism. Something to keep in mind ten moves into the chess game. We've certainly got enough to do right now, but...just saying we should start thinking of that for the future."

They stepped into the elevator, turned to face the doors as they closed, and as people tend to do the conversation stopped. Just before the doors opened to continue their march toward the latest national security briefing Henderson stopped looking at the ceiling, turned and faced Alan, and flatly said, "You're absolutely right." The doors opened and they continued on without conversation. Both men were thinking about the recent and present threats, and things to do in the future.

The American people had been through a lot. They would go through a lot, but there was no war with Iran or Iraq. The Ebola threat dissipated in weeks, and lives returned to normal...lives with short memories. Threats and attacks of all sorts came and went. Alan's idea of future threat management did not dissipate from neither his nor Senator Henderson's memory.

***

12/31/96

The Tryphine's New Year's Eve celebration was as much a social occasion as it was a private business meeting. Lord Terrence had little to do with the planning as the institution had its own event planner. For the Tryphines, business was social, social was business, and to that end the event was held at the London banking house.

All of the guests did business with Tryphine House Banking in one way or another. Those business relationships, however, served more as introductions and as easy small talk when other conversational tact fell short. Most people knew each other, but barely most. Almost half of the thousand-plus guests had never been to the banking institution for any reason other than economic.

Ionic columns and roman arches with red marble accents defined the first three floors of the octagonal atrium inside Tryphine Banking House. Above the third floor, old English oak balconies wrapped around for another six floors. At the top a stained glass dome gave the year-round illusion of forest canopy with translucent leaves in countless shades of green. At night the outside of the dome was lit with slowly rotating spotlights, giving the entire inside the illusion of a breeze through the treetops. Others said it made it look like it was raining money.

For the holiday season the balconies were adorned with green/gold ribbons and red bows. Tables surrounding the center of the atrium had matching décor. Music was provided by a twelve-piece orchestra accompanied by a grand piano and even a crystal glass armonica, the latter of which gave a magical tone to the entire room.

Gentlemen from around the globe were nearly identical as it was a white tie and tuxedo affair. The ladies, however, ran the gamut in apparel. Some older women wore dresses that were generations previous in their fashion. Some of the younger women wore more cutting-edge fashions or more sultry apparel. By and large, however, the crowd was conservative in nature and equally conservative in their dress.

After the passing of his cherished wife, Roese, Erwin Zimmermann focused more on work. The social networking nature of his financing operation did make it necessary for him to appear at certain social occasions. The Tryphines' New Year's Eve gala was perhaps the most business/social gathering on his calendar.

Arriving alone hadn't mattered much to Erwin. He was, of course, reminded of how Roese wasn't with him at the event they'd been to so often together, but so many of the faces were familiar that he was able to see beyond the missing. The host was, after all, one of his finest friends.

Erwin walked in, handed his coat, and took his place in the greeting line. At the other end his friend, Lord Terrence Tryphine, and his wife, Lady Joan Tryphine, met their guests. Upon seeing Joan it was hard for Erwin to ignore the fact that his Roese and Joan had been such fast friends, and he was reminded yet again—as it seemed every minute of every day—that she was gone. The pain was less, though. Reflecting on the moment he noticed that he was more reminiscent than holed by her loss.

The line advanced.

Love is an insane, indescribable, and unpredictable thing. The love one has for a mother is different than that one has for their father, different between love of brother and love of sister. A first love is always special, and a true, soul-binding love is rarely the same as that first love or of a puppy love. A million ways to love others, and all bound by the same word: *love*.

The line advanced.

Like everyone who loses a spouse, Erwin didn't believe he could ever have that same spousal connection a second time. For some people it's not at all unusual to have a second, third, fourth spouse or more; for some people it's easy to move on or let go of past loves. Erwin loved Roese deeply, far more deeply than many people love their wives, and it had always been that way with the relationships he'd had before her as well.

The line advanced.

Before love, there has to be attraction. Since Roese's passing Erwin hadn't been attracted to other women. Wealthy as he was, and as ever-present as he'd been in his social circles, Erwin meandered about in a sea of supermodels and generally beautiful people, but his heart stirred in a search for a different kind of beauty. He appreciated the beauty of magazine cover standards and renowned women of the world, but only in the same way that one could appreciate the beauty of a rare car's fine lines, the sleek shapes of sexy aircraft designs, a perfectly designed garden, or a bouquet of flowers. He found sunrises and sunsets to be marvels, but of the women he met and interacted with since Roese, none stirred him. Erwin just had no particular attraction.

While the line advanced again, hundreds of wait staff circulated through the crowd. Drink orders were delivered. Innumerable trays of different appetizers were circulated. Every one of the staff smiled and seemed genuinely happy. Erwin had always noticed that at most similar occasions the staff tended to remain somewhat stoic and even ghostlike in their maneuvers as if they preferred not to be noticed—not to make any sort of impression on guests. Knowing the Tryphines as he did Erwin chuckled for a moment, as he had no doubt the staff were enjoying handsome bonuses for their participation during the holiday.

Eventually Erwin reached Terrence and Joan Tryphine, his friends and hosts. First he met Lord Tryphine and the two shook hands.

"Erwin, how are you? We're so glad you could make it. Happy New Year to you. I'd like to introduce you to a few of our new clients later...perhaps after our toast?"

"I'd like that. Thank you for the invitation as usual. After the toast then."

Erwin smiled and sidestepped to Lady Tryphine. It was interesting to see which guests she hugged, which she kissed, which guests shook her hands, and which guests were given a firm embrace. Erwin was the latter.

"Oh, Erwin, I'm so glad you could come. We must have a dance later. Will you, please?"

Just then a loud, crushing pop went off. The entire atrium fell silent as nearly two thousand people searched for the source. Unseen security staff were now clearly seen frozen and on alert more than staff or guests. From the highest balcony in the atrium, all the way up near the stained glass dome, a woman's voice called out in sincere apology, "Sorry, everyone." Looking up—like everyone else—Erwin saw Anna Von Ursel waving down to everyone. She'd dropped a 250-year-old crystal champagne flute almost a hundred feet to the marble floor below. Only by sheer luck and thicker winter attire did everyone manage to escape without so much as a scratch. Before her thick German/Polish accent had finished echoing, a few staff members had already restarted the party's participants by rushing over to the impact area with towels, dust brooms, and dustpans.

Joan's eyes gently closed and she sighed. When she reopened them she was reminded of Erwin's presence, of his marital status, and she noticed that while everyone else was getting back to the party, he was still looking up at the balcony. It made Joan half-smile.

"Her name is Anna Von Ursel."

Erwin stopped looking up at the woman above and looked at Joan.

"That name sounds familiar. Have you any idea where our paths may have crossed before?"

"I'm not sure, Erwin. She and I have been friends since before I even met Roese. I know that she and Roese and I all went to Dinkleman's together. We probably met up together several times. Maybe Roese mentioned her once. Perhaps that's where you recognize her name. Anna and I had lunch here last month, and she helped me go over the arrangements for tonight with the staff. Come to think about it she asked how you were doing since Roese."

Erwin tried to consciously hide the unexpected sense of curiosity with his practiced business face, but...Joan knew him, and she knew men.

"What is Dinkleman's?" he asked.

Joan, pulled him behind and away from her husband, out of earshot for anyone waiting in line to greet them. Then she whispered to him, "Are you serious?"

"Yes, what or who are the Dinklemans?"

Joan bit her bottom lip, her tongue moved to her cheek, and then she smiled. Whispering to Erwin once more, she said,

"Dinkleman's is a 'ladies' store.' Let me put it this way since we all know what each other bought. Do you remember Roese with some 'special evening wear'? Black with—"

Erwin cut her off. "Ahhhhh, I see." He laughed awkwardly at first, then soundly. "Yes. Yes, Joan, I know exactly what you're talking about, and I remember the night, and I remember the day she came home with it. That's what 'shopping with the ladies' meant, hmm?"

She nodded and smiled proudly. "Let's go upstairs, and I'll give you a proper introduction. Anna clearly needs a new refreshment." Then she turned to her husband, got his attention, then got the attention of everyone in the receiving line. "My apologies, dear friends, but I think I should see to our little Luftwaffe bomber upstairs before we get blitzed again."

As she and Erwin headed for one of the lifts to the top floor of the atrium, everyone was still either genuinely or at least politely laughing at her humor. London's blitz from Hitler's air force was more than a half century earlier. Time had healed the wounds, leaving the horrors of that first major air war to levity amongst the modern residents of London and even a descendant of Hitler's Luftwaffe: Erwin. Halfway there Joan began giving Erwin a social description of Anna that sounded almost like a dossier.

"Anna Von Ursel is the daughter of Ludwig and Gertrude Von Ursel. Ludwig was Prussian, but just before the war broke out they were here in London meeting with PMs in a last-ditch effort to stop it. I'm not really sure if they were Prussian or German or Polish, though. They were from a small town west of Gdansk, and that area changed after both wars. When Hitler and Stalin did invade, Ludwig was tried in absentia as a traitor and sentenced to death if they came back. Hitler seized all their lands, and they were left with nothing. This left them quite disturbed, and I do believe he was the only German royalty who flew with the RAF during the war. Technically he flew for the Free Polish Air Force, but they flew Spitfires and took orders from the RAF so it's like he was in the RAF. Perhaps I shouldn't have joked about Anna being a Luftwaffe bomber? No. No, she'd laugh at it too."

"What did they do after the war?"

In the lift Joan's background report continued.

"After the war they tried go home, but everything they had was in either East Germany or Poland so they came back here. That's how I came to know them and Anna. Her father's family had worked with Tryphine House a long, long time ago, and Terrence's father was able to help them borrow against an old family trust they had. With some help Anna's father met some people. He came to know the Mediterranean players well, and after the war they did very well. Terrence's father continued to help with some of their investments, and really everyone did very well. Anna went to a great number of private schools all her life, and from what she's told me she and her parents weren't at any sort of odds, but they never really came to know each other very well. Her parents both passed away years ago, before The Wall came down. And now she's alone. I mean she has no one, understand?" Joan smiled slyly at Erwin.

"Joan, I just asked how her name sounded familiar. You know I'm not looking for anyone. No one could replace my Roese—"

Lady Tryphine interrupted him. "I know, Erwin, and you're right: no one will ever replace Roese as your wife or my friend. But I also know people need other people. Anna and I are friends. She was friends with Roese, and she's a good person. She's got no one to go to parties with and neither do you. You're both wonderful people, both here alone, and that's silly."

The elevator had climbed at its usual faster-than-normal speed, but it had seemed painfully long to Erwin. Finally the door opened, and Joan led the way around the atrium. On the other side Anna leaned on the old English oak railing and watched the festivity below. A few servants and staff went about their duties on this floor, but no other guests. She was literally as well as figuratively alone.

Standing five-foot-eight and weighing approximately 150 pounds, Anna was no supermodel, but neither was she unattractive; not in the least. Anna took care of herself, was healthy, and had an approachable, common prettiness that drew people to her. As much as her black hair and hazel eyes were enhanced by salons, there was nothing anyone could do to make her more friendly, fun, intelligent and playful. Anna was not some tart searching for a man to cling on to. She was alert, and hadn't dropped the glass as a result of having had too much beverage or any natural sense of being scatterbrained. No, that was the result of smooth gloves on a glass and little more—

a remarkably common occurrence at such events...though extremely rare from such height. Given the few guests on their floor, Anna spotted Joan and Erwin coming out of the elevator and walked around the balcony to greet them.

"Anna," Joan began with a smile. "Is our party so boring that you feel you have to try and find new ways to execute our guests? Are you trying to put others out of their misery?"

"Joan, my glass was empty. I wanted a refill, and I thought you were going to toss me up a fresh one. Perhaps you were distracted, and that's why you didn't catch it?"

All three chuckled at the light conversation. Then Joan made the introduction.

"Anna, this is Erwin Osterman. He's been a friend of Terrence and me for as long as we can remember. Erwin, this is Anna Von Ursel."

Anna presented her hand, which was gently shaken by Erwin, then she looked back at Joan with feigned contempt. "That's it? That's all I am to you Joan? He's been 'your friend since as long as you can remember,' and I'm just Anna? How about, 'Erwin, this is the best friend a woman could ever have, my life's mentor, someone I've known for as long as I can remember, Anna'?"

The polite chuckles returned, and it was Joan's time to feign contempt. "Oh, Anna, I'm so sorry. You're all that and more. I'm still in shock at my close call with the heirloom crystal raining down on me."

"I really am sorry about that, Joan."

"I know you are. Accidents happen. No one was hurt. Besides, it gave me a chance to bring Erwin up here to meet you."

"Truthfully, Joan, we met a long time ago. Apparently I'm the only one that remembers," Anna replied. "It was at Erwin's *Schloss* outside Vienna. Roese had a tea, and I was invited." Anna turned from Joan toward Erin and continued.

"*Herr* Zimmermann, you were busy in your office the entire day, but it's a good thing as I'm sure we would have bored you to no end, but you did come out to introduce yourself. I'm so sorry about Roese. I miss her too. I was at her memorial service as well, but we met at the tea, and that's a far better memory regardless. How are you?"

Erwin was a swamp of emotions. He was happy to have had fresh memories of his Roese brought up, sad to remember the funeral, happy to have met a friend of hers, sad that she wasn't there to share the moment with her friend, and he was bored, nervous, and curious. He hadn't expected anything remarkable at all from the annual party, and already he knew he'd be rethinking the night on his plane ride home. Intrigued; he was also intrigued.

"I'm fine, thank you, but I am sorry I don't recall our having met before. Roese and I had many celebrations and teas over the years. I did tell Joan that there was a familiarity about you, however. Beauty always does leave its shadows. Perhaps that's what's left in my mind from the tea." Erwin couldn't believe he'd just said what he had, but before he could dwell on any guilt or shame or embarrassment, Anna saved him. She began speaking in German to him.

"Oh, thank you. It's completely understandable. I think of Roese often. You're doing as well as can be expected then?"

They continued in German, and Joan slipped out of view, back into the lift, then back into the receiving line below. "Yes. Thank you. I've tried to focus on my work, and there's been charity work of course. My attention is of course on Roese's cancer and finding more successful treatments.... I continue to get out to as many events as I can. There are still responsibilities we have to attend to, and those pass the time. How have you been since the tea?"

"I've been well, thank you. It's just as you said, we have responsibilities. The Tryphines have been immeasurable in helping to manage my estates, and with a few assistants there's really not much for me to do. Joan and I and a few others, we do a great deal of shopping together—at least once a month. I continue to try and find a hobby, but no single thing interests me enough. I like trying lots of things. I do some traveling as well."

Erwin took her by the hand, suggested they rejoin the party, and when she agreed the two went back downstairs. The rest of the night continued with the two establishing a unique bond as friends, a friendship unlike one he'd have with other men or other women.

The real miracle of the night was that he wouldn't notice until the following morning when he was back home at his *Schloss* in Austria. For most of the evening he managed not to forget but to not dwell on the fact that New Year's Eve was the anniversary of Roese's death two years earlier.

***

4/8/1997

Officer Brian Assana sat in his parked patrol car. He and his partner were responding to a theft report at Moishe's Market at the intersection of East 125th and Superior in Cleveland, Ohio (across from Pupo's African Boutique). They'd just compiled and filed a police report on the incident, and his partner had walked inside to give a copy to the store manager. The day was unseasonably warm, 72 degrees, and sunny with a slight offshore breeze making its way through the streets from

Lake Erie just a few blocks to the north. Brian was using the MCD computer in their cruiser to see if there was any other information, any new wants, warrants, or special things happening in the area on that day—anything they should bear in mind before heading off to the next call.

It was lunchtime. Traffic increased slightly. Pedestrian traffic increased largely. While this part of Cleveland was in continuous economic depression there was still life—and lots of it. East Cleveland had once been America's Millionaire's Row: home to the Rockefellers, their rich friends, and of course, bankers. It was one of America's centers of capitalist royalty, with mansions and all the high-end businesses that catered to the rich and famous of the nineteenth and early twentieth century. Then the Rockefellers moved. The high-end businesses that catered to their needs moved to downtown Cleveland. Then the steel industry died, and manufacturing that supported it was decimated. The community fell into ruin, and continued falling from metropolitan apex to abyss. In the late 1990s it was a husk of abandoned buildings, makeshift retail, and once-proud middle-class homes, all turned into slums.

Lacking tax revenue from businesses and wealthy residents, the city's services declined too. Few of the fire engines actually worked (on average only one or two were available to answer calls). Most of the ambulances didn't work. The police force was down to sixty officers for over thirty thousand residents. With the economic decline came economic desperation; i.e., crime. When people needed food, and they had no money, and/or had used up all the available hospitality of others...they inevitably stole. Joining gangs meant security, income, and most of all: the pride that comes from belonging to something respected (even if respected out of fear). It was a dangerous place with desperate people—most of whom were good people, but most of whom were desperate nonetheless.

Brian's partner was only gone for a minute or two, but he knew he had to be extra alert while both were separated. Looking through the intersection, down Superior Avenue, to the east, Brian saw what could only be described as a junkyard car stopping at the traffic light facing him. It wasn't at all unusual to see such mechanical marvels in the area—in fact, it was more the norm. A nice new car was far more freakish.

He noticed that its rear wheels were riding low. It was likely a combination of bad tires and bad springs. Next he noticed that the tiny 1985 Chevy Cavalier had at least five young men inside. This too was nothing unusual, and all that weight in a junk car was surely taking its toll. Brian paid attention to it—partially in awe, partially in curiosity, and certainly professionally.

The light turned green. The car lurched forward and stalled. When it did, the entire front right wheel came off, rolled through the intersection, and was westbound on Superior Avenue. His partner returned at the same moment, laughing. He'd seen the car fall apart as well.

One by one all of the car's occupants came out. Each surveyed the damage. Two argued. Two laughed, and one looked around suspiciously. Now Brian and his partner weren't laughing. Their guard went up.

Next to the car, at the opposite corner from where their police cruiser was parked, a pair of well-dressed white men were doing some sort of surveying at an empty lot where a gas station had once stood. One of the men from the broken car approached them. His pants hung low, exposing his underwear, and the man appeared to be holding them up, but Brian and his partner saw a pendulum-like motion in the man's front right pants pocket, and they knew he was carrying a gun.

The surveyors spoke with the man, and then he left. It looked like he was asking them for help with the car, but it was clear the surveyors didn't have much in the way of tools. The two groups of men spoke from time to time as the vacant lot left few ways to avoid conversation for the surveyors.

Brian and his partner could have driven away to the next call. They chose to wait instead. It just wasn't wise to leave a situation after seeing that one of the men was likely armed. They didn't want to approach them either—even to offer help—lest they have to get into a situation with at least one armed man. No crimes had been committed so there was no reason to call for backup. Their job was to deter any crime at this point.

After almost half an hour, another car pulled up behind the disabled one. It stopped in the middle of Superior, blocking westbound traffic, but no one dared complain. One of the men in the second car got out, went to the trunk, and pulled out a heavy, wheeled, hydraulic garage jack like the kind mechanics use to lift cars when doing major repairs. He wheeled to the front of the disabled car and jacked it up, but there was no way to put a new wheel on as the entire hub assembly had come off. Instead, three of the young men who had been in the disabled car got behind it and started pushing while another steered, and another held the jack in place. They turned and headed north on East 125th as if this sort of thing happened every day.

Brian's partner laughed a little again.

"Shhh," Brian said. "Watch."

The men in the second car got back inside. When the light turned green the driver floored the accelerator and zoomed past Brian and his partner. Starting at the middle of the intersection they heard the pop of gunfire. Brian and his partner ducked as a steady stream of fifteen pop's was heard outside. They could hear the car racing away in the distance, but couldn't see it all. It was gone. No one was hit. No one was hurt, but there was no one to chase. The car was as junky as the one that had lost its wheel with no single color, and not even recognizable as any particular make or model.

Both officers swore vehemently. They reported the incident, but given that there were only six squad cars in all of East Cleveland at the time, there was nothing they could do. Instead they were sent to deal with a domestic disturbance called into 911. Apparently the 911 caller claimed that someone was digging up graves in the Glennville Cemetery near East 132nd and Shaw Avenue. Specifically, she claimed people were digging up zombies.

Officer Brian Assana, former USMC Marine Sergeant Assana, had been to war, but now he was on a different, more intimate frontline. He thought to himself: sometimes desperate people stole from local grocers, sometimes desperate people get creative with their transportation, and sometimes desperate people rebel/repel against authorities...like him.

Later that day Brian's partner of four years turned in his two weeks notice. He'd had enough. He no longer saw the point of just sitting in a car and getting shot at. It seemed futile to him.

Brian saw it differently. He thought of the surveyors. He thought of the people in the market. He thought of the good people in the area he protected. It wasn't chasing down shooters that kept people safe all the time. Brian felt that if he and his partner hadn't stayed, waited, watched, and been targets then the surveyors could have been robbed and killed. The market could have been robbed again—possibly with deadlier results. How many innocent bystanders would have been at risk? Brian was a true believer. He believed even sitting in the car made a difference; the difference between anarchy and even a sliver of peace...of security.

***

4/10/1997

Army Ranger Sergeant Phillipe Aristide sat in yet another African jungle. This time he was part of a six-man LRSD in the Republic of Congo (formerly Zaire, formerly the Belgian Congo, formerly Land of Leopold). Their mission was to patrol an area in northeast Congo next to the Rwandan border and gather intelligence. The mission was to last a typical six days. They had been inserted by helicopter the previous night, and would be exfiltrate by helicopter once again at a different location fifty miles to the south.

Phillipe's team was unusual. Most American LRSD teams only served a year or two together. This team had been together for three. Most teams did not have racial requirements, but since Phillipe had taken over, the team had been comprised entirely of African-Americans and himself (Haitian-American) with the intent of blending into the native population if necessary. Most teams were "strongly encouraged" to use only American military equipment, but Phillipe had found that black T-shirts and brown shorts worked better in Central Africa. Beat-up G3 rifles found in local markets were fairly accurate, and sometimes more reliable than even the venerable AK-47 in the region's harsh conditions. The only US Army gear with the team was the radios. Even the digital cameras were Swiss made. All of the men were single, Army nomads, and all specialized in Africa. These unpopular lifestyle adjustments made finding replacements extremely hard, so Phillipe's team wound up spending more time in the field than others, and was given leeway on almost everything.

After the American Black Hawk Down disaster in Somalia, the international aid mission there crumbled. American forces were withdrawn, and hundreds of thousands were left to die in anarchy and famine. When the civil war broke out in neighboring Rwanda, America's president refused to send in a stabilizing combat force for fear of another political embarrassment, and millions were killed. Millions more fled across the border into the Republic of Congo, where Phillipe and his men were now patrolling. Forces from Rwanda covertly crossed the border and began slaughtering Rwandan refugees in Congo.

This led to a war where several African nations backed Congo, and almost as many other nations backed Rwanda. It also fueled a civil war in Congo. From 1993 to 1997 millions of Congolese died in the fighting that would later be called Africa's World War. In the end nine nations were involved as were twenty major armed forces and hundreds of smaller armed groups. Truces and peace agreements had been made and broken, and the overall objective of Phillipe's Ranger team was to determine if the latest agreement would hold.

The Rangers had spent years in the African bush. It was their home away from home. It was no longer stranger than fiction; a prehistoric setting in modern times. The people were familiar to them too. Everyone lived in absolutely destitute conditions. Wholly one-third of the people in Africa didn't even have access to clean drinking water. As much as the team had seen the lowest forms of humanity in every way, shape, and form, so too had they seen people who barely even had clothes behave with the greatest attention to manners and charity toward others.

The LRSD's route was chosen by Phillipe. Others had suggested he stick to the roads so he could monitor traffic and move faster and farther. A brigade commander who was new to AFRICOM (Africa Command) had suggested moving to high ground, a small mountain that overlooked Lake Kivu and the nearest city, Kashke. Phillipe knew that the reason his team was being used was not to gather intelligence that a satellite could get just as well or better. If his team was being sent, it was to get a firsthand look at the area from a man's perspective—not a car's or a bird's, but a man's. He chose a patrol route that took them from the helicopter insertion point through the jungle toward the village of Bunyakiri, then a nearby village where the UN had a base of operations for relief workers, and finally toward an abandoned mine thirty miles deeper into the jungle. The generals admired his grit, and the desktop analysts figured him for some sort of masochist. He presented the plan professionally, confidently, in a matter-of-fact fashion, and they approved it without question.

The helicopter had dropped them off in the middle of nowhere. The nearest known settlement was ten miles away. Mountains to the east and a river running east to northwest was in front of them. Beyond that were fields and the Butuatta Road, a winding dirt track with more than thirty thousand residents living in shanties along the sides of it. There were no known military or police units within sixty miles.

By midday the LRSD had already made six miles, and they planned on making another ten to fifteen before stopping after dark. Their entire trek had been through the hilly jungle—the densest jungle on all of planet Earth. The sun was high in the clear sky, and the heat was a choking humid heat that was no stranger to Phillipe and his men. Visibility was clear, but limited to barely ten feet because of the dense jungle.

They stopped for a moment and formed a circle for security. Everyone hydrated, and the radio operator made a communications check. It was a routine they'd practiced countless times. It was as second nature as closing a door behind you when you enter a room.

Suddenly everyone stopped and they all fell silent. The assistant radio operator had heard a noise and raised his left hand in a fist to signal the others. Everyone's ears tried hard to find something unusual in the jungle orchestra, but only the assistant radio operator heard it...and Phillipe as well. He heard something rustling perhaps ten meters to their north. Using hand signals he communicated this silently to the others. Everyone mentally prepared to use their weapons as they faced the possible sound.

The team's scout/sniper crouched and moved forward silently into the brush. He was quieter than a snake. In a moment he was completely gone—swallowed into the jungle. Seconds felt like hours. Phillipe wanted to go in after him, but he knew if there was a problem he'd hear about it from the scouts/sniper. Finally, they saw one boot and then another appear as he crawled backwards toward the team.

Phillipe put his ear next to the man's mouth to hear as quiet a whisper as he could make.

"It's a fucking gorilla," the scout/sniper replied. "There's one right fucking there, female. The silverback is about another fifty feet away. He's fucking huge."

Quiet as he was, everyone in the team heard. More importantly, they saw the man's eyes. They were bulging. It was clear to all that he was...concerned.

Using hand signals again, Phillipe told the men to quietly leave their position and move away from the gorillas, and they did so immediately, with great conviction. Phillipe was the last to leave, preferring to stay as a rear guard to face off a possible gorilla attack. As sure as Murphy's Law would have it, Phillipe moved one foot back to follow his team, and he stepped on a beetle.

The bug's exoskeleton cracked with a loud, snapping *pop*, like a firecracker. As if they were connected, the silverback gorilla screamed and charged toward him. The brush sounded like a truck was ramming through. As he beat his chest it sounded like the truck had a flat tire. The animal's scream was a guttural howl that made Phillipe's ears ring as if he were on the shooting range without hearing protection.

Phillipe stood to face the attack, and his men—only a few paces away—turned, rose, and stepped toward him as well. The LRSD team was next to Phillipe at the exact moment the 450-pound gorilla broke through the jungle. It raised its arms high, screamed, flashed its fangs, roared, beat its chest, and looked down on the puny humans with great disdain and greater rage.

No one fired. No one flinched. No one showed fear no matter how abundant it was in each man. The gorilla stopped and huffed, and it repeated its howling show of force. Again the men were motionless. Finally, the gorilla huffed at them and sat down barely two feet from Phillipe.

Everyone stared. The gorilla knew humans were dangerous. While biologists would describe the gorilla as a mammal or at least an animal, the men faced a jungle monster.

"Get out of here!" Phillipe shouted at the gorilla as he waved his arms and weapon in the air. "Get out!"

The gorilla snorted, huffed, and slugged back into the jungle. It disappeared just ten feet away. Everyone sighed. Then Phillipe motioned them to continue moving away. Break time was over.

After an hour they came to a clearing. The jungle was ending. The first obstacle was the river. They were still high enough in the mountains that the river was really just a fast-moving stream—about thirty feet across. From where they came out of the jungle they could see that a tree had fallen into the river and that another flowing downstream had jammed against it. They crossed there.

On the other side was a large field interspersed with the occasional bush and/or tree. They moved from one to the other for two more hours. The jungle was rough terrain. This was as easy it could be without being a garden path.

At nightfall the team came upon four abandoned shanties and made camp. There was no fire. Two men were awake at all times. Aside from the occasional radio communications check, there wasn't any talking. Even the local wildlife was taking it easy.

Just before sunrise, as the sky was just starting to glow in that pre-dawn light, gunshots rang out in the distance to the west. First there were a few, then twice as many, then heavy machine guns. Some well-armed unit had clearly come into contact with someone or something else. It was clear they were firing every round they possibly could. The firing tempo was intense. Then it stopped all of a sudden—as if on command, but...such discipline in an armed unit was extremely unusual in this part of Africa.

Phillipe decided to check it out. Everyone was already awake. The sun was rising, and they were about to continue their reconnaissance patrol anyway. In less than a minute they were on the move toward where they had heard the shooting.

Less than an hour later they came to an overgrown dirt road. It was clear there hadn't been any traffic on it in months, but at least there had been traffic a few months earlier. If there hadn't, the jungle would have swallowed it already. They followed the grass path that was once a road.

Another hour later things took a turn for the strange. Phillipe was taking his turn on point when a tall and slender African man stepped out from behind a tree next to the road. He wore a green Hawaiian shirt with blue shorts and flipflops and carried a three-tall spears.

"What do you want here?!" He asked in French.

French was a common language in this part of Africa, and everyone on Phillipe's team was required to speak it as well as two other African languages.

"We came to see who was fighting this morning." Phillipe answered.

The man detected Phillipe's American accent and answered in an English that was easier to understand than most American dialects. "You're Americans?" he said with a sudden smile. "I'm Francois Huvuvo. You guys are a long way from home."

Phillipe knew there was no point in pretending to be local anymore. "Francois, it's nice to meet you. I'm Phillipe. What brings you to a place like this?"

He laughed. "You guys know how it is. You come to Africa to help out, then get sucked in and go native, I guess."

Everyone politely laughed and then Francois continued. "I came here after college with the Peace Corps. We were going to bring water to the natives, dig wells, stills, that kind of thing. Then Rwanda happened, and everything fell apart. I'm with the Nuvovelii tribe now. They used to live in the mountains, but the poachers, then the Hutu and Tutsi from Rwanda, brought their war here. I guess we just became friends, and I stayed with my friends. Originally from Portland. You? What brings you to Africa's World War?"

"You know how it is. Just here taking a look around," Phillipe answered.

"C'mon, I'll show you what's up."

They began walking up the road. On the way Francois asked what was happening in the US and around the world. He'd clearly been out of touch for at least a year—

probably more. Phillipe tried to get information from him too, and Francois was eager to give out as much information as he could. He obviously missed America, but he'd also made Africa his new home. Intelligence agencies would call Francois an "asset."

About three miles up the road they came to a clearing with several buildings. Bodies of armed gunmen were strewn about everywhere. It was hard to walk without stepping on an empty shell casing or blood from the hundred-plus child soldiers who were dead.

"This is what went down earlier this morning, guys," Francois began. "The Nuvovelii had become friends with some of the Hutu refugees here. One of them heard that a Tutsi militia was nearby, and we came to check on the refugees. As you can see we were too late. The Tutsi killed them all, and worse."

He pointed to a pile of bodies and body parts with streaks of dark blood coming from the pile.

"Now, the Nuvovelii are a very peaceful tribe, but everyone has limits, and this should be well beyond everyone's limit of tolerance. So, just before dawn the Nuvovelii took justice into their own hands."

Phillipe looked around. He and his men—as with all American Special Forces—had been trained not to show emotional involvement in local political issues. That included massacres.

"I don't see any of the Nuvovelii carrying guns?" Phillipe asked.

"That's Africa, man," Francois answered. "You can hear guns day and night, but you never hear the spears."

The LRSD's assistant radio operator looked around. "Spears against guns? It doesn't seem very fair. How many did you lose?"

Francois tilted his head in bewilderment. "None, and you're right, it wasn't fair at all. They had no idea we were all around them."

They walked around the dead bodies and the relaxing Nuvovelii warriors—all dressed in T-shirts and jeans.

Phillipe stepped up to Francois. He knew Francois had seen their radios. He was clearly an intelligent guy and knew that the team was an American military unit, a special unit, a Special Forces unit. "Francois, what's going on in this area? That's what we're here to find out."

Francois walked away, over to one of the shanty buildings. He stopped at one of the corpses, flipped it over as if it were a log or a box or some normal object. Then he grabbed a yellow backpack—the kind an elementary schoolkid would have back in the states. He tossed the bag to Phillipe, who caught it and opened it. The bag was filled with American $20 bills.

"Someone is paying Tutsi Rwandans to come across the border and drive out the Hutu refugees. They want everyone out—Hutu, Congolese, Nuvovelii, everyone—and they'll pay cash to get it done. They want everyone out of the Bunyakiri area. All of these refugees, they all died for...how much is in that bag? $1,000, maybe $2,000?"

Phillipe got out his camera. He took pictures of everything and uploaded them to command—to the armchair generals. He took pictures of the bodies, the weapons, the money, and the landscape, and he took pictures of Francois and the Nuvovelii and their spears. The pictures weren't just sent up the chain of command, however. They were imprinted in his mind. As a favor he emailed copies to Francois' personal email address. Those were mostly smiling pictures of him and his new friends—new family—but also of the massacre.

Phillipe wouldn't find out for some time, but his photos found their way to various news editors and subsequently...the world.

***

4/11/1997

As he had done countless times before, former CIA case officer Jim Smith landed at yet another third world airport and did his best to be invisible. He sought to attract no attention to himself at all by looking the part of a Canadian, British, Australian, or American businessman. This time it was Khartoum International Airport in Sudan. Unlike before, this time he was no longer working for the CIA. Today he truly was a private American citizen on a business trip.

During his time at the CIA he'd been sent on all kinds of intelligence gathering and other special missions. This one was little different. Defender Security, the private company he worked for, had been contracted to prevent a cargo container from reaching its destination in Sudan. It was a typical CONEX cargo container arriving at the port of Sudan, almost four hundred miles to the northwest. The blue container, number 8-99-1539440, was due to be offloaded from an Iraqi-flagged cargo ship any day. Final destination was allegedly going to be somewhere in central Khartoum. That was all Defender Security could tell him. He didn't know where the information had come from, who it was important to, or why, only that Defender Security had hired him to do another job, and it paid very, very well.

Jim got off the plane, checked through customs, and rode in an airport limo/van to his hotel in the north end of Khartoum overlooking the Blue Nile River. There, he checked in, went up to his room, and called his contact at Defender Security to see if there was any update on his mission—no...his job.

"Dan, it's Jim. I'm in town [Khartoum] on business. Is there anything new?"

Back in Virginia, his contact answered.

"Hi, Jim. Yeah, we've got some news for you. The ship already docked, and your shipment is already in town. It was last seen on the north side of town, above the river, in the light industrial area."

"Okay, anything more specific, or should I just ride around for a few days until I find it?"

"Sorry, Jim. No time for that. We're getting close to actionable stuff on this. There's some intercepted calls, foreign service intel, sat intel, and financial intel that all point to a bad thing, and they need coordinates. Best we can tell you is that it's someplace between al Inkaz Street to the west and the Block 6 shanties to the east. That leaves about two square miles, but we need it down to the specific building it's in."

"Dan, this isn't a secure line."

"I know. It's okay. Anyone who could hear is already sharing info. Oh, and did I mention that since the ship arrived and unloaded early, there's a time crunch?"

"Always is, Dan. Always is. Okay, I'll get to work right now. Thanks."

Jim hung up the phone, sat down at his desk, and opened his briefcase. Inside was a three-ring binder with all kinds of fake customs documents, inspection forms, and chemical material safety data sheets. All were prepared before he even left the US, and only one page was in Arabic. That page, complete with a Sudanese customs stamp, detailed a carte blanche inspection authorization by the Sudanese government in search of illicit pornographic items. Jim's plan was to masquerade as a special customs agent working to protect Sudan from the twisted morality of the West.

The phone system in Khartoum was a nightmare. Instead of wasting time navigating it, Jim went downstairs to have the hotel staff do his calling for him. While he waited in the lobby a young man behind the counter worked the phone. Finally, he left his post and walked over to tell Jim that a rental car would be dropped off in a few minutes. Jim thanked the man and continued drinking his tea. When it was done, he stepped outside from the air conditioning into the equatorial desert heat, and he waited for the car.

Moments later a white Toyota sedan pulled up. Jim met with the driver. Unlike in Western countries, there was no sales pitch or discussions of insurance or fuel costs. The driver just handed him the keys, and then left him to start walking back to the rental agency a few blocks away. The cost would be charged to the hotel, and then to his room in turn.

Jim sat down inside, cranked the air conditioning, and began driving around Khartoum. First he did several circles around the hotel to see if there was a poorly trained driver tailing him. Then he made four wider circles around the city, and still felt that no one was following him. Finally, he headed up Ebed Amin Street and across the Armed Forces bridge into the northern, light industrial area of the city where the blue container was last reported. Jim's plan was to ride up and down the streets looking for blue containers, and memorizing where they were. He had no idea if he'd see a hundred or none. After an hour, he'd spotted only four. Most of the containers seemed to be red, rust, or white.

The first container was behind a small machining factory, and it looked like it had been there some time—

possibly was even being used for storage rather than transport. The second blue container was on a truck at an air conditioner manufacturer's lot. The third blue container was on a truck parked in the street next to an auto repair business. Finally, the fourth container was parked near a medical plant that produced anti-malaria and other drugs.

It was easy for Jim to rule out the first container. The second at the air conditioner plant needed further examination. As the day was getting late, and the lot wasn't gated, Jim drove his car right into the air conditioner plant's parking lot, right up to the blue container. A quick check of the container's number showed it was clearly not the one he was looking for. The third container parked outside the auto repair place was easy to check out with a slow drive-by, and that one as well had the wrong serial number. Either the container he was looking for was outside the pharmaceutical plant or the container was still missing.

Unlike the others, this last choice was parked in a gated parking lot. It was going to take more than a simple drive-by to see if it was the cargo container that so many people were concerned about. Where it was parked interested him as well. A container being used for junk storage was of no concern to anyone. The same could be said of one parked outside an auto repair place in Khartoum, Sudan. One parked in an air conditioning manufacturer's lot could be of some sort of manufacturing interest, but the people that were paying Defender Security, and him by extension, were spending a lot of money, and the only place of value was the pharmaceutical plant.

Jim pulled into the open parking lot for employees and guests. Then he took a moment to get into character and (more truthfully, he thought) to enjoy the last bits of cool air in the car. He was wearing a lightweight business suit and tie, and he knew it was going to be hard in a few moments. Bodies unconsciously sweat more when lying, deceiving, or under stress, and high temperatures only exacerbated the effect.

It was a short walk from the car into the building's lobby. Inside, he spoke English to the receptionist, and asked to meet with the plant manager. It was clear the receptionist didn't understand him, so he showed the young man his fake, anti-pornography, customs inspection form, and the man motioned for him to wait. Jim unbuttoned his jacket and sat down on a small chair with torn vinyl in the closet-sized vestibule/lobby. After thirty-five minutes of baking he was about done, and the door opened with three confused workers standing before him. Only one spoke—clearly the translator, Jim thought.

"Who are you? What do you want?" he asked.

Jim smiled and stared at him until he started to smile back—albeit pensively. When he did, Jim reached his hand out to shake.

"My name is Jim Smith. I'm with the United Nations Illicit Trade Committee. We work with your government to prevent cultural contamination through trade."

"We do not understand," the translator replied.

You're not supposed to, Jim thought. Then he showed them his three-ring binder with all the forms they couldn't understand, and the one form they could. All three men leaned in to read it.

"I'm here to check a container we think has prohibited items inside."

The translator explained to his supervisors as they were looking at Jim's fake document. All three conversed for a moment. Finally one man emerged as the clear leader, and Jim took note by facing him directly and speaking to the man in charge instead of the translator.

"The government of Sudan and United Nations want me to look at a blue container number 8-99-1539440. It arrived here today."

The Sudanese started looking suspicious of Jim, so he waffled back to his amiable personality instead of playing the part of powerful bureaucrat.

"I'm sure it's a paperwork thing, but you know how they are on the other side of the river: everything has to be checked and double checked. Did you get a container in today? A blue one?"

While two of the Sudanese still debated what was happening, and what they should do, the translator replied, "Yes, one came in not long ago."

"From Port of Sudan, yes?"

The translator asked his two superiors, one of whom argued back to him, but the other nodded in the affirmative unconsciously.

"Who are your authority?" the translator asked.

"I am with the United Nations, but I work for Sudan." Jim pointed to the South, indicating he was working on behalf of the Sudanese government. Then he pointed to the spot on his fake document that listed the container's number, and motioned for the man in charge to look at it. The man looked at the paper, at Jim, and Jim looked back with an innocent, questioning smile. It was the complete opposite of his real intention.

Again, the three men spoke, then the translator began again.

"He says that is the container that a truck brought in today, but it is not for us. We share the lot with others."

The three men pointed to the north and west, where other businesses were adjacent to the parking area.

"We cannot open. It is not ours. You should go talk to them."

Jim smiled broadly, and vigorously shook each man's hand, compelling them to smile back and erase suspicious or ill feelings at the quick meeting. Then he left with a small, fake bounce in his step.

Back in the car, Jim immediately hit the air conditioning. It was late afternoon and still well over one hundred degrees. He pulled out, gave a wave in case anyone was watching, and then drove around the block again. To the north of the parking area was a large Trucial Energy fuel terminal. To the west were a series of aluminum buildings all padlocked shut with no visible office entrances. Jim headed back to the hotel. There was nothing else to see.

An hour and a shower later, he finally called his Defender Security contact.

"Dan? It's Jim."

"Hi, Jim. What'd you find out?"

"Process of elimination brought me to a pharmaceutical plant that shares a parking area with a few other unknown businesses and the fuel terminal to the north. I got eyes on the container, but only serial number confirmation came from the people at the pharma plant. They confirm the number, and that it arrived today. They also claim it's not theirs, and I believe 'em."

"Okay. Thanks. That'll have to do for now. Can you stay there a few more days in case they want to expand the contract?"

"Sure. No problem. I might change hotels just to shake things up a bit, but yeah, I can stay."

"All right, thanks. Stay cool." The line went dead.

Jim kicked back on the bed and turned on the TV. Sudanese television programming had a lot to be desired. A lot of it was BBC based in homage—if for no other reason—to its past history as a British colony. Eventually he found the BBC News with Arabic captions on the bottom. It was nice to hear his native language, but then he heard what was happening.

The president of the United States had signed an executive order under the International Emergency Powers Act calling for all Sudanese assets in the US to be blocked, and imposed a ban on bank loans and all US trade with the country. This was done, according to the American State Department, because of Khartoum's "...continued sponsorship of international terror, efforts to destabilize its neighbors, and abysmal record on human rights." In response Sudan's ministry of external trade claimed that trade between the two nations amounted to only five percent of Sudan's total exchanges. Future international transfers through American banks would be averted and further Sudanese transactions would be handled with other currencies instead of the US dollar."

People with professional careers in politics, diplomacy, military, or in particular spycraft view news reports as pieces of puzzles to real-world events. Jim heard this news report, and added it to what he knew: powerful players with the ability to monitor phone calls in Sudan had a common interest in finding a container that came off an Iraqi ship, and wound up in a holding area between a fuel terminal, a drug manufacturer, and a few unknown light industrial buildings.

Jim barricaded his door and settled in for a night of half-sleep. It was never a good idea to completely let one's guard down in a foreign land when conducting any sort of espionage. It was a lesson he'd learned the hard way years before, and would be reminded of again someday.

In the morning, after taking a long shower in lukewarm water, Jim turned on the BBC to listen to as he got dressed and finished getting ready for the day.

"American diplomats are expected to continue others in the international community to join in sanctions against the Sudanese government even in the face of strong opposition. Overnight, Chinese and Russian officials refused to join in the sanctions, and promised to block any efforts to justify the efforts at the United Nations Security Council. Several Saudi and Gulf Emirate states have offered to work with the Sudanese to maintain Sudan's economic cash flow by converting Sudanese holdings that are in dollars to more internationally recognized and tradeable petrodollars."

Then the BBC switched to more European topics.

Once dressed, Jim thought about the news and his job in Khartoum as he moved his furniture barricade away from the door. He decided it would be worth it to drive around again in the area where the aluminum buildings were adjacent to the parking area where the blue container was waiting. This time—after he drove around the city for an hour to make sure he wasn't being followed—Jim did one lap around the block where the parking area was, then he parked across the street from the aluminum buildings on its west side.

Sitting in his car, Jim took in all his surroundings. He noticed the women who were carrying groceries, and their male escorts who constantly seemed to be the target of bickering. There was very little traffic, mostly pickup trucks, a few cars, and the occasional panel van. There were a few male pedestrians who looked like average low-cost Third World laborers. After a while he saw a man walk into one of the buildings. Half an hour later he saw another man, then a few minutes more and three more men. It was when he saw the group of three that he recalled all the men entering the building were of military age, bearded, and all of them had the kind of faces that veteran soldiers have. They stared off with slightly blank emotion, faces bearing shades of guilt, confidence, and conviction.

Rather than risk drawing suspicion, Jim drove back into downtown Khartoum. There he drove laps around the city again to make sure he wasn't being followed. It was boring, but the risk of being followed as well as the threat that entailed made the maneuvers far less dull than they would have been in everyday life. Finally, after an hour he headed back across the river and left the aluminum buildings far behind. He had no intention of stopping to park where familiarity of his presence would have undoubtedly drawn suspicion, but he wanted one last look. Nothing new was happening, and he drove by.

Ever wary of being followed, Jim noticed a black Mercedes pull out of one of the buildings and get behind him. He wasn't sure that he'd been spotted, but knew that if he had...this was exactly what would happen first. As a precaution, when he got on to the four-lane Armed Forces Bridge, he moved to the slow lane and went slower and slower until all the cars passed him—including the Mercedes. Once it was several cars ahead of him, Jim began his pursuit of what might have been his pursuer.

Once they were back across the river and into the modern portion of Khartoum, Jim followed the Mercedes until he watched it turn into the United Arab Emirate consulate. Now he had something. It was time to call his Dan at Defender Security. His contract job—mission as he thought of it—was getting very interesting. It was time to change hotels.

This time Jim found a hotel that was more like an American motel, but still luxurious by most Sudanese standards. He checked in, parked his car, found his room, and immediately called Dan. It wasn't even noon local time, but back home it wasn't even 5 a.m.

"Whoever the fuck this is had better have a damn good reason for calling."

"Dan? It's Jim. I got something."

Dan's head had been buried in his pillow when he answered the phone, but he immediately sat upright, and woke up in less time than it took his heart to beat once.

"What's up, Jim?"

"I checked out the aluminum buildings west of the parking area where our container is. Did some drive-bys; even sat around for a while. I spotted a total of seven military-age males who look like they've been around. They all went inside, a few at a time. When I drove back around a little later the street was empty, but a nice Mercedes pulled out. I thought I'd been made, but I wasn't. When I slow buffed 'em they went past, and I was able to follow 'em all the way to the UAE consulate."

"No way!"

"Yeah, and get this...Saudi plates." "Please tell me you got the number..."

"C'mon man, really? Get a pen." Jim laughed and read the Mercedes license plate number to Dan.

"Also, I changed my location so don't try and contact me at the last known, okay?"

"Nice work, Jim. Get your ass home now. The ball's in a bigger court with bigger players now. Lemme know when you're in, and we'll settle up with what we owe you plus a bit for getting the plates and stuff."

The phone went dead.

Jim's contract was officially over.

***

8/10/1998

Alan had worked for Jerry Henderson for eight years, but it sometimes it seemed like a lifetime. As he walked through the senator's office doors, he noticed the door frame and for a split second wondered how many times he'd passed through to discuss horrible world events. It was another day, another tragedy, another meeting, and another moment of marveling at just what a strange trip his career had become. Once a mere congressional office accountant, he was now privy to the most secret happenings in the world; not just privy, but part of the game that was world affairs...world history.

And yet, in the end it was just another Monday morning meeting as well.

"G'mornin,' Alan. What's the latest?"

"Good morning, Senator. We learned a bit more about the two bombings in Africa over the weekend."

Alan closed the door before continuing.

"Looks like the president got a solid warning about it beforehand in his PDB [presidential daily (intelligence) brief] last week. CIA, NSA, FBI, even DOJ attorneys had been getting intel that something big was going to happen. They did in fact catch one of the bombers. He's wounded, and I suspect that the local authorities are not being very nice to him. Not sure if we'll get extradition, if we want it, or if he'll survive to get the opportunity. In the meantime, it looks like it was in fact a Muslim extremist group. They say it was planned for August 7 to protest the anniversary of American forces moving into Saudi Arabia as preparation for Desert Storm. I'm not so sure that's it, though."

"What do you mean?"

"Well, sir, FBI looks at terrorist attacks as crimes. CIA looks at terrorist acts first as deniable means of nation-states basically waging war without going into full-blown war. NSA monitors everybody, but not so much everything. I'm a numbers guy, so I look at what the Treasury Department looks at; I follow the money. Look, I'm completely convinced—as is everyone—that this Islamic terrorist group or groups did the attacks, and I take 'em at their word when they rave on and on about why they're suicidal psychopaths, but there's a difference between a nutjob stabbing someone or shooting someone and someone from an impoverished Third World country who suddenly has enough extra cash on hand to buy a few trucks and ten or twenty tons of high-grade military explosives. Someone funded these attacks. Now it could be the CIA since, well, they're the CIA and at some time or another work with every group of unaligned killers out there. I doubt the FBI funded them if only because the current director is such a stickler. I even knew a guy who quit after he was demoted for not having the right colored file folder on a case he was working on."

They both laughed, but it was short lived. Alan's reasoning was sound, and Washington, DC, agencies were tribes. Getting them to work together was like herding cats.

"Okay, Alan, so what's your thought then? Why'd someone want to blow up American embassies in Africa if not for political-religious ideology?"

"No, I think the bombers did it for their ideology. But without money the attacks simply wouldn't be possible. FBI can look at the crime, CIA the players and/or states involved, but I've been following something else."

Alan stopped for a moment and pondered if it was the right time or not. He'd been brainstorming a theory for years, and while pieces of his puzzle fit there was no way he could be certain that he wasn't just making random pieces fit together, or if what he suspected was real. He bit his lower lip, looked at his brief case, opened it, and pulled out a three-ring binder.

"Sir, my first job here was to study a company that had a relationship with one of the previous administrations: Trucial Energy. It's why you and Wayne Kowalski sent me to Iraq. The experience opened my eyes to a world that few see and almost no one really watches. Presidents have power, but it's temporary at best and subject to rule of law, politics, and popularity. Banks have much more longevity and power, but they do have international laws specific toward banking, and that serves as a little check and balance. There are, however, massive businesses with annual budgets that are sometimes more than most countries. A simple insurance company with a few funds in their holdings makes most states' budgets look like change found under sofa cushions. There are lots of entities other than nations that have more power than nations."

The senator leaned forward to look at Alan's binder. "Go on," he said with eyes squinting.

"Okay, the flowchart starts to look like spaghetti, but if I'm right...well, imagine Trucial Energy as a country, a monarchy. Imagine all these different, highest level business entities as countries with monarchies. Some actually are in fact! I think that mega-businesses like Trucial Energy don't just engage in economic and financial competition, but that from time to time the competition turns to combat. I think some outside entity has been doing that for almost a decade now, and I think the bombings are related."

Senator Henderson's head remained looking at the binder, but his eyes looked up at Alan—not in disbelief at the entire idea, but in curiosity mixed with confusion. He couldn't see how the bombings in Africa were at all related to Trucial Energy.

"What's the connection to the bombings and your theory?" he asked.

"It's the casualty list. Combined there's over two hundred dead and at least five thousand injured. When the CIA, or FBI, or NSA, or any intelligence agency looks at the list they look for criminals, known terrorists, people they've been watching, political leaders, those kind of people. When I saw the list, I saw fifty-two names that I knew—well, at least I'd heard of them."

The two men stared at each other for a moment before Alan continued.

"Look here. Twenty-two in Kenya and thirty in Tanzania. Most of those people are from Trucial Energy. I made a few phone calls and looked into it. There were meetings in both embassies at the same time: 10:30 a.m. local. The attacks happened about five to ten minutes later. It was a conference call meeting between multiple groups. That's how the State Department actually first found out about the bombing: DC was on the call as well."

Senator Henderson's doubts were evaporating. "Who else was on the call?" he asked.

"A law firm in New York where Trucial Energy is essentially the only client, and the Office of Economic Development in Kigali."

"Kigali?" It took a moment for the senator to recall the name, but only a moment. "You mean in Rwanda?"

"Exactly. I asked a friend at Foggy Bottom if there was anything on the threat board in Rwanda yesterday—anything out of the ordinary. She said nothing out of the ordinary, but they average a threat a day against one government office or another, and out of all the government offices in the entire country of Rwanda yesterday, the only threat was against the Office of Economic Development in downtown Kigali."

"Well, it's pretty clear there's something going on, but what? Did you figure that out yet too?"

Alan flipped to a page farther back in his binder. It was a map of East Central Africa with a line running from a spot just west of Rwanda on the western edge of the mountains that divided the Republic of the Congo from Rwanda, and at the other end of the line was the Tanzanian port of Dar es Saalam.

"Right around the time you were elected to Congress, back when you were still working real estate and commodities, do you recall hearing about the Congo and the discovery of the Bunyakiri gold discovery? Probably not—the press called it "Queen Victoria's Gold," thinking it was off Lake Victoria, but it's really in the western mountains near Lake Kivu, which is next to Lake Victoria. They made hay out of it in the financial press, and it got some coverage internationally, but was largely drowned out here in the US by election coverage. I don't have any solid proof, but I think Trucial Energy is planning on building a rail line from the mine in the Congo, through Rwanda, through the Maswa/Serengeti Nature Reserve that's jointly controlled with Tanzania, and all the way to the port of Dar es Salaam."

Senator Henderson leaned back, took a deep breath, and crossed his hands as he looked Alan in the eye. "That's great circumstantial evidence, Alan, but it looks like a lot of cherry-picked points. And to be connected by the attacks means someone else has to know about it besides you; besides you and me. It doesn't sound like any of our agencies are even looking at it."

"That's right, sir. I share your concern. By the way, that law firm in New York that was on the conference call—the one I said has basically one client."

"They do have a few others. Mostly real estate corporations."

Alan flipped to another map in his binder, showing another map.

"This is a map of some of the land that has been negotiated through that firm"

The map showed a row of disconnected, geometric shapes running from the Congo through Rwanda to Dar es Salaam.

There were a few breaks in the row between properties. Most notably there were no red boxes in the jointly maintained nature reserve.

Senator Henderson's mouth opened as his jaw dropped and his eyes widened.

"I'll be damned."

"Like I said, sir, I'm just as concerned that these could be pieces of a puzzle that I'm forcing together, but they fit very well."

"Any estimate on the gold's value?"

"In 1993 they estimated about a million ounces after operating costs. That puts it in the top five globally."

"My God."

"And not many people know about this. Fifty-two people fewer than a few days ago. I'm sure that for security reasons Trucial Energy is keeping the details closely guarded. Even if the conference call was planned to arrange for a cross-country easement or other permissions, it's not likely anyone in Tanzania or Rwanda knew the value of the proposed rail line and port access."

The two men stared at each other, believing the logic of the data, marveling at it, and at the same time in disbelief of the scale.

"There's more, sir," Alan continued. A US Army LRSD team was patrolling the border area and checking on Rwandan refugees who'd made it to the Republic of Congo. They found a massacre near Bunyakiri, the area where the gold deposit was found."

Alan pulled out a stack of Phillipe's photos showing the massacre, weapons, and money.

"I had the Treasury look up the serial numbers on the money that the killers were paid. It was from a withdrawal made by a Trucial Energy employee in New York."

He paused to see the senator's reaction, then Alan went on some more. "Then there's the container. The State Department had a contractor in Sudan before the bombings. He reported seeing a shipping container that Naval Intelligence suspected might be carrying weapons and explosives. I've no idea why DoD would work with State or use a contractor, but...it's Washington, so who knows. Anyway, their contractor also connected the shipping container with a Mercedes that had UAE plates. No one ever asked, 'Hey, what's a nice UAE Mercedes like you doing in a place like Nairobi?' Again, it's Washington."

"You think Trucial Energy was paying to kill everyone in the area of the mine, and that someone in the UAE is waging a war on Trucial Energy to stop them? Is that right, Alan? Look, these bombings are already a big deal politically. The president's getting hammered on national security. The press is all over the State Department since they denied additional security for months. In the Arab World these different Islamic groups who are claiming responsibility are getting all kinds of press. You know as well as I do—probably better—that the intel agencies are running in circles to distract from the fact that they missed this. Meanwhile, here you and I are...with this."

"I know."

"Okay, well, draft up a summary report and pass on copies to the White House, the DCI [director of Central Intelligence (agency)], and the attorney general, and send some off to the House and Senate leadership. Don't be too specific; just a one-page summary for now unless someone asks. After that, look into it some more. Put together a team with whatever staff you need. No one else is likely to look into this while the big, bad Muslim terrorists are in the spotlight. It's gonna be you. You're the one who's gonna find out the details of the mine, the rail line, and most of all who else knows. Once we know that, we can sell it to the IC [intelligence community] a lot easier, and they'll be able to hit the ground running."

"Yes, sir. We've got an intelligence oversight committee meeting in an hour. I'll start on it after the meeting. Maybe we'll learn something new."

"Good work, Alan."

***

10/31/1999

Halloween always meant trick-or-treating to children. It meant costumes and fun to most adults. In Detroit it meant Devil's Night and hundreds of arson calls for firefighters. It's also meant busy nights at hospital emergency rooms for doctors, and busy nights for police as well. High employment turnover at the East Cleveland Police Department meant that Officer Brian Assana was already a veteran with all the benefits that come with it; benefits like having to pull double shifts on active holidays like Halloween.

Weather in Northeast Ohio was always a crapshoot. Some Halloweens were snowy, others rainy, and yet others were in the fifty- to sixty-degree range. This year it was frigid, twenty-five degrees with a stiff westerly wind. It was the kind of cold that stung exposed skin and forced little kids to wear winter coats over their costumes.

It was one o'clock in the afternoon, and Brian had another twelve hours to go before going home. He'd miss trick-or-treating with his kids—again. At least they understood. Right or wrong they saw him as a hero policeman, and Brian was the kind of person who both knew he could never live up to the image in their minds and that he had to try. That was his nature.

This afternoon Brian and his latest partner were sitting at a gas station at the intersection of Hayden Road and Shaw Avenue. Years earlier the station had been remodeled. The old building was boarded up, and now a gas station attendant was positioned in a small booth between all of the pumps. The bathroom, however, was located in the old building. Over the years its door had been vandalized and replaced with a piece of plywood and a latch and padlock instead of a real doorknob.

In the middle of the night someone who desperately needed or wanted gasoline, but had no money, waited until the attendant answered nature's call. Then, once the attendant was away from his little booth, and in the bathroom, that someone came and put their own padlock on the door, locking him inside. Next they proceeded to fill up their car, and anyone else's car. There was no way of telling if the perpetrator(s) charged other people for the gasoline or if they just gave it away.

At noon the attendant's replacement arrived, couldn't find the attendant, and called the police. Officer Assan's partner found him locked in the bathroom, cold, miserable, and extremely angry. The station's manager showed up soon. He was equally angry and fired the man on the spot. Just as things were on the edge of turning into a fight, the station's owner arrived and took issue with the police.

Brian and his partner called for backup. Soon another pair of patrolmen arrived as did the shift supervisor. Customers desperately needing/wanting gasoline were getting frustrated as well, and a crowd was gathering—many of whom were dressed in costumes. It didn't take long before a clown shoved a wolfman, and a fight broke out.

The supervisor called for the van, and the second it pulled into the gas station lot, the crowd scattered. The clown headed north toward the lake, and the wolfman headed south. Several superheroes were seen heading west, and a gaggle of princesses were dragged by their moms across Hayden Avenue and down the cross street to the east. The paddy wagon was the great equalizer in crowd control.

By 2 p.m. the van was gone. The extra patrolmen were back on their route. The supervisor was leaving. The owner had hired the attendant back, and the manager had quit. Most of all, customers were getting gasoline again.

All that for gas, Brian thought to himself. Then again, he realized, gasoline is the way people get to work. Work meant money, and money meant food/shelter. It was a social lesson that policemen like Brian needed to understand. Every cop learned right away that desperate people do desperate things—particularly for survival. Survival, however, does not just mean food, water, shelter. It includes medicinal and recreational drugs, gasoline, and more. It was a lesson for the gas station attendant as well.

***

3/15/2000

Erwin Zimmermann was asleep. He'd been physically exhausted by all the adrenalin from the night before, but mentally his head had been far too alert. To help with that his doctor had rushed to his *Schloss* (castle/manor house) in the middle of the night and prescribed him a heavy tranquilizer. Anna too had rushed home, and she had curled up with him to help comfort him. She had been visiting their friends, Terrence and Joan Tryphine, in London, and they too were there as well.

The house and business office staffs were at their homes—some far more shaken than Erwin. The *Schloss* was, instead, filled with German police—local and federal. Unmarked vehicles filled the parking turn around out front, and though it had all happened more than ten hours earlier there were still photographers documenting every possible clue.

Lord Terrence Tryphine, Erwin's close friend, had taken charge of the estate in the wake of the night's violence, and he'd already arranged for private cleaning staff to put things back in order. Outside on the lawn ambulances and police cars still surrounded Erwin's helicopter. There were giant smears of blood all over the helipad—in some places turning the large yellow "O" shape painted on the ground into the dark brown of dried blood. Inside the helicopter, four people wearing white Tyvek suits had been working for hours trying to clean up the blood and brain tissue of half a dozen brains that had splattered out from exploding skulls and twice as many bullet holes. Not all of the brain and bullet fragments would ever be found.

Joan came down the red-carpeted stairs with Anna, and they met Terrence halfway down, under a massive painting of Emperor Franz Josef. The two were holding hands. Anna was silent, seeking a way to face the ordeal.

"He's awake now, and getting dressed as if nothing happened," Joan said to Terrence.

"That's like him. Let's let him have a moment. We can go downstairs. There are caterers from the village to help out for a while."

The three of them went down the rest of the stairs and into a dining room. One wall was adjacent to the ancillary kitchen, where dishes, normally brought up from the downstairs kitchen, were given one last check before serving. Another wall opened to the butler's pantry room, and the back wall opened up into a five-sided bay with floor-to-ceiling glass overlooking at least a quarter mile of manicured lawn in 180 degrees.

Morning frost was still melting, and the grass sparkled with billions of reflective, microscopic drops of water. A golden sun was still behind the pines far in the distance, but orange-pink clouds glowed on a purple, blue, and pale sky. The view helped Anna and everyone feel that it was a new day, and put the evening's terror and death in the past.

The caterers had set up a buffet. Rapid cleaning services and the smells of coffee, eggs, and sausages left no trace of death's sickly sweet stench. By the end of the day all the strangers would leave, and life would be back to normal. Terrence would even have the helicopter removed by noon and one of his own brought in to replace it until Erwin could buy a new one.

While Joan and Anna were filling their plates as well as the plates of others, Terrence watched the stairs, and when his friend eventually did come down he went to be the first to greet him. There was much to say, and he made a deliberate effort to use that as a distraction from the night, a focal point for the day, and all the while not overwhelm him with minutia.

"Erwin, we expected the staff would stay home for a few days, so Joan and I took the liberty of having a private service help out during that time. Breakfast is being served in the dining room over there. The police are still documenting things, but we're told they'll be done in another hour or so. Among the many people here are some of your legal team, and of course there's an insurance man here to see what needs what. He brought a cleaning and restoration service with him, and they too should be done shortly."

Terrence didn't dare question Erwin's stamina. It wasn't the proper thing to do between men of their station, but he did look into his eyes. This too was what was proper for men in their positions. What he saw was either Erwin in denial or a remarkably clear-minded man. Knowing his will, Terrence knew it was the latter, and it gave him pride to view Erwin as a friend. They stared at each other for a moment, and then they nodded at the same time, acknowledging their support and thanks for each other.

"Thank you, Terrence," Erwin said with a smile. "I've a great deal to do today, and this will make things so much easier."

They headed toward the buffet, where a crowd of strangers was gathering. When they spotted Erwin, one of the servers from the local village stopped, and she clapped for him. Everyone else turned and did the same while stepping out of his way. Joan smiled, and Anna stepped briskly to his side.

"Please, everyone, thank you all. Thank you very much. Please, let's just move along and keep things going."

A young police officer who had been in the buffet line passed Erwin his plate while someone else handed him a cup of coffee. Two other police officers at the dining table stepped aside and offered Erwin and Terrence their seats. Slowly the applause passed, and the crowd was no longer as respectfully quiet as it had been while he was resting. Erwin sat with his coffee and looked out the window.

"Has anyone seen to Manfred? Manfred Schultz? He looked very distressed last night. Doctor, could you stop by his house right away and make sure he's fine?"

One of the men in the crowd nodded back, immediately put down his plate, then walked out of the room and straight out the door.

"Terrence, could you arrange for a phone call with George Whittaker later this afternoon—at his convenience, of course? I'd like to see if there's a way I can do something for those men who rescued us last night."

Lord Tryphine nodded, and then made eye contact with one of his staff, who immediately began calling the American Treasury Secretary to arrange the call.

"Thank you, Terrence. Joan, are you comfortable staying here? I can arrange for—"

"Terrence and I will be very comfortable, Erwin. Thank you. What about you?" she asked. "Are you going to be comfortable? Terrence and I have a chalet in Switzerland we can all go to for a while if you'd like to take some time off."

"No, there'll be no time off, Joan. I've work to do. People depend on your husband and me. My moment was last night, and it is done, and I'm moving on now."

While Erwin was talking to Joan, one of Lord Tryphine's assistants stepped up and tried to discreetly ask if there was a statement to be made to the press outside. Millions of people around the globe had watched the events unfold, and someone would need to say something.

"There's not much to tell really," Erwin interrupted. "Yesterday six people from some red faction or some terrorist group broke into my home. They took my staff and me hostage. They said they wanted access to some secret financial network of investors that just doesn't exist. When they realized that, they tried to escape in my helicopter, but German police intervened and killed them all. It all happened so fast it's still a blurred image in my own mind. That's it. That's all there is to say. Nothing else remains except our gratitude to the police who rescued us, and right now my thoughts are only with our staff—our friends. It is right to have them all in our prayers of hope and thanks."

The room was silent. Everyone had seen the events unfold on TV the night before, and rumors along with half-facts had swirled since it all ended, but to hear Erwin explain the tragedy itself made it real like nothing else could. It was no longer television drama or a fantastic gossip story. This was a man who'd been terrorized in his home, his *Schloss*—his castle.

When the drum of dining restarted Erwin looked around to make sure no one was looking or listening. Then he leaned across the table toward Terrence. The two came together, and Erwin spoke softly to him.

"These people last night, their leader, the woman, she said they wanted access to this network that doesn't exist, but the others were going through my files looking for something very specific; something old. I don't have any old documents here, but they were clearly looking for something very important and not currently on the market. Also, it wasn't the police who rescued us. I could hear their voices. There were at least two Germans, and an Austrian, but the rest were British and American. That's why I want to talk to George Whittaker at the American Treasury Department. Someone knows what these people were looking for, and even though I was there I have no idea. This will need to be looked into immediately. Do you know anyone?"

Terrence looked around to ensure their conversation was still fairly private.

"Andrew Lawrence works at our office in the Lloyd's building. He's former SAS and I'm sure still has an ear to those players. I'll personally ask him when I get home. He might be able to tell us more. In the meantime, even though you denied it before, I'm having some Defender Security people come in to make sure you and Anna are safe. They might be able to look into this document issue as well; find out what it is these people want. Until we do, as long as there is a dangerous player out there who thinks you have some document that they want, you two need more security. Do we agree?"

Erwin smiled, and they shook hands. "Of course we do, my friend. Of course we do. And thank you again for all of this. I dare ask one more thing, however: When we are done with this, could you arrange a car for me? I want to go to each person's house and make sure they are fine. Poor Manfred was pushed around a great deal, and Klaus...Klaus Rosenthal, my head gardener; he even tried to save me with a paring knife from the kitchen. The old man survived Hitler's camps and almost got himself killed trying to fight a man with a machine gun who was a quarter his age and with nothing more than a paring knife! Of course it did no good at all, but my God! I am obligated to see to these people immediately."

Terrence smiled, motioned to his staff, and as one of them ran from the room to get a car, he nodded to Erwin.

***

6/24/2000

In June, 150 miles north of Norway's North Cape, the northernmost tip of Western Europe, the sun was up twenty-four hours a day. Ronald Van De Burgh, twenty-one, looked out the window of a Sikorsky S-61N helicopter. It was just before 7 a.m. local time. Since man first dared to sail into the North Sea, its turbulence had been the reality upon which legends were based. People knew it for being the coldest and roughest of all the world's seas, but often overlooked was her ability to become as smooth and flat as a mill pond. As cold fronts would tear through the area, the wind and seas were epic, but once the cold settled on a stretch of ocean, the sky cleared of all clouds. The waves disappeared as they lost their winds, and the glassy surface became a marvel.

Ronald, born in the Netherlands, had gone to school at the University of Amsterdam to become a geologist. Environmental matters meant a great deal to him. He saw the Mother Earth as a literal figure that needed protecting. Later, this view evolved into not just protecting from mankind in general, but specifically from heartless nations and the corporations that now controlled them. After two years he stopped attending university, and disappeared from any and all attention. He'd picked up a job at an environmental awareness organization, and, while surrounded by people of similar thinking, his passions grew. Eventually, as natural as a seed reacts to soil and water and warmth, Ronald reacted to the environmental protection cause and people and a need to do more than send out flyers or other awareness literature.

Ronald's real graduation day—the day he passed on from environmental activist to environmental actionist—that day was this one. With him in the helicopter were twenty-one of his friends. Some were from the University of Amsterdam, some from his job, and the rest were friends of his friends. The flight crew had no idea what they were doing.

Just before 7 a.m. the helicopter approached an oil platform and landed. They were quite literally in the middle of nowhere. It was June so the temperature had risen to a balmy eleven degrees Fahrenheit. The helicopter's rotor wash brought that down to minus-30 Fahrenheit. The big bus with rotors on top kept its motor running while three men from the oil platform began refueling it. One of Ronald's friends motioned for everyone to head out, and nearly two dozen orange-suited people made the short walk across the helipad and into the "OR-98 Opprinnelig Regnbueseks" platform.

The last person in closed the outside hatch and dogged it. The men outside would only realize that they'd been left outside to die long after the helicopter had been refueled and left. In the anteroom the men began removing their orange survival suits, donning normal worker coveralls and putting on Trucial Energy safety helmets. Ronald couldn't escape the oddity of removing his orange survival suit and putting on, in his case, a set of orange worker coveralls. A few others scoffed at the idea and just wore their normal clothes.

Ian Davies, a Brit whom he had met in college, was the fieriest of the crowd. He opened his carry-on bag and began handing out pistols, a machine pistol, a pair of submachine guns, blocks of plastic explosives, and an AK-47 rifle for himself. They didn't have a name for their little group. Ronald was clearly there to make a statement against the big evil Trucial Energy oil beast. Davies just took grave issue with any major form of power. Others were there for their own array of reasons.

"Right then, everyone, we've come a long way and worked hard for this moment," Davies said. "No one needs to get hurt. We'll just round up the crew and fax out our statement. Tomorrow morning we'll leave on the same regular, daily transport bird we just came in on. This place is extremely explosive, so anywhere you put these blocks will do the job just fine—just make sure the crew doesn't see where. We'll tell them about it, and they can leave on the emergency launch after we do, or they can stay here and meet their maker if they choose. It's up to them. Not our problem. Questions?"

Ronald asked, "What about the three outside?"

"I'll come back and let them in after we've herded everyone else into the compressor room. Anyone else?"

No one flinched. It seemed like a live action play or game to most. None of it seemed real. They had come a long way from Amsterdam, and were literally at the edge of the Earth. They were in a dream. It didn't hurt that most had shared more than a few sips of liquid courage on the flight over the North Sea.

They split into two groups. Ronald followed Ian out of the anteroom down a hallway with steel walls and yellow floors. They went first to the right, and then toward a flight of stairs heading down. The other group went out the other door to the anteroom and headed for the computer control room twenty feet away. Ever-present white noise from all the compressors, generators, pumps, and other machinery made any effort at stealth unnecessary. Still, everyone held their weapons at their side so as to retain the element of surprise and avoid needless violence; everyone except Ian Davies.

At the bottom of the stairs, Ian sent six of the people in his group down a long hallway to the left. They were to circle the floor, gathering workers as hostages along the way, and then meet upstairs in the large kitchen area next to the computer control room. Then he, Ronald, and five others stepped into the adjacent crew supply storage room and quickly searched among stacks of pallets to see if anyone was around. A minute later they gathered at the door—having found no one—and went down a long hallway that ran the length of the platform to the drilling supply warehouse. Here, among large stacks of crates, barrels of drilling fluids, spare parts, and rows of pipes, they found their first hostages.

Four men were discussing an inventory issue when the most senior of them noticed the unexpected guests. He lowered his clipboard and walked to Ronald, who was clearly in charge—all the while barking out comments in Norwegian. Ian Davies swung his AK-47 like a baseball bat and split the man's skull wide open. He fell to the floor with his pink-gray brain matter oozing out like a yolk from a broken egg.

Everyone—even Ronald and his friends—were in shock, and Davies took advantage of it to shove the remaining men down on to their knees. Ronald was the first to recover and began to use plastic ties to bind the men while someone else covered their mouths with plastic tape. Once complete, Davies had them roped together, and they walked out of the room looking for more hostages. Others looked back, but given the newfound clarity and realism of the moment, Ronald never did.

The small group went down another hallway that led down the east-west length of the platform. They searched two offices, a kitchen storage room, a kitchen, and a compressor room. By the time they headed back up a different stairwell, they had collected nine men with only the one supervisor killed. At the top of the stairs, the hallway zigzagged but led straight to the computer room. Here Ronald saw that the other group of people he had brought had left five corpses behind. In the hallway, on their way to the kitchen area, Ronald saw two more bodies—this time very badly bloodied.

Back in the kitchen area it was clear the other team hadn't taken any hostages. Everyone smiled and cheered as if they had won some sort of a game. A handful, like Ronald, were dumbstruck, but still smiled unconsciously with their peers.

The nine hostages looked down in shame and fear. A few minutes earlier their lives had been perfectly normal. Now, 150 miles from land, and several hundred miles from any civilization...they had been attacked. Their friends were dead. The killers were laughing, and they knew they were about to die as well.

Davies picked out the people with plastic explosives, and he picked out six more. They would split up into six, two-man teams and set their bombs. No one would know where all of them were. Ronald had been picked, and he—along with his escort, who only spoke German—went back downstairs while the others disappeared. They left the room still chattering with glee and silent suffering behind them.

The platform had four pylons holding it up. Forty feet below the peaceful water the four pylons met two submerged hulls that kept the entire platform afloat. Sixteen anchors held it in place. Ronald and his escort followed the stairs all the way down the inside of one of the pylons until they reached a submerged hull. There, Ronald found a network of pipes connecting to a compressor that adjusted the ballast in the submerged hull. He placed his four-pound block of explosives at the center of the pipe network and set the timer for twenty-four hours, just as Davies had told everyone to do.

Even if they could have spoken, Ronald and the German wouldn't have tried. Both were completely serious, even dedicated to not screwing up the instructions. Clarity had given way to that seriousness, and soon that too would give way to a more pure sense of dedication. They headed back to the kitchen area.

In the kitchen area Ronald asked where to find Ian. One of his friends said to check the computer control room next door. He did, and found Davies rummaging through filing cabinets.

"What happened to no one gets hurt, Ian?"

Davies turned and saw that Ronald wasn't angry, just confused.

"I thought I saw a weapon on that supervisor. It was just his clipboard, but my mind saw something else."

"And on this floor? The others didn't even get a single hostage. What happened?"

"They resisted, someone panicked, opened fire and now the situation's changed"

"Where are the ones we brought up? Did someone panic on them too? I don't see them anywhere." Ronald was getting a bit excited.

"There are two still alive in the control room. Look Ronald, no plan survives first contact with the enemy. We have a lot of moving parts in this thing, and something will always breakdown. It's how we handle it that matters. We have to adapt so that we get this done. One way or the other we are going to let those pigs know that they can't get away with destroying our planet, enslaving our people, destroying our cultures. God dammit Ronald! We are going to make them pay! If all they understand is money, then we'll have to rebalance their books the hard way. They just don't hear our protests, or strikes, or boycotts. You know this better than anyone."

Ronald interjected, "Yes, but this isn't just a few mistakes. Everyone was prepared for something to happen, for someone to get hurt or worse, but this is wholesale slaughter. Where will it end?!"

"Well, it's ended. So you can relax now. Think about the now and the soon to be instead."

"What do you mean it's ended?"

"They're all gone. All the bodies have been tossed into the sea. Your slaughter is over."

Ronald sighed, closed his eyes and faced the ceiling. "My God. No one will ever find them. Now there's not even a trace."

"There's a trace. Here." Davies tossed Ronald a small, grey, plastic ID tracker. "Everyone on a rig carries one of these. Miners do something similar. In case there's an accident they want to be able to track everyone's move. We took everyone's before they went over If you want a legacy, here, take the whole bag."

Davies walked over to a computer console, sat down, and began typing.

"...And this, is our mission." He pressed the ENTER key and sent an email to multiple corporate, government, and media email addresses. "That is our statement. Trucial Energy knows what's been done, and why, and they can't hide it from the corrupt governments of Western Europe because we sent it to every media outlet within a thousand miles. Fuck those bastards!"

"Ian! What have you done?! They'll kill us! They'll send in Special Forces and kill us all! What...why...I just..."

"It's all right, Ronald. I told them we'd taken the crew hostage, and that the place is wired. They wouldn't dare send a raid. If they tried, we'd see them on the radar we have on the rig. If they tried a ship, or a boat, we'd spot them the same way. They can't swim up because the water's too cold even for the best dive gear. They'd kill their own men. The only thing they can do is accept our demands."

Ronald threw his safety helmet on the ground and stormed out of the room. He went up to the helipad, making certain to ensure that the door wasn't dogged behind him, and he stepped out to the catwalk. The sun was bright, and the sea was starting to ripple—no longer a mill pond. A cold but gentle wind was steadily blowing. Below him the water was still enough that he could see the submerged hulls forty feet below the surface. Cold reality was an actual thing to him now, but so too was the insanity and uncontrolled manner of what he'd found himself doing.

'How did it come to this?' He wondered. Just over a year ago he was in college studying geology, and now he was on an oil platform in the North Sea and rigging it with explosives. Last Fall he was just licking envelopes on flyers for De Groenen, the Dutch Green Party. Then came his job at the Terrafirst Technologies filing papers, answering phones, and helping the environmental company with boring administrative tasks.

That's probably where he went wrong-if he was wrong at all. Ian Davies was in charge of the Amsterdam branch where Ronald worked, and he wasn't just a manager, but a leader; a leader who did more than create a team. Davies took that branch office and helped the people there see that saving the environment was something to fight for—not just with paper, but with action. At first it was cleaning up beaches, and attending protests, but this...this was something else.

Ronald accepted the need to fight for Mother Earth. There could be no greater cause than the planet. Even mankind was of less importance as man's existence was an anomaly not likely to live on, but the planet had been around for billions of years, and could survive billions more. Losing—or taking—lives in the cause of saving the planet was logically billions of times less important. That's how he rationalized the blood.

Copious amounts of cocaine and other pharmaceuticals that Davies doled out didn't hurt anyone's decision-making process when it came to their mission. Ronald never saw himself or the others as addicts, but they were. Ian Davies had used solid rhetoric, a morally bereft sense of logic, and lots of drugs to get people to follow him to the middle of nowhere.

Suddenly an invisible wall of dense air smashed into Ronald's face as he looked out over the catwalk and out to the sea. A fluttering roar deafened his ears. As quickly and without warning as it had come, the gust disappeared. It was time to go inside.

After Ronald dogged the hatch behind him, and he proceeded to the kitchen area. There he saw Davies leading once again. In pairs he sent people off to certain areas of the platform to stand guard in case Trucial Energy did try and retake the platform. When Davies saw Ronald he came over, put his arm around Ronald's shoulders, and he looked him square in the eyes with a look of sincere concern.

"How are you doing, Ronald?"

"I'm fine, Ian. I'm fine, thank you. Where do you want me?"

Davies smiled and directed Ronald to a map of the platform he had spread out on one of the dining tables.

"Here. This is the main slurry tank room. There're four large tanks with red and white checkerboard pattern on them. They call it mud, but the tanks actually hold chemical lubricants that the bastards pump down into the ground so the well casing can cut deeper into the planet. The muck is very toxic so don't touch anything. All you have to do is go down there for a few hours. I'll check on you occasionally, and we'll rotate the shifts every four hours. Are you sure you're fine now?"

"Yes, I'm sure. I apologize for my behavior. I've just never done anything like this before, and it's a lot to take in. I do understand now, though. It's terrible that some will lose their lives, but the greater good is the planet, and we have to see that no matter how hard and sad that is."

Davies tucked in his lips and nodded in faux empathy. Then he handed Ronald what looked like a pouch for sugar that one would put in their tea or coffee, but the substance was cocaine-not sugar. Next to the pouch in his hand was a pair of prescription drugs.

"This will help keep you awake and alert till the end of your shift, and the blue one [pill] will help you sleep when it's over. We need to be at our best mentally right now. I think you've got that sorted out, but a little extra never hurts."

Ronald thanked him and headed off to the opposite end of the platform; his guard post a floor below near the northwest pylon. Once there he moved around a pair of steel desks into a corner to make a barricade. He put three fire extinguishers in front of the door opening with the intent of shooting them and disorienting anyone who may try to come into the large room. The other entrance he blocked by tilting four fifty-five-gallon drums (one at a time), and rolling them into position. Each weighed hundreds of pounds, but by rolling them on the edge of their bottoms he built a solid barricade that would be hard to get around.

No sooner had he finished moving with his second barricade than Davies appeared. The cocaine was making time disappear. In Ronald's mind it had only been a few minutes, but in reality his four-hour shift was already over.

"How are things upstairs, Ian?" Ronald asked.

"Everyone seems fine. You look like you've made a good use of your time."

"Well, idle hands and all."

"Ronald, I've been in communication with Trucial Energy. They want to fly a team out to check on the hostages."

"That's a problem I suppose. What did you tell them? You didn't tell them they were dead, did you?"

"Of course not. They also want us to release some of the hostages."

"What about our demands?"

"They tell us if we release a hostage or two they'll send over news crew to hear us out."

"What are we going to do? We have no hostages to give them anymore. They're all at the bottom of the North Sea."

"You and I are going to be the hostages."

Ronald sighed, rolled his eyes in disbelief at the shifting of the plan. "You can't be serious," he said.

“Yes. I’m completely serious. I’m going to agree to the news crew, and when they come you and I will run out to the helicopter with the ID trackers. Once we get to the helicopter, we’ll take control, and the others can join us. We’ll leave the news crew here. They can film the scene inside, see that we’re serious, broadcast it along with our demands, and then another helicopter can come get them off.”

Ronald was incredulous. “And you think they won’t just shoot us down? This is insanity.”

“As long as we have the civilian crew on board, and they think we’ve got hostages, no I don’t think they will. This will be just as if we were leaving on the morning transport, except now they’ll know we’re serious.”

It was too much to comprehend, but Davies tossed Ronald two more gram bags of cocaine, and his concerns waned into a careless apathy. Another of their friends came in to take Ronald’s place in the fluid storage room, and he went to the kitchen area to listen to the new plan as Davies told the others. The more he heard it, the more he grew to accept and then even like it. By the time Davies was done selling it, Ronald was as high as a kite, and eager to steal a helicopter.

By 5 a.m. the next day, no one had slept. The mind-altering drugs had warped their bodies and minds until the young political, economic, ecological activists were caught between a college party and an ignorant bloodlust akin to something one would see at a pre-attack tribal dance in a third world jungle or desert. Ronald was by himself again and saw Davies in the computer control room. He was surrounded by others, but he kept to himself and was clearly alone in his world. Unlike everyone else, Ian Davies was not wired by white powder.

“What are you doing?” Ronald asked.

“I’m watching the radar. The helicopter is on its way in. Here, you can see them right now. They’re about thirty miles out now. That’s about ten to fifteen minutes away.” The two men paused and looked at each other, puzzled with the uncertainty of what was about to happen, and eager to see what would happen next. After a moment, the both smiled. Davies stepped into the hallway and called to everyone present.

“Attention everyone! Let’s have your attention for a moment. The news crew will be here in ten to fifteen minutes so everyone to their posts until I say otherwise. I will come get you when the time comes!”

Cheers, hoots, whistles, and positive battle cries were yelled out as everyone disappeared down the steel corridors to their posts. If Trucial Energy and the authorities were going to try to retake the platform this would be the moment. Davies told Ronald to follow him, and the two men went to a hatch that opened to the helicopter pad.

Davies tried to open it, and failed. He looked at Ronald. They tried to push it open together. It failed. They checked the dogs and everything was in opening order so they tried again—

this time more slowly, deliberately, and prepared for the unexpected resistance. After a few seconds the hatch swung open flooding the hallway with high pressure wind from outside. With a loud bang the hatch slammed open and would remain there for some time.

Hurricane Isaac was almost a thousand miles away, but a rain band had reached out across the North Sea and was hitting the platform like a freight train. Thirty miles wide the band of thunderstorms and heavy seas stretched across from one horizon to the other. Normally at this time of year there was no night, but the density and low ceiling of the clouds made it seem like night. Carried in a steady forty-mile-an-hour wind, knife-like rain seemed to cut at the platform. A hundred feet below them the ocean that was glass-like when they had arrived was now heaving with forty-, fifty-, and sixty-foot waves. White foam boiled on the deep green sea as some waves crested, and lines of mist streamed across all the waves. Neither men had noticed the platform's pitching and rolling before—they were simply too stoned, but now they realized the entire rig was moving in all directions.

"What the hell happened?!" Rolland yelled.

"I have no idea! It's amazing, isn't it? Look at the power!"

Ronald turned from the nightmare outside and looked at Davies dumbfounded.

"This is your Mother Earth, Ronald! She's showing us all her might—protecting us! She is alive!"

Ronald looked outside again. The darkness, the howling wind, the sheeting rain, the stone cold, he saw the power. He saw the natural power. Perhaps Davies was right. He knew the Earth was alive, and he knew that there was so much unknown science that he couldn't dismiss the possibility that something conscious was out there, protecting them with all nature's might. Ronald nodded softly and smiled.

Over the howling wind, pitching/rolling floor, the motion of the horizon, the darkness, and the terrible cold, Ronald heard a sound that didn't match the scene. He motioned to Davies by pointing to his ears and then over to the helicopter pad. The two men ventured outside, all the way to the edge and looked to see if anything was out of the ordinary. When they looked down they saw the top of the same S-61N Sikorsky helicopter! In an instant it rose up from below and suddenly above them. The wind had been horrible before, but now the blast from the helicopter's rotors pushed them back across the pad toward the hatch they had come from.

Ronald slipped on the sleet covered pad. On his way down he grabbed Davies to try and steady himself in vain. Davies hit the ground hard, and his AK-47 blew away in a flash. Together they slid almost one hundred feet until crashing into the upper platform bulkhead just a few feet from the hatch. Both men struggled to get back on their feet in the wind, rain, sleet, and snow.

Davies was the first to get up. As Ronald finally got to his feet he noticed that the helicopter had landed, but its door remained closed. They tried to steady themselves and head toward it. Then Ronald heard the sound again. It was a flash and a muffled bang from below. Davies opened the door to the surprise of both pilots. There was no one else inside. No news crew had been sent. Immediately he knew Trucial Energy had betrayed him.

When Ronald entered, Davies had already made his way through the long passenger cabin and up to the cockpit. Ian had a pistol pointed at both pilots and was yelling at them indiscernibly. While wielding his pistol around angrily, Ian put on an intercom headset, and Ronald followed suit.

"It's a fucking trap! They tricked us!"

"How can you tell?" Ronald asked.

"Just go back and shut the door! There's no time to talk about it!"

Ronald was still near the helicopter's wide door. He turned around to start pulling it up. As he did, he glanced back at the hatch and saw four men dressed in black commando gear, wielding submachine guns, and heading on to the helipad. Shocked, he failed to close the door, but at Davies's armed insistence the helicopter pilots lifted off the platform anyway. By the time Ronald got the door closed they were already a quarter mile away from the "OR-98 Opprinnelig Regnbueseks" platform.

***

6/26/2000

Erwin Zimmermann had been called to London to meet with Lord Terrence Tryphine on an urgent matter. It was something that Terrence didn't want to discuss via email or on the phone, but that wasn't too unusual in their business. At certain levels of international finance, secrecy was worth trillions; millions of millions. While not unusual, it was clearly important.

Erwin arrived at the London branch of Tryphine banking house at midmorning. Normally he would check in at the front desk, get a visitor pass to wear, and be immediately escorted to Lord Tryphine's offices. Today, he was directed to a nearby conference room on the first floor. They'd had meetings there before, but it was a bit unusual. In the past when that had happened it meant that Terrence was in a hurry.

The conference room was large with twenty-foot ceilings and green marble walls. A single table ran through the middle, but there were also rows of chairs along the walls for aides and secretaries to sit in on meetings. The walls were adorned with hundreds of small impressionist paintings that had been commissioned by Tryphine Banking House a hundred years earlier. Some were priceless; all were landscapes of the English countryside.

The room was also entirely empty except for one man. Andrew Lawrence. Erwin hadn't met Andrew Lawrence, but he knew a little about him through Lord Thornorough. Lawrence had worked with British Intelligence for his entire career, but finally decided to retire and take up life as a broker at the Lloyds branch of Tryphine Banking House. His former colleagues, friends, and family who were still active in the intelligence community often called on him for advice, and he did so likewise.

Lawrence was seated near the door, and immediately turned with an open hand toward Erwin.

"*Herr* Zimmermann, I'm Andrew Lawrence. I work for Lord Tryphine."

"Yes, I believe I recall him saying as much. Do we have a meeting scheduled?"

Lawrence smiled the coy smile that only someone who had been through spy school could manage. "Actually, no. I'm afraid this is it. Lord Tryphine has been called away, but he wanted us to meet as soon as possible. His lordship must have thought it better for you to come here. I apologize for any inconvenience this may have caused."

As they both sat down, Erwin shook his head politely to dismiss the idea that it was an inconvenience. Terrence was his old friend, but he was also Lord Tryphine of Tryphine Banking House, and when that man called, it was always wise to do so post haste.

"*Herr* Zimmermann," Lawrence began. "A few months ago when there was the terrible incident at your home. I was asked by his lordship to see if I could find out whom it was that rescued you. Now, from time to time my professional career is hindered by my knowledge and past experience in my past career. I am bound by law not to profit from that information, and his lordship has been extremely understanding to that end. He has never asked me to seek favors for him before. This was the first time ever. While there's no profit to be gained from my knowledge of the event, there are other secrets that I believe we all understand must and shall remain secret."

Erwin was humble and apologetic. "I completely understand, Mr. Lawrence. I apologize sincerely as well if this has put you in any discomfort or risk at all. Please say no more. I will speak with Lord Tryphine and see that the query is ended immediately."

"No, sir. That's not it at all. You already know that the team wasn't police from your village, or from the German government. I know that you've already spoken with the Americans about perhaps starting a trust fund or scholarship for the men who rescued you. Of course, I know much much more than that, but this is not why his lordship felt we should meet."

Erwin leaned forward, elbows on the table, and listened more seriously. He nodded, and Lawrence continued.

"An unusual situation has arisen where information unique to my position should actually be shared—albeit with reservation and control."

Erwin was getting confused, and while he tried not to show it, Lawrence was a man trained in reading people's minds through their faces.

"Right, here it is then. The other day a Trucial Energy oil platform in the North Sea was taken over. Apparently it was a group of environmental protesters-turned-terrorists. They planted bombs all over the rig, and demanded a news crew be flown out to broadcast some sort of environmental manifesto. The platform was retaken by the same men who rescued you. There were losses. All of the terrorists were killed, but two hijacked a helicopter and were dropped off someplace near the North Cape of Norway. The crew of the platform is missing and presumed to have been executed by the terrorists."

"This is of course awful news, Mr. Lawrence, but I'm not making the connection to myself or Lord Tryphine."

"Sir, in my past career, and in our careers today, I'm sure we both can agree that: a) there are no such things as coincidences, and b) coincidences do actually happen. It's contradictory, but it is true. That is to say we notice when things look related, and we are slow to dismiss them as mere happenstance. I do not believe that the oil platform and your rescue are unrelated. They might be. Coincidences do actually happen, but I'm not certain it's mere coincidence. The same elite team in both circumstances. You and his lordship are both deeply involved in Trucial Energy's finances and holdings. And both are terrorist attacks by the most extreme of protesters turned revolutionaries. Further, from my desk at Lloyds, I'm seeing more attacks on Trucial Energy assets. There have been more attacks on Trucial Energy tankers. Pipelines have had accidents where safety records had previously been remarkably solid. And, well, sir, I've spent a lifetime developing a sense of how things are happening. Like any trade, intelligence gathering and analysis is as much an art as a science. I have a sense someone is contributing to these attacks on Trucial Energy assets. Since you and Lord Tryphine have so much involvement in those assets, I could just as well be saying your assets. Quite literally, you have actually *been* attacked already."

Erwin rose from his chair and walked around the room slowly. Hands behind his back, eyes panning at each and every painting, he thought hard about what he'd just been told. Was there a relationship between the attack on his home, an increase in attacks on Trucial Energy assets (his assets), and someone else? If there was, who could it be? How? Why?

"Mr. Lawrence, I appreciate your efforts in this matter. Truly, I do. I trust you've conveyed your concerns to those who are in more direct position to confront any potential threat, no?"

"That's just it, *Herr* Zimmermann. I've had several former colleagues express their concerns on these questions. It concerns them greatly as well, but no one of higher authority seems to see the potential for coincidence. They seem to prefer option B to option A. That is why I've taken the responsibility of informing Lord Tryphine and now you as well. No one is actively looking into this matter, so in my current position I feel responsible to see to it that those who may be affected take measures to be protected."

Erwin humbly yet nobly thanked Lawrence when it was clear he had nothing else to say, and the meeting was ending.

***

9/13/00

Senator Jerry Henderson was in a meeting with Treasury Secretary George Whittaker when the phone rang. Whittaker's secretary was professional and would only interrupt a meeting between a ranking member of the Senate and the Treasury secretary if it was important. It was. Senator Henderson waited patiently.

Whittaker put the phone back when he was done. He opened his lower right desk drawer, then pulled out a bottle of private label scotch and two glasses. He put three fingers into each, gave one to Jerry, and leaned back in his chair with another.

"You're not gonna believe this," he said as he took a sip. "You know they were running off the first euro notes today, right? Someplace in Belgium?"

Jerry took a sip as well before he answered. "Yeah, town called Maahstricht. It's a big deal. Big ceremony. Lots of players—wait, what happened?"

"Bunch of wackos broke in, took everyone hostage. Like you said, 'lots of players.'"

"Dammit. Casualties?"

"Special Forces team went in and got everyone out. They think they killed all the terrorists, but they're still checking to see if any escaped. This is going to hit the euro hard. All the currency markets are gonna be in play today. The Federal Reserve board has been talking about raising interest rates too. Maybe I'll just leak it to a few people that they're thinking about lowering instead. That'll create enough opposite-direction market movement for a while."

"Don't worry about it, George. I'll leak it. I know just who to use. You don't need that right now."

The Treasury secretary said "thanks" before taking another sip of scotch.

Senator Henderson wasn't sure why it popped into his mind, but something about the attack on the euro-printing ceremony made a connection in his brain. It unconsciously reminded him of a conversation he had had with Alan months earlier in the wake of another attack where a player in world finance had been attacked. "Say, George, have you noticed that there've been a lot of attacks on financial sources in the past few years—even months?"

"How could I miss it?"

"Well, I've got a guy who thinks there might be a connection. We brought it up to the intel community at a closed-door Senate hearing last month, and they blew off the idea. What do you think?"

"It's certainly possible. They always say, 'Follow the money.' What attacks are you thinking of specifically?"

Senator Henderson wet his lips with the smooth scotch. "Well, my man noticed that the African embassy bombings in '98 coincided with a lot of work Trucial Energy was doing to build a rail line through Rwanda, Kenya, and Tanzania. That happened right after the coup and genocide in Rwanda. The attack on Erwin Zimmermann's place has ties to Trucial Energy, and there was that Trucial Energy platform that got attacked a few months back. Now there's this. Can you see any connections between these?"

"No. I really can't, but I do see your point. Ya know FBI, SEC, CIA, NSA, they all have task forces aimed at watching out for economic terrorist stuff. And let's not forget when the Japanese deliberately tanked the European and our own economies last year. There could be a connection. Do you think the Japanese are at it again?"

Senator Henderson shook his head decidedly. "Nah. I think if there is a connection it's that someone has it out for Trucial Energy for some reason. That's why I was wondering if there were any players at the Belgian rollout who might have a connection as well."

"How's the company?"

"Last I saw Trucial Energy was doing well. They're growing, but it doesn't seem too fast or too slow. Good profits, but not great. Stocks are doing well—a bit better than for other oil companies since they're diversified more than others. There's nothing unusual, really.

The Treasury secretary turned to his computer and began typing to find out more about Trucial Energy.

"Yeah, I've got them on my screen now. Nothing seems out of the ordinary. Even if any of the attacks were related to Trucial Energy I'm not even seeing any hits on their stock. There're a few dips here and there, but otherwise they seem rock steady."

"Well, I'm telling you there's a really good case for the African embassy bombings tied to them—maybe even the Rwandan coup."

Whittaker thought for a moment. When anyone else would have told him about a worldwide conspiracy to wage covert war on a massive corporation like Trucial Energy, he'd have dismissed the claim as crazy, but this was a financial expert and ranking member of the Senate Select Committee on Intelligence who was telling him there might be a secret war being waged. He had to take the idea seriously.

"Okay, Jerry, I've got to get on this, and I need you to get back and spread the word about a Fed drop in rates. Do me a favor and talk this over with your people to see if the Belgian euro rollout attack is related. I'll keep an eye out for things like that as well. Give me a call right away if you find something; otherwise, have your people send me a theory report in a few days. I'd like to know more."

The two men slammed the rest of their scotch, shook hands, and went about their days manipulating the ebb and flow of trillions in Western currencies.

***

10/1/2000

Captain Widman's Inn and Tavern had been in Georgetown (Washington, DC) since before the Revolutionary War. The original Inn and Tavern was largely destroyed by a flood shortly after the British burned the White House during the War of 1812. Still, the street-facing little stone building from which the tavern had spawned remained. Over the centuries it saw duty as a brothel, a private residence, a small storage warehouse, a hospital during the Civil War, an accounting firm after the Civil War, and again as a tavern and inn after the Spanish-American War. Since that time more and more additions had been made, and the small stone building was now little more than a waiting area for the rest of the business.

Beyond the stone house a large, twenty thousand-square-foot, four-story, modern building now stood. After waiting to be served, guests were escorted into the large dining hall. Booths for couples lined the back wall. Booths for four to six people were along the left wall, and large private dining booths/rooms lined the wall on the right. Away at the back of the hall a large open-hearth fireplace capable of roasting as many as six full-sized hogs could be roasted at once. Three long, family-style dining tables ran from the back to the front. There, meals were cooked in the open hearth by a half dozen cooks. The ceiling and walls were decorated to look like the inside of a giant log cabin with recessed lights and rustic candle chandeliers.

In one of the private dining booths/rooms Alan Conferra and five of his staff were enjoying their meals. It was Friday and there was a great deal of nonpolitical, lighthearted conversation. They liked having Alan as their boss, respected him, and he respected them as well. They'd been working together since after the African embassy bombings in 1998 when Alan was told to look for connections between international terrorism and large, nongovernment entities like banks, corporations, historic and even royal families, and the like.

It was a family-style dinner. Chesapeake crab cakes, New England corn chowder, duck sausage with boiled greens, Applewood and hickory roasted goose with apple chutney, rhubarb pie, and, of course, drinks later. (It was Washington, DC, of course!). A waiter who was carrying a large wooden tray with the roasted goose stopped to let Senator Henderson pass. Everyone stood for a moment, but he just smiled, told them to sit down, and he joined them. It wasn't the first time he'd met with Alan's staff, but it was the first—and long overdue—time that he'd met with them outside of the office.

Jerry smiled as he was sitting down, and with his South Carolina accent politely asked, "Do y'all mind if I join you tonight?"

No one objected, and it was clear the staff was excited at the request. Alan had dined with the senator many times, but was always happy to share his company. Over the past decade the two men had seen a great deal of world history together, and while the distance of his position was still there sometimes, Senator Henderson was also a true comrade to Alan.

The goose was served, and another waiter brought dining ware for the senator.

"Well, it's good to see you all tonight," the senator said. "I have to admit, though, I'm afraid we're not just bumping into each other. I had to track y'all down, and damned glad I did. This place is wonderful! I was here one time for a pig roast, and I'm telling you it was the best thing I've had outside of home."

Everyone stopped eating and waited for the senator to be settled. Even after his plate had been loaded they waited out of respect for him and curiosity at his appearance. Some felt they were about to be let go, but generally they all knew something was wrong. Senator Henderson had a reputation of being a friendly man, but he was a ranking senator, and this meeting was a first for them, so they were concerned. He saw it.

"Ladies and gentlemen, you can all relax. Nothing's wrong. You're doing a fantastic job, and you probably deserve pay raises for surviving the hours that Alan makes you work."

Everyone laughed.

"Yeah, well...forget it. Ya ain't gettin' raises."

Everyone laughed again—except Alan.

"What's up, sir?" he asked.

"Dammit, Alan! I don't even have a drink yet. All right, everybody go ahead and eat. Alan here's gonna brief me on this concert thing down in Miami."

They'd all seen it on the news. Terrorists had tried to use a custom-made biological weapon to attack tens of thousands of people at a concert in Miami. Local authorities had stopped them, and much of the action was caught on camera. The incident had succeeded in spreading mass fear through a huge volume of people, but the direct threat was stopped, and the games would go on...that was what the public knew. Alan and his staff had sat in on the last Intelligence Committee hearing of the day, and they knew more.

"Sir, given the public nature of where we are, perhaps we should discuss this at the office?"

"Nonsense, Alan. I'm sure you can brief me without giving away national security secrets."

Only two people other than the senator were hungry enough and comfortable enough to eat. Everyone else waited and listened to the conversation.

"Fine, sir. Last night at a hip hop concert in Miami a massive biological terrorist attack was stopped. According to the local police some 35,000 people were almost exposed to a biological weapon that was developed in New York."

Senator Henderson stopped eating. "Damn."

"Yes, sir. No doubt about that. The attack was foiled mostly by a special covert operations unit that we will have to discuss in more detail at the office. Officially local police handled it. This is all public knowledge or will be by the end of the weekend. That's the general story, sir. The nuts and bolts are a bit uglier. Are you sure you want to hear that part now?"

"Come on, Alan, let's have it—warts and all."

"Fine, sir. The bio-weapon was developed by Ajax Medical Research, and the attack was launched by the leaders of Ajax Medical in conjunction with the founders of Defender Security. I should also point out that Ajax Medical Research and Defender Security have been involved in several other events all leading up to this one. Again, this is information that the public will be finding out very shortly. A division of Ajax Medical Research called the Terrafirst Technologies initiated and funded an attack on the an embassy in Switzerland, the attack on Erwin Zimmermann's home in Germany, and the attack on a Trucial Energy oil platform in the North Sea. They tried to blow up a dam in Eastern Europe. Oh, and they tried to prevent the printing of the first euro notes in Belgium as well."

"Busy people. Anything else?" Senator Henderson wasn't confused, but things weren't adding up. "Why did they attack the embassies and other places? How are they related to Miami other than all from this one branch of Ajax Medical Research?"

One of Alan's staff answered. "Senator, it appears that most of Ajax Medical Research had no idea what was going on, and the Terrafirst Technologies, branch, department, whatever we call it, they were creating all these attacks to drum up a need for increased need high-level private security. Ultimately, they needed Defender Security to get the contract to protect the concerts and special events all around the world; otherwise their plan was doomed to fail. That's all it was—just drumming up a market for their fake security company product."

"They took over two embassies, an oil platform, and held a rich guy hostage all to get...you can't be serious."

"It is what happened, sir. The entire thing is crazy, but they were crazy people. For me and this team, math is logic. You see logic in politics, and with all due respect, sir, most people would agree that's a special kind of crazy. These people saw their entire plan as logical. In the end, logic is what works, and their plan came very, very close to working."

Alan's staff were more comfortable now, and regular dining had resumed. Senator Henderson ate as well. A few minutes after the summary briefing, he paused and asked Alan for some clarity on part of the conspiracy. "Again, to be clear, we think that only a few in Ajax Medical Research knew what was going on, only a few people in the Terrafirst Technologies knew what was going on, and that only a few at Defender Security knew what was going on...yet they almost managed to pull it off?"

Mouth full or not, Alan was driven to answer his boss immediately. "Yes, sir." He swallowed. "The intelligence community is reporting that you have it correct. Ajax Medical is an enormous international company with tens of thousands of employees. The Terrafirst Technologies is a technology development entity also with thousands of employees, and Defender Security's involvement seems to be with just its founder and a few others. Were it to be the case that all these people knew and were actively taking part in the attacks there's no doubt that secrets could not have been kept, and equally no doubt that if secrets were kept, they'd have been far more successful."

Then Alan leaned in to whisper to the senator. "Sir, we can go over the really bad things later in a secure location, but I think you should know that this biological attack, it was aimed to create a global pandemic. They were literally trying to wipe out all of mankind. Most of the people at the Terrafirst Technologies didn't have the big picture, but the leaders..." Alan sighed and paused before continuing. "They had a vaccine to stop the virus, but they were keeping it for themselves. We came very close to an Armageddon here."

Jerry Henderson had had these moments before. He was one of the few on the planet who had been involved in near-Armageddon situations; too many near-Armageddon situations. He wished that it would be better to let mankind know how close they were to obliteration. Maybe then people would be better to each other. Quieting that wish was the reality he knew: the closer people come to their mortality, the less humanely people behave.

Alan and his staff ate well and enjoyed the rest of their meal. Senator Jerry Henderson looked like he did, but it was the disingenuous appearance of a well-seasoned businessman and professional politician that masked his reality. Since he'd come to Washington he'd seen so many Biblical-sized tragedies that he should have become used to it. *Armageddon* was a word he heard annually if not several times a year now, but he wasn't used to it. No one ever could or should be comfortable with it.

***

11/1/2000

Jim Smith's last contract with Defender Security ended three months earlier, long before the company's leaders' involvement in the Miami Olympic Games attack. For years the pay had been large, and his personal expenses were low, so he wasn't in dire need of money. He was bored, devastatingly bored, and he needed to be working again. Spycraft is not something that is done eight hours a day. It's a lifestyle—one he'd lived and enjoyed for years—but since his last contract, and since the demise of Defender Security, he was desperately restless.

Luckily the number of high-level "security"/private military companies (PMC) had been increasing since the end of Operation Desert Storm. After Defender Security collapsed in the wake of the Miami attack, most of its former employees—like Jim—were getting scooped up by other PMCs. For most, this would seem like an increase in job competition, but Jim had been privately called to work independently for a wealthy businessman in Germany, Erwin Zimmermann.

Standing in front of the Zimmermann *Schloss*, Jim Smith waited until exactly 7:59 a.m. to press the button next to the front door. As if he'd been standing by the front door waiting to be called, a servant immediately opened the door.

"Good morning. I have an appointment with *Herr* Zimmermann. My name is Jim Smith."

"Yes, sir. You are expected. Please follow me," responded the servant.

They passed through the large central foyer, over the white marble floor with black diamond-shaped inserts. All over the walls were large classical paintings with frames that matched the gold-gilded, French-style furniture. Jim followed the servant up the stairs, under the portrait of Emperor Fran Josef, and to the library where Erwin Zimmermann had his office.

After opening the tall doors, the servant announced Jim, motioned for him to enter, and then left himself. Erwin was working at his desk, surrounded by computer screens and a phone with at least four lines blinking.

"Good morning, Mr. Smith. You're very punctual. I like that."

Jim only knew that *Herr* Zimmermann was interested in a career, high-level security official. Often that meant a body guard or someone who was more Special Forces experienced. Few people ever put out want ads for former spies. As such, he presented himself in the manner of a former military man. His stature was more disciplined. His speech was simpler, more polite, and respectful as if he were at a military drill sans uniform.

"Yes, sir. Thank you, sir."

Erwin stood, shook Jim's hand, and motioned to a chair in front of his desk while sitting back down in his own. "Please, sit down."

"I prefer to stand for now—if that's acceptable."

"Yes, of course it is. It shows that you are a man who seeks to be respected, and who respects my office."

Jim didn't reply. He merely stood with his feet apart and hands clasped in front at his beltline. Erwin sat upright and stared at him for a moment. He deliberately paused to create an uncomfortable silence, and see how Jim would react. There was no reaction.

"Tell me, Mr. Smith, why are you here?"

"Sir, your office requested this meeting. I can only expect that I have unique skills for which you see a need."

"Very correct, Mr. Smith." Erwin paused again before continuing. "Earlier this year I was visited by consultants and leaders of various firms who all felt that security should be increased here in my home. I declined all the offers. Later, there was an incident here, and people were killed. I've since learned that the entire incident was staged by your former employer as part of a larger plot. Do you have any knowledge of these events?"

"I'm afraid I do, sir."

"Tell me what you know." Erwin deliberately chose his words to be a command and not a polite request. There was more than a fair amount of ill will regarding the attack on his home.

Jim answered as if he were giving a military after-action report to a commanding officer. He was playing his part well. "Sir, without compromising professional privacy I can only say that you were approached by an Austrian man from a private military contracting service that I once worked for, and by an Englishman from a different private security service. Both saw your position as vulnerable to high crime threats, and offered their services. Almost six months ago, several armed people broke into this estate, and they held you and your staff hostage. They were later killed in a remarkably executed rescue that was broadcast on live television all around the world. Last month it was revealed that my former employer was involved in financing that incident in an effort to increase international demand for high-end, high-profile security services. My former employer's plan succeeded in that objective and was able to get a lucrative contract to provide security services at a concert in Miami last month, and it turned out that my former employer was actually behind a larger and deadlier biological weapon attack on that concert."

Erwin never flinched. Still sitting upright, he asked, "Why are you here?"

"Sir, I'm here either because you need a bodyguard or several, or you need something special investigated. Given that there are tens of thousands of better bodyguards available now that Defender Security is out of business, I suspect it's not as a bodyguard. I can do a security assessment, but it won't be any more remarkable than one many others would provide. Therefore, you've most likely sought me out for a special investigation of some sorts."

Erwin half-smiled. "Very good, Mr. Smith. Now sit down."

Jim half-smiled back and sat down obediently. The military bearing act was over. It was time for Jim to be the spook-the spy that he really was.

"Jim, if I may call you that, the people who attacked me...the two leaders demanded that I give them codes and access a secret digital network, a network they believed wealthy people like myself use to make secret deals and profit where people of lesser means cannot. No such digital network exists. There is a large network of people, who have means, and we do speak with each other, and we do profit. It's through this network of clients, associates...friends by which you were recommended and called here today."

Jim was stoic now, and attentive. "I understand, and I've often worked with the community you've just described. What is it you'd like me to look into?"

"Good. Good. My attackers, only the leaders wanted access to this fictional digital network. The others searched my home for something else: some sort of document or thing. All that I know is it was old, valuable, and very important. They made it sound pivotal somehow. I don't have anything like that here. We have fine things, but few valuable documents. This office operates with digital funds in digital markets. Look around and you see that this is a library with books and books everywhere. They came with the *Schloss* when I bought it, and I've only read a few. They are very old, and surely valuable, but when these people came in, and they searched everywhere, they ignored the books. These are the most valuable documents here."

Jim stood up while Erwin was speaking. He walked around the library and saw the walls lined with texts that were easily hundreds of years old. Surely some were priceless. What could they have been looking for?

"Do you have any more information, sir?"

"All that I have for you directly is their names, and you can probably get more from the local police, but..." Erwin rose and walked across the library to stand closer to Jim.

"Jim, as I said, there is a network of clients, associates, and these people are often friends. Like coworkers anywhere or friends everywhere, we do look out for each other. There's an American with whom I used to work. He's moved out of the financial sector and into politics, but we still see each other from time to time. We have several common colleagues as well—a community as you described it. I have another friend, an Englishman. These two friends of mine both have roots in the finance world as I do, but they also have strong ties to their respective intelligence communities. Given our common background, when certain events happen, we tend to look at those events through an economic, a financial lens."

Erwin's eye contact with Jim bordered on impolite staring, and he paused to let his words sink in to Jim. Smith stared back and nodded that he understood.

"Sir," Jim asked, "why aren't your friends looking into this? Clearly they have access to a wider range of assets. I don't work for anyone right now. I still have friends of my own as well, but nothing on the level that you're describing."

"Jerry Henderson—Senator Jerry Henderson—is on a committee that oversees the American intelligence agencies. He tells me that while most of the intelligence agencies have their own departments that look into economic espionage and so forth, they are terribly underfunded, and otherwise dismissed in favor of more traditional intelligence gathering. Jerry has taken it upon himself to put together a team that is looking at a slew of events that he believes are linked financially. Even though the thwarted attack in Miami has demonstrated that this is a sound form of intelligence gathering, he's met with a great deal of bureaucracy, and is getting only a taciturn of contribution from the intelligence community."

"And I fit into this...how?"

"You will work for me, and you, and me, and my friends, and your friends are going to find out who is financing all of these attacks and why they are doing it."

After his years of government service Jim knew all too well the intractable power of Washington, DC, bureaucracy—especially the intelligence community bureaucrats. Erwin clearly had the means of putting together a team to look into an intelligence issue like this, and after being held hostage as part of that 'issue' he certainly had motive. The Miami attack had in fact recently revealed a series of financially related attacks, so it was the time; opportunity was at hand. There was some logic to it all—more than he'd seen in other intelligence missions and jobs he'd had.

"*Herr* Zimmermann, is this a personal vendetta? I should tell you right now: I don't deal with those kinds of matters. Or maybe it's the money? Do you think someone is stealing from you? Do you see this as some sort of way of making money?"

"No, Jim. It's only personal in that my involvement was compelled upon me, and it's not about money for me. My wealth comes honestly, and is very secure. Should a larger economic connection exist, those who have the ability to detect and stop it, well, it's more of a duty for someone like myself. I'm not sure you would understand. Americans often have a difficult time grasping this particular sense of obligation."

Jim damned well knew duty, having been to the worst places on the planet while serving his country, but he masked any indignation well. Still, Erwin knew he had to explain it better to Jim.

"Mr. Smith, Jim, you are standing in a grand estate that was built hundreds of years before your country even existed. Nations, even empires, have come and gone during its existence. It was built by Baron..." Despite his trained efforts to hide his expression, Erwin could see that Jim Smith, an American of average heritage, didn't understand. He paused and reimagined how to explain things to Jim.

"Sir?"

"Jim, tell me what does the word *noble* mean to you?"

"I believe that being noble is doing the right thing, looking out for others, and if you mean nobility as a people, the common perception is a group of people usually born into money, power, and no check or balance to keep them accountable for their actions."

"Exactly! You Americans don't have centuries of nobility. You've had plenty of aristocrats, but no royalty; no noblemen. All around the globe civilizations have had people—as you say—who inherit wealth and power, and often through a title. Not in America. But you are terribly wrong about accountability. A nobleman is someone who is obligated to be noble. We call it noblesse oblige. Your culture rebelled because your King George failed to meet his noble obligations to you. Since then, you've had no experience with nobility."

Jim nodded and listened carefully; respectfully. Erwin continued. "I am not born to wealth and power. My father was a railroad worker, and my position comes of my own making. I am no aristocrat, and I am only married to nobility. However, I choose to live my life nobly. You asked if this was about my money. It is not. I was forced into this affair the night they held my staff and me hostage. Now that I am involved, I have a noble obligation to see it through, lest others fall victim as well. I am obligated to see this through now, and I will do so. Obligated, Jim."

Jim was impressed. Erwin was right that it was hard for someone with an American heritage to understand that a noble was someone who acted with nobility. It went against the grain of revolutionary independence, but he did understand Erwin. More than anything he understood that Erwin had conviction, and that was all Jim really needed to know.

"Yes, sir. Do you have any idea where you'd like me to start looking into this?"

"I'd like you to start wherever you see fit. I'll be paying your expenses, but the research, as I'll call it, is your charge. I might suggest, however, that sometime soon you pay a visit to Senator Henderson's office in Washington, DC. He might be willing to introduce you to his team, and perhaps they can give you some more valuable details. I'd like you to share all of your information with his office as well as Lord Tryphine at Tryphine Banking House in London. I'll notify him to expect you, but you two will have to work out where, when, and how."

"And the terms of my contract?" Jim asked.

Erwin was somewhat surprised. It was a fair question and to be expected.

"What did you have in mind, Jim?"

Jim had no idea what terms to request. He'd assumed a lucrative offer would have been made, but it seemed now like Erwin hadn't given it any thought. The German might be working out of a sense of righteous obligation, but he wasn't.

"Let's say $100,000 now, and another $100,000 if I find out that these incidents are connected, and another $100,000 if I find out who is behind them?"

Erwin, smiled. He hadn't made his wealth by throwing around money. He was fairly frugal if anything, but he also knew the value of things.

"Five hundred thousand for all three, but you pay your own expenses, and you must be dutiful in sharing your information not just with myself, but also Lord Tryphine and Senator Henderson's office."

Jim was very pleased. He fought back a half-million-dollar smile and shook Erwin's hand. "Thank you, sir. We have an agreement."

"Very good. Very good, Jim." Erwin led him to the door out of the library. "Manfred, my secretary, will see to your needs. If you need travel arrangements or assistance with anything, contact him."

The door opened, and Manfred stepped out from behind his desk. He and Jim shook hands as formal introductions were made. Then Manfred handed Jim a briefcase.

"Inside you'll find a laptop computer with all the information that's been gathered so far. Much of that is of a highly classified nature so be careful not to get caught with it, or to let it fall into the wrong hands. There's $100,000 in dollars as well, and a credit card with the remaining $400,000. Bank account information to the card is in the case. There is also a cellphone. It is not secure. Will there be anything else?"

"Yes, thank you, Manfred. I'll need a flight to London, and if you could set up a meeting with Lord Tryphine I would appreciate it."

"I'll see to it, sir."

Jim said his goodbye to Erwin, and then Manfred walked him to the front door.

"*Herr* Zimmermann's car will take you to the airport directly, and I'll call you with the flight information before you arrive."

"Manfred?" Jim asked, "what's it like working for *Herr* Zimmermann?"

"Mr. Smith, *Herr* Zimmermann is one of the finest men I've ever known. You'll come to see this. There are not many like him. A capable man with integrity, values. He respects others even when they don't respect him; even when he is disrespected. You have fallen into good company, Mr. Smith. I'm sure you know how utterly rare this is in the world. You should be very grateful."

"I am, Manfred. I am, but such men really are rare, and in my line of work I'm skeptical by nature. All this seems a lot like revenge or some European-style vendetta to me."

Manfred stopped at the front door. He shook Jim's hand once again, more firmly this time. Then he stared him square in the eyes.

"Mr. Smith, people like you and me and others, we would seek revenge. *Herr* Zimmermann sees a duty. It's something else entirely."

"He's paying me a lot of money, Manfred; his own money. In my experience, people who make that kind of investment want some sort of palpable return."

Manfred laughed. "It is a great deal of money, Mr. Smith. There are lots of people in your field who would do what he asks for money. He chose you because you don't work for money."

Jim laughed. "The hell I don't!"

Still firmly holding Jim's hand, Manfred smiled back. "No, sir. You don't. If you did, you'd have loaded your pockets with Iraqi gold a decade ago."

Jim's face went ashen, and his hands sweat instantly. He let go of Manfred's.

"That's right, Mr. Smith. *Herr* Zimmermann knows about the Iraqi billions you helped bring out of Kuwait. That's why you were chosen. You do things for the right reasons—not for the money. You're only a mercenary by trade, not by choice. Do you know what that truck is worth today? Your $500,000 is a fraction of a percent of a percent of that truck, and the thing you're looking into could be a hundred times bigger. No, sir, you work for the same reasons *Herr* Osterman does, and for the right reason I work for him."

Manfred opened the door wide, and stepped back to indicate that it was time for Jim to leave. Unable to hide his shock, Jim headed out to the waiting Mercedes limousine.

***

11/6/2000

Monday morning is a busy time of the week at practically every business in the world. Jim Smith had made an appointment to meet with Lord Tryphine at Tryphine Banking House immediately after his meeting with Erwin Zimmermann. He'd flown to London, spent the weekend around town, and at 8 a.m. local time he stepped through the large doors to the ancient bank. Jim was no stranger to large institutions, historic places, and centers of wealth and power, but it always amazed him. The marble décor at Tryphine House, designed and built hundreds of years earlier, had done so for generations, and continued even with Jim's colorful history.

After checking in with the security desk and getting the obligatory visitor pass to wear, Jim was escorted by four men to the elevator. Three followed him up to Lord Tryphine's floor. There they were met by four more security personnel, but the first three headed back down the elevator. They walked through large rooms lined with ornate desks and ranks of executive assistants. At the end, they were introduced to Lord Tryphine's executive assistant, who then escorted Jim into the core of the international institution.

"Mr. Smith is here to see you, sir," announced the assistant.

Terrence Tryphine was sitting at a small writing desk along the wall on the right side of the massive room. His executive desk was near the back windows overlooking the Thames. The rest of the room was filled with chairs and small tables. There was a wet bar opposite the writing desk on the left wall. The floor was covered by a custom rug that bore a Nicolosi globular projection of the Earth, and nations as they were in 1794.

Lord Tryphine finished writing while everyone stood in silence. When he completed his thought he stood up, put his hands behind his back, and said, "Thank you, everyone. Mr. Smith and I will need some time alone if you please."

As everyone left, Jim walked over and introduced himself formally. The two men shook hands and sat down on a pair of dark leather, high-back chairs.

"Mr. Smith, Erwin and I have spoken at length about your employment. I'm glad to see you involved in this matter."

Jim maintained an un-telling appearance and thanked him.

"Well then, let's get right to it, shall we?"

Jim nodded, and Lord Tryphine motioned to a file sitting on the table between the two men.

"This is a brief on what Erwin and I have regarding a number of terrorist attacks around the globe over the past few years. It's a great deal of information—some connected, some of it not connected. Truly, the failed attack on the concert in Miami was a watershed moment for us. I know some people in my government, and they have confirmed that the attack there—and the attacks that led up to it, including the attack on my friend *Herr* Zimmermann—were funded by Ajax Medical Research. Even your old company, Defender Security, received a large income from Ajax Medical Research."

Jim was not proud to have been part of Defender Security. He was never eager to be a "private contractor," or security guard, or a mercenary. After it was revealed that Defender Security leaders were involved in terrorist attacks, he was embarrassed to have their name on his resume. His face hid it, but Lord Tryphine knew the shame was there. No one could have been proud of that relationship.

"Jim, if I may call you that, Ajax and Defender Security were largely self-sufficient, but they did help each other out. I've had some of the people here at Tryphine House take a look at their public records, and we've done a little more than that as well. What we've found is that both those businesses had a great many common business interests. It wasn't unexpected as their leaders were close, and they were working hand in hand toward their own ends."

Lord Tryphine reached out and opened the file to show Jim where the common interests he had just described could be found.

"These highlighted ones are what we've found the most interesting. It seems highly unlikely that so many small and medium businesses from the Persian Gulf region all shared both medical and security relationships with Ajax Medical and Defender Security, respectively. Wouldn't you agree?"

Jim looked at the yellow-highlighted list. None of them seemed like they would be doing business with medical researchers like Ajax Medical Research, and certainly not high-end security like Defender Security. He saw a shoe manufacturer from Dubai, a restaurant in Kuwait, a publisher in Oman, a cosmetic supplier in Saudi Arabia, and at least twenty others. None of them would be doing business with either Ajax Medical or Defender Security, let alone both.

"I certainly see, sir."

"Good! Excellent. We thought so as well, and inquiries were made. We've found that payments from these companies often preceded terrorist events and then were duplicated afterwards."

"Half now, half on delivery," Jim interjected.

"Very good, Jim! That's as far as we've gone in following the money. There is another thing, however."

Jim closed the file and gave Lord Tryphine his undivided attention.

"This 'thing' that so many people look for during these attacks, none of us have the faintest idea who wants it or why."

"What do we know about it?" Jim asked.

"We've heard it's a document. We believe it's an old, physical document—not digital. It could be a few joined documents as well."

"Where are the places we know that people were looking for these documents? Is there a correlation there?"

Lord Tryphine sat back in his chair and stared at Jim as he pondered, nodding gently. While he did so, there was a knock at the door, and his apprentice entered.

"Mr. Conferra is here to see you, sir," the assistant announced.

"Ah!" Lord Tryphine cried out as he swiftly rose to his feet. "Alan is here! Perhaps Alan can add some insight to your question, Jim."

Alan stepped through the door. His three security escorts and Terrence's executive assistant left them alone.

"Good morning, sir. My apologies for being late. London traffic is something to behold."

Jim stood in his chair as well, and remembered having seen the man before, but couldn't recognize him. As he was shaking hands with Lord Tryphine, Alan turned and saw Jim. He shook Jim's hand and introduced himself.

"Have we met before?" Alan asked.

Lord Tryphine answered for both Alan and Jim. "You were both involved with that whole Saddam gold truck incident."

Alan and Jim both looked at Lord Tryphine, trying in vain to hide their surprise that he knew about that top-secret event in 1991. Though they had done nothing wrong—and in fact had gone out of their way to have done everything right—they felt like thieves caught in the act. It made Lord Tryphine laugh.

"It's all right, gentlemen. I've known for some time. Jerry, Senator Henderson and I are old friends and we discussed the matter at length. Your secret is safe. In fact, I'm relieved to finally be able to commend you both on how top-notch you handled the entire affair. Well done, both of you. Very well done."

Everyone sat down and smiled with relief and comfort that a multibillion-dollar secret was no longer a secret. Alan and Jim exchanged smiles and shook their heads in milder disbelief.

"Alan, Jim was just asking if there is a connection between the places where our friends keep looking for these documents. Perhaps you can add to this? I'm sure I've been informed, but the specifics escape me for the moment."

"Certainly, sir. Let me see here for a moment." Alan put his briefcase on the tea table between all three men, opened it, and pulled out a folder.

"Okay...February 13, 2000, the Belgian embassy was taken over. Rescued hostages reported that three of their captors were looking for something and rummaging through the entire building. March 17, 2000, was the attack on Erwin Zimmermann, where several of the terrorists searched his house for digital access codes and some sort of old documents. June 25, 2000, terrorists seized an oil platform in the North Sea. Two hostages were found hiding in their lockers. One reported that the leader of the terrorists spent a great deal of time in the computer center and searched all the filing cabinets for something. August 27, 2000, terrorists took over an amusement park in Europe. Again, freed hostages report that one of the terrorists was searching filing cabinets and desks. September 5, 2000, terrorists with ties to Ajax Medical Research...by the way, these are all attacks tied to Ajax Medical and the now defunct Defender Security...September 5, terrorists tried to blow up a dam in Eastern Europe. One terrorist was captured, Ronald Van De Burgh. He reports that people were looking for a document—some sort of map or treaty or agreement."

Jim was intrigued. He'd heard of some of the attacks, but not all. He really wanted to know more about Van De Burgh. To have one of the bad guys in custody meant that there was a monumental opportunity for intelligence gathering—his kind of intelligence gathering.

"What do we know about Van De Burgh?" Jim asked.

Alan reached into the briefcase on the table once more. Again he pulled out a folder and began reading.

"Ronald Van De Burgh, college dropout from the Netherlands. He was active in environmental groups. It looks like he got messed up with the wrong crowd. He's admitted to being involved in the Trucial Energy oil platform attack, and the attack on the dam in Eastern Europe. He's cooperating with authorities in exchange for a reduced sentence. Instead of life in prison he gets five years."

"Where is he now?" Jim asked.

"Jim," Lord Tryphine replied, "he was grabbed in Hungary by Interpol. There are disagreements on what to do with him. Right now it would be very hard to find him. There are governments and intelligence agencies working hard to keep him a secret."

"By the way," Alan interjected, "there was also an attack on the first printing of the euro. That was September 13, 2000, right after Van De Burgh was grabbed and before the Miami concert attack in October."

"Okay," Jim said. "We've got multiple terrorist attacks financially related, and at the top of the food chain are a list of small and medium businesses in the Persian Gulf. Aside from being financially related the attacks are related because in most of them the terrorists were looking for something. Right? Right. Now what's this business about a Trucial Energy connection?"

"That's Alan's idea," Lord Tryphine answered as he motioned for Alan to continue.

"I think these attacks aren't just related by money, and the search for some document, but that they have something to do with Trucial Energy. Jim, do you remember the civil war in Rwanda?"

Jim remembered it all too clearly. It was one of the most horrific places he'd ever been. Ironically, it was also his first assignment with Defender Security. "Rwanda" to him meant nightmares—very red nightmares.

"Can't say I remember it well, but yes, I remember it."

"Do you remember the African embassy bombings a year later?" Alan asked.

"Yes—what's the connection?"

"Just before civil war broke out in Rwanda a huge gold deposit was discovered to the west. Trucial Energy began buying up land between the region and Dar es Salaam in Tanzania to the east. The Rwanda civil war happened in a flash—"

Jim interrupted him. "It happened when the leaders of two countries were assassinated at the same time, and Hutu and Tutsi tribes went to war. It was a slaughter. I was there, Alan. It made Saddam's Highway of Death where you and I were look like a fucking postcard."

Alan and Lord Tryphine paused. It was clear Rwanda was a sore spot for Jim.

"My point, Jim, was that the civil war was quick, and as soon as a new government was established, one of the first things they did was grant Trucial Energy rights to build a rail line through Rwanda. When the African embassy bombings happened, they happened just after 10 a.m. They happened right after a Trucial Energy conference meeting started. A Trucial Energy group at the US embassy in Dar es Salaam was on the line with a Trucial Energy group in Rwanda, and another Trucial Energy group at the US embassy in Nairobi. The one in Rwanda had a bomb threat called in, but was not attacked. Funding for the attacks on the two embassies led to a familiar list of sources: the list highlighted in yellow that you saw earlier."

Jim nodded and his lower lip rose slightly. Then Alan continued.

"That means we have attacks financed by the same people for an attack on the Trucial Energy group in Dar es Salaam, an attack on the Trucial Energy group in Nairobi, an attack on the Trucial Energy oil rig, and possibly other earlier 'accidents' like the sinking of the Trucial Energy tanker in 1994 off the shores of the Orkney Islands; maybe others."

"Jim, what do you think of all this?" Lord Tryphine asked.

"I'm not sure yet, sir. The Trucial Energy thing could be something, or it could just be that they're so big that a certain percentage of bad things are gonna happen to them. The document question could just be that terrorists like to loot when they've taken someplace, or it could be something. The money trail is definitely the most interesting. I can see why an accountant and a banker would be so interested in that as well. It would naturally make flags go up for anyone in your fields, but I think you've gone as far as you ever will with that."

Alan and Lord Tryphine both asked at the same time, "Why? Why is that?"

"Hawala," Jim answered. The other men looked at each other, neither understanding. Jim continued. "It's hawala. Hawala's an old technique of moving money around. It's very popular in third world countries, Africa, the Mideast—even the Knights Templar did it. What happens is a guy wants to send his family or friend some money in London. He goes into a shoe repair shop in Oman or wherever, tells them what he wants to do. Then he gives the shoe repair guy the money. The shoe repair guy takes a cut, a commission, a bribe, whatever you want to call it. Then the shoe repair guy calls his friend or cousin or brother who lives in London. The shoe repair guy says, 'Hey, Achmed just gave me $100. Achmed's brother is going to come in your store and get it. When he does, I'll send you the money, and your cut.' There's no record keeping. There's no need. If someone breaks the chain there's hell to pay from the others. In this case, someone in the Persian Gulf—most likely—is going around and sending money through hawala to fund these attacks. There's no way to track it down beyond what you have."

Alan and Lord Tryphine looked at each other. They'd heard of such practices, but the idea that it was why the money trail ended had escaped both of them and their staffs.

"Look, gentlemen," Jim continued, "I'm happy to look into this further. There very well could be something here. Do you have any suggestions or ideas on where and what you'd like me to do specifically? I have my own already."

Lord Tryphine answered first. "Jim, it's as you said, we're in the financial business, and we've likely gone as far as our professions permit. We've also been blocked and dismissed at every opportunity by the intelligence community. I speak with friends of mine in the community about this, and they see nothing happening. Alan gives briefings to your FBI, CIA, and so forth every week, and they see nothing. You know what you're doing. All we can do is be here to help you at this step."

Alan followed suit. "Absolutely, Jim. If there's anything we can do, just drop me a line. I can be reached through Senator Henderson's office. *Herr* Zimmermann and Lord Tryphine have said as much as well."

Jim nodded in appreciation. "Thank you, both. I would like to meet with this Ronald Van De Burgh that's in custody. If there's anything you can do to make that happen, please let me know. I'll be reporting to *Herr* Zimmermann every week, and he's asked me to cc you on all of those as well."

Lord Tryphine rose, and the others did so as well. "Right then," he said. "We'll let you get on with what you do. Good luck, Jim."

Alan offered his well-wishes also. The three men shook hands, and Jim left the room. Alan and Lord Tryphine had other matters to discuss. They remained behind.

***

4/13/2001

Jim had spent almost half a year traveling the globe in search of intelligence information for his patrons. Most of his travel had been in the Middle East and Europe, but he'd also made a few visits to South America, and had just arrived from Rwanda only an hour earlier. Now he was in Washington, DC, for a meeting with Alan Conferra.

The Cherry Blossom Festival was just about over. Every year trees that had been sent by the emperor of Japan as a sign of peace bloomed pink petals all around the city's tidal basin. Jim took the opportunity to walk along the basin before the meeting. Pink petals floated all around like slow-moving snowflakes without the cold temperatures. The water was covered with pale pink dots, and a flowery, cherry scent perfumed the air. Residents took the moment for granted, but Jim saw the moment as one of perfection; perfect peace. As his walk ended, and he headed toward Capitol Hill, his moment ended, and he was reminded of why he was there.

He headed up the steps, through security, and on toward Senator Jerry Henderson's office (his main office was off the northeast corner of Capitol Hill at the Hart Office Building, but like all members of Congress he maintained a small office in the Capitol Building itself). Even though it wasn't even 9 a.m., the area swarmed with tourists, lawmakers, staff, and the ever-present lobbyists. Jim laughed to himself for a moment as he recognized how easy it was to see which was which and who was who. As he did so a remaining cherry tree petal fell from his hair, and for just a split second his mind flashed with the peaceful morning imagery.

Coming from the Senate side of the building, Alan entered the rotunda and the two men made eye contact immediately. They shook hands and exchanged pleasantries, and right away Alan began to motion that Jim follow him out of the rotunda.

"Here, take these." Alan handed Jim three identification cards, two with his picture already on them and two different lanyards with additional identification and bar codes on them. "Don't say another word—just follow me."

They left the rotunda and headed left. Then they went through the Small Senate Rotunda and down a flight of stairs. They passed through the rebuilt Hall of Statues. At the end of a hall, Alan waved one of his ID badges across a scanner, and a door opened. Inside, a security guard checked a different ID that both Jim and Alan were carrying. They passed through another door and then walked down an average-looking stairwell. At the bottom of the stairwell, there was another hallway. The first door they came to was a nondescript fire door with a security camera on top. Alan swiped another ID card, and Jim had to do the same before a beep sounded and the door was unlocked. Inside, there was another anteroom and two more security guards—this time watching from another room through a glass wall. Alan and Jim signed a log book and showed their lanyards, and they were instructed to remove any and all electronic devices, including phones and digital watches. Both men placed their personal effects in a tray, and a door opened to another stairwell. This time the hallway was covered with gray carpet on the floor and walls. Cubicle walls were placed perpendicular to the walls in the middle of the hallway, making it impossible to walk straight through it. Finally, at the end, three security guards rose from desks on the left, front, and right of Alan and Jim. Again they signed a log book, showed their lanyards, and finally were allowed into the last room.

The House of Representatives and the Senate both had committees of elected officials who were charged with overseeing the budget and operations of all the nation's different intelligence communities. These select civilians were charged with learning and overseeing the greatest secrets in the world. An equal number of representatives from each party were chosen, and went through rigorous screening before being allowed to hold sway over the intelligence community's leaders. As a matter of avoiding partisanship on key issues this process was normally held in hearings, but—given the above top-secret nature of the issues—standard hearings could not be held. Instead, in 1947 this secret room had been built to prevent eavesdropping. Through the years, it had been upgraded countless times.

"Jim, this is The Bubble. You've heard of it?"

"Yeah, everyone who worked at Langley [the CIA] knew about it, but few have seen it. I expected it to be...different."

"I thought it would be more high-tech, or as decorated as the rest of The Hill, but this is it."

The room was tan in color. There was no decorative trim. Simple acoustic tiles covered the ceiling, and a thick blue carpet covered the floor. Inset lights beamed down a color spectrum that was more like sunlight, and the only interesting part were all the vents in the floor and ceiling. A long table had a dozen seats for members and a seat for the chairperson, and on the other side a half dozen chairs for those who would present their briefings to the members of the Senate.

Alan led the way to Senator Henderson's seat, and pointed to one next to it for Jim.

"This is where I spend just about every morning. The senator simply doesn't have the time to be here for every briefing. Sometimes he's got other meetings or is back home in South Carolina or just can't make it. I've become the de facto sit-in."

Looking around at the setting, Jim pointed out, "This is really something else. It's impressive to be sure, but why all the cloak and dagger this time? I thought we were just going to brief."

"Not today. Today we've got a treat for you—just for you. The other members can know about it, but no one's told them. I've reserved the room for just us."

"Us?"

Alan raised his voice slightly and called toward the door from which they'd just entered. "Would you bring him in, please?"

The door opened. Four men wearing dark windbreakers and carrying Heckler and Kock MP-5 submachine guns entered. There were no characteristic yellow acronyms on their backs to say if they were from the FBI, US Marshals, or anything. A fifth man entered wearing a crumpled black suit, no tie, and handcuffs. Four more men in windbreakers and armed with submachine guns entered before the door was closed. Three loud locks sounded behind them.

"Mr. Smith, I present to you Mr. Ronald Van De Burgh."

The armed men seated Ronald down in front of Alan and Jim. One man then took up a post at each corner while two more stood next to the door, and the remaining two stood on Van De Burgh's left and right side.

Jim knew it was not the time or place to ask questions about how Van De Burgh came to be there, or who the armed men were or anything of the sort. He simply knew that this was a grand opportunity to gather human intel regarding the curious case of connected terrorist attacks. He looked at Alan, nodding slightly. Alan handed him a manila folder and nodded back

"Mr. Van De Burgh, it says here that you speak English. That's going to help a lot. Do you know who I am?"

Ronald's head sank as he shook his head.

"My name is Jim. I've just been handed your case so I apologize to you if a lot of what we talk about is redundant."

Van De Burgh looked up at Jim mostly in melancholy, but Jim saw a sparkle of indignation in his eyes.

"Have you been treated fairly—food, water? Can I get you anything?"

Van De Burgh looked away.

"Have you been mistreated?"

Van De Burgh looked again at Jim, this time with more attitude.

"What did they do to you, Ronald? You can tell me. It's all right."

Finally Ronald answered, "I don't know why you are doing this to me?! I surrendered to you. I am the one who called you and told you about the Terrafirst Technologies, Defender Security, Ajax Medical! I am the one who helped! Why am I being held?!"

The security guard to Ronald's left "nudged" Ronald's head with the butt of his MP-5. Ronald recoiled, but there was no blood. It wasn't a bad nudge.

Jim let it all happen and looked into the manila folder as it did. When Ronald was settled back, Jim continued. "Ronald, you were bad. People appreciate your coming forward to help stop that attack in Miami. That's why you're alive. You were bad, though. There's a price to be paid for killing those men on the Trucial Energy rig in the North Sea. Wouldn't you agree?"

Ronald, face down, shook his head as if Jim's words had never been spoken. His brain just could not connect them to actual thoughts. It blocked them out.

Jim knew that Ronald had been interrogated countless times. All kinds of techniques had probably been tried on him, and any good intel that was to be found was probably found a long time ago. It was clear just by Ronald's behavior and appearance. He wasn't a man to hold out. Still, he thought, if everything asked had been answered, then it was time to ask something new—something not asked before.

"Okay, Ronald, I'm going to get right to it. It's clear to me that you want to cooperate, and probably have been so far." Jim turned to Alan and asked, "Right?" Then he looked around at the security people and asked the same. "Right, guys?" No one flinched. "Well, I'm sure you have. So here it is; let's ask some new questions. By now we all know you'll answer, you want to answer, and you clearly don't want to be fucked with anymore. So no fucking around this time. You're gonna answer first time, truthfully, and we'll be done here."

Ronald's face floated like a cork on the ocean. One instant he was despondent at the lowest trough of a wave. The next moment he was moved with rage until he crested with a smiling eagerness for vengeance.

Jim started his questions. “The Trucial Energy oil rig job...how did you get your ticket on the helicopter out to the rig?”

“The Terrafirst Technologies—where I worked before—they booked the flight for all of us.”

“Who at the Terrafirst Technologies?”

“I don’t know. It’s like when you get a paycheck from a business. It has the company name on it and someone in accounting...I guess someone in accounting or some administration person; an office assistant maybe. I don’t know.”

Jim leaned forward and put the palms of his hands down on the table in front of Ronald. Then, sympathetically and sincerely he said, “I believe you. I believe you, Ronald. Now, what happened when you and this Davies guy left the rig?”

“Davies told the pilots to take us back to Norway. About a mile in from the coast we were near a small village. Davies told the pilots to land, and they did. We got out, and it flew off. Davies said we should split up, so we did. I saw him head off down a street to the north, and then around a corner, and that’s the last I saw of him.”

“What did you do?”

“I found a hostel, stayed there for the night, and then I caught a ride with two of the people there down to Oslo. Then I headed home to Amsterdam. I drove by work, and there were police everywhere so I went to a café we sometimes went to. Davies was waiting.”

Jim nodded and motioned for him to continue.

“Davies told me about a protest we were going to do at the dam in Hungary, but I knew it wasn’t going to be a protest. That’s when I called the police.” Ronald suddenly became enraged and stood up quickly. “That’s when I did the right thing! That’s when you motherfuckers fucked me over! You motherfuckers! Motherfuckers!”

Without blinking or showing any increase in energy, the two guards next to Ronald each put a hand on his shoulders and shoved him back into his chair. They appeared more annoyed than anything.

Ronald yellowed out one more bitter “Motherfuckers!” and then calmed down. Jim gave him a full minute to regain his composure before he continued.

“Ronald, let’s continue. What were you and Davies looking for on the oil rig?”

“What are you talking about?”

"The two hostages who were rescued told us that you and Davies were looking for something in the computer control room. What was it?"

"There were no hostages. Davies and the others...they killed everyone."

"Yes. There were hostages, Ronald."

Acting like a child, Van De Burgh replied back and demonstrated the naiveté of his age. "No. There were not hostages."

Jim played. "Yes, Ronald, there were."

"No. There were not. Ian killed everyone."

Jim thought about it for a moment before continuing. It was clear to him that Ronald didn't believe that there were, in fact, two survivors of the terrorist attack. "Let's move on then. What can you tell me about the dam job in Eastern Europe—the one where you were caught."

Van De Burgh jumped to his feet again, and was again slammed back into it by his guards.

"I told you! I wasn't caught! I turned myself in! I helped you motherfuckers! Dammit, I helped you!"

Again, Jim had to wait until Ronald calmed down. Then he waited a full extra minute in silence to emphasize the cooldown before continuing.

"What can you tell me about the dam job? Who paid for your train ticket to get to Hungary?"

"Davies paid. He had a Terrafirst Technologies [credit] card. Everything was paid for by the Terrafirst Technologies."

Jim nodded. "Good. Good!" He paused and ruffled through the contents of the manila folder again before continuing. "Oh. Okay, here, um, Ronald, it says here that there's a relationship between The Terrafirst Technologies that was funding these attacks and the Ajax Medical Research. Do you know anything about that?"

Ronald bit his bottom lip as frustration and anger were getting the better of him. "Yes," he answered, and Jim motioned for him to elaborate.

"The day before the protest at the dam—"

Jim interrupted. "The attack. It was a terrorist attack—not a protest."

Ronald looked down and paused. Then he gently nodded in shameful agreement. "The night before the attack on the dam in Hungary, that's when Davies told me. He told me about how the Terrafirst Technologies that we worked for was working off a grant from Ajax Medical Research. I didn't understand why a medical research corporation known around the world would give us grant money. Ian told me about the rest of the Ajax Medical Research plan to do all the other attacks and about the Miami concert attack. I didn't know the specifics of that attack, but I knew something big was going to happen there. That was all I knew then. What they wanted to do was wrong. That's why I tried to turn myself in."

Jim made his face look like it was all news to him, and that he appreciated Ronald's candor.

"Back to the Trucial Energy oil rig," Jim asked. "Were you looking for something? Was Ian?"

"I don't know what he was looking for, but Ian was going through the computers and the filing cabinets. I guess he could have been looking for something." Ronald paused and thought, then added, "Yes, yes. Ian was looking for something. I asked him, and he said to ignore it, but yes, I think he was looking for something important."

Half of the lights in the room went on and then off three times. Alan turned to face the door and asked, "What's up, guys? We're kind of in the middle of something here."

An intercom voice answered back. "Sir, they're locking down the building. Everyone's being evacuated. Not exactly sure what's going on, but procedure calls for all of us to sit tight. I thought you should know."

Alan, Jim, and Ronald looked at each other. Of the two guards next to Ronald, one turned to face the other door and put himself between it and Ronald, and the other put a firm left hand on Ronald's right shoulder. The rest remained frozen.

"Is that all you know?" Alan asked the ceiling.

"Sir, there's a report of an active shooter, another report of a hostage issue, a bomb threat, and a report of another terrorist attack. Whatever is happening upstairs just started. We'll know more in a few minutes when their attention turns from evacuation to dealing with whatever it is."

Jim and Alan looked at each other. Alan spoke first. "This kind of thing happens more often than you'd think, Jim. I think we've already had three bomb threats here this month. I'm sure it's just a precaution. Still, there aren't many places as secure as this one in DC."

"There you have it, Ronald," Jim replied. "This sort of thing happens all the time. Let's continue. Do you have any idea at all what Davies was looking for? Let's play twenty questions: Was it bigger than a breadbox? Is it flat, or square, or round, or maybe it's digital? Could it be—"

Ronald snapped again. This time he banged both fists on the table. "I don't fucking know! Look, motherfuckers, I don't fucking know! He was looking in the computer and in filing cabinets! What the fuck is a breadbox?! I don't fucking know!"

Jim smiled. "Do you know any more words besides *motherfuckers*?" Alan and the guard in the corner farthest from the door snickered. Ronald cocked his head back, faced the ceiling, and rolled his eyes.

"I don't know what he was looking for."

"Fine. Fine, fine," Jim replied, smiling. "Why Trucial Energy? There are hundreds of rigs in the North Sea and thousands around the globe. Why'd you guys go after one of the most remote on the planet? Do you have a grudge against Trucial Energy?"

This time Ronald smiled. "You motherfuckers, just—" He stopped. It wasn't that he felt bad about using profanity, but he knew now that doing so made him look foolish in the eyes of his captors. "You people just don't get it. Trucial Energy is what's wrong with this entire planet! They suck oil from Mother Earth, then burn it—choke our air. They spill it—remember that tanker off the Orkney Islands in '94? They destroyed that entire ecosystem! They rape Mother Earth, and pillage her, and no one can stop them. No one can get in their way. You! You all are just running-dog lackeys of the imperialist cabal that runs the planet, kills the planet, and you don't even know it. How many lives are lost when a tanker spills?! How many homes are destroyed to make way for their pipelines? How many wars are fought for that black sludge?! That oil comes from the ground and pollutes everything it touches. It pollutes people's minds. It pollutes souls! It's evil! That motherfucking shit is the root of all evil!"

Alan and Jim couldn't help but sit back, listen to Ronald's diatribe, and shake their heads in disbelief. Jim deliberately rolled his eyes so that Ronald could see him do it.

"Fine! Don't believe me. But I'll bet that oil rig isn't the only Trucial Energy facility hit in retaliation for the destruction they cause."

This time it was Alan who asked. "Do you have any information on more attacks on Trucial Energy facilities? That would help your situation a great deal, Ronald."

Half the room's lights flashed on and off three times once more.

"Go ahead!" Alan called to the ceiling.

"Sir, we've some more information on what's happening upstairs. They're still evacuating the building, but this is the real deal apparently. A group calling itself the Japanese Red Sun Army has put together a bomb and put it in this building.

They've taken two senators hostage. A team is being brought in to handle the situation, but you and your guests are being advised to evacuate the building immediately. Sorry, sir. You're gonna have to cut it short."

Van De Burgh's guards already had him up, were in formation, and about to exit the door. Alan and Jim were left at the table.

Alan seemed to be ignoring the message, and instead he flipped through a pile of folders.

"I guess we should probably go with them, huh?" Jim pointed out.

The two grabbed their papers and got behind Ronald's guards. The last two shuffled Alan and Jim to be in the middle with Ronald. One by one each guard put his hand on another's shoulder. When the lead guard's shoulder was tapped and squeezed, they began moving in step out of the room. The three Capitol Hill security guards who had been behind their desks earlier were now standing behind them with twelve-gauge shotguns. As Ronald, Alan, and Jim continued with their guards they saw the same thing at other guard positions. Everyone had shotguns.

The formation stopped at the last door. Again, each guard put his hand on another, and when the front guard's shoulder was squeezed, he opened the door, weapon shouldered, and they all made their way down the hall. As they approached the Hall of Statues, the lead guard lifted his right fist, and the group stopped without a word. The second and third guard moved up on each side of the lead guard, and as one, without signal, the formation continued toward the Small Senate Rotunda.

Suddenly four men in black camouflage and face shields crossed right in front of them. The guards all aimed their weapons at them at once, but the four men ignored them and continued moving on in close formation. It was clear they were part of some sort of SWAT team or some sort of Special Forces team. Again, the guards and everyone moved forward toward the large rotunda under the famous Capitol Dome.

There were muffled popping sounds behind them. Jim could hear the telltale sound of brass casings falling on marble. Behind them was the Capitol Hill reaction team or whoever it was had engaged the enemy. Alan knew it too. Ronald might have as well, but Jim's thoughts were of getting out before any bomb went off.

The guards headed through the rotunda. Now there were booms behind them. Jim knew the sound as flash-bang grenades going off. He also knew someone was about to have a bad day. As if to prove the point of his thought, he heard more muffled pops: the sound of suppressed submachine guns firing.

They went down the steps toward the doors, through the beeping metal detectors, and outside. There were police cars everywhere. One of the guards shoved Alan, then Jim. They were on their own. Before either of them could respond the guards were already shoving Ronald into an unmarked SUV. Some joined him, while others got into two more SUVs. As the door was closing for the last guard, all three vehicles screeched away.

Jim and Alan stood behind a police car and looked at each other.

"That's a helluva way to start the morning, Alan."

"Sure is." They both sighed and looked around.

"Coffee?" Alan asked.

"That or scotch."

"Scotch it is. I know a place a block away. I'm sure others from The Hill are having the same thoughts right now."

They began walking away from Capitol Hill, surrounded hundreds of police and other security forces. As they did so, Alan spoke calmly. "Ya know that Japanese Red Sun Army inside? They're on our list."

"List?" Jim asked.

"Yeah, they're on the list of groups that have gotten money from some of those hawala sources in the Persian Gulf. They're our bad guy's bad guys."

"Should we catch a cab to the Hoover Building or to Langley?"

"Nah," Alan replied. "I'll brief all the IC [intelligence community] later today. They'll ignore it again I'm sure."

"Gotcha. I'll call *Herr* Zimmermann and Lord Tryphine and let them know."

***

9/10/01

The small town of Guilford in Surrey was one of Lord Tryphine's favorite places. He had a comparably modest home there, but the small streets and small-town feel let him exist without the common attention that a British lord and high-end private banker tended to draw in larger towns and smaller ones as well. He liked walking down the hill in his backyard to the town's castle ruins on the other end of the swale. To the south, he could walk down the sidewalk on a quiet, one-way street, walk into a town tavern called The Weyside Overlook, and sit with a beer. People still addressed him as "Lordship" or "Sir." He could also sit on the patio behind the tavern and watch the river Wey slowly flow by, and tourists wouldn't recognize him. A park on the other side of the river (a creek by most standards) had ancient trees that had been meticulously pruned since being planted hundreds of years ago. It was picturesque, quiet, but not countryside quiet. It was a place he felt normal. He could escape from the responsibility that came with his title; with his power.

On this day he'd chosen to walk down to the tavern in the middle of the afternoon. He had a two-hour break between meetings, and it was an unusually sunny, fall, English day. Terrence walked to the bar, and the barman filled a "London stout" for him as soon as he saw him. They didn't just know him, but the entire staff knew his drinks, and which drink he preferred at different times of the day. They smiled at each other, and Terrence grabbed a small bucket of croutons to feed the ducks from the patio. Peace, life, living...these meant so many things to so many different people, and despite having more cash and collateral than most people on the planet, Terrence was happier with a warm beer, a barkeep's smile, and that tiny bucket of scrap, stale bread.

He shuffled past tables to get to one near the edge of the patio. His intent was simply to feed the ducks, drink his beer, and relax for a bit in the sunshine. Murphy's Law—whatever can go wrong will go wrong—had various incarnations. For soldiers, it was, "No plan survives first contact with the enemy." For rich, powerful, influential people, it was, "When searching for peace, responsibility always gets found." He hadn't even sat down when his cell phone began vibrating in his pocket.

Frustrated, Terrence pulled it out and sat down. His new phone received emails as soon as they were sent. He'd set most to go straight to his inbox for later review, but some senders deserved immediate attention. Those he'd set to have his device vibrate upon receipt. This was one. It was from Alan Conferra.

The email was brief. There had been another terrorist attack on a Trucial Energy asset. This time it was an oil tanker off the coast of Japan. A terrorist group, The Japanese Red Sun Army, had seized the tanker, and they had threatened to blow it up. Even though they were another eco-terrorist group like so many others, they too had planned massive ecological devastation as a means to their end—as a way of bringing down oil companies and even big business.

Once again Special Forces had taken down the threat. This time it was the Special Forces team leader who spotted the terrorists searching Trucial Energy computers for something unknown. Again, Alan's team of forensic accountants had traced the terrorists' funding to Persian Gulf small and medium businesses using the untraceable hawala money transfer scheme.

Alan also included more information on the most recent attack on the US Capitol Building. There, terrorists calling themselves the Japanese Red Sun Army, had also been funded from some of the same Persian Gulf-area small businesses. According to the FBI, they were being monitored for some time, and when their leader was arrested on the side of the New Jersey Turnpike, they changed their attack plans. Their original plan was to set several bombs around New York City with the intent of killing as many civilians as possible on city sidewalks.

Lord Tryphine closed his device and sat it on the table next to his beer. The sun was still shining. His beer was still there. He heard the ducks coming closer as they knew how to get fed by the patrons. Terrence shook his head and took a deep breath. He held it for a moment and then slowly let it out to release the new stress. Then he fed his waiting waterfowl.

***

9/12/2001

In the wake of the 9/11 attacks in America international markets were in complete disarray. Some said they were free-falling. It would be days before the American stock exchange would reopen; weeks before the businesses were back online completely. The thousands of bankers and investors who were killed or wounded in the attacks themselves were just too close in similarity to those with identical occupations who were still active in the world markets.

Erwin Zimmermann was like any other investor in so much as he had been trained and had enough experience to know that investments grow over time. Everyone in the field knew it, and while America hadn't been destroyed, her nation was in a great deal of uncertainty. Where others saw militant Islamic suicide bombers in a rage against the culture of the West, Erwin and some others saw things more ostensibly. Erwin saw an attack that was far more complicated for nineteen men from the mountains of a medieval Afghanistan. He saw an attack on America's control centers. The White House or Capitol Hill was clearly a political control center, and the Pentagon was the military control center. The World Trade Center in the investment district of New York City was the primary economic control center. There were no attacks on American cultural centers, or churches, or cathedrals, or monuments to American liberty and self-acclaimed greatness. The attacks were pinpoint—aimed at control over America.

Who would be behind an attack on American control centers, and why? he wondered. If it were a prelude to a military attack, then there'd have been a military attack, but there was none. America's list of enemies was long: states, nations, individuals, international entities from every corner of the globe. There was probably someone at the South Pole who hated America for some reason or excuse. His field was money and other marketable valuables, so Erwin looked for a money trail.

It hadn't even been twenty-four hours since the first attack. Many pointed fingers at one Islamic terrorist group, or a few working together, or even Islamic states. It was too soon to really know the day after. Still, Erwin went on the common presumption that the attacks were from a Middle Eastern, Muslim extremist/terrorist group. He began his search in the Middle East.

The attacks were surrounded by a flood of incorrect news reports about other attacks happening in the US and around the globe. What's 8 a.m. in New York is not 8 a.m. elsewhere, so Erwin looked for strange events in the Middle East over the preceding hours and days. He only found three: Iraq had shot down an American drone aircraft at about the same time as the attacks, and while that would normally have meant retaliatory airstrikes it seemed like it was disconnected from the rest of the attacks; just bad timing. There was also an assassination on a rebel leader in Afghanistan, and that was done by the same people many were saying conducted the attacks, as that group was based in Afghanistan as well. Lastly, on September 9, 2001, a Trucial Energy tanker off the coast of Japan had been seized by eco-terrorists who were going to blow it up, forcing Japan to close its largest desalinization plants and possibly even their largest nuclear facility.

The attack on the Trucial Energy tanker set off an alarm bell in Erwin's mind. It reminded him of the suspicions he and others had that some entity was waging a war on Trucial Energy, and that this entity was behind other attacks in the past. The African embassy bombings of 1998 were conducted by the same terrorists that were being blamed on the 9/11 attacks, and those embassy bombers were funded by the unknown entity waging war on Trucial Energy. He looked further and found that on August 4, just a few weeks before the 9/11 attacks, there was an Egyptian terrorist group, the Islamic Jihad, that tried to take over the Holocaust Museum in Washington D.C..

It only took him a few minutes to cross-check his information. Erwin was a digital document horder. He pulled out the court records from the 1998 embassy bomber trials and found the names of financial sources as claimed on the record by the FBI. Next he searched the FBI website and found the financial sources allegedly used by the Islamic Jihad. He repeated this for the Japanese terrorists who seized the oil tanker, and for the Arab Afghan Brigades who were being blamed for 9/11 attacks. They all cross-checked perfectly.

Erwin immediately picked up his phone. He was still rubbing his forehead in disbelief as he pressed the speed-dial button for Lord Tryphine. The phone was answered immediately by one of Lord Tryphine's very professional assistants.

"This is Erwin Zimmermann for Lord Tryphine, please. I must speak with him immediately."

The assistant tried to feign off Erwin's call. Normally it would have been dismissed as simple office operation communications, but Erwin was still excited about his discovery.

"No! I must speak with Lord Tryphine immediately, please. Go and give him a note wherever he is, and tell him Erwin needs to speak with him immediately. This is very, very important. I assure you that you will not get in trouble."

The assistant asked him to hold. A minute later Lord Tryphine picked up the line.

"Erwin, what's wrong? Is everything all right?"

"Yes, yes. Terrence, we need to have a meeting right away. Right away. Tomorrow morning."

"What's going on Erwin? This isn't like you at all."

"Terrence, we need to have a meeting tomorrow morning. You, me, George Whittaker, Jerry Henderson, his man Alan, and our man Mr. Smith. Tomorrow morning."

Lord Tryphine thought for a moment. Erwin was excited; he wanted to meet with the people who all envision someone waging war on Trucial Energy. He must have found something important, Terrence thought. But the Americans were very busy with the 9/11 business.

"Erwin, does this have to do with what happened yesterday in America?" Terrence asked.

"I don't want to say on the phone, but we must meet tomorrow morning—all of us. We can meet at your office, 7 a.m."

It had to be a connection with the attacks in America, Terrence thought.

"Right then, I'll make it happen with the Americans. You find our Mr. Smith. We'll meet here tomorrow at 7 a.m.," Lord Tryphine replied.

"Thank you, Terrence. Thank you. I know it won't be easy, but they need to hear this, and I don't think we should say more over the phone."

"Right. Thank you, Erwin. See you tomorrow morning."

***

9/13/2001

The next morning at Tryphine Banking House, they all met. The US secretary of the Treasury, George Whittaker, came with a dozen Secret Service agents. The head of the Senate Intelligence Committee came with a dozen State Department Security agents. Everyone had M-16 rifles with them. Alan walked between the huge armed escorts. There were representatives from the FBI, CIA, NSA, and even the ATF—all of whom participated in their respective departments' financial crimes divisions with special focus on international terrorism. Jim Smith waited in the lobby, then joined in the crowd. It took some time to make introductions and get visitor passes issued to everyone, but Tryphine staff members were experienced and professional so no one complained.

They met in one of the large conference halls on the left side of the main lobby. All of the security guards took position around the entrances to the hall, but outside—not inside. Once everyone was seated, George Whittaker immediately took control of the meeting. He was rushed, haggard, and worn, and probably hadn't slept since Sunday night. He didn't even take time to introduce everyone.

"Okay, Erwin. I should be pissed at your making us come here right now, but you're good people so let's have it. What's so important?"

With the presence of unidentified others in the room, Erwin chose to be more formal.

"Lord Tryphine, Mr. Secretary, Senator Henderson, and everyone...thank you for coming on such short notice. Over the past ten years I've kept a watchful eye out for something specific and unusual in the financial world. I began to suspect that some outside entity, a nation, state, group, something is waging a very expensive and very real war on Trucial Energy. I believe the attacks on Monday were part of that war. Please, I've prepared a briefing for you. There are extras being printed right now for those of you who are new to this concept."

Only Lord Tryphine, Secretary Whittaker, Senator Henderson, Alan, and Jim had copies. When Erwin saw the crowd, he arranged for one of Lord Tryphine's assistants to print ten more.

Senator Henderson had flipped through the brief already. "Erwin, we're not even one hundred percent sure who did this yesterday. How can you be so sure the funding is the same?"

"Senator, everyone around the world is claiming that this Arab Afghan Brigade is behind the attack. I went on the possibility that they are. Then I checked it with the data I've collected over the years through our own investigations—done at our own cost and risk I might add. The data is clear: If it was the Arab Afghan Brigades, then they got their money through the same hawala sources that were used for at least twenty-three other major attacks."

"Sir?" It was the FBI Counter-Terrorism Task Force Financial Resources (FBICTTFFR) representative. "I'm not sure on your clearance, but the attacks listed here are not done by the same people. You've got a list here that has eco-terrorists, Japanese nationalists, Islamic terrorists, Iranians, Georgians, Azerbaijani terrorists, and so on. You're even pinning the entire Ajax Medical Group attack in Miami on some ghost-like master terrorist. It doesn't make sense. There's no way some of these groups would ever work together let alone even with each other."

Alan spoke up before anyone else could—even Erwin. "He's not saying these groups are working together. All he's saying is that they all get their money from the same sources. That's the common denominator."

Jim joined in next. "Look, no one is saying that there's a terrorist coalition out there. All we're saying is that there's a sugar daddy these groups are using, or there's a sugar daddy out there using groups. Someone hands a group of Hutu rebels some cash, and you can bet they're gonna say, 'Hey, thanks. Is there anything we can do for you in exchange?' It's just that easy."

The CIA's representative knew Jim—it was obvious—but neither said a word about how or under what circumstances. "Jim," he asked, "why not just use regular mercs? You get better training, and...I see, that'd leave people in the know. Most of the attacks listed in this brief are dead-enders. Suicide attackers."

Jim nodded.

The NSA representative had been quietly typing at his laptop computer during the conversation. Erwin had listed various routing numbers, account numbers, and all of the information he could on the sources that were being used to funnel untraceable cash around the globe from the Persian Gulf region. “Mr., uh, *Herr* Zimmermann...this one account here, on page five. You’ve got it listed as a ‘House of Wisdom School’ in Qatar. That’s a front for SFS International. They’re on our radar big-time. Iraq, Iran, Syria...all the best of the worst use them to get money to their families, to pay off officials, to line their own pockets, and for their intelligence services. That’s about all I can say without knowing the clearance of everyone in the room.”

Few things pressed Jerry Henderson’s buttons like bureaucratic blocking in times when cooperation is needed. “Godammit. Erwin just did in one morning what you—all of you—have been trying to do for God knows how long. My office has been working with these people for a long time, and we’ve been sending you all our information every week, and you’ve shared nothing. You haven’t even thanked them. After Monday, there’s gonna be a lot of people looking for heads to roll because the intelligence community fucked up. These attacks are preventable, and you failed to connect the dots. You can tell them more about this SFS International now, or your boss can tell me in front of my committee tomorrow. Your choice.”

The room was silent. Here, in Lord Tryphine’s family business, his home away from home, even he didn’t break the ice in the room. Jerry Henderson had done well enough to build it. That’s when one of Lord Tryphine’s workers, Andrew Lawrence, entered the room. He and Terrence exchanged smiles as he took a seat.

“I apologize, gentlemen. I was only notified of this meeting last night. My name’s Andrew Lawrence. I work for his lordship. I used to work in your world. Someday, I suspect some of you will find yourselves looking for work in ours.” Lawrence was handed a freshly printed briefing.

“Glad you could make it, Andrew.” Terrence replied.

“We were just talking about SFS International. It appears that the House of Wisdom School in Qatar is a known front for various villains in that region.”

“Yes, sir. SFS International is best known for laundering illegal oil sales and providing a hawala money laundering mechanism mostly for intelligence branches and people who get by filling their pockets. It’s run by relatives of Syria’s leader, and it has close ties with the IIS [Iraqi Intelligence Service] as well as the Iranians. British intelligence has tracked them for a while.

They go back to just after the Great War. They're very much the antithesis of Tryphine Banking House."

"Speaking of Tryphine House," Terrence began, "let's not forget where you all are, please. We have a certain way of doing things here. You are all very welcome here, and I thank you all for coming, but Trucial Energy is a major client of mine and of Erwin's. That's how we came to be involved in all this. It's where our interests cross with your duties. We need to know who it is that is waging a war on our client—a client of strategic importance to your national interests I might add. Can you help us identify these people or can you not? Either way I'm sure we'll all continue to help you and share information we find with you even if these efforts are not done in kind."

The nameless staffers sat silently again. Bureaucrats to the core they refused to put their jobs in jeopardy without consulting their superiors; without having an excuse should anything go wrong. Finally the NSA rep answered up.

"Gentlemen." He wanted to give the security clearance caveat speech again, but dared not. "SFS International is one of perhaps hundreds of clandestine funding sources. Others are: Lama Trading Company, Al-Bir Company, and Container Company of Amman, but SFS is the most common source, and they probably just showed up on the list in your brief because they're so common. We'll take a closer look at it just the same. I've done a preliminary check on some of the others that you have listed, and we'll take a closer look at those as well. We'll put a 'Trucial Energy' tag on them too. That should flag all their communications that involve the word."

Terrence interrupted. "Tag?"

The NSA rep looked at Senator Henderson as if to nonverbally reiterate his reluctance to talk about classified information with people who had various or no clearance. The two men stared at each other for a moment. It was clear the NSA rep didn't want to elaborate.

Jim saw this and answered instead. "Sir, several countries have the ability to monitor any communications that go through satellites or by radio. These communications are sent digitally. That means the sender and receiver are really just getting innumerable signals indicating either a zero or a one that computers on both ends reinterpret into a signal, and then essentially play as recording. A few countries have enough computing power that they can actually choose a limited target area, monitor all the signals from that area, and search those long lines of ones and zeroes until they find a pattern that is interpreted as the letters spelling 'Trucial Energy.' This way if someone sends an email with the word 'Trucial Energy' in it, the people monitoring have a computer that is scanning all the emails to and from that particular location, and save a copy of that communication based only on the criteria that the pattern for those letters are in it. It works for phone communications as well. A man in Dubai calls a man in London, and as soon as one of them says the word 'Trucial Energy' a spy satellite detects that digital pattern, monitors the call, and records it. The real limitation is area. Because so much data is flowing at any one time or another, computers can only monitor so much, and the monitoring has to be limited to a small area or, best, a particular person. In the end, the NSA will have a list of all phone calls and emails, etcetera that come from SFS International and mention the word 'Trucial Energy.' Someone can then review those calls and emails, and from there we can learn who is possibly planning what."

The NSA rep closed his eyes at the secret Jim had just revealed. The FBI rep was frozen, as what was described was essentially illegal wire-tapping as there was no way to tell if one of the parties in a communication were American citizens or not. The CIA rep—the man who knew Jim—wore a pursed smile as he thought how freeing retirement from the bureaucracy must be for Jim.

Exhausted, Treasury Secretary Whittaker changed the focus. "Okay, gentlemen, let's say for now that these Arab Afghans are behind the attacks on Monday. And let's say they really did it for their own reasons, but someone else funded them for their own reasons. And you all think it's some private war on Trucial Energy that's been going on for years. How does attacking the World Trade Center, the Pentagon, and either the White House or Capitol Hill hurt Trucial Energy? Those don't seem like attacks on an oil company, but attacks on America, no?"

Erwin answered. "I believe the attacks were not an attack on the American people in general. I don't think it was an attack on American culture either or they would have gone after Hollywood, and media, and churches, and sporting events or things like that. If it was an attack on American nationalism, then they'd have gone for symbols like the Statue of Liberty or the Washington Monument and other things. I've no doubt the terrorists themselves thought they were making some sort of statement or waging a war on those things, but in my opinion, from a financial perspective, the attacks are aimed at command, control, and communication centers. The White House or Capitol Hill were targeted as political control centers, the

Pentagon is first and foremost a military command center, and the World Trade Center is America's financial command center. With all due respect to Secretary Whittaker's role, the actual financial operations of America's free market are not in Washington, but in New York. It's not government, but private."

"No offense taken at all, Erwin. None," George answered. "No offense taken at all. You're completely right, and it makes good sense, but why? What do they get if they could have knocked out our command and control?"

Lord Tryphine had his 'ah-ha!' moment. "I see. I see it now, Erwin. You're thinking the terrorists did this for their reasons, but the people who paid them and made it possible had their own reasons: a so-called trash and cash scheme. No?"

"Exactly," Erwin replied. "I suggest that we all take a look at who was dumping airline stocks, or perhaps buying military stocks before the attacks, and that we watch to see who buys airline stocks when the market bottoms out."

The CIA rep wanted clarity. "Can you describe this 'trash and cash' scheme a little better?"

Alan answered. "Trash and cash is a strategy like insider trading that happens every day, but rarely faces enforcement officials. It's hard to prove. It happens when, for example, a steel company starts spreading rumors that a competitor is having problems or that the competitor is going to close; anything that will make the stock holders of the competitor fall in price. Then the steel company sees the lower stock prices of its competitor and buys more shares—possibly even taking it over. When a company does this to a competitor it's a form of hostile takeover. When an individual or fund manager does this...it's trash and cash. There are illegalities attached, but as I said, rarely enforced and even more rarely proven."

Erwin pointed out the obvious. "Well, the markets are definitely reeling. The American market is shut down. The dollar is plummeting against the euro, and we know there's plenty of people making money off of that. Germany's market is down almost nine percent. London is down almost six percent. Everyone is down. Gold always spikes after any major event, and oil is headed for the sky."

Lord Tryphine, Treasury Secretary Whittaker, and Senator Henderson all had years of experience in commodities markets, and at once their minds thought of the oil commodity market.

They all said it at once. "Oil."

The Middle East had other exports, but the two things it sent to the rest of the world more than anything: terrorism and oil. Muslim extremists waging war on America were a dime a dozen, but someone in the Persian Gulf region who was possibly waging war on Trucial Energy? Oil was all over the entire incident. Now even the NSA rep was convinced about Erwin's records and theory.

Alan joined in. "What we really want to see is who was buying oil before the attacks, and if we need to see if those people were using SFS International as well. That should narrow the list of possible suspects down quite a bit. Then we'll know who was paying for these attacks and perhaps as many as twenty-three others."

***

10/7/2001

Alan and Jim had been in the back of a US Air Force C-130 transport plane for more than thirty-three hours. It was large enough to walk around inside the cargo bay, and they had been able to step outside while the plane refueled in Germany, Turkey, and Uzbekistan, but they were tired. Besides themselves there was the plane's crew, a few CIA people that Jim knew but didn't associate with anymore, some Special Forces people from an unspecified branch, and money. There was lots of money. A million dollars in hundred-dollar bills barely fit inside a large sports equipment bag. Alan was the only one on the plane who knew specifically how much money there was; about $500 million). Everyone else could only marvel at the six 463L pallets-each stacked eight feet high with nothing but hundred-dollar bills.

They were accompanying the first efforts of the American military effort in Afghanistan after the 9/11 attacks. It was midmorning, and even though the plane was flying high, they were still dodging mountains as they passed into Northeast Afghanistan. There was no control tower, not even a real runway—just a flat dirt area they were told the plane could land on. The sky was bright and shiny as an October cold front had just landed in the area as well.

The runway was high in the mountains, and the pilot only had to descend a few hundred feet to line up on the mountaintop to touch down. As soon as all three lights were solidly on the ground, the crew began working hard to stop the plane. Designed in the 1950s to land on grass and dirt runways, the C-130 was in its element, and the pilots were good—hand chosen for the important operation.

While the plane was still on the runway men on horses charged toward the plane from all directions. They didn't wear uniforms, but all had AK-47s and RPGs (rocket-propelled grenade launchers). The loud roar of the engines made it impossible to hear them, and the thick dust made them look more like hundreds of ghosts rather than real figures.

At the end of the runway, the plane turned around and lined itself up for takeoff. The crew spun down the engines, and then turned them off. As the dust settled, and the engine noise dimmed, it was clear the planeload of cash was surrounded. Nothing stood in the way of the plane being seized and everyone on board executed.

Everyone inside the plane prepared themselves. The Special Forces men checked their weapons and gear once more. The CIA people leaned together in a circle to go over documents. Jim checked the nine-millimeter Beretta pistol he was carrying. Alan tightened his tie and picked at his ever-present black suit to make sure he looked like a banker...even though he was almost three hundred miles from the nearest bank; the nearest place anyone would be wearing a suit and tie for that matter.

It was one of the CIA people who opened the left side door to the plane and stepped out first. He was followed by two Special Forces men who took positions to his left and right. Then the rest of the CIA team stepped out, and the rest of the Special Forces men took up security positions close by. Alan and Jim remained on the plane. The Afghan horse soldiers quieted down. It was clear that their leader knew the first CIA man who had left the plane. They hugged, and talked, and introductions were made.

Jim saw the entourage of CIA and Afghans walk around the plane to the rear. He pointed it out to Alan and the plane's enlisted loadmaster just as there were three loud thumps on the back right of the C-130's fuselage. That was the signal to the loadmaster. He stepped to the back of the plane and began operating the controls to raise the rear end of the plane and lower its cargo ramp. Alan and Jim stood side by side on the ramp with the pallets of cash behind them. What little noise there had been was lost. It seemed even the Afghan horses fell silent.

Jim walked down the cargo ramp and headed for the entourage while Alan waited on the plane, standing before the pallets not as a guard, but as a banker would stand. While the CIA people continued to speak to the Afghans, one of the men introduced himself to Jim. Together they headed up the ramp and into the plane.

"Alan," Jim began, "this is Colonel Mohammed Mohammed, the general's intelligence officer."

Everyone semi-smiled as the two shook hands.

"The general is very pleased to see you Americans have come back. We are very sorry for your losses, however."

"Thank you, General," Jim answered. "Alan here will have some paperwork for you to sign before your men can unload these assets."

Alan handed the colonel a folder with papers in it. Xs marked where to be signed and others where Mohammed Mohammed had to initial. The entire motion was fabricated. None of the money even really belonged to the US government. It was a fraction of the interest from the money that Jim and Alan had recovered from Saddam's forces after they stole it from Kuwait a decade earlier. Alan only wanted papers signed so he could say there was documentation if ever questioned, and to instill upon the Afghans a sense of formality and ownership on their part. While a home mortgage might take an hour to sign with dozens of pages, the half-billion dollars in untraceable cash was barely less than ten pages, and took only a few minutes.

When he was done signing, Alan thanked the colonel and arranged the papers as if there was some sort of proper order to the nonsense. Then he motioned for Jim and the colonel to come closer so that they might speak privately among the crowd, the cash, and the history of the moment.

"Colonel," Alan began, "Jim and I are not just here as part of what the general is discussing with our friends over there. We have a few questions we'd like to discuss with you specifically; some intelligence questions."

"Of course, my friends—whatever information or answers I can provide please, just ask."

Alan motioned for Jim to explain.

"Colonel, the recent attacks on our country, we know who carried them out, and we know that they were financed largely through a prince from the UAE, at least one Saudi prince, and several hawala transactions from the Persian Gulf. We've seen other terrorist groups who have also been funded through these same hawala sources...groups that claim to fight for communism, or the environment, and some who claim to fight for Islam."

The colonel nodded as if he already knew the situation. His poker face was outstanding.

Alan continued where Jim left off. "A few of us believe that someone is funding terrorism of all sorts around the globe. They're doing it not because they agree with these groups; they just fund them so the groups will attack targets they want attacked by anyone."

The colonel raised his hand to interrupt Alan. "Yes, of course these people are paid. They are just mercenaries. It doesn't matter if they say they take hostages for money, or if they bomb a mosque for Allah, or crash a plane into buildings in the name of Islam. That is the way it always is in any war. The soldiers fight for their own reasons. Others gather soldiers for a cause, and above them there are wealthy, powerful people who play with us all like pawns. Is there a pattern to these attacks you're asking me about?"

Jim wanted to be coy, but where he'd been trained in deception and espionage, Alan's career had advanced and evolved on blunt honesty. He spoke before Jim had a chance. "Sometimes the attacks seem focused on Trucial Energy for some reason. Other times it's attacks on currency in general. Sometimes survivors report that terrorists are looking for something. That's what's really strange is that we have completely different terrorist groups behaving similarly, and with similar funding sources."

Again the colonel nodded. His upper lip stiffened, and his beard sagged slightly. "We have seen a little of this as well over the past five or ten years. Chechens, Uzbeks, Tajiks, Arab Afghans like the ones you are now about to wage war on. These people come to Afghanistan; they do horrible things. I do not recall any looking for something, but the money usually comes from the...what is the word? You might call it a syndicate, or family, or cartel. I do not know the best word. Mafia. They are an oil mafia. That's what you would call them."

Alan and Jim looked at each other. They had to step aside as Afghans were boarding the plane with ropes—about to use their horses to pull off the half-billion dollars.

"Can you describe this group more?" Alan asked.

"We will call them groups. There are very large, very powerful groups in the world who have many large interests. Ones like gold, or diamonds, these groups, they seek to control them. They are like countries themselves without borders. They own countries. Everyone knows about government grift or corruption and favors. It happens everywhere. I'm sure it happens in America. In this part of the world, there is a group in the Azerbaijan and Kazakhstan areas. When they want something done, they pay to get it done. They could use soldiers who fight for money, but by using extremists, they can deny they were involved. There are other groups too. This kind of group is everywhere. The Gulf region has a few groups that extremists go to when they want money. The group gets bad work done, and the extremists get money."

It made sense to Alan and Jim. They'd considered that kind of relationship before. It was shown in the entire Miami concert plot and all the attacks that preceded it from a wide array of terrorists. They wanted a more specific name than "groups."

All three men looked at each other. Then the colonel continued.

"If Trucial Energy is your common theme, then who is it that wants Trucial Energy destroyed? That is your question. I think your answer would be found in a group within one of the Gulf States, but you might want to look at a man named Samed Vezirzade. He is Azerbaijani. Went to University of Moscow in 1970s. Very rich man. Very powerful man. Hates the West. If he is not the currency source for all these groups, then he will tell you who is."

As the three men shook hands again, the horses were about to pull the last pallet of cash off the plane. The CIA team was shaking hands with their old/new friends. The Afghans cleared out, and the plane's engines began to warm up. Dust rose. When the cash was gone, the cargo door was closed, and everyone found a seat to strap into.

Moments later the plane roared down the runway. Rather than climbing on takeoff, it lifted only a few feet and then flew on. The mountaintop runway slipped away underneath it, and in a second they were thousands of feet over a mountain gorge. Their mission was done. The United States had just bought allies for their new war in Afghanistan. Jim and Alan now had a name to research. In the end, theirs was the greater accomplishment by far.

***

11/18/01

Jim had been traveling the world again. From Greece to India his passport was looking like a collage of travel stamps. Some of the countries in the region had been visited so many times now that he was more familiar with certain airports than his own home it seemed. Tel Aviv was like a resort. Jerusalem reminded him of travelling back in time. Baku in Azerbaijan was futuristic. Dubai was futuristic and luxurious. Damascus was a new type of dangerous every time he visited. Kuwait was the opposite.

On this day Jim was in the former Soviet Republic of Georgia. He'd arrived at Tbilisi Airport just in the late afternoon. A small airport by Western standards, its modern wing-shaped roof and glass sides reflected the new, post-Soviet architecture that came with capitalist investments as opposed to Spartan, communist, bunker-style architecture. Late in the day the customs officials were tired, wanted to go home, and he passed through without even the normal lackadaisical scrutiny.

Jim picked up a rental car and headed for a hotel. He'd timed his visit to coincide with an international conference in underground salt dome, liquid natural gas storage solutions for oil and gas drilling operations. It was to be held at the same hotel. Jim's hope was to infiltrate the conference, get friendly with some of the oil and gas company representatives, and see if anyone had ever heard of Samed Vezirzade.

The hotel was old, perhaps a hundred years, and it reflected the Czarist Russian past of the town, but it was very nicely updated. Surrounding it was a mixture of cold Soviet buildings, ancient Persian buildings, a few modern/post-Cold War structures, and the 1,500-year-old old Narikala Fortress up on the hill overlooking the entire city.

Just off of the lobby was the obligatory, nice hotel restaurant that served all sorts of regional foods with some remarkably fine Georgian wines. Opposite the restaurant, a small gift shop/market allowed for longer-term guests to shop for snacks or other needs. There was a desk for a concierge, but Jim never saw one.

After settling into his room, Jim showered, changed into more comfortable clothes, and headed to the restaurant's bar so he could get to work. After decades of clandestine work, Jim found this kind of work simple, almost unconscious. The bar was loud. Inevitably, there was a group of businessmen who knew each other standing at the nearest corner of the bar where three people were sitting and three more standing. All six were speaking English, though two were clearly struggling. One seemed Russian, but Jim couldn't nail down the accent of the other man.

Jim walked up the right-hand side of the pack, approached the bar, and sat down behind them.

"English?" he asked them. "You guys are American?"

All six men stopped talking and turned toward him. Some of them nodded.

Jim reached out his hand to begin shaking theirs. "I'm Jim. Man, it's nice to hear people I can understand again. We are a long, long way from home!"

The men smiled and shook Jim's hand as they introduced themselves. One of them was wearing a polo shirt with his company's name, Westland Energy, and a logo on it.

"Westland? Are you here for the conference too?"

"Yes. You?" the man answered.

"Yeah. Hey, lemme refill your glasses." Jim ordered a round of refills from the bartender and demanded top-shelf booze for each. Years of experience had shown him that the easiest way to get information was to inebriate his asset, and the easiest way to do that was either with drugs or with top-shelf booze. The more smooth the liquor, the easier it was to deceive the asset into drinking too much, into talking too much.

The half dozen men went back to their conversation about salt dome storage of natural gas waste from drilling operations, but as soon as the drinks arrived Jim interrupted them with a toast.

"Gentlemen, here's to going to the ends of the world so that others may have light, heat, and happiness."

All six men had assumed Jim was in town for the conference as they were. None of them saw themselves as oil barons out to get rich—few in the oil industry ever did. Like most workers in the field they viewed their professions as energy suppliers. To that end Jim's words about light, heat, and happiness resounded and thus reinforced their belief that he was there for the conference.

Immediately after the first round, Jim ordered another round, and the six men opened their conversational circle to include him. He tried to follow and understand the technical aspects of what they were talking about, but he couldn't.

Jim turned to the man from Westland Energy and quietly asked, "Ya know, I'm having a tough time following some of this."

"It's okay, we're all engineers," he quietly replied. "What do you do?"

"Recruiter...I'm a headhunter," Jim answered. "We focus mainly in the energy field. One of our clients is working on a project, and they suggested I fly out here to learn more about it, find out who the best people are on the subject, and at least make ourselves known to them. I don't know how you are with Westland, but by and large we see a lot of job-hopping and resume-building moves in terms of waste management solutions so it seemed like a good place to be."

"I've been with Westland for six years now. They're good people. Some of these guys have job hopped in the past, but we all still see each other at events like this. I can see where you can get lost on the underground LNG storage idea. It's been around since about World War II, and it's really only now starting to spread as a solution. Higher oil prices means more LNG demand, which means it's more valuable and now you have people wanting to store the stuff instead of burn it off right at the wellhead."

Jim nodded and paid close attention, and his new asset just looked at him.

"You're lost, aren't you? How much do you know about it?"

Jim looked around and saw the next round of drinks coming. He paused for a moment, waiting to respond as soon as the tray arrived. Then he smiled, passed out glasses to everyone, and as he handed the last glass to the man from Westland, said, "How about this: How do you think I should explain it to my secretary?"

"Okay....a lot of the time when you sink a well, before you hit the oil you hit natural gas pockets in the surrounding strata. Most facilities just pipe the natural gas to a faraway location, ignite it, and burn it off. That's the big flame you always see on oil platforms at sea or a lot of the time in the deserts."

Jim nodded. Two of the other men in the crowd noticed their colleague explaining the process, and one of them joined in. "Now that natural gas is more valuable, companies that can afford to do so are compressing the natural gas into liquid natural gas, LNG. Then, instead of burning it and wasting it, we send it off to get stored until it's needed. Or we sell it to those who do need it."

The rest of the small crowd was now paying attention. Proud of their profession and loosened by liquor they began to vigorously boast about their field. "The problem is that LNG is very dangerous," one of them said. "A single tanker truck can—and has—set fire to entire mountains. When it leaks, there's no way to see it unless it's too concentrated to handle. It's super-cooled so it does show up on thermal as a black area when leaking, and when enough of it leaks you see mist like dry ice, but by that point it's too dangerous to really deal with."

"I was out in West Virginia one time, and we had an LNG line burst," another said. "A bad weld with some hot and cold weather, and whoosh! It was a ten-foot diameter line, and only at four psi, but everything within a mile was incinerated and black. We shut off the line right away, and it still took three days to burn out."

The man from Westland gave his "war story" next. "I was out on this platform in the Black Sea back in '99. They were flaring the off gasses on a boom that was a hundred feet from the main structure. We were there to set up a DJ77 compression unit that was going to connect to an old Brewster-72 storage unit. It was going to be set up at another platform that was being built adjacent. Anyway, we were testing the DJ77, and someone decided that it was time to send the gas to it without any storage unit synced."

The other five men all stopped and gave a collective "Ooooooh."

"Yep. You guessed it. As soon as our guy spotted it, he ran over, rerouted the gas to the off gas burner, and LNG shot into it. I swear the flash was as big as the entire platform! There couldn't have been more than ten thousand pounds of LNG in the line, but we were just testing the compressor so it was at five psi, not four. That was something else!"

Jim smiled and shook his head as the others were doing. "And now we're going to store it underground, huh?"

All six shook their heads, smiled with engineers' excitement, and fluttered out "yeses" and "yeahs." Then the Westland man continued explaining.

"It's a lot safer. In fact, there's never even been a single accident. There's a few different ways to do underground LNG storage. Most of the time it involves salt caverns. We go in, drill a hole down to about two thousand feet, well into a salt deposit. Then we blast water into the hole. It leeches out the salt, and we pump out the salt water brine. As we're doing this we lower the water pumping point. In this way we can clear out a salt deposit and make a cavern a hundred or two hundred feet wide and a thousand or two thousand feet down. You can fit a few Empire State Buildings in some of these things. Once they're cleared, and tested, we set up a system that allows LNG to go down into them, and then a manifold at the top where it can be tapped when needed."

Jim, who had been bored for a long time, was now impressed. "How many of these caverns are there in the world?" he asked.

The small group of engineers gaggled with answers ranging from a few hundred to a few thousand.

Jim shook his head in feigned awe. Then he let the engineers fall back into their own combination of techno-babble and "war story" experiences. Step one of getting the men to loosen up with top-shelf liquor: success. Step two of getting the men to accept him into their fold by letting them brag about their profession and experiences: success. Now Jim faced Step three: getting the men to talk in a way that would give him some sort of valuable information...preferably about Samed Vezirzade.

Jim passed out the drinks. Again, he handed the last one to the man from Westland. He felt that this man in particular had been loosened more than the others. He thought fast and hard about how to phrase a probing question; how to proceed with step three.

"D'you think the conference is being held here in Tbilisi because the 'Oil Cartel' in this area is looking to expand into LNG storage?"

"Oh, definitely," the man instantly responded. "I fly out to one of the platforms right after the conference. Westland's got a contract to run a line from fifteen different platforms to a new underground storage facility they're putting together up north. They're all Oil Cartel/Oil Mafia sites; whatever you want to call 'em. I think everyone here already had projects lined up in the region for the next six months."

"I wonder if I should go meet with some of those companies. Maybe see if they know anyone they might want to loan out or if they need someone I already have in our files?" Jim supposed.

"It's probably a good idea to at least know the people in the region. They'll all be here tomorrow. I think the 10 a.m. talk on USC Risk Management Solutions would be your best bet. There's also a meet and greet at lunch. I think we're meeting at Galaktion Tabidze Street Wine Cellar around one."

Jim had done as much reading as he could on nuanced Tbilisi subjects for conversation. He'd always found wine to be a good ice-breaker in most countries. Georgia had a history of wine-making going back eight thousand years. Unique to the region was a practice of making special pottery to age the wine rather than barrels. The pots, called *amphoras* or *qvevri*, were then buried in the ground for years. Some of the *qvevri* in Georgia had been reused time and time again for more than three hundred years. Jim used the nuanced information—limited as he was in the subject—to impress his new friends; his assets.

Shortly after explaining the process of Georgian wine-making, Jim began ordering rounds of high-end Georgian wines. The seven men never did get seated at a table or eat a proper dinner. Hors d'oeuvres were brought several times for each. At the end of the night, Jim picked up the $3,500 tab. He hadn't found out anything more about Samed Vezirzade, but he did harvest new assets, and most of all he had learned where and when Vezirzade might be the next day.

His night's work at the bar was late. Having flown for the past two days, and then been up all night drinking, Jim was exhausted. He went downstairs, and again didn't see a concierge. Instead he headed back to the bar, and asked a busboy where to find a good cup of coffee. The busboy's English was barely intelligible, but a manager was passing by, saw the conversation, and then stopped to help.

"You are looking for coffee, sir? We have some here if you would like?"

"No, thank you. I was looking for a café. I'm sightseeing today. Do you know of anything on Galaktion Tabidze Street?" Jim asked as he pulled out a map.

The manager looked at it, and told Jim of a café across the street from the wine cellar/bar/restaurant where the afternoon meet and greet would take place. Jim thanked him, and headed off toward the café. It was within walking distance, and he was there in less than ten minutes.

The Orjonikidze Café was named after one of Tbilisi's most famous or infamous residents. Sergio Orjonikidze had been a close friend of Josef Stalin during his rise to power and through World War II. While the city's architecture brought to mind the influence of several controlling regimes in Tbilisi's past, the post-Cold War Tbilisi seemed in race to modernize and reflect the jewel-like architecture of the modern Western world. Contrasting that, the Orjonikidze Café was adorned with red and yellow as if in homage or at least a play at the Cold War communist propaganda influences. The chairs were all red with gold cushions. The awnings were painted to look like Soviet flags. The wood was stained deep red. Even the cups and saucers thrift-store style were leftovers from what was once elite dining for communist leaders. They were decorated with gold trimming and red lithographs of long-forgotten politburo members.

Jim waited in line at the faux communist café in the same way he would at a name-brand coffee franchise in Seattle. It was busy. The coffee wasn't American café expensive, but it wasn't cheap. It wasn't that great either. The pastries, on the other hand, were incredible and would have held their own in a competition with average Parisian café fare.

Once he had his order, Jim sat down at a sidewalk table. He looked around, and looked at his map. The wine cellar was close by. He could watch it closely. Three times he watched a man come from the wine cellar to the café, and back again. Each time the man carried a coffee order back to the wine cellar. Jim targeted the man mentally.

When he returned around 10 a.m. for another order, Jim left his table and jumped in line just before the man. Speaking in French, Jim showed the man his map, put his finger on the wine cellar, and asked the man if he knew where the wine cellar was located. A woman who was bringing out more pastries heard the French, and casually interpreted for her frequent customer. He smiled, nodded, and pointed to the cellar. Jim asked him when it opened, and through the pastry cook's interpretation was told not until 11 a.m. He asked if he could see the place, and when the request finally made its way to the man, he was reluctant. Jim begged politely and offered to pay for the man's order. Again this was translated, and the man acquiesced.

They got their orders and walked down the one-lane street to the wine cellar. Inside, the man introduced Jim to someone who was clearly a manager or more. The man introduced himself to Jim in French.

Jim thanked him for letting him in early to see the wine cellar, and then he explained, "I'm supposed to meet someone today, a man named Samed Vezirzade."

"Ohhhhh," the owner replied in slightly broken French. "Monsieur Vezirzade is a very good man. He has been here before. He is hard, but very fair, and very generous. You will tell him I said so, yes?"

Jim nodded. "Do you know where we will be sitting?" he asked.

The owner pointed to a long table near the back of the balcony dining area. Jim began walking over as if to review the arrangements for Vezirzade. The owner was careful not to risk offending anyone who was associated with the man. Members of the Oil Mafia and other big businesses—legitimate or otherwise—were treated with the trained respect and fear that had been learned when dealing with powerful communist leaders.

Jim thanked him, and he made a call on his cell phone. Once the call went through and he heard it start ringing, he hung up and began looking around more as if on inspection. As they walked through the rest of the dining area, Jim encouraged the owner to explain/rant about the wines they would serve, the qualities of the wines, the paired cheeses and fruits. Finally, he made his way to the front door, thanked the owner, and walked circuitously back to his hotel room.

There, he called Alan. It was just past 11 a.m. in Tbilisi, and thus just past 11 p.m. in Washington, DC. Alan was still at work; the consummate workaholic.

"What's up, Jim?"

"I was afraid you'd be asleep," he replied.

"Nah, never enough. Where are you by the way?"

"Tbilisi, Georgia. Listen, do you see my number on your caller ID?"

"Yes," Alan answered.

"Okay, get in touch with someone at NSA right now. Tell them to look at my calls. The last call I made before calling you—that's the one we're interested in. They can trace its location down to a few yards. Tell them that there's a high-value target, an HVT, that's going to be at that location in an hour. We need them to monitor all they can from that meeting."

"I'll call them right away. What do we hope to get?"

"Once they have the location, the electronic spooks can access all the phones in the immediate area. They'll have contact lists, text messages, and lots more. They'll even be able to use the microphones on all the phones and listen in. We can get transcripts. I'm expecting we'll get a name that we can reverse match up with what they're getting from...ya know what, let's talk about this in person later."

Alan agreed. They hung up, and he called the NSA terrorism financial support team. No one was in, but they made calls and ensured that the area Jim wanted was monitored. By the end of the day in Tbilisi, and by the following afternoon in Washington, DC, the intel garnered would reveal explosive connections.

***

02/15/02

Ever since Erwin Zimmermann had been taken hostage in his own home, the search for the sponsor(s) of that attack and dozens more had become a professional hobby for him. It was a sideshow at best for Lord Terrence Tryphine. Alan Conferra's ever-changing professional responsibilities caused the search to alternate between full-time and part-time tasking. Since his involvement, it had been Jim Smith's life, not a hobby or occasional job. Still, all of those involved were committed to the findings. They all knew that there was more at stake than their own professional or personal initiatives.

Every week there were calls, meetings, emails, and so forth between the men, but it was rare for them all to meet at once. Jim's recent intelligence breakthrough in Tbilisi was the cause for this meeting. By successfully getting a lead for electronic intelligence gathering against the Oil Mafia, Jim had stumbled upon a treasure trove of connections. To review those connections an immediate meeting had been called by Lord Terrence Tryphine.

Where meetings organized by Lord Tryphine had previously been held at his banking house in London, this meeting required the highest level of security and secrecy. No ordinary conference room would suffice. Tryphine Banking House did multibillion-dollar business every day—almost every hour of every day. Every few days more than one billionaire could be found there for one reason or another. As such, a top-level secure room had been built years earlier.

One by one the men arrived and met with escorts in the lobby and were given their visitor passes. Each was then taken through the large octagonal room, down a hall to the right, and to an old, gated elevator. The servant would then escort each man into the elevator. When the gate was closed, the escort would then insert a key, and pull a lever to start the descent. The elevator was slow, but after going down roughly one hundred feet, it stopped. The gate was opened, and the man would be led down modern, carpeted hall with cubicle dividers intersecting the hallway and making straight paths impossible. At the end of the hall, the security escort would then type in a twelve-digit access code. Once granted access, they would pass through a wide hall with dark glass on both sides. At the end, the escort rubbed his thumb on an identification pad. With that security passed, the man was directed into a conference room where Lord Tryphine was already waiting.

The conference room was nondescript. Old tapestries hung from all four walls. Another lay on the floor. The ceiling was modern acoustic tile. The conference table and chairs were clear resin with burled slices of old English oak, stained to a light cherry red. The lights were fluorescent. It was a strange and failed effort at making a bunker look both classical and modern.

Alan was the first to arrive. He'd have preferred (as would others as well) to have had the meeting at a secure government location in Washington, DC, or even a British government secure location, but Tryphine Banking House was more secure than they realized.

After Alan, Erwin was brought down. He'd flown in straight from Germany. Anna had come with him and they were both to stay a few days with their friends, the Tryphines...after the meeting.

Jim arrived next. His sleep schedule was a mess, and he looked the part of the weary traveler. As if by the grace of God, Lord Tryphine had coffee ready and waiting for everyone in the room. After a few minutes Jim wondered if there was enough for anyone besides himself.

Finally, the last three men arrived. They were the reason for the security. Lord Tryphine's man with an ear on the intelligence community, Andrew Lawrence, had been brought in from Tryphine's Lloyd's Office on the other side of London. He came in with two others: Stan MacLean and Elijah Davies . Their specific roles in the intelligence community were never explained, but it was clear that they were going to run the meeting.

Everyone found seats. Introductions were made, and the meeting began as soon as Lord Tryphine had finished expressing his gratitude and opening his hospitality.

Eli, six-foot-two, 270 pounds, was a balding and graying black man, a bit husky. He was not an intelligence field operative, but he clearly had military service demeanor. Davies ran an obscure NSA branch that didn't exist on paper. Unbeknown to those in the room, the people who didn't exist in his group were field operatives who went into secure locations to covertly conduct electronic espionage without being detected. He spoke first.

"Gentlemen, Stan and I will be letting you all in on just a fraction of what we found out thanks to Jim's trip to Tbilisi. Having said that, it's time we got some things sorted out. This private little investigation of yours has become something bigger. Uncle Sam and the Brits are now involved in direct action because of your efforts. Because of the private origins of this investigation, because so many countries are involved, and because so many agencies in all those countries are involved...there is no coherent, top-secret operation or command and control structure. And there won't be either. Nonetheless, the findings of this investigation as well as the resulting direct actions that have taken place are to be considered beyond top secret. This is a read-in-only intelligence activity. You are all bound by penalty of death should any aspect of it leak to the public through your direct or indirect efforts. Do I make myself absolutely, perfectly, without a doubt clear?"

The table resounded with affirmatives, and then Stan began.

"Acting on Jim's suggestion a joint UK/US unit began monitoring communications and gathering signals intelligence from a meeting in Tbilisi. Your intent was to gather more information on Samed Vezirzade and a so-called Oil Mafia. You all suspected that either he or this group were sponsors of at least twenty, possibly thirty different international terrorist attacks...not the least of which were the attacks on America on September 11, 2001. In point of fact, the Tbilisi meeting was one for all sorts of villains. High-ranking government officials from eleven different nations were there. There was an international arms dealer, a former covert special operations member, three former Soviet generals, and your man Samed was the least of them all. Let that sink in for a moment."

Erwin was shocked. Lord Tryphine was surprised, but not completely. Jim had the same reaction. Alan bore a skeptic's face.

Elijah noticed it. "Alan, I know what you're thinking. You're thinking that you have the highest clearance possible and have been getting intelligence community briefings for years, and this all seems like something out of the blue. It is. Jim here struck pay dirt. The man traveled the globe on Erwin's dime. He lived out of a go-bag, a backpack, for years, and he finally got lucky. What's more is you're not going to hear much—if anything—of this in any of your briefings. Stan and I work so deep in the black ops hole that we might open up a hole in China and pop out at any time. You won't hear about us, and you don't need to hear about us...at least not beyond what we're telling you today."

Alan nodded with concern.

"Right then," Stan continued. "Let's begin with the Vezirzade man first. He's probably the easiest, and he gets us straight to the point you want to hear about."

Elijah took over from Stan. "We were able to access Samed's phone. Based on the location of each call he made over the past three months we were able to locate two of his houses. His dachas. From there, Stan sent in teams to bug two of the houses. Meanwhile, we took the list of phone calls that he made, and searched their numbers in our database. Through a little unconscious inter-agency borrowing we were able to create a list of Samed's known associates. We also took the list of accounts that Erwin provided, the suspected sponsor list, we'll call it. Then we correlated the list of Samed's associates and the list of their phone numbers and the suspected sponsor list, and we narrowed down our search to SFS International."

"We already knew this," Erwin interjected.

"No, *Herr* Zimmermann," Elijah answered. "You suspected this. You did not know it. Now we know it. We know it because we further checked SFS International's list with the people who were at the meeting in Tbilisi—the Villain's Meeting is what Stan calls it."

"Do we have a name then? Do we know who the sponsor of all these attacks is?" Terrence asked.

"His name is Sheikh Khalid bin Mohammed Al Tunb, though he believes himself to be an emir."

Everyone looked around the room. No one seemed to have heard of him. Elijah and Stan looked at each other. They both knew the bomb they were about to drop.

Stan answered the big question. "Alan, Jim, you've met him, and Lord Tryphine, you know him well. You know him as Ibrahim Ibn al Douri."

Jim and Alan looked at each other, puzzled.

Elijah smirked. "Alan, he and Lord Tryphine here picked you up at the airport when you went to Kuwait back in 1990. He was the Trucial Energy rep to the House of Saud, the Saudi Arabians."

Lord Tryphine's heart was furious with shame and embarrassment. He hid it, but still had to look away to consider the ramifications of what he'd just learned. "Why would he represent Trucial Energy in 1990, and wage a war on them afterwards?" he asked.

Elijah leaned back and sighed. Stan nodded reluctantly, then began to explain. "The short version is Alan and Jim stole his money. That pissed him off, but it was really just the straw that broke the camel's back so to say. For the rest, we need a bit of a history lesson."

Stan got up and walked to the cart where the coffee was located. Then he poured cups for each man, and began to explain as he passed them out.

"Where does one start with the history of offenses in the Middle East? One could go all the way past antiquity I'm sure. The Greeks wrote about it as much as—aw, hell...let's just start as recent as we can. There's no doubt that the end of World War I caused all sorts of trouble and changing of regimes in Europe, but it did so as well in the Middle East. After World War I Britain was obligated—"mandated"—by the League of Nations to serve as a protectorate for the Arab peoples from the Kurds on the Turkish border all the way down to what is today Oman, and then back along the eastern side of Africa. The Crown was able to keep a hold on much of that until the end of World War II, but after that, and after the cock-up that was the Suez Crisis, it just wasn't going to hold much longer. Our government was pinched for cash after the war, and we were on an independence run where every colony was going to be let loose. In the 1960s, and up to the 1970s, we pulled out. We told all the different sheikhs, emirs, and such that they were on their own. Seven of them banded together and formed the United Arab Emirates.

Others stayed on their own—like Kuwait, Bahrain, Qatar, and Oman."

Jim knew the history well. Alan did too. Lord Tryphine knew it best of all since his family's banking house was deeply involved in the commerce from the Trucial States going back to the early 1800s. To Erwin it was a refresher course in history, but he was familiar. Stan assessed the men and continued.

"There was also an emirate that controlled several of the islands just inside the Straits of Hormuz. These are the Tunb islands. Like Kuwait and Bahrain and Qatar, the emir of Tunb refused to join the United Arab Emirates. When 1971 came around, he was on his own like everyone else. The day before his emirate was officially declared independent, a small Iranian force—backed by the American investors—invaded and took his islands. The emir was in Riyadh, Saudi Arabia, when it happened. He was on his way back from Mecca. No one wanted to risk a cross-gulf war with Iran on one side, Saudi Arabia and the new Gulf States on the other. The United Nations essentially threw the emir of Tunb under the bus. To cool him down the Saudi royal family pointed out some sort of historical lineage connecting them to the emir. They embraced him as one of their own. At the same time Trucial Energy's holdings spread, and he was tasked with being a sort of an ambassador to Trucial Energy. In November of 1990, just before Desert Storm, the emir died. Rumor is he had a heart attack in a meeting, but the official word is that he died on a pilgrimage to Mecca. When one hears that, one knows it's a lie."

Elijah continued while Stan sipped his coffee. "Over the years, the emir had told his son all sorts of stories. When he died, his son—the man you knew as Ibn al Douri—sought about seeing if they were true. That's when he started on his no-holds-barred treasure hunt. That treasure is one of the reasons he was sponsoring these attacks—just one reason. The emir had told his sons that before their islands were taken by the Iranians, even as far back as the 1920s, Trucial Energy's founders had bought the rights to drill for oil on their islands. It was a fifty-fifty profit split. He'd also learned from his father that Trucial Energy was the main investor that pushed the Americans into having the Iranians take their home islands. In return, Trucial Energy got a twenty-year lease for drilling there. After the 1979 Islamic Revolution, the new Iranian government and Trucial Energy were taking all the Tunb's oil; their family treasure."

"What's this treasure hunt you're talking about?" Jim asked.

Elijah shook his head in disbelief. “That’s the bat shit crazy part Jim. The kid thinks that there’s some hidden, secret copy of the agreement his family signed with Trucial Energy’s founders back in the 1920s. He’s convinced of it. Some of the terrorist attacks he sponsored were part of his little treasure hunt. At one point, for who knows what reason, he thought it was hidden at Erwin’s house, and that’s why he helped the Terrafirst Technologies sponsor the attack there. Sorry, Erwin, but that’s how fucked up this man is.”

Erwin bowed his head in disbelief and anger. He’d gotten involved in the entire mess just to make things right for what had been done to him and his staff. Now he had to accept that they’d all been held hostage—almost killed—because of one man’s greed and lust for revenge. Harder to accept was that he had nothing to do with the offense that caused the attack. His thoughts turned to Anna, how lucky she’d been that night, how lucky he was to have her the next day, and how he could never explain to her what he’d just been told. For the first time in his involvement, Erwin felt a special type of anger.

“Even if such a document existed, what does he think he could do with it?” Alan asked.

Stan answered, “It’s very clear from his conversations that he hates the West maybe worse than anyone we’ve heard in a while. He clearly wants revenge. It looks like he thinks he can just go to the UN or someone, wave some secret treaty around, and get his islands back from the Iranians.”

Erwin caught on. “And there is the money.” He added, “No doubt this man thinks he’s entitled to half of Trucial Energy’s earnings off his former home.”

Alan flipped through his ever-thickening, three-ring binder. “That’s...I have data going back to 1943 from Tunb island production. Hold on...” He did some quick math. “This guy could demand as much as...yeah, right, $5.4 trillion, and that’s not adjusting for inflation, interest, reparations, and all the other stuff he probably wants. That’s more than the entire region produces in a year. No one would ever agree to that.”

Everyone sighed and leaned back in their chairs.

“Lord Tryphine,” Jim asked. “I’m sure it’s morning here, but I’ve no idea what time zone my body is living in right now. Do you have anything stronger than coffee?”

Everyone tried to laugh, but the enormity of the situation was coming home. This man was waging a personal war against people he believed had stolen his home, destroyed his family, his kingdom. He actually believed he could somehow extort trillions of dollars in retribution. Such dangerous men always seemed to make history in tragic and costly ways.

"I'll have something brought down, Jim," Terrence answered. "I must say, your work in Georgia really did pay off. Well done, sir. Very well done."

Stan interrupted, "You have no idea how well it paid off. As we've described, Samed led us to Sheikh Khalid bin Mohammed Al Tunb, and that uncovered a long list of privately sponsored attacks, but it's just the tip of the iceberg."

Andrew Lawrence had been silent, mentally merging what he'd just been told with the privy intelligence information old friends had shared with him as well. "It's not just Al Tunb who is sponsoring these attacks. It can't be."

"No, you're right, Andrew." Stan answered. "Al Tunb has been getting a royal family allowance from the Saudis, and Lord Tryphine here has helped him invest and grow that investment over the years. Haven't you, sir?"

"I'm afraid I have. Come to think of it, I specifically recall his request to invest in Ajax Medical a few years ago—before all that business down in Miami at the concert. He may find that some of his investments suddenly meet with bad luck by this afternoon, however."

"Sir," Elijah added, "I'll be passing on some names that we now know, and perhaps they can all meet with some financial misfortune later today. In fact, I'm afraid it will have to happen. You don't want to be tied to funding things as public as the 9/11 attacks."

"Or the other things!" Stan interjected.

"What other things?" Terrence asked.

Stan and Eli exchanged glances. It was time to tell the men the hardest secrets, the ones that made this group a read-in-only type of classified.

Everyone leaned forward except Jim and Andrew. They had a feeling they knew what they were about to hear from Stan.

"Alan, do you remember when you had to be escorted from the secure room in the Senate building? The money for that attack came from Tryphine Banking House via Al Tunb. Jim, Erwin, do you gentlemen remember Samed's meeting of the villains? It turned out Samed was working with a Russian general as well as others to get some old Soviet nukes put together and then put in play. We got one in St. Petersburg, Murmansk—another at Svetlogorsk. We think there's more in play-maybe Vladivostock. Al Tunb has also been traced to attacks that have involved VX nerve agent, smallpox, even Ebola. Everyone knows about the September 11 attacks, but all these and many more were happening in the background, and people must never find out. September 11 was a few thousand people, but with all the nukes and chemicals and biological attacks, Al Tunb could have killed millions had it not been for the intel gained by Jim's efforts in Tbilsi."

Stan paused and spoke directly to Alan for a moment. "I'm certain you haven't been briefed on most of them. You gentlemen have no idea how far down the rabbit hole we have suddenly found ourselves."

Andrew still hadn't had his question answered. "But you can't be saying this Ibn al Douri...Al Tunb is the sole sponsor here. Who are the others?"

Stan answered. "There are plenty of others, but in many cases, Al Tunb or whoever you want to call him is the common thread," Elijah answered. "The 9/11 attacks, for example, the entire attack appears to have cost less than $400,000. We see some of that from Al Tunb, some from a Saudi, some from a few people in the UAE whom we can't even describe, and some from one of Samed's friends in Azerbaijan. The point here is that the world has plenty of villains, but it's not often we find a man who has this much motivation, who has this much influence, and who has put the lives of hundreds of millions of people at risk just for chances to reach his goals."

The room was silent for a moment while the scale of what they'd been told was still trying to settle. "I'll need a copy of that list as well," Erwin asked. "I want to make sure that there's no one who I've been helping in any of this, and if there is their portfolio is going to meet with a sudden and tragic end, I assure you."

"That brings us to a bit of a conundrum, gentlemen," Elijah said. "These terrorist attacks—funded by Al Tunb and a few others—have put tens of millions of people at risk. They've started wars, for God's sake. As you said, I'd love to see them meet an unexpected financial loss this afternoon, but if you cut their funding, I think we all know they'll just find other people to manage their assets. If we seize their assets, they'll go deeper underground and be impossible to find. On the other hand, if we continue to allow them to use—for example—Tryphine Banking House, then we're funding terrorist attacks. However, if Lord Tryphine and Erwin do continue working with them, then we have a good chance at stopping their attacks in the future. We can see where the money is going, and at least have teams in cities ready to respond. That's a massive tactical advantage."

Erwin was already shaking his head, and Lord Tryphine bit his upper lip unconsciously, showing his dislike of the idea.

"I have a better idea," Jim said. "Why not just kill them? We know who these people are, we can find them, and we can just cut the heads off the snake, so to speak. Hell, Erwin could probably just call some of these people, ask for a meeting to talk about their finances, and when they show up...pop, problem solved. Next?"

Andrew laughed at the American sense of simplicity, and Elijah laughed at what he knew was a pipedream. "You know how it works, Jim," Elijah pointed out. "There's always another bad guy. There's always gonna be people who are the best of humanity, and who are the worst. This is an opportunity to control who is the worst. We can use this new line of intelligence to round up the so-called 'evil-doers,' and maybe even deter some. We've built weapons that can level cities, chemicals that can poison the planet for years, and biological weapons that can wipe out God knows how many people. We can't put those genies back in the bottle, but if we don't kill these guys, then we at least have a better chance of making sure they're not used."

"Then what do you suggest we do?" Jim asked.

"That's up to you all," Stan explained. "As we said earlier, this investigation of yours involves nations from all over the world and untold number of agencies. It's not sanctioned or sponsored by any nation...though, on behalf of her majesty's government, I do thank you all—as I'm sure Elijah does for the Americans."

Erwin shook his head. "No. No, I will not continue to support Ibn al Douri or Al Tunb or whoever he is nor will I do so for anyone else who sponsors terrorism. We are obligated by our ability to stop them, and so I will certainly no longer help them—not inadvertently, and certainly not deliberately. No. Absolutely not."

Lord Tryphine was nodding in agreement, but said nothing.

Alan looked at Jim. "When I was first given clearance to attend Senate Intelligence Committee briefings, they never asked me to take an oath. I didn't have to take one when I was a staffer for then Congressman Henderson. I have no skin in the game to deal with their money, and like Erwin or everyone in this room I'm sure, I feel obligated to stop people like this if ever and wherever I can."

Jim nodded back. "I took an oath. I'm in. If Erwin's not, fine. I understand. That might mean that my means are somewhat limited, however."

"No," Erwin interrupted. "You and I are still involved, and you still have a job, I'm afraid." He and Jim smiled.

The room looked at Lord Tryphine, who was clearly deep in thought. After waiting in vain for him to say something all eyes turned to Andrew Lawrence. “I'm in the same boat as Jim. I work for Lord Tryphine. It's up to him.”

This compelled a reply from Terrence. “Andrew, you'll always have a job at Tryphine Banking House. I need you at the Lloyd's office. What we do beyond that is really what needs consideration.”

Everyone thought for a moment. Alan broke the ice. “All right, Colonel. Stan, clearly you want us to keep doing what we're doing, and make your lives easier. That's not an option for some of us, but we do all want to help. Lord Tryphine just can't be asked to knowingly finance terrorist activities, to say nothing of ones as devastating as what you've been described. *Herr* Zimmermann has the same problem. I do have an idea, however. I propose we create a portfolio just for people like this Al Tunb guy. Tryphine Banking House can create a few new hedge funds that are offered exclusively to people we suspect of sponsoring terrorism. By creating the funds, and perhaps having Erwin manage them, Al Tunb and his friends can find themselves doing some high-risk investing with just the suggestion that these investments will bring high rewards. The funds can be filled with high-risk/high yield stocks, bonds, etc., and we'll offset the risk with bonds from some of the less savory countries that are state sponsors of terror. Since the US and UK don't normally trade with state sponsors of terror like Iran, Iraq, Syria, and others, I can set up a dummy corp in the Cayman Islands and use it to buy bonds from the state sponsors of terror to balance out the fake hedge funds we're making for the private sponsors of terror. This way we can control what the bad guys are getting, and we can close their accounts—even seize their funds at any time.”

Erwin had concerns. “We'll need some serious money to put together a hedge fund large enough to keep from falling apart at every market turn. High-risk/high-yield stocks are a balancing act at best. Keeping the buyers' list down to the people we suspect won't upset the apple cart on the market, but those few people won't carry enough investment capital to put together a profitable fund on their own.”

“I will not be loaning out Tryphine Banking House credit to start something that's designed to fail on command,” Terrence added.

Alan nodded and tugged at his bottom lip. “How much do you think we'll need?”

"I'm not sure any of us know how much these private terrorist sponsors are worth, let alone combined," Stan explained.

Lord Tryphine had seen the list and checked his banking house's files. "Combined, I suspect they're probably worth less than $5 billion US. We'll need twice that to create several fake funds and fill each with a large number of diverse, high-risk stocks as well as an equal value in state terrorist sponsor bonds."

Alan looked at Terrence seriously. "If I can get you the money, how long would it take for Erwin and you to put things together?"

"It'll take a few months, and then we'll have to coordinate on how we're going to approach these villains. That could take a few more months. We can't just send out a special email addressed to all our favorite terrorist friends and invite them to dump everything they have into our new, and fake, portfolio geared just for terrorists. They have to be lured slowly, methodically."

"I can get the money. It's out there. We just need to shift it around. I'll set up the transfers for you, Lord Tryphine, and you can get right to work on this. The only catch is that the initial investment I send you will have to be soundly recorded and accounted for and I'll have to be a recipient as well as our terrorist friends. We're skirting the edges of illegality pretty hard here, and to make matters worse, I'll have to be able to pull the money back out at any time—preferably a few hours before we sink any and all earnings our terrorist friends have. That's flat-out insider trading on anyone's playing field."

The room was silent. They were talking about all sorts of illegal trading issues, and Alan was very clearly correct: In the end, they were going to break the rules, and deliberately inflame some very powerful and dangerous people—arguably some of the most dangerous people in world...possibly even in history.

"I'm in!" Jim exclaimed.

"Mr. Smith," Lord Tryphine replied. "It's not your money on the line here."

Smith tilted his head and looked Terrence in the eyes. "No, but it's been my ass on the line for more than a few years now. If Erwin or anyone will keep paying my way, I'll keep doing it too. All our lives are on the line. Erwin's already been held at gunpoint in his own home. Alan's already been flushed out of one of the most secure rooms in the world when the Capitol was attacked. Your Lordship himself has lost friends in the World Trade Center, I'm sure. Stan and Elijah live in the dark like I do.

Hell, the only one who doesn't have skin in the game is Andrew here. No wonder he's so quiet."

All eyes turned to Andrew. "You're right, Jim. I don't have skin in the game or money on the line, but I've lived in the shadows long enough to be all in for the same reason that you are, that Stan is, that Elijah is, and really the same reason we all are: If not us, then who?"

Again the room went quiet.

Stan looked at Alan. "Can you really give someone $10 billion just like that?"

Alan nodded with his disarming smile.

Then Stan shook his head, sighed, and looked at Andrew and Terrence. "Americans."

***

8/6/2002

Twenty miles south of Aden, Yemen, the Trucial Energy tanker *Mary Ann DeNoto* headed west, out of the Arabian Sea and toward the Red Sea. The 1,100-foot-long ship was carrying more than 350,000 tons of Kuwaiti crude oil and was headed for Spain. Before leaving Kuwait, the crew of fourteen men had been joined by a small, twelve-man security detachment from a PMC (private military contractor).

Erwin Zimmermann had detected financial movement into and out of the SFS International hawala money laundering center. He suspected an upcoming attack, called Elijah, and he agreed. Then Erwin called Andrew Lawrence. Since Andrew was Tryphine Banking House's representative to the ship's insurer, Lloyds, he made sure that Lloyds demanded the ship have extra protection. It was a circuitous command and control structure, but it worked, and it was extremely hard to trace.

The sea was calm. The sky was clear. The air was humid, 120 degrees, and the breeze had the effect of a hot oven door, so the crew stayed inside while the contractors worked shifts outside. Three men were on watch at any given time, with three more ready and three resting but ready at a moment's notice.

On the bridge, the radar operator noticed them first. There were at least six small, high-speed craft approaching from the north. The ship was moving at just over ten knots. The small craft were moving at more than thirty knots, and the closure was almost fifty miles an hour. The ship's radar range could see traffic in the port of Aden and the coastline, but the small craft were only ten miles away when it was clear that they were headed for the *Mary Ann DeNoto*.

After a quick double-check of the radar plot by the ship's captain, a series of standard and non-standard anti-piracy actions were taken. The captain notified any and all ships in the area that he suspected they were about to be attacked. Crewmen were all put on alert to seal the ship. Some took up positions manning fire hoses along the side of the ship's foredeck as a way of possibly blasting pirates over the side or flooding their craft. The security detachment was immediately put on alert.

Within a minute of spotting the small craft on radar, a lookout spotted them through some binoculars. The two forces would join in roughly ten minutes. It took only four minutes to wake the rest of the security personnel and get them to their posts—even at the bow a thousand feet away from their berthing. The ship's crew was ready in six minutes. A helicopter from a Canadian frigate off the coast of Djibouti was headed their way, and it was expected to arrive in almost twenty minutes.

Then the waiting came. Everyone on the ship held their breath. Pirates, terrorists, criminals, drug runners, smugglers...the high seas were filled with people of ill will. There was no shortage of horror stories from other sailors who had their ships boarded. At the world's shipping choke points—the south end of the Red Sea being one of them—piracy was rampant. Navies from around the world sent warships to help ward off small attacks, but the pirates were as thick as fleas.

The head of the security team took command of the ship for the moment. He stepped outside of the bridge and relayed commands to the captain to announce over the ship's address system. It was better for the crew to hear things calmly from him.

"Here they come. There are seven of them. Small skiffs dead ahead. Prepare to repel boarders port, starboard, and aft."

Soon after the captain's announcement, the shooting started. One by one the security team opened fire: the distinctive, semi-auto, *pop-pop-pop* of their M-16 rifles. In the distance, a quarter mile from the captain, and a few hundred feet from the bow, the deeper, four-round bursts of AK-47 fire came from the skiffs. Each boat had four to seven people on board, all armed and firing wildly at the tanker.

Pings from copper-jacketed bullets ricocheting off the steel ship sounded like rocks or hailstones on a tin roof. As bullets came closer they made a zip sound, and when one or more flew very close they made a snap sound like a whip.

"Two boats going down the port side, five boats to starboard," called out the captain. "All fire hoses to starboard."

The crewmen with the fire hoses began working on the starboard side. Six hoses were already blasting thousands of gallons of seawater down on the skiffs. Another six were being dragged from the other side of the ship to the starboard side, two hundred feet away.

"One skiff sinking starboard side."

One by one more of the fire hoses came to life on the starboard side of the ship. Bullets bounced everywhere off the ship loaded with oil. Now the calm seas were frantic with the wake of the small boats trying to fight the *Mary Ann DeNoto*'s large wake as well as dodge fire from the security team and the flooding water from the fire hoses. A rainbow arched upward and contrasted the moment.

"One more skiff sinking starboard side. Two skiffs port side pulling away—wait, they're headed back at us."

The confusion of the moment instantly changed. A white flash—followed instantly by a deafening boom—erupted from the port side of the ship. Huge black smoke filled the air and began a climb skyward. Everyone was thrown to the starboard side of the ship. Only the security team stayed alert and was still in action. Even the men on the remaining skiffs had stopped for a moment.

"Damage control port side! Damage control port side!"

The bridge phone rang immediately. "Tanks four and five breached. Fires are under control below deck."

The captain looked at the deck, but it was hard to see through the smoke. The fires inside the ship were being fought, but the ones on the deck were raging.

"Let's get some foam on that deck right away, people."

"One more skiff starboard side," thc captain added.

A moment later the security team leader came back into the bridge. "Last one on the starboard side sunk, sir. Can't make it to the port side because of the heat—fire must be bad. I'll check—"

The security team leader was looking straight at the captain when the hatch behind him opened and the Yemenis began to charge into the bridge. He raised his rifle to fire, and it jammed. In a fluid motion the team lead dropped his rifle, letting it fall to hang by its sling, and drew his nine-millimeter Glock pistol. He fired all fifteen rounds—three at each man right past the captain's left side. One bullet passed so close it left a gray smudge along the edge of the captain's short-sleeved shirt. Before the last Yemeni fell to the deck, the security team lead was already reloading and looking for more threats.

The *Mary Ann DeNoto* would make it to port in Dubai for repairs. Ninety thousand gallons of oil were lost. The rest had to be offloaded to another Trucial Energy tanker. When the oil was offloaded, and the ship was no longer sitting low in the water from the weight of the oil, everyone could clearly see a forty-foot hole surrounded by torn three-inch-thick metal, burned and blown off paint, and black smudge/oily soot that covered the once white superstructure.

Erwin and Andrew had worked well together, and a pirate/terrorist threat had been stopped without anyone knowing how.

***

3/18/2003

Alan waited outside Treasury Secretary George Whittaker's office. The meeting was scheduled for 3 p.m., and it was almost 4. Senator Henderson was running late. Eventually he did arrive and broke the silence.

"Hi, Alan. Sorry to have kept you two waiting."

Whittaker's secretary stood up and professionally led Senator Henderson and Alan into the office. The Treasury secretary was on the phone, but he motioned for them to sit down on the chairs around a coffee table in his office. Then he abruptly ended his call.

"Jerry, Alan," he said with a smile. "Glad you were able to find the time, eh?"

They knew he was joking. George Whittaker had been in DC long enough to know how meetings run over, especially when dealing with elected officials.

"Sorry about that, George," Senator Henderson replied. "You know how some of these hearings can go. We had some protesters raise a fuss today. People never cease to amaze me, ya know?"

"The world's a funny place to be sure, Jerry," George answered. "Actually, it's Alan who I need to see the most. Let me tell you guys about what's been happening in the news and what the news isn't seeing. This'll sound familiar to you both."

Senator Henderson and Alan gave their undivided attention. They'd been to visit the Treasury secretary before, and had several meetings with him over the years, but they were out of the ordinary, and this sounded important.

"Gentlemen, I know there's a lot of focus on Iraq and what's happening over there right now. Jerry, you may be a politician, but you, Alan, and I are also money people. We see things through that prism. You've probably seen on the news the story about a dump truck filled with gold that they tried to sneak out of Iraq?"

Both Senator Henderson and Alan nodded.

"And you both might have heard about the box trucks filled with cash that were found in Syria, or the Iraqi tanker truck filled with currency from all over?"

Again they both nodded.

"Well, gentlemen, what you haven't heard is that our department has intercepted over $63 billion in illegal digital transfers from Iraqi banks. Looks like everybody who knows the combination is robbing the safe."

"Let me guess, people are already fighting for possession of the loot, aren't they?" Senator Henderson asked.

"Damned straight they are. Everybody's got a claim on it, including myself, and everybody is deserving, but my gut is telling me that it's going to be set aside for a provisional government to be put together."

"You know that's just lost money now, right?" asked Alan. "Anyone who gets it is going to toss it around like a drunken lottery winner at happy hour."

"That's already happening regardless," George replied. "State Department says they 'lost' $9 billion. The DoD says they 'lost' $6 billion. No one has any idea what—if anything—the Iraqi central bank still has. And then there's your money."

Jerry smiled. "I was wondering when you were going to get to that."

"Yeah, well, Alan...I'm gonna need you to hand over that loot you brought back in '91."

"Whenever we meet, I've always had the papers ready. There's no problem at all. I will need to know where to route the funds to once they're released."

"We're going to use the Federal Reserve 'Discount Window' in reverse. Here's the routing information."

Alan reviewed the document. It showed simple transfers to Treasury Department accounts. All he had to do was move the money around, and that could all be done digitally.

"I will need this document signed by all three of us."

Alan opened his briefcase and pulled out a form that required all three men to sign.

"And now, Mr. Treasury Secretary, I get to tell *you* something everyone would love to do themselves: the funds will be in your accounts right away, but availability may take several days."

They all laughed. It was a joke that anyone who had ever dealt with a bank's quirky funds-available policies would have loved.

They passed papers around, and within a few minutes, $6 billion were paid to the United States Treasury to be used as they saw fit.

"I have to be honest, it's nice not to have to deal with this anymore," Alan said. "That's a lot of headache, and I'm glad it's yours now."

"I still can't believe you accounted for it so well all these years. You ever need a job...you come see me. Got it?"

Everyone smiled, and Henderson was the first to speak. "Alan's mine, George."

Whittaker nodded and smiled back. "Hey, listen," he added. "Whatever profits were made from these funds are likely illegal under blanketing laws, but specific to where it came from and the situation we're in now with that same government—or lack thereof—the illegality would now come into question. I'd still keep a careful eye on any interest earned over the years. Keep accounting for it well in case someone ever comes asking, and if you guys do anything with any of it, make sure it's not mai tais, strippers, and cruises."

"How much do you figure in interest over the years, Alan?" Senator Henderson asked.

"Well, the spike in gold and oil really made a big difference. We started off earning about eight percent, and now we're averaging seventeen percent. We've got about $14 billion left after today."

George and Jerry just shook their heads in disbelief.

"Jesus, Alan..." Treasury Secretary Whittaker said. "You need a job—ever!—you come see me."

"I should point out," Alan said. "About half of that is now in high-risk/high-yield funds. If it grows, then great, and if it doesn't, that's not so great. I hope that somewhere down the line it can be used to fill gaps like we did with the Mississippi flooding relief ten years ago. And let's be clear, that's not 'Alan's money.' It's no one's. Iraq, Trucial Energy, CIA, DIA, FBI, DSS, any US department or agency could lay claim on part of it. There's no way to release the money without permission of myself as trustee, the Treasury secretary, and the chair of the Senate Committee on Intelligence Oversight. Even then, once it goes into the US government's proper accounts, we'll come under some serious scrutiny. Anyone and everyone with an agenda will do anything for it. People kill for a lot less, and the seriousness of that is not lost on me. I'm sure it's not lost on you two either."

The three men exchanged pleasantries, and then shook hands. The $6 billion meeting was over. Technically, Alan had told the truth. He had invested the interest on the Iraqi gold into high-risk/high-yield funds. What he didn't say was that the funds were ones setup by Erwin and Lord Tryphine to control Al tunb and the other terrorist financiers.

***

7/29/2003

Inside the Dirksen Senate Office Building at the American Café Dining Room, Senator Henderson, Alan Conferra, and Treasury Secretary George Whittaker were having a pre-meeting lunch. The meeting would cover recent efforts to smuggle vast amounts of currency out of Iraq. It was just another Tuesday in Washington, DC.

The room was a simple cafeteria. Its interior design boasted little more than acoustic tile ceilings, vinyl flooring, a faux gray marble façade hiding the vertical steel supports, and stainless steel cafeteria equipment. Family-style seating at laminate tables allowed for hundreds to grab a quick and inexpensive lunch. The most impressive design element was the choice of wooden chairs instead of steel buffet chairs.

While the room was unremarkable, the food was not. Among the top menu items were a half-pound cheeseburgers served "Kennedy style" (i.e., "loaded" with lettuce, tomato, onion, pickle, ketchup, mustard, steak sauce, and a scotch-whiskey glaze). Senator Henderson's came with three giant-sized onion rings stabbed to the top of the monstrous burger with a steak knife. George Whittaker had their version of Senate Bean Soup with fresh-made pumpernickel bread. Alan had the Asian-American fusion grilled chicken salad. While it looked like a regular cafeteria, the food was well above average, and so it drew some of the most powerful people in Washington, DC—and in the world.

World news had been filled with stories of oddities and amazements being smuggled out of Iraq for months. The details were often secret, but the subject in general was not. Still, all three men chose to sit at a table far from the door, the cafeteria line, or the kitchen. Their desire for seclusion was obvious to anyone, and as most patrons played in the same political game, they respected the three men and gave them their space.

Any small talk the three had was done when they met at the door and while they were in line. The moment the first bamboo serving tray touched the table, that's when the real conversation began.

"So, Alan," George asked, "how's your little private investment doing?"

Alan knew the Treasury secretary was talking about the interest from the Iraq gold he recovered in 1991. It was something the Treasury secretary marveled at. "Fine, sir. Very fine," he replied with a coy smile.

"What are you up to now?" Senator Henderson asked.

"We're just over $25 billion now."

Jerry and George smiled, looked at each other in amazement, and just shook their heads with disbelief.

"The high-risk funds are paying off, but I completely expect a correction at any time. The $25 billion is likely to be around $17 billion when all is said and done," Alan added.

"Looks like there's a lot of other people trying to do the same thing out there now. Once people were walking around the streets with stolen TVs and looted sofas, I'm sure anyone with a key was emptying their safety deposit boxes," George added.

George stared at his burger and planned his attack on it. "I saw a picture of a guy carrying a gold toilet out of one of the palaces. Can you believe that? Who the hell wants a gold toilet?!"

Alan grinned. "You're right, Mr. Secretary. It looks like it all started with the looting in mid-April. Once those airborne guys in the 82nd found the truck with $3 billion in gold up near Kirkuk, it looks like the entire area went into freefall. I saw a picture of a rental-style box truck filled with pallets of American hundred-dollar bills. Unbelievable things are happening over there."

"That's only the stuff we know about too. Imagine where all the rest is going?" George asked.

Senator Henderson had only managed to get his hands on his burger, and it was already pouring out juices like a sponge being wrung out. He stopped just before he started on it. "George, we can talk about the stuff we really know about later. Suffice it to say the press is only seeing the tip of the iceberg."

"How much do you think in the end?"

Alan answered the Treasury secretary. "Counting the digital transfers, the stuff we know about, and the stuff in the press, it's about $150 to $200 billion. A lot of that is grift from the UN, so ownership is sketchy at best. It'll be just like 1991 again where the insurance companies' payout lost debts, banks loan to the insurance companies, and countries pay the banks to cover the debts. No one in the US has been allowed to do business over there for well over a decade so your office won't have too much trouble, but the French, Germans, Russians, South Africans, their central banks are going to be paying out, I'm sure."

George continued to eat without missing a beat to speak. "I thought the same as much, guys, but I haven't gotten any calls. When I talk to my counterparts they're not sweating it at all. It's been months now, and I don't think many people are filing claims for the banks to bail out."

"Where do you think all that shiny stuff is going then?" Senator Henderson asked.

Alan wiped his face with a paper napkin. "Gentlemen, I'm afraid that's read-in-only information."

Both men stopped and looked at him dumbfounded.

"Excuse me, Alan?" the senator asked.

"With all due respect, sir. We know, but you haven't been read-in on that intelligence. I'm fairly certain you won't be either."

George was curious. "Alan, I meet with the president every day. I've never heard of this. What are you talking about?"

"I'm sorry sir, but—" Alan was cut off by Senator Henderson.

"What the fuck is this, Alan? First you've got this semi-off-the-books loot, and now you've got off-the-books intel? What are you doing? I'm going to need to be read-in on this today. Is that clear?"

"No, sir. You will not be read-in. It's an international thing. Think of it as aliens and Area 51 kinda stuff."

George Whittaker was not amused, and Senator Henderson was having trust issues with Alan. "We're gonna have to have a talk about this later, Alan."

"Yes, sir," he answered.

George tried to cool the setting. "Jerry, Alan's demonstrated he can be trusted over the years. If he says he knows, we can believe that. And if he says it's a read-in-only thing, then we know where it's going isn't on the up-and-up. That means it's going to some people we don't want it to go to, and that's enough to know. We know it's bad. Can we do anything, Alan? Can it be stopped? Should it be?"

Alan sighed. “No, sir, on all accounts I’m afraid. It is literally out of our hands.”

The senator’s mouth was stuffed and his hands a horrific mess from his burger. “I really don’t like this, Alan.”

Alan pulled out four paper napkins from the dispenser and handed them to his boss. “I don’t like it either, sir, but there are some spooks doing good things, and we have to give them some freedom to work here.”

“Who’s going to do oversight on them?” the senator asked.

“We are. I’m watching them, and you’re watching me.”

It was a tense and serious moment. Danions of untraceable monies were being secreted out of Iraq and given to bad people who wanted to do bad things. Senator Henderson, who took pride in being the chairman of the Senate Intelligence Oversight Committee, was angry. The Treasury secretary of the United States was sitting right there, and that made him feel even a bit embarrassed. Senator Henderson looked at Alan with a coldness he’d never aimed at the man.

“Oh, I’ll be watching now, Alan. I’ll be watching now.” Then he bit into his huge burger, and everything between the lettuce and the bottom bun shot out and onto the plate with one splattering plop.

George broke out laughing and dumped a full spoon load of soup on to his tie.

Alan felt the seriousness. He didn’t laugh—even as his boss lightened up.

***

8/18/03

Starting in 1994, the Summit of the Americas had been held three times. In 2003 it was held in Mexico City. Each of the summits involved more than thirty-three nations from the Western Hemisphere. Topics were unlimited, but the focus remained on social, military, and economic issues unique to the Western Hemisphere. In addition to the thirty-three-plus nations, hundreds of international organizations and businesses attended as audience members. In reality, they were there to represent their own interests to the national representatives at the summit.

As is common at most economic summits, there were protests. Anarchists, environmentalists, Marxists, communists, Leninists, and a long list of others all chose the opportunity to have their voices heard by national representatives, and—more importantly—international media. As is also common at such gatherings, some protests became violent, and police were brought in to prevent violent protests from evolving into riots (or worse). This time the police failed, and a protest grew into a violent protest and did evolve into a riot. That's when the Mexican military was brought in to stop the violence from spreading further.

Whether people saw it on their evening news, or on breaking news, or on the Internet, the images taken by photographers on the scene were graphic. Some of the pictures and video was taken by protesters themselves, put up on the web, and spread virally. Women beaten by police, young people covered in their own blood, the battlefield smoke of tear gas and people choking, it was a tragic scene evoking heartbreak for all who saw. Viewers around the world felt sorry for the protesters even if they didn't know the cause they were protesting.

Unbeknownst to almost the entire world, the protests hadn't organically grown into violence. A group called the EPLN (Popular Liberation Army) had deliberately caused the turmoil. The group described itself as "Fighters for the Native Peoples of the Americas." Typically they were limited in action to rural areas where government entities from Central and South American tribes had trouble with government influence. This was a radical change in their behavior.

Erwin Zimmermann knew why. He'd been watching a commodity trading account that Ibn al Douri/Al Tunb owned. That account made a payout to SFS International, which then sent money through the hawala system. When he notified Davies, Elijah traced the receiving account to a known suspect in the EPLN. Elijah notified Stan of the intelligence. Rather than pass on the intelligence to local authorities or international authorities, Stan made sure that a special international commando force was in position in Mexico City should trouble arise. When it did, and when the Mexicans asked for help from the international community, Stan's team was ready, and immediately sent into action.

Tear gas was still dissipating through the streets of Mexico City. Having carefully set the protests into violence, the leaders of the EPLN retreated to a temporary headquarters. It was an abandoned warehouse in an abandoned manufacturing center. When the plant closed in the late 1980s, the nearby residents/workers left too. Everything was in dilapidated condition. Rust, peeling paint, chipping plaster, collapsed roofs, rotten wood, flooded basements...even gangs and drug lords found the place too decayed to use. Rats had found the area so perfect to their needs that they had grown in numbers and even driven out stray dogs and cats.

It was not the imagery that Mexico or any of the Summit of the Americas attendees wanted to show as an illustration of the modern Western Hemisphere. It was a common reality they preferred hidden from voters, political opposition, and wealthy investors. Still, the world did see it. They were forced to do so when a Mexican police lieutenant leaked that the ELPN was behind the violence and had literally holed up there. News crews from all over the world had conveyed on the summit, mobilized to cover the violence, and now raced to the area. One brave reporter and his cameraman even made it into the area, and they were able to broadcast Stan's Special Forces attack on live TV all around the world.

The reporter started off broadcasting from inside an abandoned factory locker room. He was surrounded by trough urinals, stall-less toilets (most broken), sheets of paint peeling off the walls and hanging from the ceiling, and the constant dripping from broken pipes and leaky roofs all around.

"This is Jesus Hernandez reporting live from inside the abandoned Relámpago Machining factory where Popular Liberation Army members have fled. Local police sources tell us they are the ones responsible for this morning's violence at the Summit of the Americas."

The camera shifted from the reporter and went out of focus for a moment. Then it was clearly looking through a triangle-shaped hole in a pane of frosted glass that once let light into the locker room. Through the broken pane viewers could see down into a loading area. On the left was a series of loading docks. On the right, a small street entered the area. At the far end, there was only a wide alley opening to the left. Up close to the camera, on the right, was the main street where trucks once brought in and took out loads. All of the buildings were at least three stories high. The warehouse on the left had almost no window panes left—all having been broken by vandals years earlier. The rest of the area was dominated by Spanish-style housing in various stages of decrepit. One had even collapsed into itself on the right, leaving a space of rubble.

While the reporter babbled on about the protests that had happened, the camera shook, lost focus, and then regained it, but aimed slightly more to the right. Viewers could see the street right outside the window. There, the camera clearly showed one of the EPLN members. He was wearing an unbuttoned white shirt with a T-shirt underneath, khaki pants, a black belt, and brown dress shoes. He was in his late thirties/early forties, Hispanic, and he had a five o'clock shadow even though it was only three in the afternoon. Across his chest was slung an H&K G3A3 rifle, the same kind used by the Mexican military. He leaned on the side of the building overlooking the dock area, and he should have been watching the street approach to his back left.

As if on cue (and conspiracy theorists would later claim it was on cue), four men dressed in white/gray urban camouflage appeared in the camera frame. They moved up to the man at the corner of the building. Each of the men was carrying MP-5SD submachine guns with built-in suppressors. When the first man in the line of commandos was almost close enough to poke the terrorist in the head, he fired. The special, subsonic, nine-millimeter bullet hit almost an inch above where the man's skull met his spine, and it passed through his nose in a spray of white skull, gray brain, and three shades of red mist....all on live TV.

The reporter was shocked. His adrenalin had already been fully pumping through his body when the silent shot happened. He tried to control himself, but only managed to quiet his voice—more from fear than control. The cameraman had shuddered when it happened, but the man's body slumped and gushed blood all over his white shirt. His adrenalin left a metal taste in his mouth, and his body wanted to faint, to shut down, but he fought to be professional, and he succeeded.

As the first man's body slumped into a bloody pile of meat, the four men stepped around it. They walked slowly and deliberately down the length of the homes on the right side of the camera shot and toward the loading area. Again the camera lost focus for a moment, and then it zoomed in to see five more men in white shirts with rifles by the farthest loading dock. Silently, the four commandos fired at the five men. Each took no less than six nine-millimeter bullets. Each turned red before the camera. Each slumped, and the commandos never lost a beat; never missed a step.

Another man came running out of the warehouse and to the loading dock area. Like the others he was carrying the same rifle, dressed in an unbuttoned white shirt. Unlike the others who had only taken a few bullets, two of the commandos emptied their magazines into the man. He took at least twenty bullets and was immediately lifeless.

Two more men ran out. Clearly they had seen one or more of their compadres killed. Both EPLN members stepped out of the same door—and met the same fate. One man's rifle fell off the loading dock and fired. It was the first gunshot heard. The element of surprise was lost.

All four men, still walking, reloaded with stronger, standard, non-subsonic bullets. They dropped the old magazines on the ground. Again they never missed a step.

At the vacant lot the line of commandos turned and headed into the rubble—out of the camera's sight. A shot rang out from the second story of a building down at the far right end of the loading area, and both cameraman and reporter dove for cover. They perceived the shot was at them, and hugged the filthy old locker room floor.

"What you have just seen hasn't been filmed since the British attack on the Iranian embassy in the 1980s!" the reported exclaimed. He tried to whisper, but was unable. Another shot rang out, and the camera shuddered. When it came back, it was on its side and focused on the reporter again. This time, the left side of his face was covered in paint chips and filth.

"It appears Mexico's 'Fuerza especial de reaccion (quick reaction force)' counter-terrorism team is in action against the EPLN. We're...we're not where we were told to be, and we are inside the battle area. Uh...we will..." The reporter was starting to lose his nerve. "We will keep reporting as long as we can. Umm..."

The cameraman stood up, and the camera jostled. He headed back to the triangular hole in the glass so he could film the loading area again. First he zoomed in on the body of the first man killed by the commandos. Then he panned down and showed seven white/red lumps of human that were once Popular Liberation Army members.

The camera moved away after a moment, and up toward where they thought the last shot had come from. At the extreme edge of the view, the camera showed part of an open window on the third floor of one of the abandoned residences. Again, as if on cue, a white shirt moved in the window, then immediately out of view. Viewers could hear the cameraman explain to the reporter that he found a sniper. The conversation between the two men was muffled and couldn't be understood by viewers.

Interrupting their combat debate, the glass pane next to the one where the camera had been filming suddenly exploded. In the back of the locker room a high-velocity 7.62-millimeter bullet smashed through the tiles, through the brick behind the tiles, and lost its inertia a moment later. It could be heard pinging of metal as it fell down an unseen shaft behind them.

Their conversation was silenced, replaced by frantic shuffling to crawl out of the locker room.

The broadcast continued for another hour, but the two men never left the floor. Occasionally a shot from one of the terrorists could be heard. What the camera never showed were the hundreds of rounds fired by the commandos. The other fourteen terrorists who were killed were never seen by the world. The first ones died in the basement of the building next to the rubble lot where the commandos went inside. Their bodies sank in the twelve-foot-deep water that had accumulated in the basement over the years. More were killed at the top of stairwells and in rooms, and even the sniper was killed without being seen on TV.

The world never saw the attack end. The crew was "rescued" by regular Mexican police a few hours later. The reporter had incorrectly labeled Stan's Special Forces team as a Mexican military counter-terrorist team. The secrets were secure. Erwin, Eli, and Stan had worked well together.

***

10/10/2003

The echo from Senator Jerry Henderson's gavel seemed to still be echoing as people were leaving the room. He had just formally ended the latest meeting of the Senate Committee on Intelligence Oversight (aka the Senate Intelligence Committee). The day's topic was a familiar one: Should the American people know the truth about a terrible event, or should the US government continue to lie about it in the interest of preventing national and international panic? At the center of the issue was a small town in rural California.

Aetna Spring, California, made the news as people by the hundreds began calling 911 for assistance. They complained of severe nausea, bleeding from the nose, ears, and eyes, and general biological system shutdowns. The images shown on TV were nightmarish. Entire families were shown dead in their beds while they slept, sitting at the dinner table, or on couches with televisions still on. Men in white and yellow suits with full-face respirators and self-contained breathing apparatuses on their backs were dragging out bodies and piling them in the streets. Survivors walked around covered in caked blood and dust and without cognitive thought. All they could do was wander aimlessly until they died. More than 5,200 people died in the first hours. Few of the ten thousand survivors would live another five years.

At a hastily convened press conference, the president had gone with a false narrative. He claimed that a truck moving from the Travis Air Force Base Special Munitions Storage Facility had gone off the road near the town. The truck was carrying nuclear bomb cores to be stored at the air force base for dismantling in the near future. It was compared to the 1966 Palomares Incident in Spain where a mid-air crash resulted in an American bomb breaking open and contaminating a part of Spain. In this case, some radiation from a plutonium warhead had leaked into the groundwater and contaminated many of the people in the town. A Department of Defense spokeswoman pointed out that there had been other nuclear accidents at Travis Air Force Base in the 1950s and 1960s. In fact, the base was named after General Travis who crashed a B-29 bomber with a nuclear weapon on board in the 1950's. Everyone who was directly involved in the Aetna cleanup knew she was lying.

The reality was a typically darker story. Days before the Aetna Incident, an NSA asset had detected and seized a cargo ship that had been carrying materials to make a dirty radioactive bomb. Terrorists had planned on putting several bombs around the US, and rural Aetna was their first target. Subsequent covert operations from Elijah Davies' group had prevented the worst from happening. The debate about whether or not to tell the world about the actual threat was fuming in secret rooms all around the world, rooms like the one where the Senate Committee held its darkest meetings.

Henderson was the chairman. The issue before the committee was first whether or not to reveal the truth: that the Aetna Incident was no accident, but a deliberate terror attack as well as several thwarted terror attacks with so-called "dirty bombs," bombs designed to spread radioactive contamination rather than act as fission or fusion devices.

Senator Henderson and others on both sides of the aisle wanted to keep the truth about Aetna quiet—as they routinely had done with the vast majority of terrorist attacks; just stick with the "accident" story. Senator Elizabeth Carnegie, the vice chair of the Senate Select Committee on Intelligence Oversight, as well as others on both sides of the aisle wanted to use the terrorist attack as a means of embarrassing the agencies and departments in the intelligence committee so that they could be reduced in size, and—more importantly to her—in budget. The committee was divided more than usual, but Senator Henderson had his way, and it was officially decided to back the White House in their cover-up.

Once the hearing was over, Senator Carnegie rose from her chair and approached Senator Henderson.

"Jerry, I just can't see covering something like this up. I'm sorry. I still think if we hide it, then the American people and the world will never really grasp what a dangerous world we live in."

"I understand, Janice, but this is how the White House wants to play it. You're right—we live in a damned dangerous world. Planet Earth is not a civilized place."

"Exactly," she replied. "The people have to know that."

"Then we'll let them know by other means. Dead bodies in California...people would want war even though the whole affair is already over."

"Jerry, you and I and everyone in this room know how dangerous things are. We see it every day. Most of the people in this building know it. Everyone in the military knows it. Most every business leader in the country knows it, but the seventy-five to eighty percent of the American people who care more about the latest trends in pop music or which celebrities are getting divorced...those people will not grasp any sort of warning except dead bodies. Bodies are real. People get that. They connect to it. We need the American people to see how dangerous things are, and lying to them won't help that."

"What do you want to do, Janice? You wanna live stream a US Marine patrol in Baghdad? Maybe we should put some cameras on a few Special Ops guys' guns on their next raid so the world can see what psychopathic monsters we're fighting are really like?"

"That's not what I'm saying, Jerry," Senator Carnegie replied. Then she paused and considered the idea.

"Dammit, woman! The world is about lives, not ratings. You're actually thinking about the camera thing. I wasn't serious."

"Yes...no! Oh, Jerry, you just don't get it. If we lie about Aetna then those five thousand people died for nothing...nothing."

Alan Conferra had been sitting behind Senator Henderson throughout the hearing. "You're right, Senator."

Both Jerry and Janice answered, "I know, thank you." Then they looked at each other. Henderson shook his head, and Carnegie rolled her eyes.

Alan smiled disarmingly. "I meant you're both right, and you're both wrong. The vast majority of the American people don't get motivated unless there're bodies in the street, but you're also right in that we can't just tell the world about every nightmare that comes into this hearing room. In the end, the debate is moot, irrelevant, a sideshow. Today's hearing and discussion was a waste of valuable time and resources. We shouldn't be talking about what people can hear and what they can't. That's not what this committee is for. There are others who have that responsibility. We could have and should have seen this attack coming. It's this committee's job to oversee the intelligence community and make sure they're doing their jobs. We failed to do that.

"The DoD should have known about how an Azerbaijani nuclear scientist sold bombs. The NSA should have detected the entire plot. The Department of Energy and the State Department should have known that material was being snuck out of Chernobyl. The Treasury Department and Security and Exchange Commission should have seen the money being moved around. Even the Coast Guard should have had a better lock on the boats that just sailed right into the USA with stolen nuclear materials on board. The list goes on and on. Why didn't the Department of Transportation have the ability to simply stop a train headed for San Francisco with a dirty bomb on it? Senators, we failed to make sure those departments were doing their jobs."

Henderson had learned to expect and respect Alan's cold analysis, but Elizabeth Carnegie had never faced it. She was taken back.

"Well, I suppose you're right, young man. We all failed, didn't we?" She looked at Alan square as if accusing him of personally being responsible for Aetna Spring. He took it without fail or reservation.

"Yes, Senator. *We* all did."

All three people stared at each other for a moment while the secret hearing room rustled. Jerry had shifted his gaze from Alan to Janice, back and forth, and finally settled on Senator Carnegie .

"Janice, did you have something to add? I missed the part in the hearing today where you asked anyone how or why they missed this dirty bomb attack."

"Ha-ha, Jerry. I was waiting for the chairman to actually lead and do that."

"No, you weren't, Janice. You were asleep—again. Hell, I shouldn't complain...at least you finally attended one of our hearings. Thank you so much. By the way, I love your hair. Did you get it done? I remember it being more...gray."

Senator Carnegie huffed and shuffled out the door with her head aimed high like a snobby teenager. Alan and Jerry couldn't see it, but she was even rolling her eyes again.

"Alan, I swear...I think that woman wants my job."

"Really? You get that vibe, sir? She hides it so well."

Their sarcasm was in full force.

"Do you have anything you'd like to add to today's briefing—anything from your sources?"

"I'm going to see if we can't get you read-in on that program, sir. It's one of those tricky spots where—since you're an elected official—there could be political ramifications. A plausible deniability issue if you will. Now, do I have anything to add? We were aware of funding from a source to the hawala money laundering network in the Gulf region, and that Azerbaijani who organized the Aetna Spring attack...we saw him get the money out of the network. He wasn't on any of our previous watch lists, and if he had been we'd have spotted it right away. Then the appropriate measures could have been taken, but no. He wasn't on anyone's radar. There was no real way of stopping this."

"Why do you think George Whittaker and the SEC didn't spot that?" Senator Henderson asked.

"Three reasons right off the bat, sir. First, they're swamped. There's no way they can watch all the accounts in the world when they can barely even watch all the accounts in the US. Second, banking and trading laws in the US are tight, but that tightness works both ways; it makes it hard for the bad guys, and it makes it hard for the good guys to set traps. Last, I've never gotten the impression that they're even trying when it comes to international financial surveillance."

Jerry Henderson thought about that for a moment. No one was really putting forth a concerted national effort at international financial surveillance. Numbers bore people. Financial laws are even more boring. Add to that the language issues and electronic issues...it's just too boring, too hard, and too complex for a dedicated effort.

Senator Henderson knew all too well the in-fighting and foot-dragging that happens between federal agencies too. He'd seen the Departments fail to work together, fail to form task forces that they were supposed to form, and instead they created more roadblocks. Intelligence is gathered from all sorts of places, and that's why there was supposed to be a single Central Intelligence Agency, but politicians like Elizabeth Carnegie held the reins too tightly; strangled the necessary creativity and daring. Alan was right: Outsourcing had its benefits.

***

7/21/2004

Alan had always known Jerry Henderson as a gregarious and amicable politician. Few things ever got him down, and since they'd known each other there'd been more than a few things that could have or should have done so. He was a man with a background in commodities trading and finance, but like seventy percent of the members in Congress he had a lawyer's gift of gab. Things had changed. Life happened earlier in the month.

On their way home from watching fireworks, Senator Henderson's wife and three kids were in a car crash. They had been merging onto I-185 north of Greenville, South Carolina, and a Kenworth semi-tractor trailer didn't see them. There was speculation that he had been temporarily blinded by a flash from a private fireworks display, but it didn't matter. They went to merge, he never saw them, and he crushed the station wagon. Senator Henderson had stayed behind to glad-hand some of the local politicians.

Since then, Jerry just wasn't the same. Instead of being talkative, he was quiet. He became a listener. Instead of trying to find the silver lining to any "cloudy" event, he'd just nod, bite his upper lip, and look away. He'd developed quite a short fuse as well.

On this day, Alan and Jerry had flown from Washington, DC, to London. It was a quiet flight, partly due to Senator Henderson's newfound lack of gab, and partly because they left in the middle of the night to be at Tryphine Banking House for an 8 a.m. meeting. Elijah Davies came with them. Lord Tryphine had one of his limousines pick them up at Heathrow, and when they got inside Andrew Lawrence and Stan MacLean were already waiting.

Per the usual security checks and the issuance of visitor passes, the men arrived at Tryphine Banking House, and they made their way down to the secure conference room. Erwin Zimmermann and Jim Smith met them at the last checkpoint.

"Jerry," Erwin began. "I'm so sorry to hear about your loss. Please, please, let me know if there's anything I can do."

"Thank you, Erwin. I'm fine, but I'll let you know if I do," he replied.

Erwin looked at Alan. He was surprised to get two simple sentences from the likes of Jerry Henderson—or any politician for that matter. Erwin had a questioning, disbelieving face, and Alan just nodded as if to reply, "Yes, that's how he is now."

They continued inside, where Lord Tryphine was waiting. He welcomed everyone as a whole, then individually. Then he also offered his condolences to Jerry Henderson with a similar reaction.

Once they were all sitting, there was a moment of pause as they all looked at each other. Each recalled the innumerable email and fax communications they'd had with each other. It was almost like they each had private jokes between each other, and only when they came together like this did they all really feel like they were working together as a whole.

Senator Henderson got right to the point. "All right then...you fellas gonna finally read-me-in on this little hobby of yours?"

Jim leaned forward and took a deep breath. Gathering intelligence on the largest sponsors of international terrorism was his job, but it was also his life. He didn't know Senator Henderson very well at all, and took direct offense at the comment.

Stan and Elijah took offense as well. They knew of Senator Henderson, and had met him, and they knew about the curveball life had just tossed him, but they remained professional. They'd lost friends and family to the terrorists. Normally the Tryphine meetings were cordial, professional, and had certain camaraderie. That was gone.

"Senator," Lord Tryphine began, "no one is here to be coy. What you're about to hear is that we are doing something illegal, something that would be extremely unpopular if revealed to the world, and something that would end careers, destroy legacies, and certainly end lives."

No one had said it, but Jerry knew he'd spoken too brashly, and likely offended everyone in the room. He wasn't shamed, not even embarrassed. He did care, however. It showed on his face as he nodded gently.

Alan started to explain it all. "After Erwin was taken hostage, he felt obligated to find out who was responsible for invading his home, threatening his staff, and himself. He and Lord Tryphine—with some aid from Andrew Lawrence and his old friends in the intelligence community—did some leg work. They did some research on the terrorists who held him at gunpoint, and found out where their living expenses were coming from. They traced the money to the Ajax Medical Research, Defender Security, and the Terrafirst Technologies. From there they traced the money to several small and medium businesses in the Persian Gulf. These businesses offer age-old hawala-style money transfer or money laundering services to anyone without a trace. Erwin then noticed that several other terrorist attacks were traced to the same small businesses in the Persian Gulf."

"That's where I came in," Jim said. "Alan and I had a very frank conversation with a connected guy in Afghanistan. He led us to a guy in Azerbaijan—a rich guy. I tracked him down, and Elijah and I bugged a meeting he had in Tbilisi. From that meeting, Elijah got all the guy's digital world."

Elijah explained. "I got the man's contacts, their contacts, all their text messages, access to phone calls, even pictures and games on their phones. We tracked him as he sent money to known terrorists. He sent it to the businesses doing hawala-style transfers. That's when we had a correlation of money going in and money going out. With that, we created a database of transactions, checked it against known bad guys, and that's how we found the Holy Grail: the world's largest private sponsor of international terrorism."

Stan spoke next. "His name is Ibn al Douri Al Tunb...amongst others. He's a rich sheik from the Persian Gulf, and he's got a big grudge against Trucial Energy and the United States. And that's the real, real short version."

"So far it looks like you've done some great work, but I don't see anything illegal except maybe some privacy issues. What happened next?" Jerry asked.

Alan tugged at his lip for a moment, then shuffled his papers. "Well, sir, that's where we went off the reservation. It's also where you have to decide if this is really what you want to know because once you do you're a part of it. Once you do...your neck might be on the chopping block as well."

"Just fucking give it to me, Alan." Jerry was still in an apathetic sentiment. After losing his wife and his children there was little he cared about anymore.

"Jerry," Lord Tryphine began. "We devised a scheme to lure in private sponsors of terror, and enable people like Stan or Elijah to take action. Technically we're funding the terrorists."

Lord Tryphine paused, expecting Senator Henderson to explode, but he didn't.

Erwin continued. "Lord Tryphine and I have created a series of private investment funds. Some of these 'bad guys' as we're calling them have already been clients of ours...before we knew them as 'bad guys,' of course."

Lord Tryphine interrupted. "Al Tunb, for example...I've known him as Ibn al Douri for years. In fact, his father was the

Saudi ambassador to Trucial Energy for years. Once Erwin and I were made aware of who he is, and who some of these other people really are...well, we had a choice: we could either dump their accounts or track their accounts. Upon deliberation in this room it was decided to track the villains rather than lose them to seek funding elsewhere, which would have been easy."

"To do this," Alan began, "I set up a dummy bank and a few dummy companies in the Cayman Islands. Lord Tryphine used Tryphine Banking House to create a series of private investment funds. They were intended to be high-highs; high-risk, high-return funds marketed only to people we have strong suspicion of being terrorists or involved with terrorist activities."

Lord Tryphine explained the funds further. "Alan provided sufficient capital to stuff these investment funds with thousands of high-risk investments."

Jerry's right hand palm wiped his face. "Alan..."

"Yes, sir. I used a large portion of the money you're thinking about."

"I thought you couldn't take that without my signature."

"I can't withdraw it, but as trustee I am entrusted with moving it. So I did. You'll recall I did inform you and the Treasury secretary that I'd moved a lot of it to a high-risk, high-yield structure."

"Oh my God, Alan," Jerry moaned.

"It's worse than that," Lord Tryphine replied. "Oh, it's far worse. Once we had Alan's capital, Erwin and I loaded the funds up. He and I slowly, individually encouraged suspected villains who were in our books already...to invest in these investment funds. We told each man that the funds were exclusive opportunities available only by invitation and only offered to select customers."

"So you got them to invest in these hedge funds that you built to fail, no?" Henderson asked.

"Yes, but..." Lord Tryphine paused.

Erwin continued. "But they succeeded."

"Right," Stan said. "These villains or 'bad guys' or whatever you want to call them have flocked to these investment funds. We've been able to detect transfers into and out of the hawala system when they go from one villain to another. With the detection we can follow the money, and Stan's teams have conveniently been in the area whenever an attack has happened."

"So it works then?" Henderson asked the group.

Elijah smiled. "You remember the Aetna Spring event? Erwin saw money getting transferred from the Chinese to the

Iranian, and I had a man ready to go and in the area immediately after it happened. We prevented two other attacks because of that."

Andrew Lawrence finally added into the conversation. "Erwin saw some money getting funneled, notified me, and I made sure there were security personnel on a Trucial Energy tanker when it was attacked. The pirates were all killed, the money wasted, and our intelligence gathering asset worked."

Jerry looked at Stan knowing he had something to add. "Senator, because of Alan's plan, Lord Tryphine's and Erwin's efforts, we were able to have teams in place. We were able to rescue a UN negotiator and his aide who were taken hostage, rescue commuters here in London when Irish terrorists tried to hold them as political hostages, and we stopped a cult from destroying a medieval library in Venice—more on that later by the way. We took out terrorists at an economic summit in Mexico City, rescued dignitaries held hostage by the Chinese mafia in Hong Kong, and rescued Japanese dignitaries in Caracas and hostages on a cruise ship near Naples. The list goes on and on."

"Sir," Alan began to point out. "Many of these incidents—like the Aetna Springs Incident—were intended to start wars...regional wars, even world wars. Any funding that is being allowed to happen winds up wasted funding on the enemy's part."

"That's where it really gets tricky, Jerry." Lord Tryphine reclined in his chair. "These people—people like Ibn al Douri Al Tunb—they're often very wealthy. They have their own agendas and fund attacks that will further their own agendas. Rarely do they share beliefs with their footmen. The Arab Afghans and your 9/11 attacks were partly funded by Al Tunb before we knew who he was. It's not that he shares the beliefs of the Arab Afghans, but he used them to hit America so he could make an economic attack on Trucial Energy without being detected. Unfortunately for him, we detected him, and now we're using him. We're using him to cull out more villains, and to stop their attacks as soon as they're started."

Jerry thought for a moment. The impressiveness of it all was shocking, and stirring. "Okay then. I guess I'm read-in now. It sounds like you men have done an amazing job. Well done. Well done to you all. Alan, son, you amazed me before, and now I'm just speechless."

"Good, good, good," Lord Tryphine said. "I'm sure Alan can fill him in on any more questions. Let's move along then. Stan, you have something for us?"

"Yes, sir. A few days ago we had a team move into a hospital in Pattaya, Thailand. Over the past few months, Erwin has investigated the terrorists who have committed several different attacks, and he's traced their funds to a single person. We'll skip his name for now. Erwin saw money going to an unknown in Pattaya, and so I sent a team. A hospital was raided by terrorists—most likely the ones Erwin saw getting money—and the team took them out. Before the shooting started, however, the team was able to monitor communications from the terrorists to this bad guy. Elijah used that digital information to connect the middle man bad guy to Al Tunb. Now we suspect that the next attacks will be in Cape Town, South Africa, Milan, Italy, and at the Olympics in Greece."

"What makes this different than the others we've detected and stopped?" Erwin asked.

"These particular attacks seem to only benefit the psychosis of the middle man, and not Al Tunb. They don't have anything to do with the Americans specifically, nothing to do with Trucial Energy, and no one is searching for things," Stan explained.

Senator Henderson interrupted. "What do you mean searching for things?"

"Alan will have to explain why, sir, but essentially Al Tunb is looking for some document, and he often has his proxies trying to find it for him. He thinks it'll help him reestablish a family emirate of his in the Gulf. Oh, and he thinks that the world will somehow give him $5 trillion in compensation."

"He's got a real grudge, sir," Alan said.

"Yeah, I'm looking forward to hearing more about that," Henderson answered.

Lord Tryphine repeated Erwin's question. "So what do you think this is about then, Stan?"

"I'm concerned. That's the heart of it. This makes no sense, and if I can't see the offensive nature of it, I'll look at it defensively. That is, is he testing his security? Is he trying to distract his enemies—us? I'm concerned."

Jerry leaned in, "What do you want to do, Stan?"

"I can't see any other option than as we've discussed. It just doesn't set well, and we can't just sit back and do nothing."

"Well," Jerry asked. "What's the end game here? You're never gonna kill all the terrorists in the world even if you have their bank accounts and phone numbers. A trial would be a public relations fiasco with this Al Tunb guy, and if you just kill him he's a martyr. Where does this end? What's success or victory look like?"

"Jerry," Elijah answered. "I'd call it a win if we just get an edge. I don't want them to have the edge on us anymore, and there's no reason to beg for a fair fight with people who torture and kill women and children. I just want an edge."

"And clearly you have it, so what's next, Eli, Stan?"

"We go there, and we kill them, and we gather intel to get an edge for next time," Stan answered.

Having recently lost his entire family, Jerry had a newfound sense of apathy, his new lack of love for anything. He looked at things differently than he did a month earlier. "Me, I think they should just be killed. Just find out who they are, and go if they've got a bad record, get out there and waste the sons of bitches."

Lord Tryphine knew the seriousness of the situation. They were talking life and death in all they were doing. Alan and Erwin felt the same way, but all three still had no personal experience in killing, and their souls stepped back from any want of it.

Andrew, Stan, Jim, and Elijah had all killed—plenty. Because they knew what it was like, they hated killing. It sickened them even when it was so clearly necessary sometimes, but they knew the stain of shame that haunted them with every death. Jerry's words were sound, but distasteful to them.

"That's what I thought at first too, Senator," Jim replied. "When we first tracked some of these things back to this Al Tunb guy, I volunteered to do it myself. They're right, though. This way we can control the flow and see that he blows his cash on attacks we can stop, rather than blow his cash on ones we can't."

"Okay, Jim," Jerry replied. "I understand that part, but there's got to be a way to use this little investment trap y'all have set to get big bad guys, big villains, and not just disgruntled and easily misled mudslingers turned gunslingers."

Everyone in the room looked at each other. They knew he was right. They were controlling tens of billions of dollars and were only managing to stop attacks quickly rather than prevent them altogether. They also heard Jerry loud and clear, and Jim. Those men wanted heads. In hindsight, part of each man in the room did too.

"Look," Jerry began. "You've got billions tied up in this fund, God knows how many man-hours, and all you're getting is a tactical edge. That's like the DoD spending a billion dollars on a new trigger for a rifle. The fund might be a hi-hi, but the purpose of the fund is to strategically target the biggest—the most strategic—private sponsors of terror in the world. Am I right so far?"

Everyone nodded, and he continued.

"This might be a great idea for tactical edge, but it's a strategic targeting tool, and needs to be used more strategically somehow. What about this: Erwin and Lord Tryphine now have a list of people that the intelligence community is interested in. You're watching those guys for money transfers that have been leading to terror attacks. Why not watch all their transfers—to friends, family, and so forth? From there, we can put together a list, then a database of people who are acting together, and we can identify entire networks of these sons of bitches."

"Let's say we find out who these guys are friends with—we find out who their common friends are...what then?" Jim asked.

"Then we send in some folks to kill or capture them."

No one liked the idea. Stan was the first to contest. "On what grounds do we ask men to risk their lives here? Do I go tell a team that they're to go break into a home in the middle of the night, grab some man in front of his family, maybe even get shot at by people defending themselves, and do it all because I think the man might be bad? Because he has two or three friends the man is thus bad and sentenced to be killed or captured and held indefinitely?"

"You're right, Stan. You're right. Still, if you're moving teams into position to oppose likely terror attacks, we might just as well have you send a team, or a man, or have Eli send someone to watch one of these common friends. If the surveillance is sound, then a capture/kill mission should be sent in I think."

Lord Tryphine made a point. "We can't just go around capturing people, Senator."

"We can't just go around killing people either," Erwin added.

"I see the concern, gentlemen," Jerry answered, "But you're already playing with tens of billions of dollars—more money than entire countries. You're also way past knee-deep in violating people's privacy...a basic human right. And Stan and Eli here are already killing people. The bridge across the Rubicon has already been crossed."

"What if there is another strategic way to use this surveillance?" Alan asked. "You're right, sir, in that we do have a strategic tool that's being used tactically instead; a big hammer to give us an edge at swatting flies. What other ways can we strategically prevent or stop terrorist attacks?"

"Find, fix, and destroy the enemy," Eli added.

Lord Tryphine spoke up. "Gentlemen, it appears that this endeavor has grown remarkably. Perhaps it's time we added some more definitive structure. Surely there will be a need for full conferences such as in the past or today, but it appears that the entire show comes down to a financial side, and a group that will catalyze or make something happen from provided data. For the former, clearly Tryphine Banking House—myself, Erwin, and Alan are acting as trustees to these special investment funds. Eli, Stan, Jim, Senator Henderson, I propose that you four work together to determine what best course of action results from the financial side's findings."

Everyone nodded in agreement.

***

10/18/2004

At 3 p.m. on the dot, Alan stepped into his office. Jerry rose from his desk, walked to a couch in his office, and motioned for Alan to sit at a chair opposite him.

"What've you got, Alan?" he asked.

"Sir, not much has changed since the briefing we had this morning. Cyber-attacks are continuing all across the country, and some in the rest of the world. So far, the best thing to say is that this isn't creating any sort of panic. They've got power back on in most of the rural areas, but generally speaking everything east of the Mississippi is still blacked out. Most transcontinental railroad traffic is halted as well, and all of the larger ports on the West Coast are shut down."

Jerry shook his head in disbelief, and Alan continued, "I'm told the virus effects a certain make and model of a very specific digital controller. These controllers are used in lots of different industries, but only specific models were hit. The Vermont power company used it to connect to the Eastern US power grid. The rail network uses the controller to keep track of the trains and freight so they don't run into each other. The ports use the controllers for a similar purpose: controlling freight and tracking its movement."

"And you think that Samed person is behind all of this?"

"Yes sir, "Alan answered, "He's the one. I have solid information on that."

"Does he have any sort of connection to Tryphine's 'Special Hedge Fund for Dictators, Despots, and Villains'?"

"He does, sir. Back in 2001 when Erwin, Jim, and I made the first connection between the hawala network and Samed

Vezirzade, Jim followed up and discovered this so-called Oil Mafia in the region. That's a large part of how the investment fund trap was set, and the entire financial monitoring scheme evolved."

Jerry looked across the room at the window. It was only October, but he knew that in just a few hours it would be dark outside. Without power, Washington D.C. was going to be cast into a cold, autumn shadow. "Does anyone have any idea what to do with this guy? Any progress in stopping the attacks?"

Alan leaned in a bit, "As I'm sure you already know, the Department of Defense is working with NSA. That's always been the contingency plan. They keep telling anyone who asks that they'll have things fixed in a few hours. I've heard it at least twice already. On side of people and groups that officially don't exist I can tell you that the attacks stemmed from a single source, and he will never be a problem again."

"Let me guess, Irv's people caught up with him and did him in?"

Alan nodded, sighed, and once again leaned back. "Exactly."

The conversation paused for a moment as both men thought about how vulnerable the American people had become to small threats from so far away.

***

11/23/2004

A few days before Thanksgiving Jerry and Alan waited for a private meeting with the outgoing President, a man who respected Jerry a great deal.

They met in the ground floor/basement Diplomatic Reception Room. It was one of three oval rooms in the White House, and previous to World War I it had been a room used by servants to polish and shine silver. It was converted later and decorated largely by the Kennedys and Reagans. Most unique to the room was the oval mural on the walls, which portrayed views of 1820s America that Europeans of the time found interesting. The hodgepodge of partial decorating throughout the late twentieth century left the room considered by many of the day as awkward, and the lack of windows made it confining.

Jerry and Alan were alone in the large, quiet, sunless room, and the president finally stormed in after having pardoned a pair of turkeys as was the pre-turkey feast custom of presidents.

"Jerry! Good to see you." The soon-to-be former President walked quickly to shake hands and greet the men as they rose from their seats.

"Good to be here, Mr. President."

"And this is Alan Conferra." The President smiled and seemed genuinely happy to meet Alan. "Been looking forward to meeting you for a long time."

"Thank you, sir, it's an honor," Alan answered while shining his ever-disarming smile.

The President motioned for them to sit down. A set of couches had been brought in with a large, oval coffee table in the middle.

"Gotta say, we sure got our asses kicked by the voters the other day." The President was referring to his leaving the presidency, to Jerry's loss of his Senate seat, and the party loss of the Senate. "Still, I'll be happy to get out of here. This place is like a prison, and there're some real assholes in this town. It'll be good to get out and get away from it all."

"Yes, sir," Jerry replied. "It'll be good to get out of here. It's time."

"How're you doing? What are you going to do now?" President's face had turned serious.

"Thank you, sir. I'm not sure. I think I'll stay in Maryland. I've a house there. Maybe I'll get back into finance."

"Alan," the president asked. "What about you? What are you going to do now? You can probably write your own ticket in this town. You've got an excellent reputation, and not a very public one. You're very marketable."

"Thank you, sir. That means a lot coming from a man like you. I've tried to think about what I want to do, but I've been working for Jerry for fourteen years now. Maybe he'll get into finance, and I can go back to being an accountant again."

All three smiled. The President stood up and walked over to a wet bar against the wall. He poured three glasses of bourbon and brought them back to the coffee table—with the bottle. Jerry knew that wasn't a good sign. Politicians and men in power always poured stiff drinks before stiff news.

They drank to the American voter with a curse and a thanks. It didn't matter that it wasn't even noon. After the last crystal glass clinked on the coffee table's glass, The President paused for a moment. He looked at Jerry and then Alan—each for several seconds and without a word. Then he leaned forward and put his elbows on his knees.

"Jerry, I want you to do something."

"Yes, sir."

"I want you to go into finance, and I want you to break the law."

"Sir?"

"I want you to get into finance, start your own business, and manage Alan's hedge fund for international dictators and despots."

Jerry reached for his glass and took another drink, then refilled it with more bourbon.

"I know, Jerry. I know," the president repeated. "And you know what kind of world we live in. You know that there are some flat-out bad people out there. We have a month or two to make plans, and decisions have to be made now. The transition is already starting, and the intelligence community is already going to have all the heads of all the agencies cut off by Senator Carnegie. I need you to do this, Jerry. You're the only one I can think of who can."

Without hesitation Jerry answered again. "No, sir. I won't jump into or be pushed into a decision like this. I need time."

The President was frustrated. It was another example of his sudden transformation from a man with the power to destroy the planet to the man who would soon have little power over anything. He turned to Alan.

"What do you think about this, Alan?" he asked.

"Sir, it's a great idea. There wouldn't be any oversight, though, and that's extremely dangerous. It really leaves us hanging."

He paused.

"Jerry, as chair of the Intel Committee, you know the kind of people who are out there. You've both got clearance and have heard all those come-to-Jesus moments that we've had over the years. Last weekend we had another incident where one of Eli Davies' people managed to stop Los Angeles from getting nuked. He was the money man for that Oil Mafia group. They also tried to use half a dozen dirty bombs, and they wound up killing over five thousand people in Aetna Springs. The biological attacks, the cyber-attacks.... Hell, it's not even noon yet and I've already personally signed off and authorized twenty-three different Special Forces missions, and it seems like a slow day! These things happen every few weeks—now they're happening every few days. I'm genuinely, and I think realistically, concerned about the covert activities our nation is going to face over the next several years."

Again, the President paused, looked Jerry square in the eye for an uncomfortably long time, then Alan, and then back at Jerry. "You're worried too, Jerry. I can see it in both of you."

"Speaking of Aetna, sir," Alan asked. "How's the clean-up going?"

"It's a mess. FEMA likes to pretend they've got it all handled. The local government is gone, wiped out, but there's no shortage of lawyers and county politicians asserting their command over the situation. DoD, CDC, FBI, all of DC's alphabet soup of agencies is involved, and coordination seemed to change every few days. Then you get the different hospitals and insurance agencies involved...it's unreal. One of the first things I wanted to do when I took office was to form a new agency that would respond to...shall we say, 'less than natural' disasters. Jerry's party wanted to create something called Department of Homeland Security, DHS, but that's just another spoonful of alphabet soups so I vetoed it, if you recall."

Jerry smiled. "I opposed that effort, Mr. President."

"I know you did, but your party didn't listen to either of us."

"Sir," Alan added. "You're talking about a private group that would take action before an attack, and a public one after. What about some sort of special 'less than natural' disaster group that was funded through departmental administrative funds?"

Jerry half laughed as the President's eyes squinted and his face gave a mischievous little boy's smile. "I've got another week or two to push through something. Can you draft something, get it to me for review in a week, and then slip it into something before everyone goes home for Christmas break?"

Alan nodded. "Yes, sir, the Foreign Cultural Exchange Jurisdictional Immunity Clarification Act is coming up in the Senate first week of December. I can have something for you by this Saturday. We can slip it in as a rider. Even if there's no specific plan for it yet, Treasury can start accumulating funds for it after you sign."

"No plans for Turkey Day, huh, Alan?" The President asked.

"No, sir."

"That's how he is, Mr. President," Jerry added.

"Well, you're both coming over on Friday night. We're gonna have a small family dinner in the residence. Just the family and you two."

Alan and Jerry truly didn't want to impose, and even preferred to be alone on the family holiday, and it showed.

"No discussion, gentlemen. You're coming. It's long overdue. I should have had you over a long time ago. Now I'm going to make that right."

Jerry smiled. "You just want another crack at getting us to do this thing, Mr. President."

"I do at that, Jerry, but I do owe you at least a dinner; both of you. You've done so much—saved so many lives—you've earned this and so much more. Friday at 6 p.m."

The President rose, shook their hands, and left abruptly. He had a lot to do before he left office.

***

11/7/2005

Dante's true lowest level of Hell wasn't written in his book, *The Inferno*. This lowest level was populated not by sinners, but by people who were good; so good and loving that it was a sin. Their punishment differed: the souls of women who loved too much were condemned for eternity to wait for their husbands in hardware stores, and men who loved too much were chained to chairs in shoe stores where their wives would try on one pair of shoes after another.

So it was for Erwin Zimmermann. He loved his wife, Anna. He loved her more than life, or air. He loved her enough to actually go shopping with her. Once there he wouldn't just leave her and move on to his own interests. No, he waited for her...and waited...and waited.

On this Wednesday he was in a shoe boutique near the northern outskirts of Rome, Italy. She'd already picked out three new pairs of shoes. While they were being packaged by her saleswoman, another woman was bringing her three more boxes of shoes to try on for fit. Erwin didn't moan. He smiled. He liked seeing her smile. He loved her sinfully so.

For a moment Anna was walking around in yet another pair, and he felt a vibration in his pocket. It was his phone. Manfred, his secretary, had sent him a text message. It said that there was money being suspiciously moved in one of the accounts reserved for terrorist sponsors, and that Erwin should call him when possible. He put the phone back in his pocket, and continued to smile at Anna's happiness.

An hour later Erwin stepped outside and called Manfred.

"Sir, our favorite malefactor appears to be at it again. He withdrew the usual sum of funds, sent it to SFS International as usual, and SFS has sent it to someplace in Venezuela."

Erwin paused for a moment and looked to the sky for ideas. "Well, it can't be Trucial Energy then. The Venezuelan government has seized all the oil facilities there. They've nationalized the entire industry. Is there anything in that part of Venezuela that we know of, Manfred?"

“Sir, the only industry there is an oil refinery. It used to be a Trucial Energy facility, but hasn’t been for some time. We don’t have any information on its production levels either. As far as I can tell it’s not operating at full capacity, and might not be operating at all.”

“Very well. Thank you, Manfred. Thank you very much. Please send Eli...err, Colonel Davies the information. He might want to send a team there just in case. Well done, Manfred. Well done.”

With that Erwin turned off his phone and went to spending the rest of the day with Anna, shopping all over Rome, and ending the day with a romantic dinner.

***

12/1/2005

Ronald Van De Burgh hated America. He was guilty of having been a participant in the North Sea terrorist attack on a remote Trucial Energy oil platform, but he considered himself to have been tricked into the crimes that took place there. Afterwards, when his eco-warrior (terrorist) friends had waged more attacks, he decided it was time to switch sides, cut his losses, and try and prevent more death rather than be on the fringe of it. He made contact with authorities, and he tried to surrender to them at a dam in Hungary where his eco-warrior (terrorist) friends were planning on making another violent political statement. The attack was stopped, but rather than accept his surrender, the authorities tried to imprison Ronald for his involvement in the Trucial Energy attack.

He spent five years in a Dutch prison. It wasn’t like a Russian gulag or some third world prison. He lived better than most people on the planet. The Dutch penal system focused more on humane treatment than on punishment or crime reduction. In the 1970s their prisons were full, and no one wanted to pay to build more so an early-release program was started for nonviolent prisoners. In the 1990s this was extended to prisoners—like Ronald—who had demonstrated good behavior. In his case he had been released after only five years of a twenty-five-year sentence, and he was put on a waiting list to return if a slot in prison opened up. He should have been immensely grateful, but instead he burned with absolute, all-encompassing hatred for the duplicitous Americans who had captured him and for Trucial Energy Oil, which he was convinced had compelled his imprisonment.

Ronald sat at a café in Arnhem, Netherlands. Across the street he looked out over the Musispark Centre. The park was built with eighteenth century classical landscaping as well as a naturally blended and well-manicured pond with three ornate fountains in the middle. Geese and seagulls stretched the distance between Ronald and the water. It was a thing of visual beauty in a peaceful city, in a peaceful country, and he was free. A light snow/heavy frost of early December coated everything in a morning glisten, and ice crystals sparkled as the sun climbed higher into a clear, blue sky.

It wasn't the coffee keeping him warm, however. His body was hunched. His face was sullen and sour. His eyes were tired and angry. Ronald was a man consumed by the hate of having been betrayed by those who had thought were authorities on protection. He had trusted them one time and one time only, and they had imprisoned him for his help.

He'd been out of prison for less than two hours when he went to the Internet café and searched for the Terrafirst Technologies, the entity that had funded his pre-terrorist, eco-protest efforts. He found their phone number, called it, and found that his old friend, his old co-conspirator Ian Davies, was still around. He'd never been caught. Instead, he fled to the British Army, served several years, and then went back to eco-protesting. Davies said that he would meet Ronald at the café.

He was in Amsterdam, almost an hour and a half away. Davies made it in an hour. He pulled up and parked in the street right between Ronald's table on the sidewalk and the park. His smile was both irritating and refreshing to Ronald.

"Ronald! It's good to see you!" Davies reached around and embraced Ronald as his old friend. It was clear that he knew nothing of Ronald's efforts to turn him into the authorities.

"It's good to be out, Ian."

"I bet it is! Do you have a place to stay? What's next for you?" Davies asked.

"I just got out a few hours ago. Nothing's settled yet."

"Well, you're staying with me then. That much will be settled. How were you treated? Are you all right?"

The two men sat down. Ronald motioned for two more coffees to be brought over to them.

"Are you sure, Ian? I don't want to impose."

"Nah, I'm sure. I'm working full-time at Earth Liberation now."

Ronald laughed at the irony. "Incredible! I'd feared the establishment had destroyed it."

"Please don't take this the wrong way, Ronald, but I did have my concerns when they grabbed you. Even today I had my concerns, but if there's no black sedans or men in hats taking me away right now, then I know this meeting isn't...well, I know you've been a solid friend. Thank you."

They raised their mugs and tinged them against each other as a way of showing each would now trust the other.

"Listen, Ronald...there's a man I want you to meet; Arab, oil man, but a good person. We have the same interests, and he pays extremely well. If you're interested I'm sure he can find you a job."

"The Army's changed you, Ian. I can't believe you're connected with an oil man."

"You know what they say about enemy's enemy being a friend, well...you should meet," Davies answered.

"Fine then—any friend of yours I suppose. Give him a call. My schedule's free so we can meet any time he wants."

Ronald smiled, pulled out his cell phone, and called Ibn al Douri Al Tunb.

***

12/12/05

The tiny village of Porrentry, Switzerland, was far from any real roads, and not on any tourist maps. Located on the northwestern side near the French border, it hadn't changed much in hundreds of years. It consisted of mostly small farmhouses, barns, outbuildings, a few shops, and even a small bank. The place wasn't famous or historic for any reason at all, but it was close to several world-renowned ski resorts: La Chaux-de-fonds, Biel, and Neuchatel. Another benefit (or on this day curse) was that the village was only a forty-five-minute getaway from the International Monetary Fund (IMF) meeting in Geneva.

Because of that proximity to the meeting and skiing, five IMF delegates had decided to stay at a bed and breakfast in the village. Their plan was to spend their days at the meeting, nights either in Geneva or in Lamoura, and then three days at all three ski resorts. The plan went awry.

Mona Tresch, twenty-nine, had only been hired on as an intern for the Swiss firm that was hosting the International Monetary Fund conference. It was her job to act as interpreter, travel guide, and concierge to the three-man "packet" of IMF delegates. When they said they wanted to go skiing, but not at some large resort, she thought of the place she knew best: home. Mona had grown up in the Porrentry area, and she knew that this tiny village was quaint, authentically Swiss, and out of the way, and she remembered it as a cozy place that she wanted to share with the foreign dignitaries.

The three IMF delegates were from Turkmenistan. All three worked for their government's Central Banking Committee. Like any third world country, Turkmenistan's government was thick with payoffs and bribes and grifting. The three IMF delegates were wealthy men in any country, and extremely wealthy in their home. They'd traveled extensively on their country's wallet, and it wasn't the first time to Switzerland for any of them. In fact, the reason they wanted Mona to take them away from the larger resorts was that they'd been to them so many times before.

Mona took the three down an old trail that everyone in the village had skied before. She'd been on it thousands of times in her life, but it was still fun. At the bottom Mona had arranged for a Land Rover to meet them and bring them back up to the top. They made three runs in the morning, and then stopped for a late lunch around 12:30 p.m.

A tiny bed and breakfast run by Mona's aunt and uncle was the perfect place. Like the rest of the village, the building was hundreds of years old, and while it had been updated to modern standards the walls were still stone and roughhewn lumber—even logs in some places. Her aunt and uncle were friendly and made their wealthy guests feel at home.

Then they brought out the pear brandy. Everyone in Mona's family helped make it, and it was something they were very proud of. As in nearby France, every spring all the members in her family would get together and put bottles over budding pears hanging from trees all around the village. The bottles were strung up in the same way they had been for countless generations. Once fully grown, every single pear/bottle combination was cut from their tree, cleaned, and then filled with locally made pear brandy. And each year, every family member tucked away a few bottles to age.

The trip was entirely paid for by the Swiss government, but regulations and auditors made it impossible for Mona and her family to charge more than they would for anyone else. After the first bottle of brandy was gone, Mona showed the delegates how to cleanly cut the bottle to get to the pear. She held the bottle upright in roughly two inches of hot water. After a few minutes, as the steam disappeared, she carried the bowl and bottle outside with the men in tow. Then she pulled the bottle out of the hot water, dipped it in the snow, and it cracked right along the line where water had been. She rubbed the pear in the snow, tossed the water into the air where it came down as snow, and then brought the pear back inside in the bowl. There, her aunt was already waiting with a plate of local cheese and a knife to cut the pear into slivers. Having absorbed the pear brandy, it was the perfect pairing with the cheese. Amazed, and slightly drunk, the IMF delegates begged for another bottle, which they immediately drank, and then repeated the process. Mona and her family were impressed at how well the Turkmens were holding their liquor, but after two bottles in a little over an hour it was clear they were done skiing for the day.

Between 2 and 2:30 everyone in the downstairs/half basement dining room heard an alarm bell ringing. Everyone stopped and looked at each other, and Mona's uncle opened the door to see what was happening. Outside it was snowing heavily—light, powdery snow that muffled noise and left only the alarm bell to be heard from a few buildings up the street. Then they heard the shots.

First there were four. They were loud—like rifle shots. They were fast, and everyone knew they were from a battle rifle. Everyone in Mona's family, herself included, had been trained in the Swiss Army. The delegates were all too familiar with the sound of AK-47 rifles, and they recognized its four-round burst fire instantly. They immediately rose to their feet and asked Mona if there were any weapons in the home.

Mona's uncle was in the Swiss Army and, like all Swiss servicemen, had been mandated to keep his weapon and gear at home in case of a national emergency. He closed the door and raced upstairs to get his rifle. A moment later he was downstairs with his SIG 550 battle rifle. He was also wearing his green combat harness with extra ammunition over his thick white turtleneck sweater. More shots were heard, and Mona told the delegates to follow her and aunt to the upstairs attic for safety.

Her aunt had just put her second foot on the stairs when the door her uncle had looked out earlier suddenly burst open. A herd of gunmen, some wearing Swiss Army jackets, swarmed through the door. It was clear they were not members of the Army, and her uncle opened fire immediately.

The first man through the door took three bullets to the chest, killing him instantly. The bullets fired from less than twenty feet away traveled through him, killed the man behind him, and wounded two others. He fired a second three-round burst and wounded three more men. The noise was deafening. Mona's aunt froze, and the three IMF delegates tried to push her out of the way to get upstairs; they knew nothing of chivalry or courage.

When her uncle fired his third burst of 5.56-millimeter NATO bullets, one of the gunmen opened fire.

His AK-47 fired four bullets that splintered the ceiling and walls. Bullets from Mona's uncle killed two more men who were trying to get through the door. It wasn't skill that was keeping him alive, just luck—and a blind firing into a crowded doorway that men were trying to get through.

Another burst from the one gunman killed Mona's uncle, with the last bullet exploding his head and spraying his remains all over his wife—who was still panicked and frozen on the stairs behind where he'd made his last stand.

More men entered the smoke- and body-filled room. They shouted. Mona's aunt shouted. The Turkmens shouted. As the last of the gunmen entered, and bodies were moved from the door, Ian Davies fired his AK-47 into the ceiling. Everyone was silent. Even the wounded stopped crying.

"We are the Nationalsozialistischer Untergrund (National Socialist Underground; NSU)!" Davies couldn't help but notice the three men who had been shouting in a different language. "Who the hell are you?!"

No one answered. Davies grabbed Mona, threw her face down on the ground, and put the muzzle of his rifle into her spine. "Who are you?!" he repeated.

Mona's aunt was numb and still staring at her husband's corpse. "They're bankers with some conference in Geneva," she mumbled.

Davies began giving orders to the other gunmen. He had Ronald tie up Mona, her aunt, and the three Turkmeni officials.

Then Ronald whispered into Ian's ear, "This isn't why we came here, Ian."

"I'm aware of that. Thank you. But we obviously didn't get anything from the bank up the street. We can't just let these people go, and maybe we can get something for them. In any event we might need some insurance."

In the distance everyone heard a rifle shot. The room fell silent except for quiet weeping from Mona's aunt. Another rifle shot followed a few seconds later. They sounded like a hunting rifle from up the street. A third shot rang out—this time followed by all hell breaking loose. There was no telling how many, but this time everyone could hear countless three-round bursts from what had to be other battle rifles. There was no telling if it was more of Davies's latest terrorist group, or other locals taking up arms, or of police. Davies and Ronald ran out the door and left one of the NRU members to guard their new hostages.

Davies's plan had never been to kidnap members of the IMF. He'd led the NRU group on a simple bank raid where, according to the lie he had told them, there was a hidden horde of Nazi gold stashed away in the remote location so as to not attract attention. That was all it was supposed to be for them—a way to gain some funding in a quick and easy way at a remote Swiss village. For Davies and Ronald the objective had been different. Sheik Al Tunb had it in his mind that this particular Swiss bank held in its vault the very document that would prove his family's contract with the founders of Trucial Energy. Davies's job was to find the precious contract, but as had happened at so many other faux terrorist attacks, Al Tunb's intelligence or hunches had proven incorrect. Ronald and Davies were unable to find any special documents at the local bank branch. Now the police were responding. Well-placed NRU snipers had held them at bay for now, and what the NRU group lacked in training or professionalism it made up for in firepower and numbers.

Having driven off responding police, it was clear to Davies that a new exit strategy was needed. They would be back, and in far greater numbers, he thought to himself. Ronald and Davies met with a few of the others. By now the village was almost vacant with people fleeing to the woods, hills, and a nearby mountain road. Davies individually posted the NRU members in a defensive position and set patrols in motion. It took almost twenty minutes. Then he headed back to the dining room where the hostages were being held.

Mona's aunt was still sobbing uncontrollably. Before saying anything Davies shot her in the head, killing her with no thought whatsoever other than to silence her. Eight pounds of trigger pull, no thought, and fifty-five years of life were gone just for the deadly act of crying over her murdered husband. Mona and the IMF members were terrified into icy silence.

Davies then put his rifle to Mona's back. He was just about to execute her when she spoke up—not from courage or fear, but as a form of survival reflex. "I can get you off the mountain without them knowing," she said.

"How?"

"The tunnel. The road on the other at the bottom of the village. There's a bunker complex inside. We can go down the street to the road, then into the tunnel. There, you can let us free, and you can be on your way."

Davies and Ronald grinned.

Ronald headed for the door. "I'll get some of the men to help just in case."

Outside, the snow was still falling heavily. All of the streets and alleys were covered in half a foot of powder, and the buildings were fluffy, picturesque. All Ronald could hear was the mountain wind. For a moment he thought he heard something, but he continued walking up the narrow, cart-wide path toward the bank where some of the NRU men were positioned.

Again, Ronald thought he heard something, a click or a pop. No, he thought, there were three. Visibility was down to less than a hundred feet, but for a split second Ronald saw four ghost-like men in complete white camouflage as they shuffled their way across the path from a building on his left to the right. They were here!

Ronald knew that some sort of police response team was on the scene. The three clicks or pops were likely suppressed weapons, and he ran back to tell Davies.

Barging through the door he spoke emphatically. "Ian! They're here! We have to go NOW!"

Davies grabbed Mona while Ronald shepherded the IMF delegates. All six funneled up the stairs to a balcony. Mona directed them to the right where the balcony met a rise in the surrounding land, met the balcony, and continued down a path into the woods. They shuffled through the tall pines, and snaked their way down the hill for almost a quarter mile. When they came to the road, the path opened up from the pine trees to a walk with side rails and two hairpin turns descending to the road.

"You see?" Mona asked. "There's the tunnel. I told you. You can let us go now."

Davies just shoved her and they made their way down to the road. It was clear a plow truck had recently been through, but there was no other traffic. A little over a hundred yards down the road they came to a well-lit tunnel.

"On the left, you see?" Mona asked. "That's where the bunker starts."

Switzerland was world renown for its fortifications. The Swiss military had ensured their nation's ability to remain neutral in wars because of its own skill and readiness. For over millennia castles, forts, and bunkers had been built and never used. Between World Wars I and II while the French built their notorious Maginot Line, Switzerland expanded its fortifications. Even entire airbases were built underground with planes able to taxi out to roads and take off. Finding a bunker in a tunnel wasn't a rarity in Switzerland. It was the norm.

This bunker, like so many others, had been decommissioned and abandoned in the post-Soviet Union years. Ammunition, furniture, everything had been removed. The firing ports that allowed it to protect the tunnel entrance had been boarded up, and the door had been removed. While still a bunker in design, it was now just a shell—a place for teenagers to escape rather than for soldiers to fight.

Ronald shoved the IMF delegates inside as they heard shooting from on top the hill from which they'd just come. Davies brought Mona inside and they looked around for a place to hole up. Once found, Ronald bound all four hostages together, and then told Davies he was going to go back up the hill to the village for reinforcements. Davies agreed, and off Ronald went.

All four sat in the cement room staring at each other for almost twenty minutes. Mona and the delegates were terrified to speak lest they risk being shot like her aunt and uncle. Davies had nothing to say, but was certain he could hold his hostages simply from their own fear as long as he looked menacing. It worked. The silence was broken, again, by the sound of gunfire.

Ronald and two other NRU members appeared in the bunker a short while after.

"What happened?" Davies asked.

"Either the local police response team is very large, or we're dealing with some sort of Special Forces team up in the village. I found these eight men (NRU terrorists), but the others are either dead or captured. We barely made it out. Then, when we made it to the road, a pair of cars almost ran us over."

"That was the shooting just now?" Davies asked.

"Right. We had to stop one, then another came, hit it, slid, then another, and a truck. It's a mess out there."

Davies nodded with understanding. They heard more shooting outside, and screams this time as well. He told one of the eight NRU members to guard Mona and the delegates, and then he searched the delegates and stole their wallets.

"Make a noise, and you'll be killed. Then we'll find your families and do the same. Do you understand me?"

All three nodded with eyes bulging in terror.

Davies, Ronald, and the remaining seven headed into the tunnel. There was a shootout happening up the road just a few yards away. The men in white were up on the trail overlooking the road, and they were picking off NRU members. Davies told the seven with him to get out and help them. Then he and Ronald ran to the tunnel entrance.

Davies stopped at the edge.

"We've gotta jump, Ronald. There's no other way."

Ronald looked at where the tunnel entrance, the mountain, and the road met. It was steep, and in the poor visibility there was no way to see the bottom. It could have been thirty feet down or three thousand. The shooting intensified in tempo. Davies climbed over the guardrail, sat down on the edge, tossed his rifle, and slid away into the darkness. As bullets snapped through the air and echoed into the tunnel, Ronald hopped over the guard rail and followed into the gray.

***

12/5/2005

The Foreign Cultural Exchange Jurisdictional Immunity Clarification Act was approved by Congress at 10:37 p.m. on November 30, 2005. On December 1, with no fanfare or press present, The President signed it into law. The following Monday, Alan found an empty office at 500 C Street Southwest. He took it over and waited for someone to complain. When they did he would tell them that he was the director of Strategic Homeland Division of FEMA, just as he'd written the new job into the cultural exchange jurisdiction act. Funding was never allocated for his new government division as he had plenty to access from the interest off the Iraqi gold he'd recovered in 1991. With no funding to account for, Congress wasn't likely to audit him, and FEMA itself would be impressed, not concerned. Technically he'd have to take orders from FEMA's director, but since the director didn't even know his new division existed there was no reason to expect orders to be given.

Alan's new office was large, but not noteworthy. There was room for a staff of nine others, and the only windows looking out offered nothing more than a view of downtown Washington's rail lines. By the end of the year he'd officially have made the office his with all the paperwork to support it. Phone lines were installed before January. All the utilities were put in his own department's name so FEMA accounting wouldn't notice they were there. Computers and other communications equipment was ordered, delivered, and networked. He had everything ready.

All that was left were people. Alan kept several of the staff members from his working group in Senator Henderson's office, and they moved in after Christmas. He still had three more desks to fill. Those would come in time.

***

2/5/2006

It seemed to Jim Smith that he would always be one step behind any terrorist. Acting on a "suggestion" from Erwin, Jim had traveled to Venezuela. They had reason to believe there was going to be a terrorist attack on an oil refinery there.

They were right. There was an attack on the former Trucial Energy oil refinery facility. Nationalsozialistischer Untergrund (NRU)—the same group that had attacked IMF dignitaries in a small Swiss village—were responsible for the attack. It was clear to Jim, Erwin, and everyone in their little group that the NRU was just another group funded by Ibn al Douri Al Tunb. He'd funded every type of terrorist from Irish revolutionaries to jihadis to Chinese mafia hit teams.

The only thing the groups had in common was his money and the scavenger hunt. In Venezuela they searched an old Trucial Energy facility for him. Switzerland terrorists searched the bank for him. Now, as Jim was still in Venezuela, another group was already attacking a Trucial Energy shipbuilder in Norway.

Erwin had done well in tracking Al Tunb's money, alerting Stan, and making it possible for international anti-terrorist teams to at least be in the correct city when an attack was set in motion. Without that knowledge it would have been up to local police to handle all the different terrorist attacks. Instead, wherever Al Tunb sent people, Stan had an anti-terrorism team ready and waiting to respond to any attack. This time Al Tunb had sent people to Norway, but Stan was, again, one step ahead of him. He had twelve men in Bergen, Norway, and as soon as the police responded to a call, the team was sent to the location.

There was nothing Jim could do but watch the after-action news conference on Venezuelan TV. He switched on United News International and watched a press conference. Venezuelan army spokesman Diego Abreau claimed that it was his force that had responded to the call at the shipyard, and that they had killed all of the terrorists, despite one of their bombs having detonated during the assault. It was a complete and utter lie. Jim knew it, and mostly accepted it as just part of the scenery in all this terrorist business.

***

9/23/2006

Lord Terrence Tryphine called another meeting for those involved with tracking Al Tunb. As usual the meeting was set for 1 p.m. at Tryphine Banking House in London. Erwin and Anna had stayed with the Tryphines at their estate at Guilford in Surrey, so Erwin rode in to work with Terrence. Elijah Davies and Alan came in together from Washington and were at the banking house before noon. Jim walked up and met them just as security let them into the building. Stan arrived next. Andrew Lawrence was unable to attend, and former Senator Jerry Henderson declined the invitation.

The five who were present met in the ornate lobby. Above them was the same rotunda and stained glass window where Erwin and Anna began their relationship years earlier. The party atmosphere of that New Year's evening was long gone, and the financial business was in full bloom as men and women in expensive suits passed left, right, and all around. The banquet tables were gone, and the century-old leather lobby chairs were back where they usually were. The only live connection to that night was a string quartet tucked away in the back, quietly playing in lieu of recorded elevator muzak.

Lord Tryphine greeted everyone in the lobby personally. As his staff took down names and issued visitor passes he welcomed the group as a whole. "Gentlemen, I'm afraid I've another meeting at 3, so if we could make our way to our secure conference room and get started...perhaps?"

Per the usual checks, they made their way downstairs to the secure conference room. Lord Tryphine sat at his usual chair at the far end of the room with Erwin by his side, and Jim next to him. Alan, Eli, and Stan were on the other side.

Before everyone was even seated, Terrence began. "I'd like to thank you all once again for making your respective travels for this meeting. Let's get started, shall we? Colonel Davies , I believe you have some news..."

"Okay, I'll start: After the attack in Switzerland—well done to you and your people by the way, Stan. After that attack, Stan's people were able to just wound a pair of the terrorists involved. My people got them out of the hospital and made them disappear. We had some less-than-friendly conversations with them before locking them up appropriately. What we found is that one of Al Tunb's lieutenants, a former British soldier named Ian Davies, was behind that and several other attacks. In fact, we'd run into him several times before since 2000. He was directly involved with at least a quarter of all the missions Stan's people have conducted, either directly or indirectly selling arms and connecting various terror groups to Al Tunb and his resources."

Eli glanced at Jim for a moment and then continued. "Davies is working with an old friend of his, Ronald Van De Burgh. Van De Burgh was involved in a pair of attacks paid for by Al Tunb through the Terrafirst Technologies. I know Jim has personally had a sit-down with him, and Alan as well. These two are on the loose, and they are extremely dangerous. I have my people looking all over for them. Others do as well. Every American and British intelligence agency I can think of has them on unofficial want lists. Even the American Coast Guard has them on a want list. Interpol's looking for them. Everyone, but they seem to have disappeared. That's where I think Jim can continue."

Jim reclined and slowly rocked back and forth as he spoke. "Eli, let me know about these two right away, and I've been looking for them as well. I started with their earliest known location—that was in the Netherlands at a local Terrafirst Technologies office from six years ago. It turns out that place is a complete breeding ground for terrorists."

"It's one of Al Tunb's favorite investments," Erwin interjected. "He's funneled tens of millions of dollars into it since the late 1990s."

"Well, he's getting his money's worth," Jim added. "I went there several times, and watched. There's a coffee shop some of the people like to go to, and after a few weeks I finally heard Davies's name mentioned. Someone was talking to someone else about another café in Arnhem that Davies had taken her to once. The next day I went there, checked out the café, and watched as usual. Really good pastry there—they have an apple strudel that's the best I've had outside of Munich. We'll have to meet there sometime. Anyway, last Tuesday I spotted Ronald Van De Burgh there. Like Eli said, I've met the man. More to the point, he's met me, and I'm confident he didn't recognize me, but I haven't seen him since. Obviously I contacted all of you later that day, but—correct me if I'm wrong, Eli, Stan—you guys have been watching the café in Arnhem ever since and nothing, right?"

Both men nodded.

"Were you able to learn anything, gather any other intel while you were feasting on all that strudel?" Alan asked.

Jim smiled. "It's better with bits of pineapple than with raisins."

No one laughed so Jim continued. "I got a list of some interesting groups from the people who are still active in the Terrafirst Technologies, but that was really the extent. In this case I would say that the lack of information is information in and of itself. No one seems to have seen or heard of Davies in a while as evidenced by his lack of mention in conversations. That's suggestive of him having either gone to ground or been away and up to serious mischief. That's not a lot, but we know he's not back in his comfort zone. I think that's worth noting. Additionally we know that Ronald Van De Burgh is out there. He's still visiting a meeting place he has in common with Davies, and that suggests he's looking to make contact with him again. I'll keep an eye on the place, but I suggest we reach out to some of the intelligence services that are looking for Davies and let them know where he might show up. They can do the footwork watching for him."

Eli looked to Alan and added to Jim's report. "I'll get my people to put a digital net on both places and we'll see if anything turns up; any new leads. Maybe I'll even have one of my people pay a visit and set up a few covert cams in and around the café. I'm sure the strudel will help get a list of volunteers. It's not like I'll be asking them to stake out a training camp along the Afghan/Pakistani border."

"Well done Jim, Colonel," Lord Tryphine added. "Well done to both of you. Alan, do you have anything new for us?"

"Actually no. After Senator Henderson lost the election, I've found myself with a new role in Washington. I still have clearance, but no briefings to attend and that sort of thing."

Erwin looked to Alan and asked, "What exactly are you doing now?"

"I've an office in the Federal Emergency Management Administration, FEMA. We'll be a sort of first responding Special Forces that sends people to places where there've been tornados, hurricanes, natural disasters in general, and, if there are more 9/11s or Aetna Springs incidents, I'll be sending people in first. It's an on-the-books operation, but it's also something the President and I created before he left, so while I technically answer to the regular FEMA chain of command, they don't even know we exist. That makes us less likely to draw scrutiny, and able to have some freedom of operation. I'm still hiring, by the way. Jim, if you want a job we can talk." Alan smiled.

Erwin didn't give Jim a chance to answer. He pointed his finger to Alan's face and poignantly said, "No sir, Mr. Conferra. Jim is under contract with the Zimmermanns. Right, Jim?"

Leaning back with his head held high, Jim simply nodded and grinned.

"Stan? Do you have anything new?" Lord Tryphine asked.

"I don't, sir. I'm sorry, but Davies has been busy, and Erwin's been keeping my people busy in response. Right now the teams are home at Hereford, back here in the UK. They need some rest, if I do say so myself." Stan paused before continuing. "We need to train up some replacements as well, I'm afraid."

Terrence sat upright. "That leaves me." He paused and looked around the room before continuing.

"Gentlemen, Eli's people have been doing an amazing job. Through their operations they've come in contact with many more of our so-called villains, and our list of accounts to watch and monitor has tripled. Erwin, you, Alan, and I discuss how we'll handle these new accounts later. I would like to draw your attention to one thing in particular: Ibn al Douri Al Tunb's funding of a Pakistani group called the Harkat-ul-Mujahideen-al-Islami (HUM). According to Eli, this group has close ties to the Arab Afghans as well as other groups that have been responsible for a multitude of attacks. However, these groups have not been following the treasure hunt modis operandi. Instead these groups don't seem to be fulfilling Al Tunb's needs in some other way. No one seems to know how or why he's funding them. There is speculation that he has developed a relationship with another emir who leads that council. We just don't know. What we do know is that he is funding this URF group more often."

Alan had questions. "What else do we know about the URF's funding? Is Al Tunb the primary source now? Are there others? Is there a way we can get involved in monitoring their funds? I know Stan's people need a rest, but that's beside the point for now."

Terrence had few answers. "Alan, Al Tunb's money transfers are still going through the hawala network, and largely using the SFS International company as their primary money launderer. We don't as yet know where the URF is getting the rest of its funding, how much it's funded, or how they're transferring funds."

"URF's money is going through two banks in the UAE, a Saudi bank, and SFS International is again acting as middle man. We've been closely monitoring them. That's how we were able to add to our little group's watch list. There was some very high risk involved in that operation so please be reminded of just how sensitive our conversations have become," Eli added.

Lord Tryphine took over the meeting. He and Eli detailed each of the new additions to their "villains watch list." There were over eighty-seven additions. Some were described as suspicious. Others were curiosities—people who had transferred great sums of money to others on the watch list, or had transferred funds often. There were at least nine who were reputed, international "persons of interest" in multiple terrorist attacks.

Just before 3 p.m. they adjourned. Lord Tryphine had another meeting with some Swiss members of the International Monetary Fund, and they were already waiting in the lobby. The men made their way through the cement-walled basement, past the walls with bulletproof glass and guards watching their every move on the other side. It was nothing new to any of them.

The lobby was a busy place. People in suits crossed in all directions. Near the back of the lobby the Swiss delegation was waiting at the check-in desk. Terrence noticed them right away. Erwin noticed his wife, Anna. She was with Terrence's wife, Joan.

He went over to meet them between the columns on the right side of the lobby. He kissed Anna and asked, "Did you ladies have a nice time?"

"We did," she replied. "Joan and I went to an old haunt of ours."

Both ladies demurred and look at him slyly.

"We went to Dinkleman's...," Joan said with a grin.

Erwin smiled—almost blushed. It seemed that half of the time Joan went shopping with anyone she went to the age-old Dinkleman's lingerie store. It was a bit of a strange thing, he thought, but Anna always seemed happy—particularly when shopping with Joan, and devilishly so when they went to that store. It wasn't like he didn't enjoy it as well.

Terrence had been over to speak briefly with the Swiss delegation, then he came over to Erwin and the ladies.

"I know that smile." He grinned as well. Alan, Eli, Stan, and Jim were still near the hallway to the basement from which they'd come, and Terrence motioned for them to come over so he could introduce them to Joan and Anna. Anna waved before they could arrive as she was heading to the coat closet to fetch her and Joan's Londonwear.

While introductions were being made, four men in suits walked past them and up the "Employee Only" stairwell toward the record room. Four more men in suits randomly seemed to meander and then stand in positions close to the four guards in the lobby. Then it began. Eight men wearing camouflage jackets and carrying rifles of different sorts all streamed through the front doors and into the lobby.

The first four men began beating the guards whom they were standing next to at the time. The men in camouflage spread out. Three of them walked quickly over toward the largest group of people in the lobby: Terrence and the others. Three more surrounded the Swiss delegation and the people around the check-in desk. Two more stood by the front door. The rest disappeared into the hallways. No one went to the teller windows.

There was no time to react. The gunmen were around Terrence's group before Eli, Stan, Jim, or anyone could even turn and see them. In the center of the lobby a woman with a pink tie-dye shirt and blue jeans screamed. She was frozen like a statue until one of the gunmen hit her in the back with a Heckler & Koch G36 rifle. Only a silent alarm had been tripped, and screams heard from around the building provided the only alert for Tryphine Banking House workers.

All of the gunmen had everyone down on the floor, on their knees, and their heads facing down. Then their leaders walked into the bank. Ian Davies was followed by Ronald Van De Burgh. They surveyed the scene, decided all was going to plan, and—

"What was that?" Davies paused in the middle of the lobby. He'd heard a thump sound. He pulled out a shiny, nickel-plated, .357 Desert Eagle pistol and headed toward a door on the side of the lobby. For a moment he thought about just firing into the door randomly. It would have made a good demonstration of power, he thought to himself. Instead, he flung open the closet door and saw Anna sitting on the floor.

"Well, well, what have we here?" he said as he grabbed Anna by the hair. "Let's not have any more of that kind of behavior, shall we?"

He tossed Anna to the three guards around Erwin and the others. She had seemed fine, but as soon as she touched Erwin she began to shake uncontrollably. It wasn't fear, but adrenalin caused by the fear. Her mind was afraid, but once she saw her husband her body had let loose from its calm—a common occurrence for survivors of stress, be they car accident survivors or soldiers after a battle. Erwin jumped up to protect her, grabbed her, and tried to both comfort her and shelter her with his body.

Davies then ordered the guards by the Swiss delegation and the guards around Erwin, Anna, and the others. "Take them to the conference room like we planned. Tie them up, and make sure to tape their mouths."

The half dozen men in camouflage began kicking, shoving, and herding people into the conference room next to the closet door. This conference room was a stark contrast to the cement walls of the secure basement room, or the marble of the conference room at the front of the lobby. Instead its walls were wood paneled in a Tudor fashion. The ceiling was adorned by iron chandeliers, and historic men-at-arms' armor was displayed in all four corners; one with a pike, another a mace, the third with a sword, and the last with a warhammer. It was a dark, windowless room with soft incandescent lighting.

Ronald noticed something, or rather someone.

"Wait!" he cried out. Then Ronald walked over and lifted up Jim's head. Jim nodded to him, and he nodded back. Ronald looked at Alan as well. "I know these two." He pulled off the visitor passes that Alan and Jim were wearing. They're Americans."

"Fine," Davies replied. "Use them as examples to the others."

With that, two of the men in camouflage began to beat Jim and Alan. Neither man cried out more than anyone else would have. Alan took a foot to the head, and when he did the gunman's heel left a half-inch cut that bled profusely. The men chose to focus on Jim then as they didn't want to get too much blood on their boots. The woman in the tie-dye shirt started panting and breathing heavily at the sight of Alan's blood on the white and gray marble floor. At one point she looked as if she was going to die. The pace of her breathing and screaming compelled Davies to tell the men to stop. Alan was unconscious. Jim was in and out. The guards dragged both into the conference room, where other guards were already using plastic straps to bind the hostages.

Before the gunmen could bind and gag Eli or Stan, the two men sat next to each other in a corner of the conference room. Their heads were on the ground per instruction. Eli touched his throat and began muttering.

"What the hell are you doing?" Stan asked.

"I have a subdermal."

"A what?"

Eli smiled, though no one could see it. "A subdermal implant. My team uses small, short-range communications devices under the skin in our necks. We can talk to each other wherever and whenever we want, and if there's a cell tower we can talk to people on the other side of the planet. When my guys are sneaking into some cave in Afghanistan or an embassy in

Azerbaijan they need to be as quiet as possible. This is how we do it."

Stan grinned. "I just thought that was a double chin Colonel."

"Fuck you, Stan."

"Are you in contact with someone?" Stan asked.

Now Eli smiled. "We are always in contact. I've got a guy here in London. He's on his way now. They're alerting your people too. How long before you think they can make it here from Hereford?"

"They can make it in an hour or so. If you tell them I'm involved...." he quietly snickered, "If you tell them I'm being held they might make it in half that."

"Already done," Eli answered.

Both men smiled and had to clinch their lips shut as a guard came over to bind them. Just before Stan's mouth was taped, he looked the guard square in the eye and said, "You are going to have the worst day you can possibly imagine."

Eli snarfed and chuckled. No one else in the room saw any humor at all in the hostage situation.

Terrence was the last to be bound and gagged.

"What is it you want with us? Why are you doing this?" he asked.

Davies's back went stiff. He was still in the lobby, but he'd heard Lord Tryphine's question and felt it arrogant just in asking. He walked into the conference room, put his nose to Lord Tryphine's, and spoke while spraying spittle.

"You fucking people. You sicken me with your class righteousness. What is it we want, your Highness? We want you to fucking live like the rest of us. We want—" Davies caught himself. He wanted so much to tell Lord Tryphine all about the rich and the poor and so much more, but he reminded himself of the mission. "You know what we want. You've been fucking with the wrong people. Now we're here to collect."

Davies pulled a crumpled piece of paper from his back left pants pocket.

"You're in charge here, right, Highness?"

Terrence nodded.

"You're going to put a hundred million pounds in each of these accounts, and you're going to do it right fucking now, you filthy sod!"

Terrence was cool and professional. He tightened his tie and took the list from Davies.

"I'll need to use my computer, and transactions over a million pounds don't happen instantly. The Banking

Commission is automatically notified and has to approve them. There shouldn't be any problem, but it can take hours."

"Let's go to your computer then, Highness. I'll follow you, and it's gonna get done today or we're going to do worse than just put a bullet into everyone's head. Got it?!"

Davies shoved Terrence from the conference room and into the lobby, and they headed off to Terrence's office upstairs. Ronald decided that the lobby would better be served with human shields, so he told two of the guards to move the Swiss delegation back to the check-in desk and to tape them to it. One of the guards who had been by the front door took up position behind the check-in desk, behind the wall of Swiss banking delegates. One by one other guards brought in more hostages taken from all over the bank to the conference room and bound them as well.

Upstairs in Lord Tryphine's office, Davies wandered around and marveled as Terrence sat down at his computer.

"There's a wet bar in the corner if you'd like to help yourself," Terrence offered.

"Thanks, Highness. Now shut up and get typing."

Lord Tryphine logged into his account and began typing. While Davies circled the room and, while looking at every painting, every detail in awe, Terrence wrote an email notifying the banking commission of the gunmen and their demands. Davies was too preoccupied to notice Terrence send the email and send a copy to other bankers. The email included a list of the accounts from the piece of paper Davies had given him. Then Terrence began to write up a transaction that would transfer a hundred million pounds to each account, and delete a hundred million pounds from each account.

When done, Terrence called out to get Davies's attention. "It's all arranged. I'm sure you'll want to see."

Davies came over to look at Terrence's screen, and Davies falsely explained how the money was being deposited into the accounts and withdrawn from his (all the while the subsequent withdrawal was actually to those same accounts negating any deposits). The screen was confusing with all sorts of banking data and charts. Rather than look foolish, Davies acted like he understood; like he was satisfied.

"You seem awfully comfortable with all this, Highness."

"All banks are insured by the government and various international monetary funds. We'll be reimbursed. Besides, Tryphine Banking House has dealt with all sorts of people over the centuries. You're not the first to make demands by gunpoint, and won't be the last. It's not a common thing, but we do see it, I'm afraid. Is there anything else I can help you with?"

Davies strutted away from the desk. With a tight chin and stiff upper lip he waved Lord Tryphine away from the desk as well. "Right then, back to the conference room with ya."

He pushed Lord Tryphine out of his office, into the Hall, and when another gunman was walking by he passed Terrence off to him. The gunman was told to put Lord Tryphine in the conference room with the others. They went downstairs and Davies headed toward the records room.

Ronald was already in the room. It seemed the rows of bookcases were never-ending. Tryphine Banking House had so many records dating back over four centuries that a staff of six people was maintained solely for maintaining, finding, and adding yet more and more documents. All of them were in the conference room. Both Ronald and Davies arrogantly believed they could find what they were looking for without help. Both men began walking the rows looking for old contracts from 1923.

After ten minutes of walking, they still hadn't found anything, and the first shots from police were now ringing out. London's Armed Constable Reaction Team took almost half an hour to get to Tryphine Banking House after the silent alarm was triggered. Then they secured a perimeter around the building. In the process, one of London's constables came too close to one of Davies's snipers on the roof of the building.

He'd placed three snipers on the roof. Two had simple, bolt-action hunting rifles—more than enough for the task. The third was another British Army Iraq War veteran—an old war buddy of Davies's—and he was armed with a suppressed Walther WA2000 bullpup-configured rifle. Before that first bolt-action rifle shot was heard by everyone in the area (inside and outside), Davies's war buddy had already killed two other constables and severely wounded three members of a news crew who had tried to get a better angle on the action.

This caused the London police to withdraw from the area by more than a block. Police snipers had been unable to successfully engage Davies's snipers. As soon as one sniper would shoot at another, more would join in, and soon both sides reached a détente. Police and Davies's snipers all fell silent; they exposed themselves only for easy targets.

Davies went down to the lobby. There he was met by one of his men, who told him that the bank's security system was under their control and had been reset. They all knew that the police would eventually have to storm the bank, and when they did an armed security system would help. He then went to the conference room to double-fcheck that all the hostages were secured, and when he was convinced they were, he reduced the number of guards around the hostages to one. Finally, he headed back up to the records room.

"Ronald!" he called out. "Did you find it?"

Ronald called out from down the row of bookcases. "It's not here. I found the 1923 section. There's nothing in there. The sheik was wrong. He was wrong *again*, Davies!"

Ian Davies knew Ronald's frustration. It was his too. How many times had he been sent on fox hunts for fools? They were too many to list, he thought. Still, he did get the money. No robbery that yielded hundreds of millions of pounds was ever considered a failure.

Without ever having seen Ronald in the records room, Davies called out to him once more. "Fine, if you find anything, grab it, and we'll start on getting out of here. The pigs are already here." With that he headed back downstairs to meet the inevitable police negotiator.

On the rooftop the sniper duels had restarted. The police got reinforcements. Using radios to communicate exactly when, all of the police snipers and their reinforcements leaned out of cover and began to fire at Davies's snipers. The police reinforcements all used suppressed rifles. Inside the banking house the firing didn't sound unusually strong. There was no way of knowing that Davies's outnumbered men had all been killed.

The guard in the conference room was circling the room. When he stepped in front of Colonel Eli Davies and Major Stan MacLean there was a pop from behind the wall. Splinters flew out as a nine-millimeter bullet fired from behind the wall passed through and into the guard's forehead. He fell lifeless without ever having even a thought. Everyone in the room turned and looked.

A twenty-four by twenty-four inch wood panel near the floor, behind Stan and Eli, opened up and disappeared in the wall. No one could see how or who had done it. A dim reflection off the lens off some sort of night-vision goggles were all they could see.

Stan moved his bound hands to the opening in the wall. They were cut by a man in black hidden in the shadow. Then he removed his gag, took a knife from the man inside the wall, and freed Eli. They passed the knife to the next hostage and people began freeing each other. Meanwhile, Stan grabbed the guard's

FN FAL rifle and began to watch the door, ready to open fire on Davies or any of his men.

“Thanks, Sam,” Eli said to the man in the wall.

The three green lights nodded. Then a growling voice spoke quietly. “I can’t get you out of the building, but I can get you to safety. Everyone has to follow me.”

Eli got everyone’s attention, and then he told them all to follow him. He went into the wall first. Everyone followed. Stan was the last into the wall. When he replaced the panel to hide their escape, there was no light at all.

The space between the wood panels and the building’s exterior stone walls was narrow. It was a claustrophobic’s nightmare. At the front of the line of hostages, the man in black, Eli’s “man” Sam, snapped several chemical glow sticks and lit the passage a dim blue. Everyone could see him for a few seconds—at least his silhouette and his night vision goggles but no facial features at all. His legs were spread and pressing on the walls, and below him was a cast iron hatch lifted open.

Sam faced the line of packed people in the blue glow. “This hatch leads to the old coal storage room. It’s about a ten-foot drop so good luck.” Then he scurried up the walls like a spider and was gone in the darkness.

Eli grabbed a glowing chemical stick and tossed it into the hole to see the bottom. Then he grasped the first hostage by the hands and lowered her down into the blue-lit room below. She landed with a thud, but she managed to stand up and walk away. She’d made it. The rest followed shortly after. Again, Stan was the last.

“I thought you people just did electronic and digital spy stuff, Eli?” Stan asked.

“Yeah, well, there’s some fieldwork involved,” Eli answered coyly. “By the way, your people are here now.”

The two men smiled.

A few minutes after Davies’s last sniper was killed, while the hostages were all making their escape, a hard knocking at the main door to Tryphine Banking House began. Davies was standing on the “Employee Only” stairs when he heard it. The gunmen in the lobby looked at him, and he motioned for the man closest to the door to open it, and he let the negotiator in to talk. His plan was to wait out the police. One of the accounts that he’d just loaded with one hundred million pounds was to a Saudi diplomat, who was going to call and make arrangements for Davies and his men to leave the UK peacefully.

The camouflaged gunman slung his H&K G3 rifle over his shoulder and opened the front door. He expected to see some police department leader awkwardly dressed in a suit or white shirt and body armor, with hands held high and eager to talk about a peaceful end to the banking house occupation. Instead the gunman opened the door and froze in shock. There were five rows of heavily armed men wearing full-combat, heavy body armor and facemasks, and one with a ballistic shield. Each row had four men in it, and he was staring in stunned awe at twenty men trained, ready, and aiming to obliterate his body and being. Stan's men had arrived...with vengeance.

The man in black who was second closest to him, behind the first man with the giant ballistic shield, motioned with his finger for the gunman to be quiet. The gunman nodded slowly, and four of the men in black began pulling pins on flash bang grenades—grenades that were designed not to fragment, be forceful or destructive, or start fires, but rather to flash areas with blinding light and deafening booms. Though the men were arming the grenades behind him, the second man closest to the gunman knew they were ready, and his finger moved from his lips, where it signaled to be quiet, to pointing into the bank. Eight beer can-sized grenades flew over the gunman at the front door. As they landed, another eight were primed and tossed in for good measure.

Inside the bank, Davies heard the banging of the grenades echo on the marble floor. His mind connected the sound with the frozen gunman at the front door, and he knew it was not a negotiator on the steps outside. Davies knew they were being breached, so he fled to the most secure location in the bank: the vault in the basement.

Davies made it a full two steps toward his destination when the first of the sixteen thunderclaps reverberated in the historic marble lobby. There was no shockwave, but the combination of flashes and booms confused the signals from his eyes and ears to his brain. With his brain—as well as all the other guards—getting too many signals, he froze. The centuries-old stained glass ceiling high above shattered and rained down pieces of colored glass. Each one exploded on impact with the marble floor, creating a vivid, multicolor sparkle throughout the entire lobby.

While the last flashbang grenade was exploding, the men in black stormed Tryphine Banking House. The man with the ballistic shield entered first with three men tightly following him. They shoved aside the gunman, charged across the lobby, and executed the guards behind the check-in desk while they were standing still and stunned. It was as choreographed as a ballet, and looked a simple thing.

The second team of four men in black came in seamlessly behind the first, and they headed for the conference room to rescue the hostages. On their way the last man in the four-man, line formation fired into the gunman who had opened the door and was disoriented on the floor. It was an execution as well, and bore all the care of swatting a gnat, albeit with a twelve-gauge shotgun. They opened the conference room, saw there was no one there, and proceeded up the stairs.

The third team of four men in black came in upon the heels of the second team. They headed left. First they checked the teller windows, then the marble conference room on the left, and then they disappeared into the hallways to begin clearing offices of gunmen. Shots could be heard from the halls immediately after they disappeared.

The fourth team entered as did the first three, and they headed down into the halls on the right side of the lobby. Again shots were heard as they began hunting down and killing Davies's men.

The last team entered and headed straight for the basement. They were steps behind Davies. Occasionally Davies fired in their direction, and they responded with a hail of gunfire. It was a shooting, a hot pursuit in corridors where bullets bounced off floors, ceilings, and walls. It was a funnel of steel and lead flying in all directions.

Armed constables from the police began racing into the lobby next. Almost a hundred men in various uniforms were searching for hostages and gunmen. They found only bodies, broken glass, and smoke from the flashbangs. The police investigation was already beginning.

When the second team of men in black entered the records room, one of Davies's camouflaged gunmen opened fire on them with an Uzi submachine gun. He missed all four men, and was killed excessively. Ronald, wearing a suit, was behind a bookcase with an FN FAL rifle, but he set it down quietly while the men in black began to search the stacks of documents. He reached into his pocket, pulled out Alan's visitor pass, and slung it around his neck. Then he got on his knees and put his hands over his head just a split second before the men in black found him. Assuming he was a hostage, they escorted him downstairs and handed Ronald off to the police as such.

In just over five minutes the entire building was cleared except for the basement. Davies and another gunman had made it to the vault. The men in black headed down the long concrete corridor in plain sight. Davies was inside one of the guard rooms, and watched through a bulletproof glass window as the four men headed toward him. The glass was thick—too thick to penetrate even with their military-grade weapons. It was so thick that they couldn't hear Davies's taunts and ravings, but he was clearly animated and vocal.

The lead man of the four-man team reached the window. He stopped to look at Davies while the other three headed left down the hall to the room where the vault door was. Davies continued hurling epithets at the man in black, who tilted his head curiously in response. Meanwhile the other three men had reached the vault door, but a wall of steel bars had been closed by Davies, keeping them out of the vault room as well as the vault itself or the security room where Davies was cursing.

Another four-man team of men in black came down the hall. They ignored Davies's screaming from behind the window, and joined with the three men from the first team while their leader continued distracting Davies. At the vault door room, behind the steel bars, all of the men stopped, lined up along the bars, and pulled out gas masks from bags they carried on their lower backs. Once everyone was set, a tear gas grenade was tossed through the bars and into the vault.

While tear gas grenades in the late twentieth century worked by burning a chemical with a flame in the grenade itself, twenty-first century grenades were called cold grenades because they generated no heat, and thus had minimal risk of causing a fire. This was important as the vault contained a great deal of paper money.

The second generation tear gas grenades of the twenty-first century were also more refined in their effect. Tear gas grenades now caused far more than just tears. Their smoke was not just an eye irritant. They caused terrible nausea as fluids filled the lungs and stomach. Uncontrollable coughing and vomiting resulted as well. The flood of fluids into the lungs also caused shortness of breath and dizziness. By the time Stan's men in black stormed Tryphine Banking House it was nearly impossible to stand more than a minute in a confined space with a tear gas grenade.

Davies was in the security office attached to the vault. He smelled the gas immediately and recognized it from his British military training. He knew what was about to happen so he started stuffing a leftover bank guard's jacket into the space between the security room door and the floor. The chemical agent still found its way through, and after two minutes he'd had enough.

Davies opened the door, headed into the smoke that had filled the vault, and began firing in the direction of the steel bars. The eight men in black responded. They opened fire at the muzzle flashes from Davies's pistol. In less than thirty seconds his body was shredded beyond recognition, and the men in black were reloading. Again they saw muzzle flashes in the tear gas—this time from a machine pistol of some sort—and again they opened fire mercilessly.

The building was secure. Davies and all of his men had been killed. Only Ronald Van De Burgh, who had pretended to be a hostage, managed to escape. He gave a quick, false story to the police in the lobby, and then he walked away down the street without question.

All of the men in black searched the building one more time for anymore gunmen. The constables sent men along as well. When they were certain there was no one else, the lead element of Stan's men in black came down the basement and opened the door to the coal storage room. The hostages were rescued.

Stan's men escorted everyone to the lobby, where police were taking statements and getting contact information. Stan met with his men briefly, and then they stepped into the marble conference room off the lobby. Out of sight from the police and hostages, they removed their black outfits, donned collared shirt and slacks, and packed their gear in lightweight duffle bags.

The lobby seemed chaotic, but it was far worse outside. Police cars, ambulances, fire trucks, media vans, normally parked cars, more constables, and a line of white panel vans all filled the streets. The media had burst through their barricades from blocks away and were now wrestling with the police to get camera angles. They'd heard hundreds of shots throughout the day as well as the flashbang grenades, and like sharks to blood they smelled dramatic footage. Alan and Jim were taken straight through and put in ambulances, then rushed to the hospital, but it took almost ten minutes to move through the crowded street.

Lord Tryphine, Joan, Erwin, and Anna stood out front behind one of the panel vans. No one wept. They were too tired from the stress. Exhaustion came first; Erwin remembered that from the time he'd been held hostage in his home years ago, but it didn't make it any easier. Anna wasn't shaking anymore, and both her body and mind had processed the entire event already; it was already a thing of the past for her. Joan embraced Terrence.

They all spoke occasionally. Having been through the happenings together, they were recovering faster than some who had gone through the experience alone. Eventually, the money came up.

"What did you do about the money he demanded?" Erwin asked of Terrence.

"I put together a transaction that both moved money into the accounts and then moved it out. He was too confused to notice. They got nothing. This was all for nothing."

Over time all of them would go through the five stages: denial, anger, depression, bargaining, and acceptance. Joan was in depression. Anna was in acceptance. Terrence had fooled Davies and that bargain was his comfort. Erwin had been in anger since Davies first put his hands on his precious wife Anna.

It was more than anger. Erwin cared a great deal about money, about his noble duty to others, about the arts, and charities. He cared about his work, using digital financing to track down terrorists and prevent attacks. He loved Anna. He loved Anna more than anything or anyone in the world. It was a glowing, red hot, retaliatory rage.

After hearing that Lord Tryphine had fooled Davies, and filled with anger from the day's events, Erwin left Terrence and the ladies for a moment. He stepped aside and called his secretary, Manfred.

"Are you all right, sir?" Manfred had already seen the news. He'd also been contacted by Andrew Lawrence after Lawrence got the email that Lord Tryphine sent from his desk while Davies's back was turned.

"We're fine, Manfred. Everyone is fine. Thank you." He paused and looked back at Anna. "Manfred, in my desk, on the right side, in the second drawer, you'll find a yellow folder. Would you find that for me, please? I'll wait."

Manfred agreed, walked to Erwin's desk, and found the file in the back of the drawer. "I have it, sir."

"This was Al Tunb's people, Manfred. He paid for the attack on us before, and he's done it again. I will no longer be a nuisance to that...that...that man. The file is a list of people who have had financial dealings with him. We had hoped to monitor that list. The plan was to determine who his terrorist lieutenants are, and who are just his innocent friends and family. Well, he doesn't seem to care how innocent someone is who he hurts, so I'm going to do the same to him. He has been waging a war regardless of his victims, and no one has fought back. I am going to fight back. He wants war, and it's time he got war."

"Yes, sir, what would you have me do with this list?" Manfred asked.

"I want to empty those accounts."

"I'm not sure how to do this. These holdings are in banks all over the world. There must be.... Sir, there are almost two thousand accounts in this file."

"I want to empty those accounts, Manfred. Many of those are with Tryphine Banking House. Send the transfer requests for those, and I'll see to it that Lord Tryphine approves them. As for the others, find someone who can access those accounts and empty them. I want it done immediately. Call Colonel Elijah Davies ; I believe I gave you his number. Call him and tell him I want it done, and that if he has any questions he should call me directly. I'm certain today will have left him with a similar sentiment and he'll assist you."

"Where do you want the money to go, sir?"

"I don't care. Give it to charity, or move it to one of Mr. Conferra's offshore accounts that we have on file. Take it for you and the staff. I don't care. Mr. al Douri, or Al Tunb, or whatever that man's name is, he's gone way too far too often. It's time his friends and family felt some of the pain he's been shedding. I want everyone he knows to be beggars in the streets before the sun sets in the West." Erwin paused. "You will do this for me, Manfred?"

"Of course, sir-yes sir. Before the sun sets in the West it'll be done."

Without any reservation at all, Manfred went to work. Everyone who had ever so much as sent or received a dime from Ibrahim al Douri Al Tunb was about to lose everything they ever had in any bank. Every home, car, yacht, boat, would be seized by Erwin's banking friends. The price for crossing top-tier bankers such as Lord Tryphine and Erwin Zimmermann would be high. Erwin looked around at the crowded street scene. When he looked back at Anna, Terrence, and Joan he saw Terrence speaking with Andrew Lawrence, who had just arrived. It was clear that they were already in the process of doing the same thing that Erwin had just done. He glanced back at the front door of Tryphine Banking House and saw that every member of the Swiss delegation was on the phone. Surely they would have notified their families by now, and calls after that were most certainly in line with Erwin's economic counter-attack on Al Tunb and everyone associated with him.

***

10/23/2006

The financial attacks on Al Tunb and everyone associated with him were swift, sweeping, and devastating. Manfred was able to empty thousands of accounts from Erwin's yellow folder. Other banks and financial firms were notified en masse by email. They soon followed their friend's call as well.

Lord Tryphine and Tryphine Banking House were far more devastating. They had access to banking networks and investment networks that Erwin didn't. Then Terrence called American Treasury Secretary George Whittaker, who brought the full weight and power down of the US government on everyone remotely connected to Ibrahim al Douri Al Tunb. The Swiss spread the word openly in the world's banking community about what had happened and what was now going to happen, and wealthy friends of Al Tunb who didn't want to lose everything traded information for their wealth by the billions. Colonel Eli Davies covertly sent people to SFS International and seized all of their electronic accounting information, effectively pulling the curtain from their involvement in the hawala money transfer system. Lastly-and far less covertly, Stan MacLean sent his men in black to SFS International, and the morning after their visit international news networks reported SFS had burned to the ground after a kitchen fire in a neighboring restaurant had spread.

By October Ibrahim al Douri Al Tunb was broke. Everyone he knew was equally broke or had become an intelligence asset for his enemies. The House of Saud no longer allowed him in their kingdom, and the Gulf Emirates shared the sentiment. In the fourteenth and fifteenth centuries his ancestors ruled the Persian Gulf, the southern coast of the Arabian Peninsula, and as far south as Dar es Salaam. Now, their royal descendant was broke, homeless, and lacked allies. He was also an internationally wanted man. After sponsoring the worst terrorist attacks in human history, Ibrahim al Douri Al Tunb had finally pissed off all of the wrong people, and he did it all at once.

Ronald Van De Burgh was also on the run. He'd quickly made his way from London back to Amsterdam. The Terrafirst Technologies was still active, but he was too concerned about being caught to visit them or the café in Arnhem. Instead, he moved from hostel to hostel throughout Europe. Eventually he decided to try and contact Al Tunb himself.

It took some time, but he did. There was little money to be paid to Ronald, but Al Tunb gave him more details on the hundred-year-old oil contract that he'd always sought. Then he offered Ronald a one percent share of any settlement that Al Tunb might end up making with Trucial Energy. Ronald agreed, and a pitiful $10,000 was mailed to a hostel in Brussels where Ronald planned to stay next.

At the same time when Ronald was shifting from place to place in Europe, a storm was brewing in the mid-Atlantic. Hurricane Joyce was the last named storm of 2006, and it was to be the worst. The late-forming tropical storm brewed up off the west coast of Africa. It traveled toward Bermuda, shifted north, and then ran almost parallel to the American east coast. It was not, however, perfectly parallel, and Hurricane Joyce made landfall south of Ocean City, Maryland, just after it became a category 3. The storm surge brought terrible erosion all along the Chesapeake Bay and up to Washington, DC, forcing the federal government to close for several days. Joyce's powerful eye wall struck Washington with the force of a category 1 hurricane. Then it turned north, and was downgraded to tropical storm status as it reached Pittsburgh. It appeared as if the storm would continue to downgrade as it faded back toward the east—dumping huge amounts of cold October rain everywhere from New Jersey to Maine.

***

10/25/2006

For years Al Tunb had searched for his family's 1923 contract with Trucial Energy. He was convinced that it hadn't been lost to time, hadn't been tossed in a desk clerk's circular file, hadn't rotted to nothingness or been burned to ash. Since his father's death every day he worked toward finding it. He'd spent millions paying people to search the ends of the world for the elusive piece of paper. He's sponsored terror attacks trying to find it. Wars had been started. He'd searched the globe and come up empty-handed.

With Davies gone, and Al Tunb's allies reduced to the deepest parts of the underworld, Ronald had to think of a new plan. Prior to his life as an international terrorist for hire, before he was ever in prison, and before Ronald had ever become an activist at the Terrafirst Technologies...before all of that he was a geology student. He loved the history of Mother Earth, and he loved history as well. Al Tunb's ancestral contract between his family and Trucial Energy involved: Al Tunb's family history, Trucial Energy's formative history, post-World War American history as they had negotiated the contract, and later Iran's history. Al Tunb certainly knew his only family history. He had attacked and searched Trucial Energy facilities around the globe while waging his private war on the global corporation. And getting at records from the early days of the Islamic Republic of Iran would be next to impossible. American history, Ronald thought, was an open book for any and all to study. Then he wondered if perhaps instead of Trucial Energy or the Iranians, perhaps the Americans had at least a copy of the contract?

Ronald was sitting in a small pub in Brussels when he had the thought about the Americans. On the TV in front of him the news was being shown, and there was a report about plans for a presidential library for the most recent former President. The report described how the library would have all sorts of memorabilia, memorandum, and documents from the former president's life in office and his earlier years in the CIA. It made Ronald wonder if there was an American presidential library from the time when Al Tunb's contract with Trucial Energy's founders was negotiated by the Americans.

While sipping local wheat ale, he moved from the bar to a booth. It was late afternoon, and there were only four other people in the small pub. Its cozy atmosphere made him feel secure. He pulled out his new smartphone and began searching the Internet.

First Ronald searched to find out who the American president was in 1923 when the contract was negotiated. It was President Warren G. Harding. Next he searched to see if there was a Warren G. Harding Presidential Library. He found it to be in a small town, Marion, Ohio, and the website showed that the museum did in fact have a documents collection that was open to the public for researchers. How convenient, he thought! Lastly, he bought an airline ticket from Brussels to Columbus, Ohio, which was only forty-five minutes from the museum. Ronald smiled, downed his beer, and headed to the hostel where he'd been staying to collect the backpack he'd been living out of for months.

Getting out of Belgium and into the US was easy for Ronald. He'd learned to forge documents—including passports—long ago. The journey, however, was arduous. First he flew from Belgium to London. Then from London he flew to New York City, where his fake passport didn't raise any alarm. In New York he almost missed his connecting flight to Atlanta, and in Atlanta he had a two-hour layover before finally flying into Columbus, Ohio.

***

10/27/2006

Just before dawn Ronald began heading to the Warren G. Harding Library. He rented a car at the airport, parked it in a strip mall parking lot just north of Columbus, and slept for four hours before he made his way to Marion, Ohio. The museum was only another fifteen minutes away, but he was exhausted, and he knew from the museum's website that it didn't open until 10 a.m. The 2007 Ford Taurus that he'd rented was far larger than anything he'd driven in Europe, but the back seat was still cramped for him to sleep in. The jetlag and time difference played havoc with his ability to sleep, and after little more than three hours of resting he headed up to Marion to be at the museum when it opened.

Marion, Ohio, population twenty-four thousand, was the classic example of small-town America. Main Street was the center of attention. Road and rail networks crossed around the city. A few large industries provided most of the jobs. Farmland covered most of the town's boundaries. Like most American small towns in the post-1960s the retail spaces, the small shops, that lined Main Street, were declining in number and longevity. America's great irony was that people in small towns and the vast countryside seemed to migrate toward the larger cities, and people in the larger cities tended to migrate out to the suburbs between the cities and countryside. As large inner cities declined from urban migration, so too did the small towns, and Marion was not unusual in this sense.

Ronald marveled at America. Everything seemed so big, and so cheap. He had only known the quality of European roads and buildings that had lasted hundreds and hundreds of years. Here, the roads were pock-marked with potholes. The houses were wooden and cheaply built by comparison. Everywhere he looked he saw decay and unchecked corporate sprawl. It sickened him. It angered him.

Driving from Columbus to Marion Ronald saw more and more farmland. Here his sentiments changed. Here he saw homes and farming operations that didn't seem as corporate to him. He saw advanced, scientific, high-tech farming equipment parked next to simple, average, often well-maintained homes and properties. It made Ronald think that perhaps there were Americans who were self-reliant, who were able and eager to work with Mother Earth and not rape her for resources. He wasn't impressed enough to be happy, but his mood did balance out. Fatigue from the journey was taking a physically imposed, emotional toll.

The weather didn't help. Clouds, temperatures in the thirties, and periodic precipitation of all types were the rule of the day. Remnants of Hurricane Joyce were playing havoc with the area. One minute it would snow, the next rain, the next small white pellets fell down from above. Occasionally the sky opened up and Ronald could see blue, but a few minutes later dark, low, gray "snow clouds" would pass overhead, dimming the light and his morale.

Using his smartphone for directions, Ronald arrived in Marion just before 10 a.m., and he pulled into the Warren G. Harding Presidential Library parking lot a few minutes later. The front of the library was President Harding's original home—not a giant palace or castle or even an estate. It was a simple home like most of the others in downtown Marion—an average, late nineteenth/early twentieth century home of well under three thousand square feet. He curled the right side of his mouth and marveled at how Americans chose their leaders from such humble ranks, and marveled at the contrast to Europeans, whose aristocratic estates (actual breeding grounds for their political leaders for centuries) were the size of large American cities like Washington, DC. Behind President Harding's home was a newer building, the size of a small, modern manufacturer and lacking all the décor of the same, he thought to himself. The only other cars in the parking lot were that of a few staff members.

While entering the building Ronald found that security was extremely light. He paid a small entrance fee, and while the attendant was gathering his change she gave a practiced welcoming speech that described President Harding and the library. The attendant pulled out a flyer with museum information on it as she handed him a few dollar bills and coins. She also asked if there was anything in particular he was interested in seeing.

"I'm doing some research on post-World War I alliances and Middle East resource mandates. Do you have anything like that?" he asked.

"We do. Our records room is here," she pointed to a map on the back of the information flyer. "When you go in, we have a research coordinator who can help you find anything specific."

They exchanged polite smiles, and Ronald headed down to the research room without an escort or a security guard to be seen. There wasn't even a door on the room. He was amazed. Americans can be so naïve, he thought.

No one else was in the large room except the records coordinator, who immediately introduced himself as Dan. Ronald gave the same vague description of what he was looking for to Dan, but he asked Ronald to be more specific.

"Actually, I'm looking for a 1923 contract that the Harding administration negotiated between Emir Al Tunb in the Persian Gulf and American Petroleum. It might be under JP Oil & Gas, William Jennings and Associates, or Carnegie Coal and Heat. They all merged around the same time."

"Do you have a specific date of the contract?"

"I do not," Ronald answered.

"That's no problem," Dan said with a smile. "President Harding died of a heart attack on August 2nd, so that rules out more than a third of the year. Anything after August 2nd you would have to go to the Calvin Coolidge Library in Vermont. Let's hope we can find something for you here. Now, let me think....in 1923 people sometimes referred to the Persian Gulf as the Arabian Gulf, and the countries we see there today didn't exist. They were just called the 'Pirate Coast' or 'Persia' or the 'Truciary States.'"

They headed toward several tall bookcases packed with boxes of documents. Dan led the way. Finally they came to a nondescript desk in the farthest corner of the room. On it was a desktop computer and a microfilm viewer.

Dan sat down at the computer, and then he motioned for Ronald to join him. All the while Dan seemed to be putting his master's degree in American history to work.

"Before World War I most of the rulers in that area formed their own relationships. The Portuguese from the 1700s, then the British in the 1800s, and of course the Ottoman Turks held a great deal of influence over the entire region until after the war. They finally lost that influence at the Treaty of Lausanne in July 1923, but it wasn't ratified until the Coolidge administration. I'm going to guess that any contracts negotiated in that year, before President Harding passed away, would have been before the Treaty of Lausanne. That means we're looking for something before July."

Ronald nodded as if he understood or cared. He was trying, but it was confusing information presented too quickly, and he was simply tired. Dan noticed.

"I'm sorry. I love history. What can I do?" He smiled and continued making his way through different screens on the computer. He tried different search criteria to find the contract Ronald sought (and Ibrahim al Douri Al Tunb was looking for by extension).

"This might be it. There was a contract between Rexford Oil and Emir el Toonmt in May of 1923. The contract was negotiated by State Department Special Envoy Patrick Carnegie . Hmmm..." Dan paused. "Patrick Carnegie was elected to Congress in the House of Representatives the next year for Pennsylvania's 5th District. You might be able to find out more about this in Pennsylvania. There might be a Patrick Carnegie Museum. There're also places you can look in Washington, DC."

Ronald tilted his head as if impressed. He was, but only to a degree. What excited him was the possibility that Al Tunb's long-sought-after contract might soon be found. Even that prospect, however, didn't get enough adrenalin flowing.

Dan continued searching the museum's document archive database. Then he sighed. "Okay, we have good news and bad news. It looks like there is a contract like the one you're looking for. That's the good news. The bad news is that we don't have it here."

Ronald bit his tongue and sat back in his chair. "Where is it?"

"I think that...because it was a contract negotiated by a State Department official, it was kept as part of the State Department's archives. A few years ago the State Department began its effort to go paperless. When that began they finally started getting rid of old documents. We acquired them, but we don't have the room in this building yet. They only made it as far as Cleveland."

"Cleveland?" Ronald asked. "Where do I go in Cleveland?"

"Our State Department-related archives were sent from Washington, DC, to the Federal Reserve Building downtown. It's sort of a catch-all location for important documents to go before they're dispensed to museums and such." Dan looked down at his screen. He clicked on part of the information next to the document he'd found in the database. "Yup. It's in Cleveland, at the Federal Reserve Building. Basement level 1, room B101, document case 36, third shelf."

Finally Ronald's adrenalin surpassed his fatigue. He smiled from ear to ear. He couldn't believe it! He knew exactly where Al Tunb's grand prize was located. He was going to be rich. Trucial Energy was going to finally pay the price for their raping of Mother Earth, and governments were going to have to eat each other alive to sort it all out. He couldn't be happier.

Dan wrote down the information on where to find the document. "If you leave soon, Cleveland's only about three hours away. They won't let you take it, but you can see it and copy it by the end of today."

Ronald thanked him profusely, and headed back to his car. It wasn't even lunchtime, he noticed. While he wanted to race up to Cleveland, he remembered that he had hardly eaten in days. Ronald decided to stop and have a real meal...or what Americans thought was a real meal.

Once he stepped outside his longing for Amsterdam resurfaced. The weather and scenery were utterly demoralizing. Cold, wet wind was blowing from the north and gusting to almost twenty mph. He got in his car, and the sleet-covered roads were a new experience for him. Hunger could wait, he decided, and Ronald started heading north on Interstate 77 toward Cleveland. Not until he stopped for gas did he get anything to eat, and his experience with American gas station beef jerky didn't improve his demeanor.

Just north of Akron, Ohio, the ugly weather shifted to bad. He had entered what locals called a secondary snow belt. Another five miles, and the weather went from bad to worse as he entered the primary snow belt. The roads were covered with snow and hard to see. The wind tried to push his car off the interstate. Unaccustomed to winter highway driving in Ohio, he slowed to forty-five mph, and seasoned locals blew past him doing seventy and eighty mph. Snow changed to rain and back again, making him constantly adjust his windshield wipers. To Ronald, it seemed as though he had found himself in the North Pole.

In Cleveland, Ronald got lost. His smartphone's navigational feature wasn't current with Ohio's never-ending cycle of road construction and reconstruction. Detours had him get off on the west side of town, and as he headed east toward the Federal Reserve Building he found himself on the I-77 once again. It took him five hours to get from Marion, Ohio, to the Federal Reserve Building in downtown Cleveland.

Cleveland, Ohio....in late October and hit by an early snowstorm...was nothing like Ronald's Amsterdam. He was used to civic beauty built upon centuries of artisanship. In contrast he saw Cleveland as rust, mismatched architecture, and devoid of beauty spaces. Granted, he was seeing a formerly great city in the lowest pit of its economic decline. The housing crisis had already hit the city a full year and a half before the rest of the nation and the world. Thousands of homes were being foreclosed on in 2006. The steel mills that had built the city in the early twentieth century were all gone by the twenty-first century. Manufacturing remained, but once a home to well over a million people, Cleveland was already less than half that in population. The Great Recession had already hit, and the town was not at its finest moment. Ronald's bias and idolatry of Amsterdam and Europe made his opinion far worse.

Once he found a place to park, Ronald fought his way through the blowing sleet and snow, down the sidewalk, and into the United States Federal Reserve Building. The huge doors to get into the building were heavy. They were old and stiff. The grease in the hinges hadn't been replaced. Blowing rain had made its way into the frame and then froze. He had to push with all his might just to get inside. Once he did manage to get in, the building's steam heat hit him like an oven. The door slammed behind him, and in an instant he had gone from snowstorm to warm wooden lobby with a roaring fireplace at the end, and steam heat with a broken thermostat.

Unlike the Warren G. Harding Library, security in this building was extreme. Doors all had double security locks with both swipe card and key access. Cameras were made to be seen in every corner, as were motion sensors and what appeared to be electronic jammers since his cell phone was immediately inactive the moment he stepped in out of the cold.

Ironically the Cleveland Federal Reserve Building finished being built in 1923. The two hundred-foot-tall, thirteen-story building was typical of most mid-western American buildings of the time. It was built in an Italian Renaissance style, and decorated with cathedral-style marble lobbies as well as neoclassical conference rooms. The main lobby, however, was done in highly trimmed woodwork with a large, green, marble fireplace at the end, with hallways and teller windows off to the sides. The building also housed one of the largest vaults in the world: three hundred tons with a ninety-ton door—balanced so precisely (even in 1923) that two men could still open it by hand. Inside the vault, estimates ranged between $5 billion to $10 billion in cash as well as unknown amounts of gold and securities. The steps to the building's entrance once had firing ports for machine guns in case anyone ever thought of robbing the bank, but they'd long since been cemented over, replaced by more modern, more effective security measures. None of this mattered to Ronald. His interest was in the basement records room, B101.

He stepped to a barred teller window on the left.

A security guard was on the other side. Her eyes were staring at a computer monitor to the side. Ronald waited politely to be recognized, but she ignored him—deliberately, arrogantly.

"Excuse me?" he asked.

The guard sighed, tilted her head, and looked at him with annoyed eyes. "Yes, sir, how can I help you?"

"I'm looking for a records room, B101?"

The guard answered as if she were seeing through Ronald and reading a teleprompter behind him. "I'm sorry, sir. All unnecessary offices had been closed due to inclement weather. They are expected to reopen on Monday at 8 am." With that she turned back to her computer.

The woman's indignance set Ronald off. Though discourteous behavior could be found in all cultures in all of human history, Ronald saw her attitude as an American one. He walked the lobby looking for a door, but they were all locked. He stood by the fireplace to warm up before heading back to his car.

"Sir?" the guard behind the window called out to him.

"Yes?"

"Sir, I'm afraid you can't wait until Monday in here. The building is closed to all unnecessary operations. You'll have to go, sir."

"I was just trying to warm up first," he replied with confused surprise.

"I'm sorry, sir, but you'll have to leave."

Another woman made her way in through the front doors. She walked up to the armed guard's barred window. The guard gave her a clipboard to sign. She signed it and headed for a door next to where Ronald was standing in shock.

The guard wasn't looking anymore, and Ronald watched as the woman entered her four-digit passcode. Then she tapped her plastic access card on the lock and pulled the door open. Ronald took the moment to walk up and bump into her.

"I'm so sorry," he said with a humble smile.

The woman smiled back, replied with a simple, "That's okay," and proceeded into the building.

Ronald stormed out of the building. The door opened to blistering wind. It reminded him of opening the hatch to the helipad on the Trucial Energy oil rig in the North Sea near the Arctic Circle.

***

10/28/06

Instead of blowing out to sea, Hurricane Joyce—like so many other hurricanes—confused all computer models and meandered in place. She did move east, but she also moved southeast as well. Still a named tropical storm, Joyce waited and spun over the New York/Boston area.

Northwest of Cleveland a typical cold front (often called an "Alberta Clipper") came down from Alberta, Canada, and looked to be the final push she needed out into the Atlantic. Instead, a warm front, fueled by warm water coming north from Florida, nudged Joyce back on to land and toward Pittsburgh for a second hit. Pennsylvania, West Virginia, Maryland, New Jersey, and New York saw extensive flooding, but worst hit were Buffalo, New York, then Erie, Pennsylvania, and on Saturday, October 28 she finally hit Cleveland, Ohio.

A natural phenomenon called lake-effect snow exacerbated the storm. Lake Erie was still almost sixty degrees from the summer and fall. It was far from frozen over. As the cold air from the Alberta Clipper came down, the remnants of Tropical Storm Joyce collided with it and forced it to go directly across Lake Erie from north to south. The cold air—moving fast from Joyce's winds—streaked across the warm waters of the lake and pulled up massive amounts of moisture. This moisture was then turned to snow in the cold air, and fell back to earth once it lost the energy from the warm water. The result was that on October 26 Cleveland was hit with almost a foot of snow. On the 27th the city had two more additional feet fall on it. On the 28th, three additional feet of snow fell.

All of Northeastern Ohio was put on a snow alert. Parking on streets was banned. Events were canceled. The State Highway Patrol announced that people should only be on the roads if they absolutely had to be, such as in the case of first responders, utility workers, and so forth. Snowplows from as far away as Cincinnati were being called up to help.

The snow decreased dramatically in the late hours of the 28th and early hours of the 29th, but it was replaced by cold air that had been pulled down from the Arctic Circle. This caused drifting snow, and made the six feet of snow pile high into drifts big enough to cover semi-tractor trailer trucks on the sides of the freeways. The media called the entire affair the Halloween Blizzard.

After trying to drive in the gray, slush-covered roads, Ronald finally gave up. He was lost. His smartphone's navigation was proving almost entirely useless. Street signs were covered with snow that had been glued to them by high wind gusts. All he knew was that he was on the eastern half of the city. No one else was on the streets except police cars, and that was making him nervous.

There were plenty of abandoned homes on the east side of Cleveland; row upon row of them. At one point he counted twenty-four on a single street. He parked his car in the driveway of a boarded-up home at the corner of Norwood and Bonna, walked around back, pulled off some plywood, and made his way inside. The home had been broken into previously. Many of the last owner's belongings were still inside. Some pictures were still on walls. There was even furniture. He found a fireplace in the living room, opened its flue, and made a fire. Then he pulled up an old couch that had been beaten and broken by vandals, and stretched out. It was as good as an international terrorist on the run could really have hoped for. Besides, he was truly exhausted—physically and mentally.

***

10/30/2006

Monday morning in snowbound Cleveland was a mess. Hundreds of local schools and businesses had been closed. Only the main roads had been plowed. Government buildings and most businesses, however, were back open.

Ronald had been awake from time to time to refill the fireplace. By 8 a.m. on Monday, he was running out of things to burn. Vandals had kicked holes in a wall, and he'd even started pulling off the wood lath that held plaster in place. Half a century of drying in the house made it burn hot and fast, but he had needed lots of it, and several walls were now mere skeletons.

He headed through the kitchen and out the back of the house where he'd torn off the plywood to break in. There was no sight of his car. All he could see was a snowdrift half as tall as the house. He knew it was in there so he used the plywood from the house to start digging until he found it.

It took Ronald more than an hour to get to his car. He spent another half hour trying to start it, and another hour and a half trying to get it out to the street. The street—largely devoid of residents due to the housing crisis—was completely unplowed. The only reason there wasn't six feet of snow was that it was the most open area to the wind, and all of it had been blown to the sides and backyards of the empty homes.

With his smartphone in dying need of a charge, Ronald tried to find his way back to downtown, to the Federal Reserve Building. He knew he was on the east side of the city, and decided he could just head north toward the lake, then turn left to get downtown. The larger four- and five-lane streets were choked with traffic, so he tried to stick to the residential side streets. For no particular reason he chose to head north on nearby East 62nd Street. After crossing a five-lane road, East 62nd hit a dead end.

Ronald was confused for a moment. Then he had a thought. Whether he was freely given access to the records room in the Federal Reserve Building, or whether he had to sneak in using the woman's four-digit passcode and the security card he stole from her, he still had to get Al Tunb's contract out of the building. He had to get a government document out of one of the most secure government buildings in the entire United States. If he was caught Al Tunb would never get his document; Trucial Energy, the Americans, and the corporations that ruled the world would never be forced to pay the price. More specifically, he knew he was a wanted man, and he didn't want to get caught just for trying to slip out a piece of paper. He was going to need a distraction—something that would distract the entire city, and sitting in front of him on that dead-end street was his distraction.

Right in front of international terrorist Ronald Van De Burgh was the Trucial Energy-Cleveland Natural Gas headquarters complete with pipeline connections and valves all around behind the building. Ronald was going to need a distraction to get out of the Federal Reserve Building. A fire at a nearby natural gas headquarters would do nicely, he thought. Such a flammable place wouldn't need a lot of work to start a fire, he figured. Ronald was almost like a dog drooling before being fed.

He had no weapons to fight his way into the facility. He had no explosives to set it on fire. Walking through the front door of headquarters was not a good option either; his appearance was not a trusting one...not after having spent two nights in front of a fire in an abandoned house after weeks, months, even years of being on the run. There was a parking area, a utility vehicle garage, and an area where spare parts were being stored out in the open. Only a few blocks from the lake, the snow here was extremely heavy, and all of the trucks were gone out on emergency repair calls—often due to the weather's effect on poorly insulated home gas lines.

He drove his car back down East 62nd, over a block, and up an industrial alley/street that led to the gas company's vehicle parking area. There was no gate, no guard, and no trucks. There was no side street traffic because it wasn't even a named street—just a path for delivery trucks to move in and out of adjacent industrial areas that had long since been abandoned. Ronald just drove into the parking lot, walked to the garage, opened a door, and was inside. There he found all sorts of tools for working on vehicles and gas lines ranging in size from one-inch home lines to thirty-six-inch main gas pipelines.

One of the tools Ronald found was a modified, gas-powered circular saw. The saw was mounted in a custom-built aluminum bracket, and had two chains looping through the bracket. A cartoon picture on the saw showed how simple it was to use. He took the saw and headed out the door—back into the blowing snow.

After walking across the parking lot, Ronald made his way under a roof shelter to where multiple pipelines of all sizes came together. He searched and found a thirty-six-inch diameter pipe that connected to several others, and then turned ninety degrees and headed into the ground. It seemed his best option for starting a large, distracting fire. Ronald looped the chains around the pipe, and he tightened them back on to the saw's mounting bracket. He pressed the fuel-priming button three times as the cartoon directions on the saw instructed. Then he opened the choke halfway and pulled on the starting cable. The saw gurgled instead of starting. On the second try, it began howling. He revved it a few times and reduced the choke. Lastly, Ronald mounted the saw on the custom, aluminum, pipe-cutting bracket. When he saw the first sparks, he ran for his car as fast as he possibly could.

The soft snow and the high wind deafened the sound of the saw, and when he closed the door to his car, he couldn't hear it at all. Ronald raced out of the parking lot as fast as he could. He laughed like a mischievous kid. He smiled with a maddening satisfaction. The Americans whom he hated so much were going to pay! Ronald never noticed the signs all around that described the pipe he'd just sabotaged as not natural gas lines, but far more concentrated and flammable compressed liquid natural gas (LNG).

He drove down the industrial street/alley, then turned right on St. Claire Avenue and headed toward the Federal Reserve Building downtown. St. Claire was busy with traffic and snowplows, and there was a water main break. Cars were being rerouted northeast on East 55th rather than southwest toward downtown. The hundred-year-old, forty-eight-inch water main had cracked fifteen feet below the street, and a river was forming. He had to follow the detour as the water was headed his way—forcing him back in the direction of the Trucial Energy facility!

Any excitement and eagerness he had felt disappeared. Ronald knew the saw would cut through the gas pipeline at any moment. He slammed the accelerator down in his Ford Taurus and raced past the front of the facility. He went under a railroad track bridge, over a bridge crossing Interstate 90, and saw that the road was about to bear right along the edge of Lake Erie instead of left toward downtown. A small side street came into view as he came off the interstate overpass. Ronald tried to make the turn, but he was going too fast and only made it halfway. Instead his car shot down a ravine and headed toward the lake, stopping in a drainage ditch. To his left was Burke Airport. Behind him, the natural gas facility was about to explode. To his far left was downtown. In front of him, a storm culvert emptied storm runoff and debris into Lake Erie. The car was completely stuck, and since a wanted international terrorist might run into bad luck if he called for help, he was reduced to walking.

At 1:10 p.m. on October 30 the saw finally cut its way through the wall of a thirty-six-inch liquid natural gas line. The liquid was at four psi, and burst through with so much volume that instead of igniting from the saw's sparks, exhaust, or internal combustion, it pushed all the oxygen out of the area and smothered the saw silent. The force of the liquid natural gas release opened from an eighth-inch-wide hole that the saw had made into a twenty-inch tear. Liquid blew off the overhead awning and launched more than a hundred feet into the air, surrounded by a white cloud of vaporizing natural gas. Then it splashed back down, coated all the pipelines and valve assemblies, and began to flow outwards.

Without a further sound, it poured into the abandoned industrial areas to the east. It flowed down the streets and around the homes to the south. Cars were stalled and stuck as the liquid and cloud of vaporizing gas stalled their engines on St. Claire Avenue. It flowed north, across the railroad tracks, around buildings, and down into Interstate 90, where cars and trucks were choked and stalled.

Just before the wall of clear bubbling liquid and white gas started to pour over the road above where Ronald had lost control of his car, the fuel-air mixture became perfect, and an ignition source in some home or car or from simple static set the entire area aflame. Unlike a firework's boom, or a military-grade high explosive's bang, the inferno made a deafening *whoosh* followed by a howling, indiscernible white noise. The flames seemed to start somewhere to the south, then spread their way to the source and began climbing. As they did they also spread outward and headed toward Ronald.

It all happened so slowly that he had time to marvel and then consciously decide to take cover behind his car. The heat shot over him as he was almost a hundred feet lower in ground level than where the natural gas facility had been. Even seven hundred feet away and a hundred feet below, the heat was enough to set his clothes on fire. He rolled in the snow, but it was melting before his eyes. It was too blinding to keep his eyes open, so he closed them just as the debris began falling around and on him. When he opened them, the snow-covered area he had been standing in was a steaming, burning, smoking pile of debris, mud, and bright light. Half of his car was burned so badly that the paint had come off. It had acted as a shield, but just seven hundred feet away he had to look up. The flame from the broken and burning gas line was almost a thousand feet tall—taller than any of the buildings in Cleveland. Ronald ran to nearby Lake Erie, jumped into the pollution around the culvert, and began wading into it for shelter from the heat and the light. Water temperature was in the fifties, but it was a lot better than standing under a deafening, thousand-foot-tall, white-hot blowtorch.

The blast from the Trucial Energy Liquid Natural Gas facility was the equivalent of a twenty-kiloton atomic bomb detonating at a thousand feet. An estimated 13,450 people were killed instantly. Another 54,500—including Ronald—were seriously injured. The fireball was over six hundred feet wide and rose almost three thousand feet in the air, leaving a furious column of continuous, high-pressure flame over a thousand feet tall. Every building and vehicle window within 2.5 miles of the facility was shattered. Anyone who was outside or near a window within two miles of the facility instantly had second-degree, blistering burns on any exposed skin. People who were within one mile of the fireball received third-degree burns. Thousands of residential homes within the two-mile radius were collapsed, blown away, and those that were not were set ablaze. Stronger buildings within a mile also collapsed and burned.

The FBI offices were only a quarter mile away, and their building was completely erased from existence. One of the four Internet hub stations for the Midwest was in a building half a mile away, and when it collapsed all Internet service from Detroit to Pittsburgh was cut. Most of Cleveland's hospitals were in the blast and burn radius, and suffered greatly. All of the rail traffic from Chicago to the East Coast had to be rerouted since the tracks were less than five hundred feet from the fireball. Every window at Burke Airport had been blasted away, half of the buildings and hangars had collapsed, and the control tower toppled. Communications lines and power networks that passed through Cleveland left all of Northern Ohio powerless, and created a communication blackout from Toledo to Erie to Buffalo, New York.

A late-season ore carrier that was passing on the Cuyahoga River had a bridge fall on it and it was sinking, creating a dam in the river from which most of the region's water drained into Lake Erie. The city's iconic Terminal Tower was set on fire when flammable materials burned after the windows were broken and heat from the thousand-foot fire set them ablaze. All road transportation from Detroit and Chicago had to be diverted down to Dayton, Columbus, and then to points east. And of course, two million people in the region were left without gas heat in the middle of the Halloween Blizzard of 2006.

That blizzard brought with it never-seen-before side effects. The cold air, laden with moisture that had risen from Lake Erie, dumped rain on the burning city, and within an hour a two-inch casing of clear ice covered everything within forty miles to the south and east of Cleveland. The contrast in arctic air and a two thousand-degree fireball also sent winds hurling, with steady winds increasing to thirty mph and gusts over sixty mph. Parts of Cleveland that had been covered in six feet of accumulation or as much as twenty feet of snow drift saw that snow turned to water in seconds. Streets were flooding, freezing, and flooding again. Buildings and rubble were becoming encased in ice from freezing mist and rain. Just south of the fire where the snow had turned to rain, it was snowing harder than ever, and in one place more than three feet of snow fell in an hour. The dynamic atmospheric conditions caused thunder snow and a crescent of parked thunderstorms to the south. Smoke filled the air, and what had been a cloudy day seemed like dusk. The bright light from the thousand-foot flame could be seen from Canada, and the glow from the burning city could be seen from West Virginia.

The Federal Reserve Building was not exempt from the damage. It was, however, the best-equipped structure to handle the explosion. The windows were bulletproof, and while all of them would have to be replaced, none were broken through. Heat and blast did little to the building's pink marble façade and thick brick walls. Inside, the power switched to backup, and emergency protocols had all of the employees racing to make the building and its valuables secure. Within ten minutes it was entirely locked down; the hundred-ton vault was filled and closed, and the workers were assembling to find out what to do next; to find out what had happened and when it would be safe to leave.

Police Sergeant Brian Assana was in the Cleveland Courthouse waiting for a court appearance regarding a domestic violence arrest he'd made the week before. When the liquid natural gas facility went off, he was sitting on a bench in the hallway. The fireball wasn't a flash, but rather a rapid glow that lit the hall and front lobby. He instinctively stood and looked to see what it was, but by the time he reached his feet he had to turn away from the blinding light. At the same instant his hand rose and covered his eyes, the blast hit the building and blew out every single window. First he felt the cold weather blow in, then the heat. The light was still blinding, and the hot/cold alterations continued until finally it was cold and snowing into the building.

People screamed through it all. Even two miles away the noise from the burning sheet of flame was loud. It sounded like a quarter-mile-tall vacuum cleaner. The interior lights instantly went out. People were running into rooms, hiding behind giant marble columns and on the stairwells.

Everyone was in shock. Few had seen anything like it. Brian had. He'd seen burning oil wells in Kuwait, and this seemed like the exact same thing. The sight brought back old emotions from the battlefield, and it confused his mind; blocked all thought...creative or logical. While everyone sought shelter, he stood motionless, physically confused.

After a few moments the clarity of duty he'd had in Kuwait came over him. Battlefields are by nature the peak of chaos, and everyone on a battlefield knows it well, but survivors only do so by luck and by being able to focus amidst the fog of war. Brian had done both. He didn't know what had happened, why, or even what to do, but he knew he had to do something.

He tried to make his way to his patrol car, but glass, debris, snow, wet marble floors, and confused lawyers seemed to slow or block him at every turn. When he finally did make it out of the building, he saw his car. Some unlucky homeowner had the roof blown off their house, and it had landed on his car. With that the best he could do was direct people to find shelter away from the fire to the east.

A police lieutenant saw him and ran over to him.

"Come with me!" he yelled over the noise of the fire.

Both officers made their way back into the courthouse, and down a stairwell near the front lobby.

"This is the City Emergency Command Center (CECC)," the lieutenant told Brian. "A lot of people are going to be haulin' ass to get here. I need you to stand here, and make sure not just anybody gets in here. You got it?"

Brian nodded and took up a position at the bottom of the stairs in front of the steel fire door that led into the CECC. The lieutenant ran into the deputy safety director on his way up the steps. They spoke for a moment and then the deputy director headed down. Brian pretended he knew what he was doing and made him stop to identify himself. Once done he let the deputy director enter. Ninety percent of authority was attitude, he told himself—an early lesson from his police academy days.

Leaders who were in the courthouse were the first to appear and face Brian's scrutiny: the deputy police chief, deputy fire marshal, deputy mayor, and three councilmen. Almost half an hour later others had managed to get through the debris in still-standing buildings as well as the rubble, snow, flooding, and fires in the streets. The mayor arrived and without fanfare passed through the nondescript steel fire door. Then the police chief came, complimented Brian, and entered with three of his staff. Someone from the Cuyahoga County Sheriff's Office came down the stairwell. A line was forming in front of Brian. Business leaders were trying to get in and get involved. There were people from the county water department and the local power company, and at least a dozen people from different communications businesses wanted in as well.

The federal agencies all seemed to arrive at once. Only one FBI agent in 150 miles had survived and she led the way—taking charge of the federal government officials as if she too knew what she was doing (Brian smiled because he knew that she was just acting with authority; no one really knew what to do). After the Federal Reserve Building was secure a US marshal, a Department of Secret Service agent, and a Treasury official had made their way to the courthouse. They followed her inside. The building had plenty of people in shock and fear, but the feds showed no sign of that at all. They impressed Brian.

More officials from Cuyahoga County came in. Someone from the County Commissioner's Office came with two people from county sewer operations. Almost an hour had passed by the time they got to Brian, and—like many people—the initial shock had worn off on them. They asked Brian if he knew what had happened, and he told them it looked just like one of the oil well fires he had seen in Kuwait, but he didn't know for sure. They nodded and looked at each other. As they entered the door behind Brian, the man from the Commissioner's Office told his aide that they'd better get in touch with someone from Trucial Energy.

Less than ninety seconds after the fire started, the president knew about it. Four satellites circled the globe to monitor any and all missile launches. During the boost phase of a rocket launch into space the plume of fire gave off a specific infrared signature as well as a specific pattern of radio interference. The satellites were positioned in a way that any rocket launching toward the upper atmosphere would be detected by two satellites, and its position immediately triangulated. Atmospheric atomic explosions were detected in a similar fashion, as were large oil well fires, and in the case of Cleveland, Ohio...a large fire from a large, underground, salt cavern—a liquid natural gas fire. NORAD was notified as it happened. The computer indicated it was a large, non-nuclear explosion similar in scale to a twenty-kiloton bomb. The duty officer in Cheyenne Mountain, Colorado, notified his chain of command, who notified the President immediately. The White House notified FEMA and called Ohio's governor to both notify and offer any and all federal assistance.

The FEMA director of the Homeland Emergency Logistics Personnel was riding in his small, private, Gulfstream V jet from New York to Chicago. Rough weather from the remnants of Tropical Storm Joyce had the plane flying high at forty-five thousand feet. Here the sky was blue, and the waves of heavily laden clouds were far below. They were north of Pittsburgh, Pennsylvania, when the pilots saw the flash and glow from the fire in Cleveland.

The copilot called on the intercom. "You'd better get up here, sir."

Alan Conferra left his seat, made his way forward, and opened the cockpit door.

"Sir, we just saw a bright flash over in that direction. It was huge. Cleveland air traffic control isn't answering anyone on the radio either."

"You think a plane went down?"

The pilot joined in the conversation. "No way. Something really big blew up in or around Cleveland."

"Hey," the copilot interrupted. "Check it out." He pointed to the plane's on-board computer display. He had switched it to show weather radar, and it was receiving live data from several satellites as well as ground stations. The copilot cycled it to show combined data from a wider range. It showed a circle forming over Cleveland and the clouds were moving around it.

"Jesus...," the pilot remarked. "Did they get nuked or something?"

"I'll make some calls," Alan replied. "You guys better change the flight plan and take us overhead. We need to get a look at this."

The plane changed direction by a few degrees while Alan went in the back. He opened up his laptop computer and logged into the FEMA network. A few minutes later he saw that someone had already issued an Emergency Ready Response Initiative (ERRI), setting in motion a national response to an unknown fire or explosion in the downtown Cleveland area. There wasn't a lot more information, but he watched in real time as towns, cities, and states began adding blackouts, etc., to the map on his screen.

Help was on the way. Even without communications, word spread quickly about the fire in Cleveland. When the fire erupted a local TV station was broadcasting an after-lunch talk show live. The station was only five hundred feet from the Trucial Energy facility. The bright light was seen by everyone in Northeast Ohio, and it ended a split second later with a scream, flying debris, and then static. Cable news networks tried to call the station for statements and soon found that no phone calls were getting through to anyone in Cleveland.

A single cameraman/reporter in Akron, Ohio, former US Army Ranger Phillipe Aristide, was twenty miles to the south. During his time in the Army, Phillipe had built a reputation with war correspondents—sharing his personal photos of combat areas with them. When he'd seen enough of war, he left the Army and through his media contacts got a job doing video work for a Chicago TV station. He still saw too much death, so he quit and sought a lower-paying job in the quietest place he could find: Akron, Ohio.

Phillipe contacted his network and told them that he couldn't get in touch with anyone at the station in Cleveland, and that there was a bright glow to the north. He went to the top of the tallest building in Akron and sent them video. For a split second of that video, the thousand-foot-tall fire could be seen under the smoke and clouds. Seconds later every cable news network was sharing the feed.

The state of Ohio began to organize relief efforts after the White House notified them of a problem. When they saw the glow and the fire on TV, the governor immediately declared a state of emergency, and mobilized the Ohio National Guard. He ordered all nonessential businesses to close immediately, and he ordered everyone in Ohio to go home and stay off the streets. The Ohio Department of Transportation began sending two out of every three snowplows to the Cleveland area. Hospitals sent ambulances. Hundreds of fire trucks were ordered north from other cities in the state and from small towns. Massive amounts of help were being sent blindly toward the fire. No one knew how bad things were, but Phillipe's video and lack of communication made it clear that the situation in Ohio's largest city was very bad.

Each time someone went through the steel fire door, Alan heard the conversation in the CECC growing louder and louder. When the men from the county opened the door, Brian heard the distinct sound of yelling and tables being overturned. He looked inside and saw a fight between two men. The police commanders were trying to break it up, but the lieutenant who had originally posted him at the door was already heading to the door to call Brian in and break it up. It was a case of a man in a suit being too good to get his own hands dirty as well.

Brian rushed through the door and through the crowded room. It was lit only by emergency lighting, and it was clear not much was getting done besides talking. Everyone had their suits on as the temperature in the now open-air building was falling rapidly. He shoved his way passed the police chief, pushed the deputy mayor out of the way, and grabbed the bigger of the two men, a Cuyahoga County Sewer Department official, from behind with a chokehold. Everyone else managed to restrict the other man, a Treasury Department representative. Both men had family in the blast area. Both men knew those family members were either dead or critically injured, and in the latter case they were most certainly buried in rubble to either freeze or burn. The stress level for everyone in the room was extreme.

Though Brian had individually seen ID from every person in the room, he didn't remember their names. Someone in some planning process had decided it was a good idea to have "HELLO MY NAME IS" stickers for everyone to wear, but everyone put their title or role on instead of their names. It was the FBI agent who addressed the crowd—not the mayor or any other leader.

"Gentlemen! We have a serious problem, and people in desperate need. There is no time for this sort of behavior!" Though one of the youngest people in the room, the woman in her late thirties/early forties spoke with the authoritative sound only a wife, mother, or grandmother could carry. Everyone listened, heard her, recognized that she was right, and went back to their discussions.

The police lieutenant came over and thanked Brian after he released the sewer district staffer.

"Thanks, Sergeant."

"Looks like you might want me in here now."

"I think you're right," he answered. "What's your name?"

"Sergeant Brian Assana, sir. East Cleveland PD."

The lieutenant bit his upper lip. "I'm sorry, Brian. It doesn't sound good for your part of town."

"It doesn't sound good for anyone today," Brian answered. "It looks like one of the oil well fires I saw back when I was in Kuwait."

"Yeah, they're not really sure what it is, but there's obviously a lot of fuel somewhere or it would have gone out an hour ago."

A few people from the building's IT department came in without being checked, but the lieutenant didn't seem to care anymore. Then another man in a suit brought in a Trucial Energy utility worker he'd seen walking down the street in a daze.

Everyone noticed his steaming and burnt coveralls. The room fell silent as their heads turned. The crowd parted as the mayor crossed the room and walked over to talk to him. "It's gonna be okay, son. We're working on this now."

The man looked back at the mayor. He knew his face from TV, but he saw the mayor as just another man, not a civic leader or political celebrity. "No," he said and paused. The man stared the mayor in the eyes. His nose was bleeding, and the hair on the back of his head had been burned off. "It's 1944 all over again."

"What are you talking about?" the mayor asked.

The fire marshals could be heard in the background, "Shit."

The mayor called to the fire marshal. "What's he talking about?"

The fire marshal sat down and put his hands on his face, and instead the deputy fire marshal answered.

"Nineteen forty-four. There was a twenty-foot-wide liquid natural gas storage tank at the East Ohio Gas plant on East 62nd. It leaked, found a random ignition source, and blew up everything from St. Clair to the lake. They found a manhole cover nine miles away. That's probably what we have. That plume of flame looks to be in the same area."

Eyes rolled; heads fell back on their shoulders. Others sighed, and more than one man cried.

The FBI agent knew her office was right in that area as well, and while she thought of her friends and colleagues, she was still focused on the situation. "This seems a lot bigger than the area you just described."

Heads nodded, and looked at each other, and the Trucial Energy worker stood up to explain. "That was just a small above-ground storage tank back in '44."

The Cuyahoga County engineer was in the room staring at the floor. "They stopped using above-ground storage tanks after that. Instead, some genius came up with a way to store liquid natural gas—LNG—below ground. That's why the fire's still burning so strong. It's being fueled by LNG stored underground."

"Why is this so much worse than the one in 1944 then?" the FBI agent asked.

"The tank that leaked and blew in '44 was small. The underground storage area is probably a thousand times bigger."

The county engineer interjected. "The one that blew in '44 was twenty feet in diameter. The underground storage area is a two hundred-foot-wide, thousand-foot tall cavern dug—or more like washed out of the salt deposit that's under the city and the lake. It's the difference between a twenty thousand-gallon LNG spill and a two million gallon spill."

The Trucial Energy worker looked at the engineer. "Exactly, but in '44 the gas leaked out, and then blew. Here, it was still under pressure, and is still venting."

"I've never heard of anything like this," the mayor said.

"It's happened," the fire marshal said as he reentered the discussion. "Moss Bluff, Texas...two years ago. Burned for almost a week. Yep. That's what we've got. It's just like that one was: two- to three-mile radius."

There were a lot of whispered calls to God and Jesus amongst everyone in the room.

"How many people were hurt when the Texas one went?" The mayor asked.

The fire marshal shook his head. "Just a few. It was out in the middle of nowhere."

The county engineer was familiar with the storage facility as it was frequently inspected by his department. "Ours was one of the first underground LNGs approved not just by the county, but anywhere in the world. The '44 fire scared everyone, and people thought this was safer. They were right until today."

"Yeah, but it's not just the LNG underground," added the Trucial Energy worker. "It's not like we just put it there and leave it. There are pipelines going south, east, and west that supply as far away as Detroit and Pittsburgh. The regional operations center in Columbus should already have been alerted to the drop in pressure from the fire. Their monitors would alarm to a possible fire right away, and they've probably already shut down all three supply lines, but it'll still take a few days for those lines to empty and get burned off by the fire. It'll take a few days for the underground storage to burn off too, I'm sure."

The Trucial Energy worker had been correct. Regional Trucial Energy controllers did notice the drop in pressure. They did suspect a gas line break of some sort, and they did cut pressure to the main lines in the region that passed through Cleveland. They also alerted state of Ohio and federal government offices that there might be a major gas line break in the Cleveland area. Lastly, they started rerouting utility trucks from around Ohio, Pennsylvania, Michigan, and Indiana all to the Cleveland area.

People monitoring the North American electric grid noticed the moment the fire started as well. They saw a large portion of the power grid fail in the same way it had failed in 2003. Back then a bug in the software that managed the Akron area connection to the national grid caused the system to fail. A series of grid safety measures were caused to fail as well at the time. It was the second largest electrical blackout in human history, cutting off power from all of Central Canada, the American Midwest, and most of the Northeastern United States. Since then, safety measures had been improved, and the grid had seen some modernization. However, electricity still moved at the speed of light, and electricity in Ohio, Michigan, Indiana, Kentucky, West Virginia, Pennsylvania, Maryland, New Hampshire, Vermont, Massachusetts, and Maine all lost power for hours. In total, sixty million people were in the dark in an early winter.

The safety director stood by a white board at the far end/front of the room, lit only by a pair of emergency lights. "Okay, everybody. It looks like we know what the problem is or at least what it most likely is, and what's gonna happen over the next few days. It also looks like most everyone who can get here is here so let's run it down. Sound off when you've got an answer."

He searched and found a marker and then began calling out, "Firefighting status?"

The deputy fire marshal answered, "Unknown. Radios aren't working well."

"Police status?"

The chief of police answered, "Unknown. Same problem. Communications are a mess."

"Okay then. Communications?"

One of the IT people answered, "Internet's out. Phones are out. Radios are probably getting interference from the fire. Something that big, and in that much motion, is bound to cause static."

Someone in the back of the room chimed in, "That's why there's so much thunder and lightning."

The list on the white board grew as the safety director continued. "Okay, communications....none. How about transportation? The storm was already making it difficult, and I'm sure the buses aren't running in the blast area. Anything at all from them?"

No one answered, so he wrote down, "Transportation—unknown" on the board.

"Medical?"

The county engineer spoke up again. "The big hospitals are all in the blast radius or downwind from the fire; if they made it through at all."

The safety director went back to the white board. "Electricity? Well, we know that's out, and we've got to get someone working on that. Gas, hopefully cut off by now. Water?"

A Water Department official called out from the back of the crowd, "We had a main break in the area earlier today. That's going to impact firefighting. I doubt if any of the hydrants are still operational. For the city as a whole, we'd likely advise a boil alert if we could send it out, and if anyone could hear it."

"Looks like communications are going to be the key here. We can't do anything or even know anything without them, and we can't even call the state for help yet. So first order of business is communications."

"We have to evacuate," the mayor pointed out. "We have four hundred thousand people in this city. God knows how many are dead and dying. With this storm, and no heat, people will freeze to death in their homes. We have to evacuate."

Everyone nodded, but issuing an evacuation was next to impossible. There was no communications to let people know. People couldn't even use radios to hear because the fire would give them mostly static. Sending police cars down the streets wasn't an option because they were clogged with snow, debris, flooded, and packed with rubble. Even if people could be told to evacuate, they couldn't drive out on those same streets, and people walking out would pose a bigger freezing threat and die in the streets instead of their homes. There was silence for a moment as everyone looked at the list of problems and realized evacuation wasn't possible. Nothing was possible until they could get in touch with surrounding communities, the state, and the federal government.

Twenty minutes after changing course for Cleveland the crew of Alan Conferra's Gulfstream V saw the clouds glowing below.

"Still no answer from Cleveland Air Traffic Control?" Alan asked.

"No," the copilot answered. The radio's all messed up; static on all channels. We can't even get a radar downlink from the satellites."

Alan sighed. "How do you guys feel about going down and taking a look?"

"Better buckle up. That's some really rough stuff in those clouds."

Alan nodded and headed back to a seat on the left-hand side of the plane next to a window. He strapped himself in tight and made sure his bags were strapped in to other seats as well.

The plane came in over Lake Erie and began a ten-mile-wide circular descent. At forty thousand feet they met the first turbulence. At thirty thousand feet as they headed south it seemed to get easier, but when they headed back east, south of the city, the turbulence became a nightmare. The plane headed north, over the east side of the city, and it eased a bit. Visibility was nonexistent in the heavy and changing types of precipitation. The cycle continued as they circled three more times. The pilot increased the rate of descent when they were over the lake for the fourth circle, and when they began their left turn to parallel the coast they broke through the clouds at 1,500 feet.

A massive, circular fire engulfed the eastern side of the city, and the fire from the LNG facility was so bright that all three men in the plane had to put their hands in front of their faces to block it from their view as they would if they stared toward the sun. All of the tall buildings in downtown smoldered.

They passed two miles east of Burke airport. The eastern part of it had been stripped bare—down to the mud under the grass. The tower was nowhere to be seen, and one of the hangars was on fire. All of the planes were in the lake on its north side.

"We need to get in there," Alan called to the pilots.

Both men looked at each other. The wind was impossible. They could feel the pilot's window on the left getting warm even three miles from the fire. All electronic landing systems were out. The crosswind was unknown, but they could see white caps on the waves at the airport's edges. Still, they were professionals. The pilot had been a naval aviator for eight years, and the copilot had been a US Air Force A-10 ground attack bomber pilot. No two pilots were more capable of Alan's request. More than that, however, they knew Alan was a special FEMA director, and that the city needed him. Duty called, and they didn't so much as blink.

"Okay," the pilot said to both Alan and the copilot. "I'll bring us down on over the lake—circle over it instead of the city this time. Then I'll get it down as low as I can, and we'll make a pass from the east. If we can, we'll land. If we can't we'll try it again. If there's too much debris on the runway we'll have to fly low under the clouds and see if we can wander our way out to Hopkins International to the west."

Both Alan and the copilot nodded. Then the plane banked sharply to the right. The descent didn't seem fast, but the water and waves got bigger very quickly. So too did the buffeting from wind coming over the crest of the lake all the way from Canada. The pilot got the plane down to five hundred feet, then one hundred, then fifty.... Burke's runway shot under them. He dropped the gear, the flaps, and the power to the engines, and the plane made a rough but very short landing. At the southwest side of the airport he turned the plane to face northeast and into the wind with its tail to the fire.

Alan sighed, and even though they did so very quietly, so too did each pilot.

The pilot looked over his shoulder and at Alan. "Okay, boss, what now?"

"Well, I've got to find someone in charge. What do you guys want to do?"

"It's probably best we don't let the plane sit here and cook. I'd like to make our way to Hopkins or out to Toledo. Flying through that cloud cover is a bitch. I'd like to stay low and go along the coast as much as possible."

"Sounds good," Alan answered. "You guys get the plane someplace safe, but close, and listen to your phones in case I call for a ride. It could be a while, though."

Both men nodded with understanding while the copilot prepared to open the door to let Alan out into the freezing and burning air.

He grabbed his briefcase, shook both pilots' hands, and waited for the door to open. When it did, it was like opening an oven door. It was snowing, raining, and steaming all at once. Alan didn't wait for the steps to be lowered. He jumped out and ran to take shelter behind the one building that seemed the most intact, the terminal. Before he made it there, his plane was already turned around and had started rolling down the runway to safety.

Dressed as well as usual, Alan was wearing his typical black suit, white tie, slacks, dress shoes, and an overcoat. He made his way into the terminal through a blown-out emergency exit door, and immediately removed his overcoat. He wrapped his briefcase in it and used them as a heat shield. Still, even surrounded by steam and flame and under a towering column of white hot fire...Alan refused to loosen his tie.

It was clear no one was alive in the terminal. Anyone who had survived had fled. There was no way they headed east through the fire, or south into it. Alan was faced with the same choice; he had to go west toward downtown. Using cars, buildings, planters—anything he could find—to use as a heat shield, Alan made his way a few hundred feet to the Rock and Roll Hall of Fame.

The largely glass structure was a mess. Piles of rock and roll artifacts lay strewn about in ruin. A J-160E acoustic guitar that John Lennon had used to record "Give Peace a Chance" was crushed, burned, and half covered in drywall. A CGBG concert poster for the Ramones was on the floor in a broken frame, under shattered glass, and roasted from the fire outside. Historic concert t-shirts rested in the bottom of a broken display case. Prince's motorcycle from the movie *Purple Rain* was toppled and covered in ash.

After a moment's respite to cool off on the north side of the building where it was snowing, he headed south, up the East 9th Street hill and into downtown. Again, he made a stop-and-go run using cars and trucks as heat shields. Once in downtown, he had to avoid a collapsed building and work his way farther east. A few minutes later he found himself near the courthouse and other clearly government buildings.

There was next to no one on the streets, but Alan did spot two men in suits running into one of the government buildings, and he ran to follow them. He'd hoped to see if they knew anything about the city's leadership; how they were, where they were, anything. They ran into the courthouse, and he followed. Still too far away to call to them, Alan saw them run into a stairwell, and he followed. There was a fire door at the bottom of the stairwell, and he opened it to see the room crowded with officials. The two men he'd chased were standing just inside the door.

"Who are you?" one of them asked.

Alan was wet and steaming. As he patted himself down and brushed off his suit he answered, "Alan Conferra, FEMA director, Homeland Emergency Logistics Personnel . Who's in charge?"

The other man Alan had chased answered while pointing people out to Alan. "That's the mayor, and that's the safety director at the white board. You got here pretty quick. Did you bring some help?"

"No, I was in the air and we saw the flash. Came straight in. FEMA in DC already has an ERRI issued so help's already being organized. They'll get here as soon as they possibly can."

The safety director interrupted the discussion. "Can we help you?"

Alan made his way through the crowd to the front of the dimly lit room. He shook the safety director's hand and gave a comforting smile. "My name's Alan Conferra. I'm the FEMA director for the Homeland Emergency Logistics Personnel . As I was just telling those two by the door, I was on my way to Chicago when we saw the flash from the air. We came straight in as fast as we could. The answer to his question and to all of you is, no. No, I did not bring anyone except myself, but I can tell you that FEMA in Washington is aware and has begun mobilizing resources to get here as soon as possible. The governor has surely been notified as well, and I'm sure he's doing the same. You should also know that there are complications."

He felt air leave everyone's lungs. "We circled the city several times, and it looks very bad out there....very bad." Alan walked over to a large map of the city on the wall next to the door through which everyone had entered. He studied it for a moment and asked for the safety director's pen. Then he drew a circle where he had seen the city burning around the Trucial Energy facility. Someone in the crowd muttered, "Oh, my God." More than one man put his head in his hands or on a table.

"This is roughly what I saw from the air. We were just below the clouds and the turbulence was extreme. The airport is destroyed. There's no one there. We made it in, but I had some amazing pilots. I don't think it's usable—certainly not safely."

He paused. "There's more. I personally went over this bridge and saw that the rail lines are damaged beyond use. The streets are filled with abandoned cars and debris. The white board over there says 'unknown' by transport, and I'll tell you flat out that it's impossible."

"What is FEMA advising us to do?" the mayor asked.

Alan thought for a moment. "The plan for a nuclear attack is to evacuate. We can't do that. It's just not possible. Besides, I've no doubt that people who can already have left. Those who cannot..." He put his head down and sighed. "They're not going to. I believe we find ourselves in a live or die situation, not one with many wounded survivors. Without communications all we can do is secure this location and wait for help to come in the next few hours."

"We need to evacuate!" The mayor was emphatic.

Alan looked and saw the fire marshal in uniform. They stared at each other, and then the fire marshal answered the mayor. "He's right, Mayor. The surrounding communities will do the right thing. The suburbs will send as much help as they can. With the extreme heat, and the extreme cold...anyone who was wounded was trapped, and they're already dead. People who can get away aren't just going to be sitting in the dark in their basement while the neighborhood is burning. They're already leaving. Common sense is our best defense right now."

Brian inadvertently snickered, but the entire room heard him.

The chief of police immediately yelled at him. "You think that's fucking funny, officer?!"

"Sir, with all due respect...I work that area. My friends are...my friends were right there." He pointed to the map where his station had been—well inside the ring of fire Alan had described. "Look at this map. Do you know the people who live in this area? I do. I know them by name. I know every fast food cashier and every drug dealer. I also know that a lot of them are not as well educated as most people."

Brian pointed to another spot on the map between East Cleveland's border and the ring of fire Alan had drawn. "Do you know why this is the highest crime area in the city? Because criminals are stupid, that's why. Common sense is an uncommon virtue in high-crime areas. These people won't evacuate on their own. They won't even evacuate if we order them to. It'll be just like the high-crime areas in New Orleans after Katrina. There are good people there, nice people, but there're also a lot of people who are a dumb as rocks. I'm talking about your lifelong hoods."

The mayor jumped into the conversation. "What do you think we should do, Sergeant?"

Brian shook his head. "Mr. FEMA here has a good idea. Sometimes doing nothing is actually doing something. This building's wrecked. It's going to be dark soon, and colder, and these emergency lights aren't going to last. We need to secure it. We need to be as ready as possible for when help does come."

"And the people who won't evacuate on their own?" the mayor asked.

Brian asked the safety director for a different colored pen, and was handed a purple one. Then he drew a purple shape around the red circle Alan had drawn. "This area here...it hasn't burned yet, but it's next." The shape of Brian's purple area excluded downtown, but encompassed all of the residential areas south, east, and northeast for three miles from the Trucial Energy facility. He drew lines through the purple area, marking it off. Then he erased part of it and wrote in "DARK ZONE." "This area is where people who haven't left will not leave. We've got to focus our police effort there. I'm talking martial law for a few days. That sounds extreme, but this *is* extreme." Brian switched to the red pen and began boxing off other areas. "As soon as the National Guard gets here we should delegate units to security and recovery operations per zone." He looked to the chief of police. "How's that sound to you, Chief?"

The chief nodded and half grinned. It probably wasn't the best plan, and all plans need to be adapted as situations evolved, but the chief liked having a plan rather than no plan. "I like it. Something's better than nothing, Mayor. Let's go with this for now. We'll change it as the situation warrants."

The mayor had reservations. "Martial law? I just don't see that it's come to that yet."

Just as the safety director was about to explain that it was a fairly standard procedure in disasters of this scale, Alan stopped him. "Sir, it's a precaution, and a necessary one. I can't tell you how many times I've seen the breakdown of civil order happen in the blink of an eye. Gangs turned into warlords in Somalia. Racial tension turned to genocide in Rwanda—same thing happened in the Balkans. Look at the looting in Baghdad, or in New Orleans after Katrina. The reason governors are advised to immediately activate the National Guard for things this big is to maintain civil order and the continuity that it brings to people's lives. I'm sure Ohio's governor is doing it already. There are good people out there, perhaps ten to one outnumbering the bad, but there are bad people out there too. They will take advantage of this situation. I strongly advise you to go with the martial law plan described by your own police department, which knows the city best."

For a split second, cell tower communications came back online. Every single person's phone rang. Collectively they all answered "Hello" at almost the same time. The tower had already failed again, and no one heard anyone who had called them. A few were able to get text messages, however. Alan was one of them.

Like everyone else, he was looking at his phone. There was a message from Colonel Davies, Eli. Alan hadn't heard from him in weeks. The message changed everything for Alan. It simply read, "VANDBRG IN NYC. LAST SEEN OHIO."

While the discussions in the room restarted, Brian went to put the markers back by the white board. Alan was still standing by the safety director's written assessments. He and Alan didn't recognize each other from when they met in the Kuwaiti desert fifteen years earlier, but the familiarity of each other's faces made conversation more comfortable.

"You said you patrol that area?" Alan asked him.

"Yes, sir."

"Why are you here then?"

"They didn't have grunts to do security; all chiefs—not enough Indians."

"How long have you been a cop?"

"A little over ten years. I was in the Marines before that. Why?"

Alan leaned in to speak softly into Brian's ear without anyone noticing. "I'm with the Homeland Emergency Logistics Personnel of FEMA. I need men with guns. If you're not assigned, I need you with me. If I'm right, this fire was no accident."

Brian froze and stared at him for a moment. "Homeland Emergency Logistics Personnel...you're from the government and you're here to HELP?"

"Officer, if you're in, keep your mouth shut and follow me outside."

Alan started toward the door and stairwell, but Brian stopped him.

"If you're right, that woman over there is the last FBI agent in the area. She's got a US marshal and a DSS guy with her. We should grab them as well."

Alan nodded in agreement. Then he waved over the crowd to the FBI agent until he got her attention. When she looked back at him, he motioned her to come over. As she did, he pointed to the others with her and told them to come as well. Then Alan and Brian went out the door, up the stairs, and to the lobby.

While he waited, Alan sent a quick text message to Eli. He knew it wouldn't go through for a while, but at least it would go through faster than a call since towers processed messages before connecting calls. The message read, "WHERE OHIO? M IN CLE NOW"

The marble walls and floor were strewn with papers, glass, snow, and wet floors. It was cold with occasional gusts of temperatures over a hundred degrees. Alan put his overcoat back on. Then he directed everyone to a conference room for lawyers and began explaining the situation to them.

"Here it is...first off, what I'm going to tell you is a very, very short version of a classified, read-in-only matter. Do we all understand? If you mention any of this, you will not be arrested and prosecuted. You will disappear. That's how classified we're talking about."

They looked at each other with puzzled, doubtful, skeptical looks.

"Again, my name is Alan Conferra. I'm FEMA director of Homeland Emergency Logistics Personnel. This division deals with special events like this. I've just been informed that an international terrorist by the name of Ronald Van De Burgh left Europe and was last seen here in Ohio sometime in the past few days or hours. I've asked for more information, but who knows when we'll get it."

The FBI agent and US marshal had their interest piqued now.

"What's he wanted for?" she asked.

"He's been involved in at least a dozen different attacks, mostly aimed at Trucial Energy facilities, banks, and International Monetary Fund things. Hundreds have died in these attacks. Millions of lives have been put in danger repeatedly."

"I've never heard of this guy," she added.

"Did you see the attack on Tryphine Banking House on TV last month?"

"He was there?"

"Definitely."

"How can you be sure."

"I was there too." Alan pointed to a scab on his forehead at the edge of his scalp. "He gave me this, and a lot more. This man is extremely dangerous. You might see him from time to time on an Interpol list or some other wanted poster, but he's wanted in the black ops world."

The Treasury Department official was curious after hearing about the attacks on banks. "What's he want? If he's hitting banks he might have gone for the Federal Reserve Building."

"He might have. That would be his style. What's he want? He was working for...he was working for a disgruntled man who has a bad family vendetta against Trucial Energy."

They all looked at each other. Alan was trying to be vague, but he'd overdone it. He knew it.

"Okay, there's an Arab out there who thinks he's an emir of an island in the Persian Gulf. His father died a few years back, and just before he did, he told this man that his family had sold oil rights to Trucial Energy after World War I. This man thinks that there's a copy of some contract from the Roaring '20s that will give him back trillions of dollars in reparations and give his family back their little Gulf state. Ronald and another man were his foot soldiers, and he'd send them out anywhere in the world where he thought this paper might be—all sorts of crazy places. That's what Ronald wants: some hundred-year-old Trucial Energy contract to a Persian Gulf island sheik."

Everyone dropped their shoulders and sighed. There was a "Jesus Christ" muttered from one of them.

Alan tried to calm them. "I didn't say he was all there, just that he's dangerous."

"You think he might have hit the Trucial Energy place here in Cleveland because some nut thought there was a contract there?" Brian asked.

"He's done things exactly like that before," Alan answered.

The Treasury official was still curious. "Why are he and this other man hitting the banks?"

"Well, we took out the other guy in London last month. It's just Ronald now. Most of the time they seemed to just think the contract was in some records room here or there. In London...well, he might have been after me and a few other people as well."

The Treasury Department official continued. "He still might be headed for the Federal Reserve Building then. We have all sorts of federal documents archived in the basement." He paused and thought for a moment. "Wait a second...when was this contract supposed to have been done? Sometime in the '20s?"

"Yeah, 1923."

"Warren G. Harding. Warren G. Harding was president in 1923. The Harding Library is here in Ohio, but we keep a lot of his documents because they don't have space. If he's not looking for a contract at the Trucial Energy facility, then the most likely place he'd be looking for a contract like that would be in the Federal Reserve Building. He *is* going to go for the Fed."

"Where is it?" Alan asked as he looked to Brian.

"About four blocks south and as many east."

Now it was Alan's turn to drop his shoulders and look at the ceiling. "Look, this guy's been face to face with dozens of the most elite Special Forces guys the world has ever known, and he's escaped each time. Well, all but once. Anyway, we're gonna need a lot more than your pistol, Brian."

This time the US marshal proudly added to the discussion. "We've got an arsenal in that building as well as people trained to use it. We locked it down as soon as the fire started. He'll never get in."

"You don't know this guy," Alan replied. "All right, let's get over there. We can at least make sure things are secure and get everyone as armed as possible."

Brian, the FBI agent, the US marshal, and the Secret Service agent all drew their pistols and led the way out of the courthouse toward the Federal Reserve Building. Again, they used cars and sidewalk planters for heat shields. They headed down Ontario Street for about six hundred feet. When they got to Superior Avenue they headed northeast—directly toward the fire. It was too hot, and they had to stop behind each city block to use the buildings for cover. Three times they ran a block, then took cover and cooled off. Finally, they reached the Federal Reserve building and ran to the door. It was hot to the touch, but the Secret Service agent removed his jacket and used it as a glove to open it.

The door was even stiffer than usual. Brian helped, and the instant they could get inside the six of them piled through. They were met by a crowd of guards and armed civilians. Luckily they all recognized their friends, and deemed both Alan and Officer Assana as non-threats.

The Secret Service agent led Brian, Alan, and the FBI agent to the armory while the Treasury official headed to the Warren G. Harding collection in the basement and the US marshal ordered all the security efforts double checked. Everyone was sound about not giving the details that Alan had explained to them.

In the armory, Alan and Brian showed all the forms of identification they had and filled out forms to be held accountable for everything they used. Brian and the FBI agent were already wearing bulletproof vests. The Secret Service agent handed each of them Heckler & Koch MP-5 submachine guns as well as combat harnesses so each person could carry twelve thirty-round magazines filled with nine-millimeter bullets.

Brian looked at Alan, who was putting his coat over his vest and harness. "Have you ever fired a weapon?"

Alan looked at him and gave him a comforting smile. Then he sheepishly looked away, and back again to Brian. "Not very often, but I don't think it's going to matter much if we have to face Van De Burgh."

"He's that bad?"

"Officer, there are myths and legends and reality, and sometimes reality is the worst."

The FBI agent and DSS agent were listening. They looked at each other. She grabbed a small backpack and filled it with more ammunition.

"Okay, so what now?" Brian asked.

Alan thought for a moment. "Well, they're checking to make sure he has as tough a time getting in here as possible. Let's say he started the fire as a distraction, on his way here. How would he get here? What route would he take?"

The DSS agent pointed out, "There's a map of the city in the front guard booth."

They headed upstairs and ran into the Treasury Department official, who handed Alan a box. "These are all of the Harding administration contracts and correspondences to the Middle East; everything from Egypt to Persia."

"Is there a safe or a vault somewhere where you can put this?" Alan asked.

Everyone in the room smiled.

The Treasury official's smile was the largest. "I'll take care of it," he replied before taking the box away and putting it in the two-story, three hundred-ton vault with the ninety-ton door.

The DSS agent came back with a map of the city. He pointed out where they were located, and where the area where the fire seemed to have started.

Brian looked carefully. "If he started it in this area, he could've just come all the way down St. Claire Avenue. We're only a block south of it."

"No," the FBI agent interjected. "There was a water main break at St. Claire and East 55th this morning. I had to go around it to get to the jail for an interview this morning."

"Yeah, you're right," Brian added. "There was a break there. I remember. So, if he set the fire, and ran into the detour...that would have taken him toward the lake. He'd have to go up to North Marginal Road, and then all the way down past the airport, then work his way through downtown."

"To the best of my knowledge, this man's never been to the US. He'd be lost as hell," Alan replied.

Brian looked at him. "Okay, fine. If he's lost he's lost, but he'd be lost somewhere between this intersection...on this road...all the way down along the airport to East 9th....where the Rock Hall is."

Alan pointed to the map. "I landed here, headed through the terminal, to the...the 'Rock Hall,' and came up that road. Half the airport is completely wiped flat. The other half is empty.

I didn't see anyone from when I got off my plane all the way to the courthouse."

Everyone sighed, and Alan reached into his pocket. He'd felt his phone vibrate. There was a message from Eli. It read, "FACIAL RECOGNITION SOFTWARE ID'D KUNST: COLUMBUS AIRPORT, GAS STATION INDEPENDENCE, OH AND FED RSRV BLDG CLE—IRV"

Alan put the phone in his pocket and bit his bottom lip. "It's confirmed. He's after something here."

The FBI agent started to ask, "How do you—?"

"Facial recognition shows him having been here, in this building, in this spot on Friday. I don't know when specifically, but someone does."

The FBI agent called out to everyone in the lobby, "Who was working this security booth on Friday?!"

"I was, ma'am."

Alan walked up to her as she was coming forward. He smiled to calm her and indicated that she wasn't in any trouble. It had the desired effect and put her at ease. "Do you remember anyone coming in and asking about Warren G. Harding?"

"Yeah, there was this guy. European, I think. A lot of the offices closed early because of the blizzard. He tried to hang around, but I kicked him out."

Alan's head shook as he smiled. "He didn't get it. All that, all this...and he didn't get it." He shook his head some more, and his smile faded suddenly. "All those lives, and he still didn't get it."

Brian looked at the map again. "It's been hours. If he started the fire as a distraction, he'd have been back. If he got detoured and lost, he might have been caught in the blast. The guy's a fugitive. He only would have tried a big distraction if he knew he couldn't get in and out the front door. A few hours after the fact he's got to know he definitely can't now. He'd be running."

Everyone nodded in agreement.

"Okay, how?" Alan asked.

"Well, anything east of East 55th and the fire blocks his way. Same thing if he heads south. He still has to go west toward us." Brian pointed at the map and continued. "If we ignore the route you already took from the airport to downtown, then that puts him somewhere on North Marginal between the airport terminal and East 55th. It's been hours so if he made it through the blast, he could be anywhere, but this is where we should start. There's not a lot of cover either. He'd have to be down on the breakers along the lakeshore, or in some ditch or maybe there's some structure still intact. There's a pair of marinas here and here, and there's an apartment building here and here."

Looking around at the others, Alan asked for a suggested plan.

"The heat that close to the fire is going to be hard," offered the FBI agent. "We can head down to the terminal where you started, and then north to the lake and work our way along the breakers. It'll be the farthest land from the fire, and we'll have cold air on our backs at least."

Everyone looked at each other, nodded, and headed for the door. There were handshakes and goodbyes from some of the people in the Federal Reserve Building lobby. Many doubted the survivability of where they were about to search. Alan wondered if it was indeed a suicide mission.

Once again they headed out into the burning city. As before they used buildings to block them from the heat, and then ran across streets as fast as possible to limit their exposure to the giant flame a mile and a half to the east-northeast. Alan, Brian, a US marshal, an FBI agent, and a Secret Service agent all headed up East 9th Street. When they reached the bridge that crossed over the railroad tracks and the freeway, there was a collective gut-check.

With his amiable smile Alan looked at them all. He knew them to be brave and dutiful just by the nature of their careers, but he also knew they were human. "I know it's a long way, but I've done it before. We can do it again." Everyone nodded and they ran across the bridge for the shelter of the Rock Hall. Three times they stopped—twice behind vans and once behind a half-burned panel truck. On the north side of the overpass they took shelter in the remains of the train station that had been shredded and blown onto the road.

While they were cooling and catching their breath, there was a terrific banging and smashing sound below and behind them. When they turned to look they saw three large Ohio Department of Transportation snowplow trucks heading north on the southbound side of the freeway. They weren't just plowing snow. The lead truck was on the left, with another behind and to its right. The third was behind and to the right of the second. They were pushing cars off the freeway and making a lane. Behind them were three airport fire trucks from Hopkins Airport. Help was arriving.

Over the rushing wind and the roar of the fire at the Trucial Energy facility, the FBI agent suggested that she, the US marshal, and the DSS agent check the "Rock Hall" while Brian and Alan check the Coast Guard facility on the northeast side of the street, closer to the airport. Everyone liked the idea, and they split up. They also ran as fast as they could—into the driving snow, with the scorching heat on their right sides from Trucial Energy.

Brian made it to the Coast Guard station first. All of the windows were gone, but the building was built to federal government regulations, and it was sound. There was a lot of debris inside—broken glass, paper, furniture tossed about—and window blinds seemed to have come apart, making a particularly messy scene. It was clear from the debris that no one had been in the building since the blast. Brian led the way and checked all the rooms.

In an upstairs office area there was a pile of cubicles that had been knocked down. Brian paused to check for survivors or for Van De Burgh. While he did so Alan found that a single window had remained unbroken. All that had happened to it was a single hit from some sort of debris, creating a large crack from left to right. He paused to look out, raising his hand to cover the bright light from the fire. As he did so Brian saw a long, low shadow moving. He looked more carefully—someone was out there!

"Hey! I just saw someone run through the parking lot toward the water!"

Brian came over and looked out the window to where Alan was pointing.

"There...see? He's headed for that...what is that?"

"I see him. That's the USS *Cod* submarine. It's a memorial. Well, someone's trying to use it for shelter. He just went in. C'mon, let's go."

Brian and Alan headed downstairs, but stopped before leaving. Brian put his left hand out to tell Alan to stay where he was while he moved down a hall to the north end of the building.

Just after Alan lost sight of him he heard from down the hall, "Stop! Police!"

There was a gunshot, then a burst of gunfire from Brian's MP-5. Another shot rang out, and Brian came running down the hall toward Alan. He motioned for Alan to get down behind a desk as he did the same to his left. As they did, three young men came down the hall, blindly firing pistols sideways in their direction.

"Motherfucker! Pigs gonna die today!" More pistol shots rang out.

Alan watched Brian out of the peripheral of his vision, and when Brian rose up, so did he. Both men opened fire on the looters. They scattered, and one went down like a bag of rocks.

"They got Alex!" one of them cried out.

Another, slower, steady stream of pistol shots came toward Alan and Brian, but Brian rose up and fired until the magazine in his weapon was empty. The shooting stopped, and they walked forward to view the looters' bodies.

"It's gonna be like this all over the city," Brian said as he shook negatively.

"Don't have to tell me," Alan answered. "I can't tell you how many times I've seen it before. Cities come apart."

"C'mon, let's go check out the sub," Brian said as he headed off.

They went outside into the parking lot between the Coast Guard station and the submarine—using burned-out cars as heat shields again. From there Brian led the way up the gang plank, past the conning tower, and toward an access stairwell into the sub, halfway between the conning tower and the bow. Steel tube safety railings had been bent and twisted from the blast. Both men had to squirm their way into the sub while rubbing on the hot steel. They seemed to constantly get burns from touching steel and brass edges. Inside the submarine, they had to take a ladder down through a second, smaller, narrow, oval hatch.

There was no power on the sub, and they were in darkness. Brian's service flashlight was all they had, and their vision was limited to whatever was in the circle of light it gave. At the bottom of the ladder they found themselves in the forward torpedo room. To their sides, disarmed torpedoes rested in their racks. Behind them were the torpedo tubes and a bulkhead of knobs, handles, and valves. Directly in front they could look down the sub's main corridor and see almost all the way to the rear torpedo room.

They made their way down the corridor, checking every alcove on their way. On the right-hand side they saw a galley. Brian froze with his light aimed inside. Alan, who was behind him, came up and looked inside. Sitting at a chair with his head in his folded arms on the table, was a man. His back and left side were charred. His clothes were torn and blackened. His face was blistered, and his eyes were closed. Alan recognized him as Ronald Van De Burgh.

Quietly he stepped past Brian, into the galley, and sat down at a chair at the opposite end of the table. Ronald sighed. He'd known he was caught the moment he saw Brian's flashlight glow through his closed and exhausted eyes.

He'd had enough. Defeated in every possible way, with his eyes still shut, he spoke softly in a soot-laden voice. "I surrender."

Brian let his MP-5 fall slack on its sling. Then he switched to his service pistol, and reached for his handcuffs at the same time. Since Ronald's reputation was that of a man who was a maximum threat, he tossed the cuffs onto the table.

"Put 'em on," he said flatly, coldly, and with anger about to boil over from beneath his surface façade.

Ronald painfully sat upright. He looked at Brian, and then turned to look at the cuffs. That's when he saw Alan.

"You...?"

Alan's comforting smile was more fake than it had ever been. "Yes, Ronald. It's me."

"Who are you? What is your name?"

"I'm Alan."

Brian kept aiming his nine-millimeter automatic at Ronald. "I thought you said you knew this piece of shit?"

Alan's face didn't change. "We've run into each other a few times."

"London was the last time," Van De Burgh added. "How's your face?"

"Better than yours right now. You look like shit."

Ronald's pain and fatigue had gone past caring. He just wanted it all to end.

"You should know, Ronald, I have the contract. Al Tunb will never see it now."

It was shattering news to Van De Burgh. He felt a wash of cold all over him and his heart slowed. His vision blurred and began to fade from the peripheral of his view. As he began to waver Brian smacked him on the back of his burned head to bring him back to attention.

"Where is Al Tunb, Ronald? I'd like to tell him I've got it myself."

"I don't know. I just only spoke with him on the phone. He moves around. I have no idea."

Brian smacked him again, and this time Ronald cried out in pain.

"What's his number?" Alan asked.

"I don't know. I have no...I just don't know." Ronald's arms folded and his head dropped into them on the table.

Brian smacked the back of his head a third time. This time Ronald snapped to attention, turned to face Brian, and yelled at him. "This is torture! You can't do this! You are American and you are police, you cannot torture! You are a filthy fucking imperialist American, but you cannot torture!" He began to waffle between outrage and smug laughter.

Brian looked at Alan. "Do you think we'll get anything out of him?"

Alan shook his head. "When Van De Burgh was in custody before he was belligerent, he was easy to make talk." With that Alan determined they probably weren't going to get anything from him. Van De Burgh probably did not know how to get in touch with Al Tunb.

"Okay then," Brian said. "Torture time is over, okay? Okay? One last question though: Did you start this fire?"

Van De Burgh smiled. "I did, but I had no idea this would happen. I had no idea it would work so well."

Brian stared for a moment.

When he was a Marine and they were about to cross the sand berm into Iraqi-held Kuwait, Brian's company commander addressed them. He said, "On the other side of that fence and that pile of sand is a battlefield. Once you cross into it, you are not in the normal world anymore. You are in a war. There you will have to remember, either you are a killer or you are killed." The Marines had taught him how to fight and how to kill; how to be a killer. When he crossed that line in the Kuwaiti sand, he felt the clarity of the killer he'd been trained to become.

While he was staring down the sights of his 9mm Glock pistol at Ronald Van De Burgh, he felt the clarity return. Just as the smell of a melting piece of kitchenware could make him sick, or the bang of fireworks could terrorize his father, the sight of the gas fire, the smell of a city burning, the smell of Ronald's burned body...it all brought back the clarity of the killing commitment he had once felt.

Then he thought of his wife, his little girls, his son, his father, and his friends at the station. He hoped someone had made it, but he knew inside that the man at the other end of the sights on his weapon had blown them all up; set them on fire. The concept of his wife and/or his girls being trapped in rubble and burning because of—

Brian fired and executed Ronald.

EPILOGUE

5/4/2007

Help for Cleveland had poured in during the first hours and days after Ronald's fire. The Trucial Energy salt cavern burned for four days with the column of fire getting lower and lower each day. Finally, its fuel was exhausted. Hundreds of fire trucks and tens of thousands of first responders—augmented by the Ohio National Guard—had the city's fires out after a week.

Clearing debris and rebuilding took place while the fires were being doused. Much of the debris was hauled to Burke Airport and dumped in the lake as fill, and when spring came the following year the airport was able to expand. Large swaths of the city were plowed flat. Abandoned homes and manufacturing facilities were pushed away, and green fields grew in their place. Federal financial aid spawned a rebuilding boom, and with it a skyline of giant cranes, green fields, and shiny new buildings. Cleveland, which had been burned down, was reborn.

Working with former Senator Jerry Henderson, Alan managed to pull political strings and see that a new emergency plan for such disasters was put in place. The president, the governor, state representatives, and Ohio congressional members all flocked to the city in May for the signing. It was an unusually sunny and warm day, the opposite of those darker days in every way imaginable.

Alan declined the invitation. After Ronald Van De Burgh was killed "resisting arrest," he made his way back to the Federal Reserve Building, had the box of Harding administration contracts removed, and left town as soon as he could. He flew out from Hopkins Airport the following afternoon and straight to London, where he met with Lord Tryphine and Erwin Zimmermann. They searched the contracts in the case, found the legendary Trucial Energy contract, and secured it in Lord Tryphine's vault. Enhanced security measures after the attack by Davies and Van De Burgh the previous year made it far more secure than even the three hundred-ton vault in Cleveland.

Awards were given to Brian Assana who, as it turned out, had not lost his family, nor most of his friends. Through varying twists of fate, their communities rallied together and kept each other alive in the face of Hell unleashed. Many others were given awards as well, promotions too. What he was most proud of, however, was that Alan had asked him to join him in the Homeland Emergency Logistics Personnel. Alan and some of his wealthy friends made the six-figure job economically lucrative as well.

www.ingramcontent.com/pod-product-compliance
Lightning Source LLC
Chambersburg PA
CBHW070639310726
48982CB00001B/333